ASHLEY HERRING BLAKE is an award-winning author and literary agent at Rees Literary Agency. She holds a master's degree in teaching and loves coffee, arranging her books by color, and cold weather. She is the author of the young adult novels *Suffer Love*, *How to Make a Wish*, and *Girl Made of Stars*, and the middle grade novels *Ivy Aberdeen's Letter to the World*, *The Mighty Heart of Sunny St. James*, and *Hazel Bly and the Deep Blue Sea*. *Ivy Aberdeen's Letter to the World* was a Stonewall Honor Book, as well as a *Kirkus Reviews*, *School Library Journal*, NYPL, and NPR best book of 2018. Her YA novel *Girl Made of Stars* was a Lambda Literary Award finalist. She's also a coeditor on the young adult romance anthology *Fools in Love*. She lives on a very tiny island off the coast of Georgia with her family.

CONNECT ONLINE

AshleyHerringBlake.com

🐦 AshleyHBlake

📷 AshleyHBlake

📌 AEHBlake

DELILAH GREEN
DOESN'T CARE

Ashley Herring Blake

PIATKUS

PIATKUS

First published in the US in 2022 by Jove, Berkley
An imprint of Penguin Random House LLC
First published in Great Britain in 2022 by Piatkus

1 3 5 7 9 10 8 6 4 2

A CIP catalogue record for this book
is available from the British Library.

ISBN 978-0-349-43256-4

Printed and bound in Great Britain by Clays Ltd, Elcograf S.p.A.

Papers used by Piatkus are from well-managed forests
and other responsible sources.

Piatkus
An imprint of
Little, Brown Book Group
Carmelite House
50 Victoria Embankment
London EC4Y 0DZ

An Hachette UK Company
www.hachette.co.uk

www.littlebrown.co.uk

For Rebecca Podos, who goes with me into every great unknown

DELILAH GREEN
DOESN'T CARE

CHAPTER

ONE

DELILAH'S EYES FLIPPED open at the buzz on the nightstand. She blinked the unfamiliar room into focus, once . . . twice. It had to be at least two in the morning, maybe later. She fumbled for her phone, silky white sheets tangling around her naked thighs as she twisted to silence the vibrating, which seemed loud enough to wake up—

Oh shit.

She'd done it again. The name of the woman lying next to her slipped and slid in her memories from the previous night, the letters nearly impossible to grasp through the art show at the tiny Fitz gallery in the Village——a few of her photographs on the walls, a handful of patrons nodding and praising but never actually intrigued enough to buy anything, the champagne that never seemed to stop flowing—followed by that florid bar up on MacDougal Street and a whole hell of a lot of bourbon.

Delilah glanced over her shoulder at the sleeping white woman next to her. Dark blond pixie cut, creamy skin. Nice mouth, full thighs, phenomenal hands.

Lorna?

Lauren.

No. Lola. Her name was definitely Lola.

Maybe.

Delilah bit her lip and grabbed the still gyrating phone, squinting at the name flashing on the bright display in the dark.

Ass-trid

She barely had time to smirk at the way she'd spelled her stepsister's name in her contacts before she hit *Ignore*. An instinct. In Delilah's experience, a phone call at two in the morning was rarely a good thing, particularly when Astrid Parker was on the other end of the line. And who the hell even called anymore? Why couldn't Astrid text like a normal human?

Okay, fine, there might have been several unanswered texts in Delilah's messages, but in her defense, she was a useless sack of skin lately, with another month's rent looming and preparing for the Fitz show, at which her work only appeared because she knew the owner, Rhea Fitz, a former fellow waitress whose dead grandmother left her enough money to open her own gallery. The past few weeks had been a scramble of waiting tables part-time at the River Café in Brooklyn and working freelance portrait jobs and weddings, all of which barely paid enough to cover her apartment and food. She was one catastrophe away from having to move to New Jersey, and if she ever wanted to break into the ruthless New York City art world, New Jersey wasn't going to cut it. She'd sold a piece or two, sure, but her photography was *niche*, as one agent had told her while declining to represent her, and *niche* wasn't an easy sell.

So, yeah, she'd been too busy busting her *niche* ass to talk to her stepsister. Plus, it wasn't like Astrid even liked her all that much anyway. They hadn't seen each other in five years.

Had it already been that long?

Hell, it was late. Delilah dropped the phone to her chest while Jax drifted into her thoughts for the first time in a while. Months. She squeezed her eyes closed tight, then opened them and stared up at the ceiling, which was covered with those glow-in-the-dark star stickers. She sat up, a cold panic shooting through her veins. Was she in a college dorm? God, please no. Delilah was nearly thirty years old, and college girls . . . well, she'd been there already, lived that part of her life. She preferred women her own age, always had, and was happy to leave behind all the fumbling and fluttering lashes she remembered from her early twenties.

She relaxed as the room came into focus, felt the softness of expensive sheets under her fingers. The bedroom was filled with modern furniture, all straight lines and cream-colored wood. Sophisticated art dappled the walls, expertly hung. An open door led into a living area, which Delilah now distinctly remembered as the scene where—Lana? Lily?—had pushed her onto a very posh white couch and slid Delilah's underwear off, tossing it over her own bare shoulder.

Definitely not college-level kind of furnishings. Not even Delilah Green–level kind of furnishings, and she was a full grown-up. Also, what Lilith had proceeded to do with her mouth was definitely not a college-level kind of skill.

Delilah flopped back down onto the bed, boneless at the memory. Her eyes had just started to feel heavy enough to close when her phone buzzed again. She jolted fully awake, peering at that same unlikely name and pressing *Ignore* for the second time.

Layton stirred next to her, turning over and squinting at Delilah, mascara smeared under her eyes. "Oh. Hey. Everything okay?"

"Yeah, sure—"

Her phone went off again.

Ass-trid

"Should you get that?" Linda asked, tousled hair falling adorably over one blue eye. No way this sex goddess's name was Linda.

"Maybe."

"Then do it. When you're done, I've got something I want to show you."

Lydia—sure, why not—grinned, pulling down the linens to her hips for a split second before tucking the sheet back up to her chin. Delilah laughed as she tossed the covers back, slipping out of the bed completely naked. She very nearly answered the phone like that, but then grabbed a silk robe—definitely not a college-level kind of robe—that hung over a gray upholstered chair in the corner. She could not and would not talk to her stepsister in the buff.

Sliding on the robe, she went into the small living room-slash-open kitchen and climbed onto a stool, resting her elbows on the cool marble counter. She breathed in . . . out. She shook out her hands, rolled her neck. She had to prepare to talk to Astrid, like a boxer heading into a match. Gloves on, mouth guard in. On the counter, the phone stilled, Astrid's name disappearing, only to pop back up like a greeting card from hell. Best get this over with, then. She slid her finger across the phone.

"What?"

"Delilah?"

Astrid's velvety voice filtered through the phone. Like an American Cate Blanchett, except more stick-up-your-ass and less queen-of-bisexuals. Exactly the kind of voice Delilah always knew adult-Astrid would have.

"Yeah," Delilah said, then cleared her throat. Her own voice was somewhere between six-cocktails-parched and years-of-sleep-deprivation-raspy.

"Took you long enough to answer."

Delilah sighed. "It's late."

"It's only eleven in Oregon. Plus, I figured this was the best time to catch you. Don't you turn into a bat after midnight?"

Delilah snorted. "I do. Now if you'll excuse me I'd like to get back to my cave."

Astrid didn't say anything for a few seconds. Long seconds that made Delilah wonder if she was still there, but she wasn't going to be the one to crack. They'd only spoken on the phone a dozen or so times since Delilah left Bright Falls the day after high school graduation, hopping a bus to Seattle with her *Bright Falls High* duffel bag on her shoulder, while Astrid took off for a postgrad trip to France with all of her horrible BFFs. Isabel, Astrid's mom and Delilah's wicked stepmother, had armed both girls with enough cash to keep them out of her hair for two weeks. The only difference being, Astrid came back, prepared for college at Berkeley like the dutiful daughter, while Delilah flew to New York and rented a one-bedroom dump on the Lower East Side. She was a legal adult, and there was no way in hell she was going to stay in that house one second longer than she needed to.

It wasn't like Isabel mourned her leaving.

Neither did Astrid, as far as Delilah could tell, though every now and then, this would happen. Texts that went ignored and turned into awkward phone calls where Astrid tried to pretend she hadn't made Delilah's already lonely childhood a living hell. Delilah had been back to Bright Falls five or six times in the past twelve years— a few Christmases and Thanksgivings, a funeral when her favorite art teacher had died. The last time was five years ago, when Delilah fled New York with a freshly obliterated heart, mistakenly thinking the familiarity of Bright Falls might serve as a balm. It hadn't, but it had given Delilah an idea for a photo series that had changed her ambition from *struggling freelance photographer who barely made rent to successful queer artist with an amazing apartment in Williamsburg.*

Which she still hadn't achieved, but she was trying.

"So . . . are you coming?"

Astrid's voice cut through her musings, and she blinked Lucinda's kitchen back into view. "Coming . . ." A dirty joke rested on the tip of her tongue, but she bit it back.

"Oh my god," Astrid said. "Are you serious? Tell me you are not serious."

"I—"

"Delilah, tell me!"

"I'm trying if you'd shut up for two seconds!"

Astrid blew out a breath so loud, it buzzed in Delilah's ear. "Okay. Okay, I'm sorry, I'm just stressed. There's a lot going on."

"Right," Delilah said, racking her brain for what the hell was *going on.* "Um, so—"

"Nope, no, no. You are *not* canceling on me, Delilah Green. Tell me that is not what you're doing."

"Jesus, Ass, take a Xanax, will you?"

"Please don't call me that and do *not* cancel on me."

Delilah let a beat of silence pass. Maybe seeing her own art on actual gallery walls, tiny as they may be, followed by great sex had just addled her brain a little, and whatever the hell Astrid was talking about would come roaring back to clarity. She pulled the phone from her ear and hit the speakerphone button, then checked the date on her calendar app—Saturday, June 2. Wee hours. Friday the first was definitely a date that had been cemented in her mind for months as she prepped for the Fitz show. But there was something else there, something June-ish and Astrid-shaped and—

Oh fuck.

"Your wedding," Delilah said.

"Yes, my wedding," Astrid said. "The one I've been planning for months and for which Mother insisted I hire *you* as a photographer."

"Don't sound so excited."

"I have another word for it."

"You're not really helping your case here, Ass."

Astrid huffed into the phone.

"I'm still crushed I'm not a bridesmaid," Delilah deadpanned, but with the revelation of her stepsister's impending nuptials to some poor sucker, her heart picked up its pace as both terror and relief flooded her system.

On the one hand, a Parker society wedding in Bright Falls was the absolute last thing she wanted to do right now. Or ever. She'd rubbed elbows with a few agents at the Fitz show and sold one whole piece—granted the patron was currently sleeping in the next room, but Loretta one hundred percent forked over her money before even batting a single lash Delilah's way. At least, Delilah was pretty sure that's how it happened, as she was too busy freaking the fuck out that someone traded actual money for something she'd created.

Regardless, now was not the time for Astrid-slash-Isabel bullshit. Delilah felt as though she was on the edge of something, *being* someone, and Bright Falls was a soul-sucking pit of despair where she was absolutely no one.

On the other hand—the hand that tried to keep Delilah fed and clothed—Isabel Parker-Green had offered her a ridiculous sum of money to photograph Astrid's wedding and two weeks' worth of pre-wedding events. As the details from when Astrid first called Delilah about this happy event floated back to her now, there were definitely five figures involved. Low five figures, but still. Pocket change to Isabel Parker-Green and to most Brooklynites, but to Delilah, who could stretch a dollar for days, it was an IV to her dehydrated bank account.

Along with the money, which Astrid almost certainly knew Delilah couldn't refuse, Astrid had also delivered an oh-so-subtly manipulative, "Mom says your father would've wanted you at my wedding." Delilah still resented her for it, mostly because she knew Isabel was right. While he'd been alive, Andrew Green had been a devoted family man to the point of ridiculousness, insisting on nightly dinners and spring break vacations, Christmas Eve traditions and checking homework and learning how to plait hair just so Delilah wouldn't be the only girl at the Renaissance Faire field trip without a braid crown.

A wedding would be nonnegotiable. You showed up for family, even if you got paid for it and gritted your teeth the entire time.

"Pre-wedding events start on Sunday," Astrid said now. "You agreed to be there for all of it, remember? The details I emailed you indicate you're booked June third through the sixteenth. I signed your contract, agreeing to all of your terms, and—"

"I know, I know, yes," Delilah said, running a hand over her hair. Shit, she did not want to go back to Bright Falls for two whole weeks. And it was Pride month. She loved Pride in New York City. Who the hell started all this wedding nonsense that far before the actual day anyway? Well, Delilah knew exactly who.

"Astrid—"

"Don't you fucking dare."

"That mouth, Ass. What would *Isabel* say."

"She'd say that and a lot worse if you're about to cancel on her only daughter's wedding on such short notice."

Delilah sucked in a breath, even though she tried not to.

Her only daughter.

She wanted to fight the sting, to let the words slide right over her, but she failed. It was a reflex, this feeling, left over from a childhood with two dead parents and a stepmother who never really wanted her in the first place.

"Shit," Astrid said, her tone regretful and irritated at the same time, as though Delilah had made her forget that Isabel had been Delilah's sole guardian after her father, Isabel's second husband, had died of an aneurysm when Delilah was ten years old.

"There's that mouth again," Delilah said, laughing through a thick throat. "I think I might like this new stressed-out Astrid."

Her stepsister didn't say anything for a few seconds, but the silence was long enough for Delilah to know she'd be on a morning flight out of JFK.

"Just be here, okay?" Astrid said. "It's too late to find someone decent to replace you."

Delilah wiped her hand down her face. "Yeah."

"What was that?"

"Yes," Delilah practically yelled. "I'll be there."

"Good. I already booked your room at the Kaleidoscope—"

"What, I'm not staying with Mommy Dearest?"

"—and I'll email you the itinerary. Again."

Delilah grunted and hung up before Astrid could hang up on her, then dropped the phone on the counter like it was on fire. She twisted the lid off a half-full bottle of gin that sat next to the sink and took a shot, no glass required. The liquor burned all the way down, searing her nostrils and watering her eyes.

Two weeks. It was just two weeks.

Two weeks and enough money to get her through three months of rent.

She snatched up her phone, the damn traitor, and went back into the bedroom. Lanier's robe hit the floor, and she found her own strapless black jumpsuit that showed off the tattoos inked all over both her arms in a rumpled pile next to the dresser. After slipping it on, she spent about ten seconds looking for her underwear, her favorite purple lacy cheekies, but they were nowhere to be found.

"Fuck it," she said, slinging her bag over her shoulder and pulling her mass of dark curls into a messy bun. She located her red four-inch heels by the huge black-and-white framed photograph leaning against the wall. The image showed a white woman in a thin white dress, mascara running down her wet face as she stared at the viewer. She was in a bathtub, gown completely soaked and sheer, nipples barely visible above the milky waterline while her fingers curled around the rusty white tub. It was Delilah's, one of the four pieces in the Fitz show. Memories of Leila-Lucy-Luna forking over actual money and then promptly shoving her tongue into Delilah's mouth drifted into clarity. The damn name still played hide-and-seek.

"Hey," the woman said, lifting her head from the pile of pillows and squinting at Delilah in the city-light, hair a tousled mess. "Wait, are you leaving?"

"Um, yeah," Delilah said, popping on her shoes and double-checking that her wallet was in her bag, her keys, her Metro card. "Thanks, this was fun."

Leah grinned. "It was. Sure you don't want to come back to bed?" She lifted an eyebrow as the covers fell just low enough on her chest to reveal a lovely swell of skin.

"Wish I could," Delilah said as she edged toward the door. The offer was tempting, but her brain was already gone, back at her apartment, running through what the hell kind of clothes she needed to pack for this wedding and all the brunches and showers and, dear god, bachelorette parties Astrid had planned.

Astrid and her posse of mean girls.

London's face fell. "Oh. Okay, well . . . text me?"

Delilah turned her back to the woman and headed into the hall-way. She lifted a hand as she opened the front door. "Absolutely. Will do."

She knew she wouldn't though.

She never did.

On the subway ride back to her apartment in Bed-Stuy, it settled on her, the reality of what she was about to do. Going back to Bright Falls was one thing, but spending two weeks at Astrid and Isabel's beck and call? That was quite another.

And Delilah had absolutely no intention of making it easy for them.

CHAPTER

TWO

CLAIRE DRAINED HER wineglass for the second time that night, then set it down on the rough wooden table a little too hard.

"Relax," Iris said, sitting across from her, stirring the orange in her vodka soda.

"What do you think I'm trying to do?" Claire asked, tipping some more Syrah into her glass. She knew she'd regret it—red wine always gave her a headache—but Ruby was spending the night over at Josh's apartment for the first time in two years, and she'd told Iris she wanted to go out, clear her head, get away from Josh and his relentless *I'm a great guy!* smile and sparkling hazel eyes. So here she was, half drunk at Stella's Tavern, Bright Falls's only bar, while the neon jukebox in the corner piped out horrible country music and she tried not to hyperventilate.

"I don't think the alcohol's doing the trick," Iris said. She turned her head and surveyed the crowd, which consisted mostly of guys playing pool and a bunch of college students home for the summer.

"No, I don't think it is."

"You want to go somewhere else?" Iris squeezed her hand. "We could just go back to your place and watch a movie."

Claire shook her head. She felt jittery, like that time she and Josh had tried pot during their senior year in high school and her heart raced at a thousand beats per minute for the next two hours. She had to get some energy out, and sitting on a couch drinking and eating leftover pizza wasn't going to cut it.

"I just need a distraction," she said.

Iris's eyebrows popped up. "What kind of distraction?" Her voice was teasing, and Claire knew exactly what direction her friend was headed. Iris was always reading one romance novel or another, and was famous for constantly trying to cultivate happily ever afters for her friends, even if just for one night. "Like . . ." Iris rolled her hand over and over, prodding Claire to go on.

Claire rolled her eyes but smiled. "Okay, yes, fine. That kind of distraction."

"Yeah?"

"Yeah."

Iris clapped her hands once, then rubbed her palms like some wicked villain. "Yes! It's been forever since we got you laid."

Claire shushed her and leaned forward. "Keep it down, will you?"

"*Keeping it down* isn't going to land you in the sack with someone."

"Oh my god, will you—"

"Hey, Bright Falls!" Iris called, cupping her hands around her mouth as she stood up. Heads swiveled toward her, mouths already smiling like they did anytime Iris Kelly spoke up. "Who wants a chance with this fine-looking lady next to me! She's in desperate need of a good fu—"

"Iris, oh my god." Claire tugged on her best friend's gauzy tank top, half hoping she ripped the hem in the process. Iris plunked down into her chair while Claire's face burned like the center of the sun. Everyone stared, and more than a few lifted a brow in her direction. Matthew Tilden, who used to make extremely inappropriate comments about Claire's ass back in middle school, turned around on his barstool and tipped his beer toward her, while Hannah Li, a kindergarten teacher, for god's sake, smiled so prettily before lowering her long lashes to her cheek, Claire's stomach flipped.

"What the hell, Ris?" Claire asked.

"I thought you wanted to meet someone?" Iris said, her smile dropping away as she leaned across the table, her fiery red hair falling into her face. Iris did everything at one thousand percent, while Claire simmered at around ten.

"I did. I do. It's just . . ." Claire sighed. She wasn't great at this. Dating. Romance. Sex. She'd never had a one-night stand, never had a fuck buddy. She'd had a kid at nineteen; she didn't have time for fuck buddies. But lately, she'd been thinking about trying to date again. *Thinking.* She hadn't acted on anything. She hadn't had the time. Between running the bookstore and parenting a preteen, she collapsed into bed every night around ten, as soon as Ruby was asleep.

"How long has it been?" Iris asked.

Claire's mouth opened, then snapped shut quickly. It had been a while. No, longer than a while.

"Uh-huh," Iris said. "A long-ass time. Who was it?"

"What?"

"The last person you slept with. Hell, the last person you went on a *date* with."

Claire took another swig of wine, knowing the answer would scandalize Iris's romantic heart. "Nathan."

Iris nearly choked on her liquor. "Nathan? My assistant Nathan? The Nathan I set you up with because you're both ridiculously detail oriented and thought maybe you could bond over your filing system or something like that, whom you took to dinner at a lobster roll food truck in Astoria and never called again, making it incredibly awkward for me at the shop the next week? That Nathan?"

Claire sat back in her chair, slipping off her dark purple–framed glasses and polishing them on her shirt while she said nothing.

"That was six months ago, Claire. *Six*. I had no idea it was this bad."

The timing had been off with Nathan, that was all. He was a perfectly nice man—gorgeous, that's for sure, and Claire had definitely been attracted to him—but Ruby had just had her first major blowup with her best friend that week, catapulting Claire into uselessly trying to figure out how to help her daughter navigate the particular kind of hell that was fifth-grade friendships. And she'd been finishing up a small remodel in the bookstore, which had been her biggest project since taking over the business from her mom. It was important, a lot at stake.

"And I know you didn't sleep with him," Iris said.

Claire lifted a brow. "Is he a kiss-and-tell kind of guy?"

"No. He's classy as shit. However, I distinctly remember you being wound just as tight as you always are the next day."

Claire presented her middle finger to her friend.

Iris took a sip of her cocktail and then leaned forward. "Just please—*please*—tell me that the last time you had sex was not with the father of your adorable, precious, star-of-my-heart daughter. Tell me that wasn't the last time."

Claire froze, a confession on the tip of her tongue. But then she realized it wasn't even true. She waved a casual hand. "Oh, come on, Iris, you know it wasn't."

"I know no such thing."

"I tell you everything." Or almost everything. She and Josh split up nine years ago. Her heart pinched, just thinking of it. All the yell-ing, the crying. Ruby and her tiny two-year-old eyes so wide and scared while her too-young mom and dad ripped each other apart.

"Well, I must be having a memory block," Iris said, glancing around the crowded bar. "Where the hell is Astrid? She usually writes these things down."

"What, my sex life?"

"All of our sex lives, including her own." Iris lifted her hand, pretending to write in the air and putting on a posh accent that sounded nothing like Astrid. "Monday, May 3, 9:23 p.m. I let Spen-cer penetrate me tonight, which was quite thrilling. Next time, I might go a little wild and venture into reverse cowgirl. He keeps asking for anal, but I—"

"Oh my god, stop," Claire said, laughing. "She does *not* write that in her planner."

"She writes *something* postcoital. I guarantee it."

"She likes order. You're the one who personalized her planner."

"Yes, and I put a little box at the bottom of every day that says *Intercourse: yes, no,* or *maybe,* just for her."

Claire cracked up. "You did not."

Iris winked and took a sip of her drink. They'd all been best friends since fifth grade, when both Claire and Iris moved to Bright Falls the same summer. The only time they'd been apart were the four years Astrid and Iris went off to college while Claire dealt with a little surprise in the form of her daughter. Her friends came back to Bright Falls after graduation, cementing their trio back together, and Claire had never been so relieved. Astrid and Iris tried their best to be there for her during Ruby's first couple of years, but she refused to let them put their lives on hold. Plus, she'd had Josh.

Until she didn't.

Still, she'd made it, having a baby at nineteen and falling completely in love with her daughter, surviving her breakup with Josh. But she'd never been happier to see her friends settle back into Bright Falls. Astrid, armed with a shiny business administration degree from Berkeley, took over Lindy Westbrook's very lucrative interior design firm when the older woman retired, while Iris worked as an accountant until she had enough saved to open up Paper Wishes, her paper shop next to Claire's family's bookstore on Linden Street in downtown. Iris was hugely talented—she sold her own line of personalized planners and had over fifty thousand Instagram followers—while Astrid had almost single-handedly revitalized half the houses in Bright Falls.

Claire pretty much ran River Wild Books now, the store her grandmother had started back in the 1960s, and was trying her best to bring it into this century. Her mom let her do what she wanted, but what she wanted—putting in a café, hanging local art on the walls, getting some e-commerce going—took money, and lots of it. So far, she'd managed to brighten up the shelves and walls, setting up a little reading area with soft leather couches in the middle of the store, but that was it. Still, it was a start.

Claire slugged back another swallow of wine, which drained the glass. "Nicole Berry."

She said the name quietly, its sound still causing a slight twist somewhere in the middle of her chest. She'd not only had sex with Nicole, she'd dated her too. For five whole weeks before Claire reached the point where she wanted to introduce her to Ruby, and then Nicole had promptly freaked out. She'd liked Nicole. A lot. Could've even loved her if Nicole had given them half a shot.

Iris pulled a face at her. "Nicole."

"Yes, Nicole," Claire said, her voice lighter than she felt. "She was hot, right?" And god she was. Silky hair, long legs she used to slide around Claire's hips in a way that made Claire—

She clenched her thighs together at the memory. God, it had been too long.

"Um, sure, yes, gorgeous," Iris said gently. She knew how much Nicole leaving her had stung. "And that was two years ago. *Two*, Claire. You haven't"—she shook her boobs a little, and there was plenty there to shake—"in two whole years?"

"Oh please, no one has time for sex, Ris" was her brilliant retort.

Iris gave her an *oh you poor thing* kind of look. "That is absolutely not true, and you know it. I have sex all the time."

"*You* have a boyfriend."

"And you have a vibrator."

She lifted her empty glass in salute. "That I damn well do."

"And it's very, very tired."

Claire laughed but couldn't deny it. She'd had to charge her vibrator's battery at least twice in the past month.

Iris clinked their glasses together, and Claire emptied her lungs for the first time all evening. Ever since Josh had shown up back in town two months ago—swearing that he was staying this time, that he was starting a construction business instead of just picking up odd jobs with his friend Holden's building company he could easily walk away from, that he really wanted to be there for Ruby—she'd been on edge.

And with Astrid spinning like a top out of control lately, her wedding to Spencer looming like a dark cloud on the horizon . . . well, let's just say Claire was due a few drinks.

"How's it going?" Iris asked, reading her mind like always. "With Josh?"

Claire shrugged. "Ruby adores him."

"And we'll leave it at that?"

Claire blew out a long breath. Josh was the father of her child, and she'd always love him. But goddammit, if he got Ruby's hopes up one more time just to vanish on her again, she'd kill him. Like, literally kill him. Slow and painful. She'd had enough unreliable people in her life, and she didn't want Ruby growing up with the same ghosts.

She checked her phone. Other than the time and a picture of her daughter's smiling face, the screen was blank. No texts from Josh. Her vision swam just enough that she knew one more drink would turn her sloppy, and she couldn't do that in front of Josh. He'd never use it against her—at least she didn't think—but she was trying to set a good parenting example here.

"I should go," she said.

"What about your distraction?"

She waved a hand. "It can wait."

"Astrid isn't even here yet."

Claire rubbed her temples, everything in her life coalescing into a headache behind her eyes. "I want to check on Ruby over at Josh's before she goes to bed."

"Check on Josh, you mean."

"Can you blame me?"

Iris shook her head. "And I never will. You know that, right?"

Claire pulled some cash from her wallet. "I do."

"I love your sex-deprived ass."

Claire laughed. "You better."

"Forever and ever." She reached out and stilled Claire's hand on her wallet. "So let's take this slow."

"Take what slow?"

"Dating. Finding someone you like."

"Okay," Claire said carefully. "What do you—"

"One number. That's it. Just get someone's phone number tonight and go from there."

Claire's shoulders immediately curled around her neck. Everyone she'd ever been with, she'd met organically. Josh was her high school boyfriend. Nicole was a local author who wrote vegan cookbooks and had come into the bookstore to sign her latest on plant-based desserts. Claire handled the signing, they started talking, and that was that. Iris had set up Claire with Nathan. She'd never picked up someone in a bar, but having watched Iris do it at least a dozen times since high school, she'd always wondered what it was like, the thrill and excitement.

Claire forced herself to relax. This was why she'd come out tonight, after all. She wanted . . . something. Needed someone—even it was just the *possibility* of someone—to make sure she didn't fall back into bad habits with Josh. She wasn't in love with him; she knew that. But her body got stupid around him. Always had.

That didn't change the fact that the idea of walking up to some stranger and essentially saying *How you doing?* made her feel like she needed to puke.

"Starting tomorrow," Iris said, sensing her impending freak-out, "we're locked into a solid two weeks of wedding tomfoolery."

"Tomfoolery?"

Iris ignored her. "I'm talking brunches, lace doilies, manicures, and a sexless bachelorette party."

Claire laughed, remembering how Astrid had strictly forbidden anything phallic at her last hurrah. No penis straws, no penis cakes, and absolutely no dildos. Iris was hugely disappointed.

"Not to mention," Iris said, lowering her voice and leaning forward, "we've got to have the big t-a-l-k with Astrid, for which she'll probably hate us for the rest of her life."

Claire closed her eyes and breathed in slowly through her nose. Ever since Astrid had shocked even Iris into speechlessness a few months ago by announcing that she was marrying Spencer Hale, whom she'd barely dated for ninety days and with whom her best friends had only minimally interacted, Claire and Iris had been functioning on a constant low level of panic. He was handsome and rich and the only dentist in town and couldn't seem to get through a meal without putting some ridiculous demand on Astrid.

Hand me the salt, would you, babe?

Ask the waiter to bring another beer, would you, babe?

You didn't want the rest of your fries, did you, babe?

And what's more, Astrid complied every single time, even though the fucking salt was right in front of his golden-boy face.

Iris and Claire kept saying they were going to talk to her about it, make a plan, but weeks turned into months, and they still hadn't figured out how to explain to Astrid that the supposed love of her life was a total dickwad. Because he was the worst kind of dickwad, surreptitious and smiling. Half the time, Claire couldn't put her finger on what irked her so much about the man, only that she felt like she was hanging out with a poisonous snake anytime she was in the same room with him, which wasn't exactly a reason to tell Astrid to run for the hills. Besides, Astrid liked facts, numbers, and neither Claire nor Iris had any to give, just bad vibes they couldn't shake.

"Your point?" Claire asked.

"My point is that the next couple weeks are going to suck, and there's no way you're going to find someone in Vivian's Tearoom or at a spa at Blue Lily Vineyard."

Claire balked. "Hey, some sexy stuff can happen at spas."

"Not at the kind Astrid frequents."

"You never know."

Iris leaned forward. "So you're telling me that you'd get busy with your masseuse if they were into it? Like"—she flicked her eyes down to Claire's purportedly neglected nether regions and waggled her eyebrows—"*busy*."

"Oh, for sure."

"Bullshit."

Claire lifted her hands and let them drop. "Okay, fine, so I'd like to go on a date first. Sue me."

"I know. You're not wired for casual, and that's okay. Hence, a phone number. I know you hate Tinder and Her and Salad Match."

"I don't hate them, I just—wait, Salad Match?"

"Find your salad soul mate. It's a thing."

"Oh my god."

"Exactly."

Claire rubbed her eyes under her glasses. The dating world was terrifying. Not that she'd ventured into it very much. She'd dipped a toe in with Nicole, and that was enough. "I'm raising a kid here, Ris."

Iris's eyes went soft, and she reached out and squeezed Claire's hand. "I know. You've worked hard. You've sacrificed a lot, and you've got a great kid to show for it."

Claire's throat went a little thick at the emotion in her friend's voice. "Ris—"

"Which is all the more reason to enjoy a nice non-self-induced orgasm."

Claire smiled, and Iris got that gleam in her eyes, the same kind she got whenever she was working on a planner design or bought a brand-new set of Tombow markers. That *never say die* kind of sparkle.

"Okay." Claire sat up straight, rolled her shoulders back and her neck from side to side like she was getting ready for a boxing match. "Okay, I can do this."

"Hell yeah, you can."

"I'm hot, right?"

"Hot and a badass bitch."

She shook out her hands. "Just one number. How hard could it be?"

"Easy. Everyone in the whole damn room wants your number."

"I wouldn't go that far."

"I would." Iris reached across the table and slapped Claire on the back, shouting, "Go get 'em, tiger," over the din, and then sat back to sip on her drink with an excited grin on her face.

Claire turned in her chair and faced the lacquered bar, watching its activity for a few seconds. She looked over her shoulder at Iris. "One number."

"One number. That's it. A *valid* number. As in someone you actually find hot or interesting or whatever floats your mom boat these days."

Claire stuck out her tongue at her friend.

"Save that for better uses, my love," Iris said, winking.

Claire laughed. "Fine, fine." She turned back around with a deep breath. Stella's was busy tonight. It usually was on the weekends. Or any other night, for that matter. Bright Falls was charming, and she loved it, but with only a handful of shops, most of which closed at six p.m. on the dot, and just a few restaurants, the one bar in town was bound to be packed on a regular basis. She scanned the tables around the bar top, hoping to spot Hannah Li again. She'd definitely feel more comfortable approaching a woman or someone nonbinary. Since coming out as bi when she was a junior in high school, she'd always felt more drawn to other queer people or femmes. Josh being one of the few, albeit huge, exceptions. Still, she knew every queer woman in this town, and half of them were already married or partnered—including Iris, who'd figured out she was bi her sophomore year in college and would always and forever be more sister than potential partner—so the chances of someone single actually hanging out in Stella's tonight was slim.

And Hannah was nowhere in sight, not at her original table, not at the bar.

Claire started to turn back to Iris, ready to give up, when her eyes snagged on a pair of tight black jeans.

The woman was white and had just reached the bar, a rolling suitcase by her side. Her hair was dark and curly, volume for miles. She had her back to the room, and Claire couldn't take her eyes off the way she leaned over the bar to give her drink order to Tom, the bartender that night, pressing up onto the toes of her black boots. Tattoos vined down her bare arms. God, Claire loved a good tattooed arm.

And those jeans. Those jeans were nice.

"Attagirl," Iris said from behind her.

Claire turned. "You don't even know who I'm looking at."

"Please." Iris tipped her glass toward the tattooed woman. "You have a type, and that person is it, all broody and mysterious."

Claire opened her mouth to protest, but when Iris was right, she was right. She smoothed her hands over her own jeans, made sure the collar of her blouse was lying flat, and adjusted her glasses. Then she stood up and started toward the bar.

CHAPTER

THREE

STELLA'S TAVERN SMELLED exactly like it did the last time Delilah was here—booze, sweat, and sawdust from the lumber mill on the outskirts of town that big, burly workers were constantly tracking in on their boots.

She hadn't exactly planned on stopping by a bar the moment she got out of her Lyft. But it took about fifteen seconds of glancing around the darkened Bright Falls city center to remember that the whole damn place shut down when the sun disappeared, even on a Saturday. The inn where she was going to stay sure as hell didn't have a liquor license—it was more of a glorified B and B—and there was no way she was dealing with her step-monsters without a little liquid courage.

Once inside, though, she hesitated, her limbs suddenly rubbery as the laughter and music hit her ears. It'd been five years since she was last in Bright Falls. She'd fled New York, fled Jax and her gorgeous lying mouth for this—the coziness of the town, all these faces who'd known one another for lifetimes, this club she'd never quite felt like she belonged to, but felt fascinated by nonetheless. Ever since she and her father had moved here from Seattle when she was eight, a shiny new ring on his left hand, it had been this way, like she was standing outside a warmly lit house in the rain, tapping on the window. And it got even worse after her dad died two years later, leaving Delilah with a stepmother and stepsister who had no idea what to do with her.

Delilah took a deep breath and eyed the bar. It was a short thirty paces from where she stood, a sea of bodies between her and a drink. She was a New Yorker. An artist. A struggling artist, yes, but an artist nonetheless, goddammit. This town, her *family*, would absolutely not bring her to her knees. Not anymore.

She took off her gray bomber jacket and slung it over her suitcase. Humid, boozy air oozed over her bare arms, but it was better than suffocating in a coat. Angling her body to touch as few people as possible, she kept her head down and walked swiftly to the bar. Once there, she exhaled in relief, the bartender's face a stranger instead of some dude she went to high school with who would only end up squinting at her like she was a puzzle he couldn't solve. She'd been practically invisible in high school, a ghost with a cloud of unruly dark hair and blue eyes she kept on the dingy tile floor, the strange goth, while Astrid sparkled like a star at the ball.

"Bourbon, neat," she said, setting her suitcase next to a stool and resting her arms on the bar. The guy—*Tom*, his name tag said—smiled and winked at her, then made a very large show of pouring her liquor into her glass from a height of about two feet.

She simply stared at him, tapped her short gray-painted nails on the shiny bar top.

He set her drink in front of her and leaned in. Floppy hair, trimmed beard, deep brown eyes. Probably cute to someone who appreciated the male form.

"Thanks," she said, tossing it back. It burned all the way down, lighting her up in a way that made this whole godforsaken wedding seem bearable. She knew it wouldn't last though.

"You from around here?" he asked.

She fought an eye roll.

"I'm not your type," she said.

His smile faltered. "No?"

"No."

"I think you might be."

She tapped her glass for a refill, and he obliged with even more showmanship than before, flipping the glass *and* the bottle in the air. Oh, how she wished he'd drop them. When he gave her the drink, he lingered, eyes on hers expectantly. She sipped her bourbon more slowly this time, staring him down with a look that could blow a hole through the wall, in hopes he'd scamper off.

He didn't.

She sat down on the stool, knowing this was probably going to have to end with her coming out to a complete stranger, just like she'd done so many times before, which would most likely be followed by some horrible threesome joke this douche nozzle thought was sexy.

As she filtered through her list of *I'm gay* scripts in her mind, someone stepped up to the bar next to her. Out of the corner of her eye, she saw it was a white woman—light brown hair up in a messy bun, thick sideswept bangs, dark purple–framed glasses, and a vintage-style coral blouse with white polka dots. Delilah turned her head just a bit more, taking in dark high-waisted jeans that hugged curvy hips, soft arms, and nails painted lavender, chipped at the tips.

The woman turned too, their eyes locking.

Delilah sucked in a quiet breath.

The woman was gorgeous, yeah. Deep brown eyes, long lashes,

high cheekbones, and a fire-engine-red mouth with a full bottom lip Delilah immediately wanted to tug between her teeth. She remembered fantasizing about doing that very thing back in high school, every time Claire Sutherland would come to Wisteria House to do whatever the hell Astrid and her coven got up to while Delilah sat alone in her room. Claire was one of the girls who, unbeknownst to her, helped Delilah figure out she was queer. Claire had been curvy and nerdy-sexy, and Delilah could see she still was, her hips and ass a little wider than they were back then. She looked amazing.

And now, twelve years later, judging from the friendly smile gracing Claire's pretty mouth, she one hundred percent did not recognize Delilah.

At all.

This wasn't that surprising. Growing up, Delilah had watched Claire and that loud redhead, Iris, hang out with Astrid mostly from afar. After Delilah's father had died when they were ten, Isabel was completely shut down in her own grief for a while, so Astrid and Delilah had been mostly on their own for that first year. Astrid latched on to her new friends for comfort, and Delilah retreated into the books her father had given her, the fantastical worlds where orphans were heroes and the awkward kid always came out on top. She was curious about Astrid's friends, particularly as Delilah had never had any. She'd lost her mother at age three, and her father's own quiet nature meant the two of them fell all too easily into their own world. Delilah was observant, watchful, and her father had always celebrated that. But after he died, everything about Delilah suddenly became strange and unwelcome. She heard the whispers when Iris and Claire came over—*Why is your sister so weird? Is that her peeking around the corner? Oh my god, you can't even see her face she has so much hair.* Astrid would shush them, Isabel would say benign things like,

Oh, Delilah, don't you want to watch the movie too? but then the three other girls would go silent, obviously frozen in fear that Delilah would say yes, and Isabel would do nothing to actually enforce her suggestion.

So Delilah kept her distance, only answering questions when asked, which wasn't all that often. Eventually, the loneliness got so heavy it felt like she might suffocate just sitting in her room by herself. She had nightmares about it, dying and no one realizing it for weeks and weeks.

By the time she and Astrid got to high school, they'd all fallen into a routine. Delilah kept to herself as much as possible, drifting through her own internal world and only interacting with a few kids in her art classes. Isabel enforced family dinners every night and did her charity work and obsessed over Astrid's success and beauty and status. And Astrid, despite the times Delilah saw her buck up against her increasingly controlling mother, blossomed into the town's sweetheart, always smiling and surrounded by adoring fans.

Including Claire Sutherland. So of course she didn't recognize Delilah now. Plus, Delilah's late twenties had been kind to her. She finally figured out what to do with her curly hair, how to make it look more like, well, *hair*, as opposed to a bird's nest, and every tattoo that now spiraled up and down her arms she'd gotten in the last five years. She knew she looked different than she had as a teenager, as a twenty-five-year-old the last time she was here. Less makeup, better-fitting clothes.

Still, the blankness in Claire's eyes stung like a slap.

"Hi," Claire said, then lowered her eyes, lashes fanning her cheeks, lips curving into the tiniest of smiles. She tucked a loose strand of hair behind her ear and took a deep breath.

Delilah lifted a brow. Was she . . . ? Yeah, she was. Claire Sutherland was blushing, pink blooming on her round cheeks as though she'd been out in the wind. She took in the way Claire was standing—one knee bent, her hip popped out slightly, her forearms resting on the bar just close enough to Delilah's that she could almost feel the little hairs along Claire's skin. She glanced up at Delilah, smiled and turned even pinker, and glanced back down.

Claire Sutherland was hitting on her.

Her. Delilah Green, the Ghoul of Wisteria House. That's what Astrid and Claire and Iris had said about her one time. They were all fourteen or so and were in the kitchen—the kitchen Delilah's *father* had designed—and Delilah slipped in to grab an apple. The three girls had been talking, laughing, making a total mess while they baked snickerdoodles or oatmeal butterscotch-chip cookies or some shit. But the conversation, the motion, it all stopped dead when Delilah entered the room. Her cheeks burned—she remembered that, the fire that felt like it would consume her anytime Astrid's friends were over. She could never tell if it was from embarrassment or anger or desperation to belong.

"Hi, Delilah," Claire had said then.

Delilah remembered that too. Claire often said hello, but again, she could never figure out *why.* Delilah lifted her hand in greeting, the stiff, awkward gesture of a lonely fourteen-year-old girl, grabbed one of the six-dollar organic Honeycrisp apples Isabel insisted on buying from the bowl on the kitchen's island, and fled.

"God," she heard Iris say as she left. "Why does she always skulk around like that?"

"Iris," Claire had said, but laughter edged her voice.

"What? She's like a ghost, haunting the hallways of Wisteria House. No, wait, she's like a ghoul."

"What's the difference?" Astrid asked.

"I don't know. Ghouls are creepier?"

Then Iris made a wobbly *wooooo* noise and all three girls dissolved back into laughter. Upstairs, Delilah closed herself in her bedroom and bit into her apple, crunching so hard she remembered worrying she might crack a tooth.

And now, here she was, the Ghoul of Wisteria House sitting in Stella's Tavern while a very cute Claire Sutherland smiled at her.

"Hi, there," Delilah said, spinning on her stool so she could face Claire. This also gave Claire a full view of her face, which, come on, hadn't changed all that much since high school. Sure, her naturally thick eyebrows were a bit more under control and she'd learned how to go easy on the eyeliner, but still.

She tilted her head at Claire, giving her every chance to figure it out.

Claire just tilted her head too, the tiniest smile on her lips.

"What are you drinking?" Claire asked.

Delilah watched her for a beat. She could tell her. She *should* tell her. She should open her mouth right now and say, *Hey, remember me?*

Or.

She could flirt with this gorgeous woman—maybe even more than flirt, fulfilling every daydream teenage Delilah had about Claire Sutherland—and see what happened. Claire was clearly attracted to her. She wouldn't be standing here right now, lashes fluttering, if she wasn't. A warm and fuzzy feeling filled Delilah's chest, thinking about waking up in bed next to Astrid's mean girl BFF . . . and *then* telling her.

Added bonus? Astrid would be so pissed.

"Bourbon," Delilah said.

Claire motioned to Tom for the same, leaning over the bar as she waited. Once the glass slid between her fingers—Tom frowning at Delilah as he very unceremoniously poured the drink—Delilah noticed Claire's hands were shaking.

"Cold?" Delilah asked, motioning to her bourbon.

Claire laughed. "No. I think . . . I think I'm nervous."

Delilah nearly cackled. This was too perfect.

"About?"

Claire took a sip of her drink and then turned to face her. Delilah spread her knees, just a little, just enough that Claire was almost between them. She expected another blush, but Claire simply looked down and lifted a brow.

"Or maybe I don't have any reason to be nervous," she said.

"Maybe not," Delilah said.

Claire's eyes narrowed, and Delilah wondered if she was putting the pieces together.

"It's always a risk," Claire said, "talking to another woman in a bar. Not that I do this all that often."

"A risk?"

Claire nodded. "You could be straight as an arrow."

Delilah laughed but gave nothing away. "And you're not?"

"Oh." And the blush was back. "No, not at all."

Delilah remembered when Claire came out as bi in high school. It was a glorious day, a beautiful, rainbow-hued day. Not that Delilah had any delusions that Claire would ever go for her back then, but Delilah had figured out she liked girls in the seventh grade, and the fact that Claire Sutherland was a baby queer too? Young Delilah savored the knowledge, tucked it away, used it to give her confidence when she got to New York, when her ghoulish Bright Falls days were far behind her and she realized she was pretty damn charming and could flirt like hell, that other queer women and enbys actually *liked* her.

"Hmm," Delilah said, resting her chin in her palm. "That's quite the predicament."

Claire laughed again. It was a nice sound. Completely without pretense. She wasn't playing a game here. She was just . . . *cute*. "You're not going to help me out?"

"I haven't decided yet."

"Well, I'd appreciate you throwing me a bone. I'm not very good at this."

"Good at what?"

"Flirting."

Delilah made her eyes dramatically wide. "*This* is you flirting?"

"Oh god," Claire said, dropping her head into her hands.

"I'm kidding," Delilah said, taking a sip of her bourbon. "I know exactly what's going on here. You're trying to recruit me for a cult. I get it."

Claire lifted her head and laughed, eyes sparkling behind her glasses. "You got me. I've got the Prophet out back ready to shave your head and brand a unicorn on your ass."

"A unicorn?"

"It's a queer cult."

This time Delilah laughed. "Well, in that case, sign me up."

Claire's lips parted, just a little. "Really? So you're . . ."

She trailed off, waiting for Delilah to fill in the rest. Delilah leaned in until her mouth was right next to Claire's ear, her knees brushing Claire's hips. She smelled like a meadow, like fresh air, some delicate flower just underneath. Delilah made a show of breathing her in. Or maybe it wasn't even a show. This woman was funny and sexy and adorably unsure of herself, and for a split second, Delilah forgot who she actually was.

"I'm very, *very* queer," Delilah whispered, releasing the words slowly while her bottom lip brushed the shell of Claire's ear. The other woman inhaled softly, the sound fluttering low in Delilah's stomach.

Claire pulled back, her dark eyes all pupil. "That's very good to know."

"Isn't it?" Delilah said.

They watched each other for a few moments while Delilah thought about how she was going to play this. The *What's your name?* question was coming any moment, and she was having too much fun to ruin it with the truth. But before she could make a decision, a familiar voice cut through the country song twanging from the jukebox.

". . . where's Claire? Tell me she did not get hung up babysitting Josh."

At the sound of her name, both Claire's and Delilah's heads swung toward the voice. Astrid stood about ten feet away, shucking off her raincoat, no doubt Lululemon or some shit, her mouth running a mile a minute to a redhead—Iris Kelly, the final member of Astrid's triad—who was already sitting and drinking some clear liquor.

"Oh, there's my friend," Claire said. Delilah just hummed, watching her stepsister pour the rest of a bottle of Syrah into what must've been Claire's glass, filling it nearly to the brim.

"Easy, killer," Delilah heard Iris say.

"She's a little stressed," Claire said. "She's getting married in two weeks."

Delilah turned to look at Claire, who was still beautifully oblivious. "Is she now?"

Claire nodded, then leaned in and whispered, "To a total douche."

Delilah's brows shot up. She hadn't met Steven . . . Spencer? No, Simon. It was definitely Simon. She hadn't even laid eyes on him, but this little tidbit of information, coming from one of Astrid's posse, was . . . interesting.

"Really?" she asked. "How so?"

Claire shrugged. "Spencer's just"—dammit, it was Spencer— "demanding."

"Sounds like a match made in heaven, then."

The words slipped out, and Claire frowned, eyes narrowing softly. Her mouth opened, but before she could say anything, Astrid's voice split between them again.

"You will not believe what my sister did," Astrid said, taking a long pull of wine. "Well, *almost* did, but still, it's just like her to—"

Her tirade cut off as her eyes landed on Delilah.

"Wait . . ." Claire said, leaning back. Delilah watched her, could see the pieces coming together. Her pretty mouth dropped open, and her eyes went wide behind her glasses. "Oh my—"

"Delilah?" Astrid said. She stood up, wineglass still in hand. She was dressed in dark skinny jeans, a fitted white T-shirt, and a tailored black blazer that probably cost more than Delilah's whole closet. Her blond hair was shoulder-length, shaggy bangs brushing her brows. Gold hoops hung from her ears, and a huge-ass diamond sparkled on her left hand.

"Hey, sis," Delilah said, then lifted her glass in salute before knocking back the rest of the liquor. She was going to need it.

CHAPTER
FOUR

CLAIRE'S CHEEKS BURNED as she stared at the woman, whose flirty smile had turned into a full-on smirk. Anger, confusion, surprise—it all streaked through Claire like a flash flood.

This was Delilah? As in Astrid's reclusive stepsister who took off the second she turned eighteen and never looked back? Or barely looked back, at least. Claire remembered Astrid mentioning Delilah's promises to come home for Christmas or Thanksgiving each year and then only showing up once or twice. There was that spring trip about five years ago, but Claire didn't think she even saw Delilah then.

Not that she'd tried to see her. After Delilah had spent their childhood pretty much acting like Astrid didn't exist, Claire had very little reason or desire to seek the woman out. Besides, about five years ago, Claire was dealing with the fallout of another one of Josh's disappearing acts, trying to comfort her devastated six-year-old. An earthquake could've broken the town in half and she might not have noticed.

She blinked at the woman—at *Delilah*—trying to figure out how she'd missed it. The tattoos, those were new, and she could actually see her face now, whereas back in high school, Delilah's hair usually curtained around her features, hiding her from the world. Claire didn't even think she knew what color eyes Astrid's stepsister had, but now, she could see them clear as day.

Blue.

Like, sapphire blue. Dark and deep and fixed on Claire, a challenge in the set of her straight brows.

"Good to see you again, Claire," Delilah said as she set her now-empty glass on the bar.

Claire tried to think of something to say back, something smart and pithy, but all that came out was a brilliant "Uhhh . . ." as Delilah hopped off the stool and slid into a dark gray jacket. Claire's pulse was still in her throat, her breath fluttering in her chest from the woman's mouth brushing up against her ear.

Delilah. Delilah Green's mouth.

"What are you doing?" Astrid said as Delilah made her way over to the table.

"I'm drinking," Delilah said.

"Holy shit, you look different," Iris said.

"And you look exactly the same," Delilah said.

"I'll take that as a compliment," Iris said, grinning up at her.

Delilah shrugged and took a sip of Astrid's wine. Claire was still frozen by the bar, her fingers clammy on her own glass. She went back through the night, every moment since she saw Delilah walk into Stella's. Was she *that* into the woman that she hadn't made the connection? Clearly, because she still felt the tiniest thrum between her legs, an ache that started up the second Delilah had turned to face her, knees spread wide and taking up all the space in the world she wanted. The complete opposite of high school Delilah Green.

The complete opposite of grown-up Claire Sutherland, if she was being honest.

She shook her head, swallowed back the last of her bourbon, and walked over to the group.

"How was your flight?" Astrid asked her stepsister.

Delilah laughed. "We don't have to do this."

Astrid blinked, but then her mouth tightened. "Fine. Good night. You'll be there tomorrow?"

Delilah sighed, took another hearty swig of Astrid's wine. "You emailed me the itinerary for the next two weeks. Three times. I know where to be."

"I don't know what you know."

"See you tomorrow at noon," Delilah said as she took one more sip.

"Oh shit," Iris said. Even Claire tensed. Astrid made sure the week's itinerary was burned into all of their brains, and *noon* was definitely not the right answer here.

Predictably, Astrid's face contorted. "It's ten. Ten a.m. for the brunch at Vivian's Tearoom. Remember? Delilah, tell me you remember."

From behind the wineglass, Delilah smiled, and Claire nearly screamed at her. She was playing Astrid like a fiddle.

"Ugh, just be there, okay?" Astrid said, snatching her drink back. A bit of red wine sloshed over the rim, spilling onto the rough wooden table.

"Sir, yes, sir," Delilah said smoothly, then started for the door with her suitcase. She glanced at Claire once, something flaring in her eyes Claire couldn't name. Claire lifted her chin, trying to appear completely unaffected, like she openly hit on her best friend's sister on the regular and, of course, she knew who Delilah was the whole time. But then Delilah lifted a brow and pursed her lips as if to call bullshit, and Claire was the first one to look away.

Once Delilah was gone, she sat back down at the table and took her wine from Astrid. She wanted to chug it like water, but she still needed to drive home and she already felt a bit hazy. Bourbon and Syrah probably didn't mix very well. She couldn't tell if her head was spinning from the liquor or Delilah.

"So . . ." Iris said as they all settled around the table again. She had a purely evil grin on her face. "Did you get the number or not?"

"Oh, shut up," Claire said and then gulped down the wine anyway.

"What?" Astrid said, signaling Gretchen, the server who kept everyone at the tables happy, for a third glass. "Whose number?"

"No one's," Claire said, widening her eyes at Iris. Astrid was already pulled tight enough to snap with the wedding—not to mention that she still had no idea that her best friends despised her future husband. She certainly didn't need to deal with the fact that, not ten minutes ago, her wicked stepsister had gotten Claire all hot and bothered with one little whisper. If ever there was a sensitive subject in Astrid's life, it was Delilah Green. And honestly, Claire was doing her best to forget the entire interaction as well.

Luckily, Astrid seemed to be sufficiently distracted. She leaned her elbows on the table, fingers massaging her temples. "I have a headache. She's been here for ten minutes, and I already have a headache."

Iris reached out and squeezed Astrid's arm. "It's going to be fine."

"I don't know what I—" She took a deep breath, followed by a sip of wine. "I don't know what my mother was thinking, asking her to be the photographer."

"Me neither," Iris said, and Claire shot her a look.

"She was probably thinking that she loved Delilah's dad," Claire said softly. "And Delilah is . . . well, she's . . ." She widened her eyes at Iris, silently begging for help.

"She's . . . part of the . . . family?" Iris said slowly, her intonation tilting up at the end like it was a question.

Astrid's shoulders slumped. "Yeah. She is." Then her back went ramrod straight and she waved a hand. "At least, that's what my mother says, and she's the one with the checkbook. God knows Delilah wouldn't come without some other incentive."

"Your mother still uses a checkbook?" Iris asked, and Claire kicked her under the table.

"You know she almost bailed?" Astrid said, ignoring Iris. "I've been trying to get in touch with her for weeks now, emailing, texting, leaving voice mails. I had to call her at two in the morning her time last night just to get her to talk to me."

"So she's a vampire," Iris said, tipping some ice cubes into her mouth from her glass. "Explains a lot."

"Ris," Claire said, shooting her yet another look.

Delilah and Astrid's sisterhood wasn't typical. Delilah's mother died when she was only three years old—cervical cancer, if Claire remembered correctly—and her dad married Isabel, Astrid's mom, when she and Astrid were eight, so they'd practically grown up together.

Astrid told them that Delilah was a quiet kid from the beginning, attached to her father like a barnacle, which Claire supposed made sense. She understood single parenting. She also understood being a young girl with only one parent to rely on—it was a precarious, desperate, somewhat panic-fueled existence. But then Delilah's dad died suddenly of an aneurysm when the girls were ten, and there were no grandparents, no aunts and uncles, so Isabel had sole custody of Delilah.

Claire remembered the first time she ever went over to Astrid

Parker's big Georgian-style brick house to swim in the crystal-blue pool in the backyard. Delilah was a shadow, peering at them through that mass of hair around the back patio's stone pillars. Astrid had asked her if she wanted to come play once or twice, but Delilah never did, and Iris hardly ever had very nice things to say about her. Eventually, the shadow disappeared, and that's how it went for years, on and on. Delilah was a ghost, a wraith. Claire always tried to be nice to her—Iris was a little more teasing, but they were kids and Delilah was strange. They didn't know how to handle strange.

Since becoming a mother, Claire had sometimes thought of Delilah. At least she thought of the awkward girl she'd been growing up. Claire's own daughter was a quirky kid, artistic and precocious, easily lost in her own head. She wondered if that's all Delilah was, and she simply didn't have the right parent to help her navigate it. Isabel wasn't exactly the most maternal of mothers, and Astrid had been just a kid herself.

Now, Astrid shook her hair out of her face and held up her glass. "It's fine. It'll be great."

"It will," Claire said, clinking her glass with Astrid's.

Iris joined in, but she shot Claire a look and mouthed *phone number* before taking a sip.

Claire flipped her off.

———

ALL THREE WOMEN were sufficiently buzzed by the time Astrid's phone buzzed on the table. She snatched it up to read the text, glassy eyes turning a little crazed, if Claire was being honest. She and Iris locked gazes. They knew exactly who it was. They also knew their night of drinking and best friend revelry was about to come to an end.

"I've got to go," Astrid said. Iris mouthed the words right along with her. Claire fought a laugh. Because really, it wasn't funny. "That was Spencer."

"It's only nine thirty," Iris said.

"I know, but he's tired," Astrid said, gathering her purse.

"And?" Iris said. Claire wanted to kick her. Astrid was already stressed enough.

"And I'm tired too," Astrid said, standing up. "See you in the morning?"

"Eleven a.m. sharp," Iris said.

"Don't even joke," Astrid said.

Iris laughed, then stood up and kissed Astrid on the cheek. "Ten o'clock with bells and penis necklaces on."

"You're a horrible person," Astrid said, but she was smiling.

"You love me."

"God knows I do." Astrid came around to hug Claire before disappearing out the door.

"Another round?" Iris asked.

"I should go too," Claire said. "I've got to open up the bookstore before the brunch."

"You know Brianne can do that."

Claire nodded but said nothing. Brianne, her very capable manager, *was* doing that, but she was starting to feel itchy. Nine thirty was Ruby's bedtime, usually. She wanted to say good night. She wanted to make sure there was a good night to say, that Josh wasn't going to let her stay up until midnight watching crappy movies and eating bowls of sugar like he did the last time he'd been in town.

Okay, fine, he didn't feed her bowls of sugar, but he did forgo dinner for homemade chocolate chip cookies.

"You're full of shit, you know that?" Iris said, but she took out her wallet. "You okay to drive?"

Claire blinked into the still-packed bar, gauging herself. She wasn't sloppy drunk, but her head definitely felt floaty enough that she didn't want to risk getting behind the wheel. "No, but I can walk to Josh's." He lived downtown, about two blocks away.

Iris lifted a brow. "But you can't walk from Josh's back to your place."

Claire shrugged. If she ended up sleeping on the couch, waking up to make sure Ruby got up at a reasonable hour and ate some protein before the brunch, so be it.

Outside, it was dark, a light drizzle frizzing up Iris's hair and fogging up Claire's glasses. Claire linked her arm through her best friend's as they walked down the cobbled sidewalk. Streetlights spread an amber glow through the town center, turning the light rain into golden droplets floating through the air. A few businesses flew rainbow flags for Pride. At the corner of Main and Serenby, Iris slapped Claire's ass in goodbye.

"I'm going to go have sex, just so you know," Iris said, jutting her thumb toward the entrance of the building where she rented the top-floor apartment with her boyfriend, Grant.

"No one likes a bragger," Claire said.

Iris laughed, but Claire noticed her eyes tighten, as they always seemed to lately when it came to Grant. He was a chemical engineer in Portland, and they'd been together for two years. More importantly, he was desperate to have kids. He wanted to get married and pop out at least four redheaded amalgams of him and Iris, go on vacations to Disneyland during the summer, and coach Little League.

Iris . . . did not. She loved her brother's twins, visited them in San Francisco often. She spoiled them, sent them lavish birthday gifts, and had pictures of them all over her refrigerator. She doted on Ruby and was *Aunt Iris* in every way. But she didn't want her own kids. She never had. It was a sore spot with Grant, and Claire worried it was getting sorer.

"Everything okay with you two?" she asked.

Iris waved a hand. "Same argument, different day."

Claire pulled Iris into her arms and kissed the top of her head. Iris softened, just for a second, then pinched Claire's butt before pulling away and heading off down the sidewalk.

Claire watched her for a second before she moved on too, passing River Wild Books, her recent favorite reads displayed in the window, along with a rainbow flag she'd set up three Prides ago and had decided to leave up year-round. Paper Wishes came up next, its green-and-white-striped awning fluttering in the damp breeze. Josh's apartment was one more block down in a recently renovated building, above a new acupuncture studio that just set up shop a couple of months ago, around the time he rolled into town. It probably wouldn't last. Hardly any business ever did in this little corner of the block, and the townspeople liked to joke that the space was cursed.

Incidentally, Andrew Green's boutique architecture firm had been the last thriving business to take up that space—Delilah's father.

Claire shook off yet another Delilah-shaped thought and let herself in the outside entrance, then climbed the stairs. At Josh's door, she stood there for a few seconds, listening. Music trickled into the hallway, that indie folk rock that Josh loved, and she could hear Ruby laughing.

So, no nine thirty bedtime, then.

Rolling her shoulders back, she lifted her hand and knocked.

And waited.

And then waited some more.

She considered just opening the door and barging in—she grew the kid inside in her own body, after all—but she decided to try one more knock before going all SWAT team.

Finally, the music turned down and the door swung open, revealing the father of her child covered from head to toe in makeup. His lips were pink, his eyelids a glittery purple slash, and royal blue sparkled on his fingernails.

"Hey," he said. He was breathing hard and grinning, like he'd just been laughing. "Everything okay?"

She let her eyes flick down to his painted toes. "I should be asking you that question."

He blinked for a minute, and she saw it bloom into his eyes—that fear that everything wasn't okay, that he'd done something wrong.

"It's late" was all she said when he just stood there.

"Oh. Yeah, well"—he jerked his thumb toward his living room, in which Claire could see some sort of blanket fort draped between the couches—"we were having a makeover."

"I see that."

"Lost track of time."

"Mm."

He tapped a finger on the doorframe, and she lifted a brow at him.

"Oh shit, sorry," he said, opening the door wider. "Come in, sure."

"Thanks, I just wanted to say good night."

"Right," he said, but his voice was flat.

Inside was all fresh paint and sparse furniture—which Claire was pretty sure Josh rented along with the apartment—but even the simplicity of Josh's space couldn't hide the mess. The small kitchen, which opened into the living room, was covered in used pots and pans, red sauce splattered on the counters. Bits of dried pasta clung to a colander, and the oven was still on.

Claire clutched her stomach, wondering if the appliance would've continued to churn out *gas* heat all night long if she hadn't come by. She took a few steps, checked to make sure nothing was actually cooking—there wasn't—and pressed the off button with a little more vigor than necessary.

"I hadn't cleaned up from dinner yet," Josh said. "Obviously."

She just nodded. She could already feel it—anger, sadness, terror, something else she couldn't name—brimming to her edges. Any minute it would slosh over, but she worked hard to tamp it down, just like she always did.

"Mom!" Ruby said, poking her head out from under the blanket fort. She was covered in makeup too, the job much more pristine than Josh's own face. She assumed they'd made over each other. Josh was a good illustrator, his hands nice and steady.

"Hey, Rabbit," Claire said, walking over to the fort and bending down. Inside, fairy lights glowed, fastened to the cotton walls with clothespins, and a nest of quilts swirled around Ruby like a cloud. She was in her pajamas at least. "What's all this?"

"Dad made it. Isn't it cool?"

"The coolest."

"He cooked too. Did you know he could cook?"

She did. When they were together, he would cook all their meals. She hated cooking. Always had. When it was just her and Ruby, she made do, forced herself into Taco Tuesdays and had perfected many a casserole, but that was just throwing stuff into a baking dish. Josh *cooked*.

"I remember something about that," she said as Josh sat down next to her, crossing his legs like a kid and grinning. His hair was long on top, short on the sides, and looked stupidly adorable in the soft glow from the fairy lights. His hazel eyes twinkled at her. *Ruby's* eyes. Their daughter had gotten his hair too. Thick and wavy, strands of gold slipping between the brown.

"He made this homemade sauce with all these fresh tomatoes and garlic and olive oil and ugh"—Ruby flopped back onto the quilts, holding her stomach—"it was *so* good."

"Sound delicious," Claire said. "Isn't it time for bed?"

Ruby stilled and sat up, but it took a second to get her body to do what she wanted. She was all arms and legs, that awkward, lanky phase settling on her the last few months. "It's summer."

"I know, baby, but—"

"And I'm at Dad's." Her daughter glared at her, this withering stare that Claire had become very accustomed to lately. "Dad's rules."

Next to her, Josh cleared his throat. "Um, Rube—"

"We were about to watch *Inside Out*."

Claire glanced at Josh, and he just smiled that ridiculous smile he always smiled whenever this happened. The one that said, *I'm just a big dumb kid myself. What are you gonna do?*

"It's ten o'clock," she said.

"It's the *weekend*," Ruby said.

Claire let her eyes travel over the fort. Ten o'clock was no big deal, she knew. Neither was ten thirty. Eleven, for an eleven-year-old, was pushing it. But a movie would last until midnight, and Ruby was a beast when she didn't get enough sleep. Cranky and whiny and prone to tears at the slightest problem, all of which Claire would have to deal with tomorrow when Josh dropped her off. All of which he would know if he was part of their lives on any consistent basis. But now, sitting here in front of the, admittedly, most amazing blanket fort she'd ever seen, *she'd* be the bad guy if she said any of this. Just like she always was when it came to Josh.

"Rubes," Josh said, leaning toward his daughter. "Maybe we should call it a night. Your mom's right; it's late, and we can watch a movie anytime."

Claire pressed her eyes closed, waiting for that to land. She knew Josh was just trying to help, but now that he'd sided with her, he'd just put a stick of dynamite on top of a ticking bomb.

"Ugh, fine!" Ruby yelled, untangling herself from her own legs and crawling out of the fort and standing. She balled up her little fists, jaw tight. "Why'd you even come over here?"

"Ruby," Josh said sharply.

"It's just one night, and now you have to go ruin everything like you always do!" Ruby's eyes brimmed with tears, and Claire's heart lurched. It was true that over the past few months, her daughter had grown a little moodier, a little more temperamental. She'd read this was normal for her age—hormones were starting up, and god knew middle school was the worst few years in Claire's own life, but this, these instant tears and the yelling over a simple bedtime suggestion, this happened every time Josh came to town. It's like Ruby ran on a constant low level of panic, always worried he was going to leave, always *waiting* for him to leave, so that every moment he was actually with her felt like a rare jewel, a prize, and anything Claire did to try and maintain a modicum of normalcy was met with tantrums and eye daggers.

Claire stood, tried to reach out for her daughter. Sometimes a hug worked.

"I'm going to go brush my teeth," Ruby said, slapping her mother's arm away.

And sometimes it didn't.

"Want to come and watch me and make sure I floss?" Ruby said.

Inside, Claire flinched, but she knew she couldn't let Ruby get away with talking to her like that, no matter the circumstance.

"That's enough," she said.

And it was, apparently, because Ruby rolled her eyes and stomped off toward the hallway that led to the bedrooms. A door slammed, causing Josh to jump. Claire, she was used to it.

They stood there for a second in silence while Claire wracked her brain for what to say. She wanted to take her daughter home, tuck her into her own bed, and watch her sleep, but she knew that wasn't an option. Not unless she wanted to declare war, and she didn't. Not tonight.

Josh cleared his throat. "Hey, I'm—"

"I'll see you tomorrow," she said, turning and heading toward the door. She knew better than to even try to say good night to Ruby, and honestly, right now she was so pissed off, she didn't trust herself. She hated fighting with her kid, but she hated *this* even more—this feeling that she was the boring parent, a stick in the mud, a wet blanket thrown over all the glitter and fairy lights of Ruby's time with her dad.

"Claire, hang on."

She stopped at the door and dug inside her bag for her keys. She was sure as hell sobered up now. "We've got Astrid's wedding brunch in the morning at ten, so I need Ruby home by nine."

"God, Astrid's getting married?" Josh said, stopping with her at the door and leaning against the wall.

She flicked her eyes up to him. "I told you she was."

He nodded, even though she knew he didn't remember. "Poor guy."

"Oh stop," she said, but cracked a smile. Josh had grown up with all of them in school, so he knew Astrid was a lot. Particular, high-maintenance, wound tighter than even Claire, but *poor guy* wasn't even nearly accurate in this situation. More like *poor Astrid*.

"When's the wedding?" Josh asked.

"Two weeks."

"Am I invited?" he asked, grinning.

"I wouldn't count on it," she said as she opened the door. He held it for her, his arm over her head, and she got a whiff of his familiar scent—clean laundry and mint from his aftershave. Even with all that makeup on his face, her knees went wobbly, just for a second. She'd loved this man once upon a time. He was her first kiss with a guy, first time with a guy, first relationship with anyone. She'd made out with Kara Burkes her junior year in high school, at a Halloween bonfire not long after she came out, but she'd never dated anyone seriously until Josh.

He leaned closer to her, his smell wafting over her even stronger. Her eyes fluttered shut, and she knew she had to get out of here now. She'd made this mistake too many times, sleeping with him on one of his trips back, the emotion and stress of having him reappear in their lives and what it might mean gathering like a storm until it broke and they tumbled into bed together. Not even Iris knew about that. The last time was over two years ago, right before she started dating Nicole.

"Claire," he said, stepping closer, his voice like butter. *This* was why she'd desperately needed to get someone's number at Stella's tonight. She squeezed her eyes closed, Delilah Green flashing in her mind. That had certainly backfired.

"Look, I'm sorry about tonight," he went on. "I didn't mean to make it worse."

"Didn't you?"

Hurt filled his eyes. "No. Come on."

She sighed and fiddled with her keys. "I know. It's just . . ."

"I get it. I'm unreliable. But not this time. I swear it."

She looked up at him, all their history growing thick between them like life-choking vines. He reached out and tucked a stray piece of hair behind her ear. She almost leaned into him. It would've been so easy.

"I've got to go," she said, backing away and then slipping out the door before she could do something stupid like kiss him. She knew it wouldn't go further than that, not with Ruby in the apartment, but still. She didn't need the complication. She didn't want it either. She was just horny. That was all. She knew she didn't love Josh, not like that. But her skin was hungry. Iris's phone number quest had sufficiently riled her up.

Or maybe it wasn't only the quest.

When she got back to the small Craftsman she'd scrimped and

saved for years to make her own, her body still felt electric, plugged in. Once in bed, she slipped a hand between her legs, desperate to get rid of the ache so she could sleep. But when her fingers started moving, it wasn't Josh she envisioned. It wasn't even some nameless fantasy woman she made up in her head for times like these. No, this person had a riot of dark curls and sapphire-blue eyes, tattoos vining up her arms like snakes.

CHAPTER

FIVE

WHEN DELILAH FIRST opened her eyes, she had no idea where she was.

Chintz.

Lots of chintz.

Huge pink flowers swallowing her whole in a sea of quilts and pillows. Even the wallpaper bloomed like a spring garden. It wasn't an altogether rare occurrence for her to wake up in someone else's bed, but it's not like it happened every day either. And the women she usually spent the night with were not the type to drench their homes in floral patterns.

A headache swelled behind her eyes, her stomach roiling as she sat up. She vaguely remembered mixing bourbon and wine last night, which was how her mind wrapped back around to Stella's Tavern and the Kaleidoscope Inn in Bright Falls.

Jesus.

She fell back on the pillows—which smelled faintly of gardenias or some other cloying flower—and rubbed her temples before checking her phone. Just after nine a.m. She still had plenty of time to get ready and be on time to snap banal black and whites of heteros nibbling petits fours at Astrid's brunch.

God, Astrid's brunch.

She squeezed her eyes closed, breathed in through her nose nice and slow. For a second, she considered staying in bed and skipping out on the whole thing. Astrid was bad enough, but Isabel was sure to be there, and Delilah never knew how to act around her perfectly-put-together stepmother. It was like talking to a smooth marble statue—beautiful, cold, perpetually constipated expression locked into place. There was a time she remembered Isabel smiling, even laughing, looking at Delilah's father like he not only hung the moon, but made it sparkle and shine just for her. Isabel had truly loved Andrew Green; Delilah knew that full well.

It was Delilah Green sans Andrew that the woman never understood, nor did Delilah understand Isabel. And Isabel always seemed more than fine with their mutual misunderstanding, which was what hurt more than anything.

Delilah pulled the covers over her head and opened up her email, hoping for something from the Fitz about a sale, or perhaps a response from one of the photography agents she'd contacted with her portfolio in the last few months.

Nothing.

She clicked on her sent mail tab, opening the latest email to an agent she wanted to represent her so badly, she'd give up sex for a decade. She read through her message again, feeling a bit calmer at her professionalism, her clear knowledge of the industry. Then she clicked on the included link to her online portfolio, scrolling through the images of her best work.

They were all black-and-white, all queer women or nonbinary people, all featuring wedding dresses or suits and water and some sort of chaos. Her favorite was of a Black woman and a white woman, both in tattered lace gowns, sticks and leaves tangled in their hair, holding hands and wading into Lake Champlain in the middle of a thunderstorm. Not the safest shoot she'd ever done, but goddamn, it had been worth it. The light was perfect, the rain droplets like silver bullets shining in the air, the desperation evident in the way she'd had the models—Eve and Michaela, two women she knew from waitressing at the River Café—cling to each other. The effect was lovely and terrifying all at once, trauma and hope. It was beautiful.

It was *good*.

And yet, her inbox continued to accumulate cobwebs.

She switched over to her Instagram account, where she tried posting a photo a day. Weird shit she snapped on the sidewalks. Unique shots she got at queer weddings. Anything that matched the brand she was trying to build for herself—queer, feminist, angry, and beautiful.

Niche.

Her stuff didn't appear to work for most stick-up-their-ass NYC agents, but it sure worked for the Internet. She had close to two hundred thousand Instagram followers and couldn't keep track of the comments anymore. Her queer stuff got the most attention, and lately people had been asking whether or not she sold her pieces in an Etsy shop. It was affirming, but the idea of running her own e-commerce business—shipping, taxes, invoices—it all made her head spin.

She pulled up one of the pictures in her photos app she'd taken at JFK yesterday, a tripod-selfie in Terminal Four in front of the word *Queens* printed on the wall in huge blue and black mod letters against the white background, her in all black and gazing off to the side with one booted foot on the wall and looking . . . well, really queer and angry.

And sort of beautiful, if she was being honest.

She worked on the photo in Lightroom for a few minutes, adjusting the contrast, the tone, then uploaded it with no caption because she never wrote a caption. She was just about to click her phone's screen dark when a new email notification popped up. It wasn't from an agent or anyone at the Fitz gallery, but the subject line grabbed her attention like a yank on her hair.

Possible showing at the Whitney

Delilah sat up straight, floral comforter sliding to her lap, her fingertips tingling as she stared at the impossible words. They were real, though, sent from an official Whitney email address no less. Her hand shook as she tapped on the message.

To: delilah@delilahgreen.com
From: alex.tokuda@thewhitney.org

Dear Delilah,

Hello, my name is Alex Tokuda and I'm one of the curators at the Whitney in New York City. For the past several months, we've been preparing for our *Queer Voices* exhibition, due to launch on June 25, which will showcase queer photographers and their work from all over the country.

Delilah had, of course, heard of the Whitney's *Queer Voices* exhibition. While New York City was home to over eight million people, queer photography was still a small world—*niche* to the true assholes—and the fact that the Whitney itself was creating an entire showcase centered on queer voices was . . . well, it was huge. Delilah would've given anything to be part of this show, but she couldn't even submit work for consideration. The Whitney dealt with agents, seasoned gallery owners, famous photographers. They didn't take emails from queer women in torn black jeans working weddings and serving up sparkling rosé at the River Café.

She swallowed hard and kept reading.

> I do apologize for the weekend email, but in the spirit of full transparency, I'm a bit desperate here. Yesterday, a mutual acquaintance, Lorelei Nixon, shared one of your pieces, *Submerged*, with me, and I was very impressed. I'm writing to ask if you'd like to be part of the exhibition. I understand this is late notice. Usually, we book our artists months in advance, giving them plenty of time to prepare, so again, I do apologize. Just this morning, one of our previously scheduled artists had to pull their work from the exhibition due to a personal family matter, and I immediately thought of you. I feel your style and perspective is integral to this show, and this experience would be a wonderful opportunity to share your work with a broader audience. As this is a collective show, we're asking each artist to prepare ten pieces from their body of work.
>
> Please let me know your answer as soon as possible. We would need your pieces ready for matting and framing by June 20, at the very latest.
>
> Best,
> Alex Tokuda
> Assistant Curator, The Whitney
> they/them

Lorelei Nixon . . . Lorelei Nixon. Who the hell was Lorelei Nixon? Delilah scanned the email again, landing on the piece Alex referenced, *Submerged*. Of course Delilah knew the piece well. It was hers, after all, and she'd named the damn thing—a bride in a rusty bathtub full of milky water, mascara sliding down her face, eyes on the viewer. What she didn't know was why the hell someone named Lorelei had it available to show to—

Lorelei.

Realization flashed hot through Delilah's veins.

Lorelei.

That was the name of the woman who bought *Submerged* and promptly took Delilah home to her bed. Blond pixie cut, talented fingers. Not Lola or Leah or Laura, but *Lorelei.*

Which meant this was real. This was actually happening. The Whitney wanted Delilah's photographs on their walls. Granted, they only wanted them because someone else more important or high profile had to drop out, but who the hell cared about that?

She, Delilah Green, was going to show at the Whitney. The *Whitney*. LaToya Ruby Frazier, a Black photographic artist whose work blew Delilah away—and who happened to be just a few years older than Delilah—had shown at the Whitney. Sara VanDerBeek, Leigh Ledare. This was huge. This was potentially *the thing* that could alter the course of her entire career. This was a life changer.

And she was in fucking Bright Falls.

She felt a flare of panic as she scanned Alex's email again for the details. June 25, which was nearly three weeks away, but they needed her work by the twentieth, which was a mere four days after Astrid's infernal wedding. She chewed on her bottom lip, wondering just how much grief Astrid would give her if Delilah crapped out on her right now.

Not that she cared all that much about her stepsister losing her shit, but as Delilah's mind ran through dropping the bomb on Astrid, booking a flight back to New York, then walking into her apartment without the fifteen grand Isabel was paying her for this wedding gig, she knew she was up shit creek.

Delilah needed the money. Plain and simple. The Whitney might open a lot of doors, even give her some sales, but sales weren't guaranteed, and the show itself wouldn't pay her rent and ensure she could buy a grilled cheese sandwich from her local bodega for dinner.

Still, there was no way she was passing this up. She had some pieces that she really loved already—maybe even a couple that she'd shown at the Fitz—and she'd have a few days once she got back home to fine-tune them, take some new shots if she needed to, work in the co-opted darkroom where she rented space in Brooklyn.

She just wouldn't sleep for seventy-two hours. Or eat. No big deal.

The Whitney.

Her chest swelled, and she felt an inescapable need to squeal. So she did, nice and quiet, while she wrote Alex back and enthusiastically—but totally professionally—accepted their invitation.

She'd just hit send when someone knocked on her door. Delilah froze, trying to remember if she'd requested room service or something in her slightly inebriated state upon check-in last night. Nothing rang a bell, and she vaguely remembered hanging the *Do Not Disturb* sign on her doorknob. Better to hunker down in this sea of cotton flowers until they went away, but she'd barely decided on this plan when she heard the unmistakable sound of a key sliding into a lock and the door swung open, revealing Astrid with two to-go cups from the Wake Up Coffee Company, the local coffee shop, stuffed into the crook of her left elbow, a key dangling from her right hand.

Delilah dropped her phone and yanked the comforter up to her chin. "What the fu—"

"I knew it," Astrid said, cutting Delilah off. "I knew you'd still be in bed." She set the coffees down on the dresser—the entire piece of furniture might as well have been one giant papier-mâché flower—and fisted her hands on her hips. "It's nine thirty."

"How the hell did you get a key to my room?" Delilah motioned to the rose-gold key ring, which, unsurprisingly, was shaped like a rose.

"Nell is a client of mine."

"Nell."

"The owner?"

"Ah yes, good ole Nell."

Astrid sighed. "Most people actually know one another in this town, Delilah, and I redesigned her living room–kitchen combination last winter."

"So a few throw pillows and a leather couch equals a complete and utter invasion of privacy? Isn't that illegal?"

Astrid pulled a face, making it very clear that what she was about to say next pained her greatly. "I'm your sister."

Delilah rubbed her eyes—that word had always settled funny on her gut. "Well, you *should* have redesigned this god-awful hotel room."

Astrid's shoulders loosened, just a fraction, before looking around at the garden party. "Jesus, it's truly heinous."

"I think I dreamed I was getting strangled by a tulip all night long."

"Oh, these are peonies," Astrid said, running a hand over the pillow on a rattan rocking chair by the window.

Delilah flipped her off. "I guess it's better than the Everwood. That place is like something out of a horror movie."

The Everwood Inn—the only other inn within a fifty-mile radius of Bright Falls was just on the edge of town—was nationally famous for the Blue Lady, the purported ghost of a scorned early twentieth-century woman who haunted one of the Victorian house's bedrooms, searching for her long-lost lover with a glowing blue lapis lazuli stone around her neck. It was also creepy as hell, with dark wood furnishings, ancient carpets that probably dated back to the Blue Lady herself, and cobwebs in every corner. Pru Everwood, the owner, still ran it as an inn, as far as Delilah knew, but it was little more than a tourist trap these days.

"I'd love to get my hands on that place," Astrid said, swiping her hand over the dresser, then rubbing her fingers together, as though checking for dust. "It could be really beautiful if Pru would ever consider renovating."

"Pru was a hundred years old when we were kids. I doubt she's up for a big project," Delilah said, pushing back the covers and swinging her legs off the bed.

"Whoa, hey, oh my god." Astrid shielded her eyes like the sun was attacking her.

"What?"

"You're naked."

"I have on underwear."

"And no top."

"I'm sorry, I didn't expect company wielding a fucking key."

"Okay, fine, just get dressed or we're going to be late."

"I thought I'd go like this."

Astrid's arm dropped and she glared.

"All right, all right," Delilah said, grabbing her black bralette off the floor and slipping it on. Then she struck a pose. "How's this?"

"I will sneak in here at two in the morning and staple all your underwear to the walls."

"Sounds noisy. I'd probably wake up."

Astrid's nostrils flared. Delilah grinned, her plan unfolding perfectly. If she was going to photograph this wedding—particularly now that she had a ton of work to do for the Whitney show—then, dammit, she was going to have fun, and she could think of nothing more entertaining than getting under Astrid's skin. And Isabel's, if at all possible, though the woman was like a highly polished granite wall. Astrid, on the other hand, was easily ruffled.

"Is that for me?" she asked, motioning toward one of the coffee cups.

Astrid picked up a cup and held it to her chest. "You only get it if you put on pants."

"It better be my favorite drink."

"Pants. Or a dress. If you own one, that is."

"God, I hope that's my favorite drink. If it's not, I might have to go back to New York."

"Like I know your favorite drink."

"Americano with two inches of steamed soy milk, obviously."

"You're such a coffee snob."

Delilah shrugged. It was true. Her Brooklyn flat was full of sloppily-put-together IKEA furniture, but damn if she was going to drink shitty coffee. She'd rather go without.

"What are you doing?" Astrid all but screeched as Delilah pulled her bralette over her head and tossed it back on the floor.

"This shirt doesn't work with a bra." Delilah slipped on her favorite black silk tank she'd planned to wear today, specifically for its modest neckline and bordering-on-inappropriate low armholes that revealed half her rib cage. She turned to grab her high-waisted linen pants out of her suitcase and nearly smiled as Astrid's horror grew. She must've seen the side boob.

"We're going to *Vivian's*," she said.

"I know." Delilah pulled on the cream-colored pants, tucking in the tank and smoothing down the pleats before slipping on a pair of black heeled sandals and draping a few thin gold chains around her neck. The final look was sleek as hell. And by Astrid's resigned sigh, she agreed.

"Just don't turn to the side when Mom's around, okay?" she said.

"I wouldn't dare." Oh, she would though. She would totally dare.

"And do something with your hair."

Delilah smiled with all her teeth. "You're a delight."

Astrid winced. "I'm a little on edge, okay?"

Delilah decided to ignore this, heading into the bathroom and brushing her teeth for the full dentist-prescribed two minutes. Then she added a touch of mascara and some cherry-red lipstick—god, Isabel would love that—before checking out her hair in the mirror.

It was huge, curls and corkscrews frizzing out all over the place. Usually, she slept with it all piled on top of her head or wrapped in a silk scarf to avoid waking up in such a way, but last night, well, she'd been jet-lagged and half drunk, not to mention a little amped-up from Claire-freaking-Sutherland.

"So who's going to be there today?" she asked Astrid as she took out a bottle of her favorite blueberry hair gel, squeezed out a penny-size blob, and mixed it with some water before smoothing it over each section of her hair.

"Well, Mom, of course," Astrid called. "And Spencer's mother, grandmother, and sister. The girls."

The girls.

"Ah, the coven."

"Don't call them that," Astrid said, appearing in the doorway. She was wearing an ivory bandage dress, simple pearls around her neck, a single diamond solitaire sparkling on her finger.

"What? Covens are powerful, feminist, badass groups of women."

"Somehow, I don't think you meant it like that."

Delilah grinned at her in the mirror. "So . . . Claire's looking well."

Astrid's posture went rigid, her eyes narrowing on Delilah's reflection.

God, she made it too easy. Delilah tilted her head innocently, widening her eyes like an ingenue. "*Very* well."

"Don't," Astrid said.

"Don't what?"

"Claire is not your type."

Delilah turned around and folded her arms over her chest. "Oh, I think she is."

"Well, you're not hers."

Delilah's eyebrows popped up. "You don't think so?"

"No way."

"That's not what it felt like last night."

Astrid straightened even more, if that was possible. She was like a dry twig in the winter, ready to snap. "What about last night?"

Delilah shrugged and turned back to the mirror. "Just, you know."

"No, I don't. Claire would *never* go for you."

Now, that stung a bit, but Delilah tried not to let it show. She fiddled with her hair a bit more, twirling an errant curl by her ear into the right pattern. "And why not?"

Astrid laughed, a bitter sound. "Um, because she actually *likes* people?"

Delilah's mouth dropped open, a clever retort right on the tip of her tongue, but nothing came out. It took her a second to get her composure back, to remind herself that she needed the money from this job, that she wasn't the same girl she'd been in high school, that she didn't need Astrid's fucking approval, and that Claire Sutherland had very clearly been into her last night.

A fact she had no doubt would drive Astrid absolutely crazy, not to mention Isabel, who adored Claire and Iris like they were her own. And here came the big, bad dyke Delilah Green to corrupt her sweet little girls. God, that woman must've really loved her father to have wanted Delilah at the wedding.

"I think I'm exactly Claire Sutherland's type," she said.

"I just meant she's not into casual, Del. And . . . well, *you* are."

Delilah gritted her teeth. She hated when Astrid called her Del. Her stepsister hadn't said anything that wasn't true, at least as far as she knew. She'd never told Astrid about Jax, whom Delilah met seven years ago at a queer wedding she was working. What started as a standard hookup with the maid of honor led to Delilah falling hard and fast for the first and only time in her life, a shared apartment in Brooklyn within six months, and dreams of years spent entangled on the couch watching movies and rushing home from a job to kiss a familiar mouth.

Jax, as it turned out, had other dreams.

Before her, Delilah hadn't done relationships. And after . . . well, she definitely didn't do them after. They simply weren't worth it, and Jax had made it clear Delilah wasn't worth it either, even after nearly two years together. Delilah liked sex though. She *loved* sex, and New York City was full of queer people just like her, women and enbys who simply wanted that—skin and breath and mouths, one night with someone else filling your bed without a single sticky string attached.

But Astrid, her *sister*, part of the tangle of reasons Delilah didn't do relationships in the first place, telling her she could never get someone like Claire Sutherland? The implication made her feel like she was fourteen again, an oddball, Astrid and *the girls* standing around the kitchen and laughing.

Delilah turned around. "You're wrong."

Astrid shook her head. "Leave her alone, okay? She's been through enough."

Delilah frowned. She remembered hearing Claire had a kid

young, didn't go to college like the rest of the coven, and stayed in Bright Falls to run her family's bookstore. Oh, damn, yeah, that was rough, having a job and a roof over your head and a successful business. "All the more reason for her to have a little fun."

"Just drop it, will you? Let's go."

But she didn't want to drop it. She wanted to be *right*. For once, she wanted to win against Astrid Parker, to be someone other than the woman who needed her stepsister's money to pay her rent this month, the girl on the outside. Even the whisper of a victory, ghoulish little Delilah Green wooing one of Astrid's perfect princesses into her bed, felt like a drug in her veins.

"Let's make a bet," she said.

"A bet," Astrid said, her voice flat.

"I'll bet you I can get Claire to realize I'm *exactly* her type by your wedding."

Astrid rolled her eyes. "Are you serious? I'm not betting on my best friend's love life. What's even in that for me?"

"Winning? Being right? I know you love that."

"I've already won," Astrid said. "She'd never do it."

"Why not?"

"Because she loves me and she's my best friend, two concepts I know are completely foreign to you."

She spit the words, and they had their desired effect, Delilah's lungs feeling suddenly airless. She didn't let on, though, keeping her face perfectly passive as she got herself together inwardly.

Besides, this time, Astrid Parker was wrong. True, Delilah hadn't expected her to actually take the bet, but it was enough that it was out there, a challenge that Delilah was damn sure she was going to win, especially since Claire was the one who started this whole thing last night at Stella's, fluttering her lashes at Delilah the way she did.

"Can we just go already?" Astrid said. Delilah smiled at her reflection in the mirror, pulling on one of the armholes of her shirt to reveal just a little more side boob.

Astrid huffed through her nose before spinning and all but stomping back into the bedroom.

"Ready," Delilah singsonged, looping her camera bag over her shoulder.

"Here," Astrid said, shoving the coffee cup at her stepsister.

Delilah took a sip of the drink, the bitterness of plain black coffee making her shudder. Most definitely not her favorite.

WHERE THE KALEIDOSCOPE Inn was drenched in flowers, Vivian's Tearoom in downtown Bright Falls was drowning in crystal. Chandeliers, salt and pepper shakers on the white linen–covered tables, vases full of cream-colored mini calla lilies, and flickering ivory candles inside round crystalline globes as the centerpieces. Everything was cream, white, ivory, or gold, as though an elite wedding planner came in and projectile vomited all over the place.

Delilah had only been inside the room for a total of thirty seconds before Isabel descended.

"There she is," her stepmother said. Delilah braced herself but soon realized Isabel wasn't even talking to her.

She was talking to Astrid.

"Cutting it a little close, aren't we, dear?" Isabel said, gliding over like a bat through her cave. She was dressed in an ivory pantsuit—the color matched Astrid's dress perfectly, because of course it did—and three-inch ivory pumps. The woman was already a solid five feet nine without her precious stilettos and pushing sixty years old, but god forbid she ever went anywhere without heels. No, Isabel Parker-Green had to positively tower over her minions, or else they might just forget their place.

Astrid tensed, her shoulder like a brick wall against Delilah's.

"In my day, brides arrived early to every single event so as to greet their guests," Isabel went on. She reached out and smoothed the already-smooth fabric at Astrid's hip. "But what do I know, right? I guess I should just be grateful you didn't meet Spencer on some website." She said *website* like it was a four-letter word, which Isabel absolutely never uttered.

"Sorry, we stopped for coffee," Astrid said, exhaling heavily.

Isabel frowned. At least, she seemed to try to frown. Delilah saw a twitch near her pink-painted mouth, but the skin there simply bounced back into perfect formation, Botox-infused soldiers ready for inspection. "Coffee? Before coming to a tearoom? Astrid, really, I'm—"

Delilah plopped her camera bag onto the nearest pristine gold-and-white table. Crystal rattled against crystal. "Where shall I set up?"

She said the words so sweetly her teeth ached. And she planned to pair them with some dagger eyes in Isabel's general direction, but as soon as she'd made her presence known, she regretted it. When Isabel swung her Sauron gaze toward her, Delilah's heart immediately started pounding. Her palms grew clammy, and she had an almost uncontrollable urge to curtain her hair around her face. She resisted. She was nearly thirty years old, for Christ's sake. She was a New Yorker now, a grown-ass woman. She had a show coming up at the Whitney. She could handle a small-town society priss.

Except this small-town society priss had been her parent during the most formative years of her life, entrusted by her sweet, naive father to provide and care for his only daughter, and Delilah was still waiting for that *care* part to kick in.

Isabel's eyes skated down Delilah's tattooed arms, lingering, Delilah was almost positive, on the blooming black-and-gray wisteria that trickled down her left forearm, ending in a sun's curling rays at her wrist. Wisteria had been her father's favorite, the reason he'd named his home what he did, carefully planting the purple flower so that it vined over the front of the house like a guardian. When Delilah got her first tattoo five years ago, it was always going to be wisteria. Not for the house that she couldn't wait to escape, but for her father who dreamed of a family, the life he wanted to give her.

"Delilah, darling, is that you?" Isabel said, something like a smile attempting to settle on her frozen lips. She came at Delilah with open arms, settling her hands on her stepdaughter's shoulders as she air-kissed both sides of her face. "It's been so long, I hardly recognized you."

She drew out the *so* for what felt like a thousand years.

"It's me" was Delilah's brilliant retort.

"You're looking . . . well," Isabel said.

"Why, thank you, *Mother*," Delilah said back. Isabel winced slightly. She'd never asked Delilah to call her Mom or Mother or anything other than Isabel, and Delilah knew exactly when to bring it out. "You too."

Isabel bared her teeth, her own special version of a warm smile. "You're coming to Monday's dinner, yes? Tomorrow night?"

In the extremely detailed itinerary Astrid had emailed her, nestled in between Sunday's brunch and a two-day trip to a vineyard in the Willamette Valley was a Monday night dinner at Wisteria House. Delilah was hoping to avoid Isabel's lair during her time in Bright Falls, but the wedding itself was taking place in the backyard, not to mention the rehearsal and tomorrow's dinner.

Still, the thought of walking into that house always made her stomach cramp.

"Yes, she'll be there," Astrid said when Delilah just stood there with her mouth pursed, adding a subtle elbow in Delilah's ribs.

"With bells on," Delilah said.

"But not literal bells," Astrid said, her elbow digging deeper.

Delilah side-eyed her stepsister, because really? Then again, the thought of showing up with actual bells somehow attached to her person, clinging and clanging a glorious cacophony and disrupting the museum-like quiet of Isabel's dungeon, did sound like something Delilah would be into. And with Isabel's age-old air of entitlement and Astrid over here bossing her around like she owned her—which she sort of did for the next two weeks—Delilah could sense that familiar anxiety bubbling up again in her chest, the pressure to please just to earn a sideways glance.

And the feeling really pissed her off. Oh, there would be bells all right.

"I'm so glad," Isabel said, then waved a hand at Delilah's arms. "These are new." The wisteria was just one of many tattoos. She had more flowers spiraling up her left arm; a bird arching over her right shoulder, an empty cage just underneath; a little girl holding a pair of scissors, the cut string of a kite floating off near her elbow; a tree half covered in verdant leaves, half winter bare; more birds twisting between even more trees and flowers, flying free and wild. She loved her tattoos. Each one made her feel like herself, like her own person, a feeling she only experienced after leaving Wisteria House.

"They are," Delilah said.

Isabel's mouth twisted—or tried to—and she nodded while continuing to scan Delilah as though for inspection. "Well, they're lovely. And how nice to have them on full display here at Vivian's." She flashed her teeth in a way that indicated it wasn't nice at all.

Delilah flashed her teeth right back. She was not going to let this woman win. She was going to be in this fun-forsaken town for fourteen days, and this time, *she* was going to win, goddammit.

She retrieved her camera from her bag, attached the right lens for candids, and looped the strap over her head, making sure to lift her arms nice and high and angle her body so Isabel got a full view of her side boob. She might have even . . . jiggled a little. She knew she'd hit her mark when her stepmother sucked in a breath, promptly turned on her stilettos, and marched off toward a woman Delilah assumed was the wedding coordinator, judging by her French twist, professional attire, and iPad.

"I thought you were going to keep that hidden," Astrid said, nodding toward Delilah's ribcage.

Delilah smirked, wrapping both hands around her camera to hide the fact that they were shaking. "Oh, come on, you knew I wasn't going to miss an opportunity to ruffle Mommy Dearest's couture feathers, now was I?" Then she shimmied her shoulder back and forth, just once, causing her admittedly small breasts to undulate under her blouse.

Astrid's mouth twitched, and for a split second, Delilah could've sworn her stepsister nearly smiled, but then the front door opened and the smile was gone, replaced by her usual worry-brow, that tight set to her lips that made her look exactly like Isabel. She rolled her eyes at Delilah and then headed toward the women now spilling into the room in a flurry of tea dresses and lace.

Delilah grabbed her moment of freedom and sped toward a table with a champagne fountain where a tower of glass flutes rose tall and proud, already filled with sparkling golden liquid and a splash of orange juice. She stowed her camera bag underneath, the ivory satin cloth hiding everything away, before taking a flute off the top. Normally, she'd never drink on a job or while working on a piece.

But this was anything but normal.

From across the room, she caught Isabel watching her with that quintessential judgy expression—mouth puckered, eyes narrowed. Or maybe that was just the Botox. Either way, Delilah tipped her glass to her and then downed the drink in two gulps. The bubbles burned her throat, but her limbs warmed pretty quickly. She took a few deep breaths, readying herself to do her job. She could blend into the walls, like any event photographer should, go through the motions until this day was over. She'd done it a thousand times before. Two hours, tops. Surely, this bland crew wouldn't brunch for longer than that.

After she felt sufficiently steeled, she turned around. A couple more people had arrived—an older woman with a coif of dyed blond hair she assumed was the mother of the groom, a woman around Delilah's age who looked about as happy to be there as she felt, and an elderly lady who seemed to be ripping Isabel a new one for not already having a drink in her hand. Delilah liked her immediately.

She lifted her camera and snapped a picture of the interaction, capturing Isabel's fake smile and tight jaw. How lovely. How very mother of the bride.

Delilah grinned to herself, thinking of all the less-than-flattering moments she could immortalize over the next two weeks if she so chose. She'd worked a lot of weddings over the past ten years, and if there was one thing she'd learned, it was that they brought out the worst in people.

She started a slow circle around the room, snapping the food display—there were petits fours, of course, all gold and white and ivory icing and embellishments—and the table settings. Figuring she should get some shots of the bride herself, she made her way toward Astrid. Iris and Claire were both there, the three of them huddled together and talking in low voices. As Delilah got closer, their tones sounded tense, stretched, and she readied her camera to freeze the moment in time.

But then Claire shifted, and Delilah caught a glimpse of her face around Astrid's blond head. Her eyes were red and damp, and she dabbed furiously at them with a tissue, trying to keep her tears from forming a mascara trail down her cheeks.

God, she was gorgeous even when she cried. Delilah angled her head to get a better look at her—hair up in a twist, soft tendrils around her face, a hunter-green lace dress that looked like something right out of *The Great Gatsby*, tea length with lace sleeves that stopped at her elbows, a fitted lace bodice that showed just the right amount of cleavage, and a little satin bow at her curvy waist. She had a garment bag tossed over one arm.

"I knew this would happen," Claire was saying. "Goddammit, I knew it. I knew he'd do this. I'm so sorry, Astrid."

"Hey, come on," Astrid said, her hand on Claire's arm. "It's fine. I don't care if Ruby's late."

Iris snorted next to her, and Astrid elbowed her.

"I don't," Astrid said again, her eyes on Claire. "I just want her to be part of this."

Claire nodded. "He's on his way. He said he was, anyway."

Astrid smoothed her hand down Claire's arm while Iris said something about liquid courage and made a beeline for the champagne table. Through the space her absence created, Claire lifted her eyes and met Delilah's. Maybe Delilah was imagining it, wishing it into being, but she swore Claire's pupils widened a little behind her glasses and her mouth parted, just a little.

Just enough.

Oh, Astrid was so, so wrong. Delilah was totally going to win.

CHAPTER SIX

CLAIRE WAS GOING to kill Josh. Eviscerate him. Flay him alive. Cook him in a cauldron with his own juices.

This morning, she'd woken up before seven and texted him.

Good morning! Are you two up?

A simple, easygoing message. Nothing too demanding. She'd even prefaced the question with a jolly greeting, for god's sake. He hadn't responded for another hour, but that was okay. Eight o'clock was still plenty of time to get Ruby up and moving and home by nine so she could change into the dress Astrid had bought for her to wear at the brunch. It was lavender, all lace and satin, and Ruby positively hated it. Claire didn't have the heart to tell Astrid. Two years ago, Ruby would've loved the dress, but now it seemed her daughter balked at anything other than jeans, dark colors, and Claire's old nineties band T-shirts Ruby had found in a box in their attic six months ago. Claire had managed to convince Ruby to suck it up and be polite—the dress cost more than Claire's own vintage outfit, after all, and Ruby truly loved Astrid—but Claire also knew that Ruby's mood swung like a pendulum these days, and it would be better to get dressed at home rather than at Vivian's.

Hence, her request that Josh have their daughter home by nine o'clock that morning.

But nine o'clock came and went.

Where are you? she'd texted him at 9:01.

On it! he'd texted back, but clearly, he wasn't *on it*, because when the clock struck nine forty, Claire had to leave or risk being late, and one of the maids of honor could absolutely not be late to a wedding event in Astrid Parker's world. Claire drove to Josh's apartment and banged on the door at nine fifty. No one answered, and she was on the verge of a panic attack, because now she not only envisioned that eye twitch Astrid got whenever she was stressed, but her mom brain ran through a million horrifying scenarios, everything from a car accident to Josh kidnapping their daughter and taking off for Canada.

Where the fuck are you? she'd texted when she parked outside of Vivian's, her hands shaking and tears swelling into her eyes. Maybe the *fuck* would get his attention. She hardly ever used the word, reserving it for times like this when she fantasized about hacking off a vital part of Josh's anatomy.

On our way! he texted back. Claire wanted to wrap that happy exclamation point around his neck. Stopped for donuts! And then he'd had the gall to follow that up with a donut emoji and a green heart.

Now, she stood in the middle of Vivian's extravagant ballroom, marble under her heels, eyes red and puffy, while Delilah Green captured it all on film.

Or maybe not. She hadn't actually lifted the camera to her face since she'd spotted Claire, but she *was* standing awfully close while Claire unraveled, looking ridiculously hot in a black silk tank and sleek cream pants that made her already willowy frame even more elegant.

And those tattoos, Jesus. Claire's eyes snagged on one in particular, lightning bolts and rain droplets falling from a gray cloud into an ocean-filled cup. A storm in a teacup.

She'd barely noticed any specific designs last night. She'd been too busy trying to act like she wasn't an exhausted mom of an angsty preteen while she hit on Astrid's estranged stepsister. And that Delilah had clearly known who she was . . . No, she couldn't think about that right now. She needed to focus her energies on not committing homicide. She looked away from Delilah just as Vivian's front door burst open behind her, Josh and Ruby spilling inside and laughing.

"Morning, ladies!" Josh called when he spotted them, pulling his aviator sunglasses down his nose, revealing those twinkling eyes.

Iris growled.

"Joshua," Astrid said, folding her arms and glaring.

"I hear congrats are in order," he said, but then he held his hands palms up and moved them up and down like a balance scale. "Or condolences to the groom. Either or."

"Goodbye, Joshua," Astrid said.

"What, I'm not invited?" he asked, presenting that panty-dropping grin that had gotten Claire into trouble in the first place.

Astrid said something back, because Astrid could never keep her mouth shut once Josh opened his, but Claire ignored them both. If she talked to Josh right now, she'd claw his face off. She'd learned not to engage with him when she was this mad. She always came out feeling like she was overreacting, like she didn't know how to relax and whatever Josh had done was actually no big deal.

And lately, nothing pissed her off more.

Claire made her way to her daughter and wrapped her in a hug. "Hi, baby."

"Hey, Mom." Ruby was dressed in her usual black jeans and black T-shirt, this one featuring Bush's album cover for *Sixteen Stone*.

"Have fun?"

"The funnest. We got donuts, and Dad let me have coffee."

Claire ignored that last part. "Good, I'm glad. Let's get changed, okay?" She held out the garment bag and smiled brightly.

Ruby took the bag, but her shoulders slumped. "Do I have to?"

"Honey, we talked about this."

"I know, but . . . the dress itches. And I hate the color. It's a little kid's color."

"It is not. I wear lavender all the time."

"Yeah, but you're my *mom*."

She said *mom* like she might've said the word *scorpion*.

Claire forced a smile and took Ruby by the elbow, walking her over to the hallway that led to the bathrooms. "It's just for today. I promise."

"Dad said I didn't have to wear it."

Claire gritted her teeth. *Kill him. Cook him on a spit.* "Dad is not in charge right now. And this is for Aunt Astrid, okay? You love Aunt Astrid."

"If Aunt Astrid really loved *me*, she'd let me be myself."

Claire felt the color drain from her face. She could almost hear exactly how Josh would've said those words to Ruby, kindly, gently, like it was the most natural thing in the world to simply do whatever you wanted, whenever you wanted, consequences and other people be damned.

"Ruby, I . . ."

But she didn't know what to say to that. Didn't know how to combat it. All her mom wisdom flew right out of her head, and she felt a weight settle on her shoulders, that heavy feeling of being unable to win.

"Can I see it?"

Claire's head snapped up to see Delilah Green standing about five feet away, leaning against the hall entryway with her head tilted at Ruby.

"See what?" Claire asked.

But Delilah wasn't talking to Claire, apparently. She looked straight at Ruby and asked her question again, nodding toward the garment bag in her arms.

"I . . . I guess?" Ruby said. "Who are you?"

Delilah smiled and walked toward them. "Wicked stepsister." Then she winked at Ruby, and Claire's daughter actually broke out in a full-face smile, eyes crinkling and everything.

"Oh, I've heard about you," Ruby said, still grinning.

"Ruby," Claire said, but Delilah just laughed.

"Have you now?"

Ruby nodded. Claire couldn't remember ever talking about Delilah around Ruby, but god knows what Iris had said at their house on one of their cocktail nights. After even one drink, she got even more loose-lipped than normal, and Ruby liked to lurk when she was supposed to be in bed. Claire had caught her more than once over the years, sprawled out on her stomach in the hallway just out of sight, her chin propped up on her hands, eyes wide and hungry like she was listening for secrets about buried treasure.

"What have you heard?" Delilah asked, tilting her head.

Ruby opened her mouth, and Claire saw it happen—the realization of whatever she had to relay to Delilah wasn't necessarily kind. Pink spread over her daughter's cheeks, and her throat bobbed in a hard swallow.

"Um . . ." Ruby said, and Claire knew she had to step in, do something, say anything. She wracked her brain for a distraction, but then, Delilah's smile . . . fell.

An unpleasant sensation swooped through Claire's belly, shame or guilt or embarrassment, she wasn't sure. She was sure, however, that Delilah also realized that whatever Ruby had heard wasn't flattering.

"Never mind," Delilah said, waving a hand, then tugged on the garment bag in Ruby's arms. "So show me this dress."

Ruby exhaled heavily. So did Claire, if she was being honest. She definitely didn't want a reprisal of Iris's drunken—or in some cases, stone-cold sober—tirades about the Ghoul of Wisteria House. Not that anything that Iris said was necessarily untrue—Delilah had left Bright Falls and Astrid, despite their strange childhood together, and never looked back—but seeing Delilah's teasing smile plummet, as though a heavy blanket settled on her in the middle of a sweltering summer . . . well, Claire hadn't been prepared for that.

"It's horrible," Ruby said as she unzipped the bag. "Just look."

Delilah reached out a hand, pulling the lace and satin into view. Claire couldn't be sure, but it looked as though her fingers shook, just a little, as she touched the dress. Her brow furrowed, mouth dipping downward.

"God, it is," she said.

Ruby burst out laughing, and just like that, any empathy Claire had vanished.

"Are you serious right now?" she said as quietly as she could. Really, she wanted to scream. She didn't need this. She just needed Ruby in the dress.

"I wouldn't lie about something so important," Delilah said, meeting Claire's eyes. There was no malice there, no sarcasm. Just . . . well, hell, Claire couldn't tell *what* was there. Delilah held her gaze for a beat longer than felt natural, her full mouth tipping up at the corners, just barely. Freckles spilled over her nose and onto her cheeks. Claire hadn't noticed them last night in Stella's dim lighting. Now, though, she saw them plain as day, and had a ridiculous desire to trace a pattern with her finger.

Claire shook her head and stepped back. "Ruby, we need to get changed, okay?"

"Mom," Ruby said, her voice a whine, and Claire felt even more blood rush to her cheeks. This was going to turn into a fight; she could feel it. A huge, tear-streaked fight, right here in Vivian's, at Astrid's first wedding event. She took a deep breath to calm her wobbling stomach, trying to think of what she could say to Ruby, the magic words to make this all fine, but her mind was blank.

Horrifyingly, her eyes started to sting, a swell just behind them. She was so tired. She was so, so tired of being the bad guy.

"Hey," Delilah said. She took the dress fully out of the bag and draped it over her arm. "Let's see what you and I can make of this. What do you say?"

She was looking right at Ruby again, Claire forgotten. Ruby's arms dropped and her face brightened.

"Yeah?" Ruby asked. "Like what?"

"Well," Delilah said, heading toward the bathroom, "I happen to have a lot of experience in remaking a piece of clothing I hate into something I sort of like, and I'm thinking you've got some ideas up your sleeves too." Her eyes flicked down to Ruby's nail polish—bright turquoise alternating with a deep plum—then up to her hair, which Claire hadn't even noticed yet. Her daughter's locks were long and loose on one side, but on the other, an expertly woven fishtail braid arched down to her shoulder. She didn't even know Ruby could do a fishtail braid. And when she looked even closer, she spotted a silver-and-black-striped ribbon twisted through the plait.

"Maybe," Ruby said, grinning, and then Delilah swept Ruby into the bathroom, the heavy oak door thunking shut behind them.

Claire stood there for a few long moments, trying to figure out what the hell just happened. She felt silly, slightly embarrassed, that she hadn't thought of just *asking* Ruby what she would change about the dress. It was a dress. It was already made. Astrid bought it for her, and god knew, it probably cost more than all of Ruby's other clothes combined, which were a blend of Target and Old Navy, cheap stuff that she'd just grow out of in a year. Claire loved clothes, loved finding unique pieces in thrift stores and vintage clothing shops that made her feel like herself, but she never really *remade* anything. She'd never even thought about it.

Still, underneath the need to do a massive face-palm, there was something else, something stronger.

Relief.

Delilah was actually going to get her daughter into the dress. There would be no public argument that ended with Ruby screaming that she hated her. Claire pressed her hands to her stomach, breathing into the new space she felt there.

"Claire?" Astrid came down the hall, her heels clicking on the marble floor. "Everything okay? We're ready to start."

Claire nodded and jutted her thumb toward the bathroom. "Ruby's just getting changed."

"Oh good. I really hope she likes the—"

But her voice was cut off when the bathroom door swung open. Ruby stepped out first, Delilah behind her. The dress had been completely transformed. Well, not completely. The bones were still there. *Only* the bones. The lace overlay was gone, leaving the satin slip underneath, sleeveless with a scooped neck and falling to just above Ruby's knees. Instead of the matching lavender pumps that had been in the bag, Ruby wore her black combat boots, the ones Claire had gotten her for her birthday last April.

The effect was . . . perfect.

Ruby looked like herself, much more than Claire ever imagined she could in Vivian's Tearoom. What's more, she was *smiling*, and that was enough for Claire.

"What . . . How . . . When . . ." Astrid spluttered, her mouth hanging open. "What happened?"

"Delilah fixed my dress," Ruby said proudly. She popped her hands on her hips and struck a pose. "Isn't it amazing?"

"Yeah, *sister*, isn't it amazing?" Delilah said, her mouth pursed like she was trying not to laugh.

"I . . . well . . ."

Claire saw Ruby's smile start to dim.

"It *is* amazing," she said, taking her daughter's hands and holding out her arms out to get a better look at her. The smile brightened again. Claire twirled Ruby around once before leading her back into the main room, her daughter leaning against her happily.

She looked back over her shoulder, just once. Catching Delilah's eye, she mouthed *thank you* at the exact moment Delilah lifted her camera and snapped a photo.

CHAPTER SEVEN

DELILAH LOWERED HER camera and inspected the photo on her screen. Claire had her arm around Ruby, her head turned over her shoulder. Her mouth was open a little, lips pursed slightly, her *thank you* just released into the air. With her hair up and those nerdy-sexy glasses, her gold heels and that lacy dress swelling over her hips before hitting her calves, she looked incredible.

Classic.

Iconic, even.

And the photo was damn good. The lighting was perfect, the soft glow of the hallway gathering around Claire and Ruby, like it was protecting them.

But what was even better was the expression in Claire's eyes as she looked right at Delilah. She was grateful, sure. Delilah had clearly helped her avoid some sort of preteen catastrophe, but the gleam in Claire's gaze was more than that. It was *interest*.

Delilah smiled down at her screen, enjoying whatever dance the two of them were engaged in. Astrid was dead wrong—Claire was intrigued, at the very least, and Delilah could definitely work with intrigued.

Still, she wasn't exactly sure why she stepped in to help Ruby with her dress. She'd been covertly snapping photos of Astrid's argument with Josh—whom Delilah vaguely remembered as a baseball guy from high school—figuring Astrid would *love* to memorialize how her mouth twisted up and her forehead filled with little wrinkles as she berated him.

But then it all came together: Claire crying, the girl—who couldn't be more than ten or eleven—looking absolutely miserable as Claire pulled her toward the bathroom with that garment bag. Delilah knew Claire had a kid, that she'd gotten pregnant right after high school and decided to keep the baby. Delilah hadn't felt anything about the news then—other than maybe a slight morbid glee that Claire's decision meant she wouldn't get to attend Berkeley with the rest of the coven.

Before she knew it, Delilah had drifted away from Astrid's bickering and toward Claire, fascinated with someone her age having an almost-teenager. Or maybe she was more fascinated with how Claire's dress perfectly clung to her ample chest. Either way, there she was, watching Ruby slowly melting down over a dress.

She had a flash right then, one of Isabel lingering in her doorway with clenched fists while a thirteen-year-old Delilah sat on her bed, ripping up the dress her stepmother had wanted her to wear to a charity event for which she was on the board.

You couldn't do this one thing for me? Isabel had asked. *After everything I've done for you?*

"Can I see it?" she heard herself asking, and that was that. She and the girl had gone into the bathroom, and once Delilah had asked her what she actually *wanted* the dress to look like, Ruby chattered nonstop about the boots her mom had gotten her for her birthday this past April and something simple that didn't make her armpits itch.

Now, as Claire and Ruby wandered back into the tearoom, Astrid cleared her throat.

Delilah lifted her eyes and saw Astrid's clenched jaw. So, helping Ruby had come with the added bonus of pissing Astrid off. This day was going better than she expected it to. "Yes, dear?"

Astrid's eyes narrowed. "Really? You just happen to be the one who tears up the dress I gave Ruby?"

"She hated the dress."

"She—what? She did not."

Delilah gave her an *oh come on* look. "Did you see the *happy* girl who just walked out of the bathroom?"

"Yes, but I—"

"It's a dress, Ass. Let it go."

Astrid pressed her mouth flat. "Just take the pictures, okay?"

"Oh, I've already got some good ones." She flipped through the photos on her screen and landed on one of Astrid talking to Josh, her mouth wide open and her nostrils flaring. "See?"

Astrid looked, then lifted her arms before letting them slap back down to her sides, exasperated.

"Damn, you really hate that guy," Delilah said.

There was a beat of silence before Astrid said, "Well, he's unreliable and irresponsible and doesn't give a shit about anyone but himself, so yeah."

Delilah very nearly made a joke about Astrid swearing again— *And in Vivian's! Fetch Isabel's smelling salts!*—but then her stepsister's words registered, hanging heavy in the air between them, spat with a little more force than Delilah thought the guy was worth. Astrid crossed her arms and stared down at the floor, her teeth working her lower lip.

Something uncomfortable settled in Delilah's stomach.

"Just get back to work, okay?" Astrid said, already turning away and walking off down the hall. "I'm not paying you to be a goddamn tailor."

THINGS WENT SOUTH from there.

Delilah did her job, just like Astrid asked. She slinked around the room and snapped photos of a whole lot of dainty nibbling on crustless cucumber sandwiches and delicate sipping of mimosas. Like any event photographer worth their salt, hardly anyone noticed her, while she noticed everyone, everything.

Every laugh.

Every time Isabel put her hand on Astrid's back or smoothed a hand over her hair.

Every chair filled, not even an extra one in a corner in case Delilah might like a break.

Every *I'm so proud* her stepmother uttered.

Delilah captured it all, just like she was supposed to.

Still, she felt like she was suffocating. She couldn't get Astrid's words out of her head, couldn't forget the anger and hurt that laced every syllable, like she wasn't talking about Josh at all. Looking at Astrid now, she seemed fine. Happy. She had everything she needed. Friends, an adoring mother, a fiancé, a beautiful wedding brunch that would bleed into even more beautiful wedding events, culminating in a beautiful wedding. Knowing Astrid like she did, this was everything her stepsister could ever want.

Delilah's skin itched and her lungs felt tight. She arranged shots, changed lenses, bent and arched to get the right angle, all the while sweat gathered on her upper lip, under her arms, the same sick feeling she remembered so often from her childhood.

The only person who seemed to notice her was Ruby, who kept trying to catch her eye with a funny face, her features all twisted up and adorable. Delilah managed to smile at her—she was a sweet kid—and snapped a few pictures of her silly expressions to humor her.

She got a lot of Claire too. Once or twice, Delilah could've sworn that the other woman had been looking at her, had just swung her eyes away right when Delilah's camera centered on her, but she couldn't be sure. Either way, she got far more shots of Claire than she probably should have, but what could Delilah say? Claire was a beautiful subject, and focusing on her seemed to calm Delilah's swirling thoughts. In fact, concentrating on making sure the chandelier's light reflected on Claire's shiny hair just right was all that was keeping Delilah from picking up one of those little quiches—whose crust looked just like a goddamn seashell, for Christ's sake—and yelling at the top of her lungs, *What the fuck is this all for?*

She remembered events like this while growing up. Remembered them vividly, Delilah stuck in an itchy dress, sitting at one end of Wisteria House's long dining room table while Isabel and Astrid sat at another, surrounded by adoring townsfolk who thought Isabel was the soul of class and charity.

Isn't it so amazing how Isabel took in that poor girl after her father died?

Isabel didn't have to do it, you know.

She is an odd little thing, isn't she? God bless Isabel.

Delilah had heard it all over the years, praise and adoration, the musings at Delilah's demeanor, the judgment that her gratitude for Isabel didn't bubble over like champagne from a fountain.

Despite walking calmly and snapping photos dutifully, her breathing became quicker and more ragged as the minutes passed. She focused on her task, the simple movement of aiming and clicking, but it didn't help. Then she tried thinking about the Whitney show, but at this moment, New York felt like another planet, three weeks a lifetime away. She could feel Astrid's eyes on her. Isabel's. Dyed-blond coif lady, who, if she was Spencer's mother, would surely know all about Delilah by now, her poor dead parents, how *magnanimous* Isabel was in *taking her in*, like she was a fucking lost orphan Isabel found on the streets.

She passed close by the champagne tower, which was just as tall as it had been at the beginning of the event, Vivian's staff replacing a glass as soon as one was taken. She lifted one off the top again and gulped down the drink, swishing the bubbles around her mouth as she stared at the golden liquid through the expensive glass.

Then, before she could think too much about it, she let her hip bump the table as she turned back around. It was subtle, clearly an accident, but it was enough that the glasses rattled against one another and then . . . toppled.

Gloriously. Horrendously. Like Sauron's tower finally vanquished, the flutes crashed downward, champagne splattering and glass shards spilling all over the table and marble floor with a triumphant cacophony.

The room fell silent. Delilah lifted her gaze, her expression completely flat, and looked right at Isabel, whose own expression had apparently broken free of its Botox prison—nostrils flaring, skin flushed, barely-there eyebrows so low they dipped into her lashes.

"Oops," Delilah said, then snapped a picture of the alcohol-and-glass mess at her feet.

DELILAH DIDN'T BOTHER getting any more shots after that. She helped the staff clean up the mess—the least she could do, as this disaster was her fault and one hundred percent worth it. Even better, the *accident* had brought the brunch to an abrupt close. When the floor was once again pristine, however, she didn't want to deal with Astrid or Isabel. As guests began to get up from the tables and Isabel pasted on a smile again, Delilah grabbed her camera bag from under the table, packed it up, and all but sprinted out Vivian's front door, desperate for some non-perfumed air and some liquor.

She spilled outside and sucked in the warm, early-summer breeze. In New York, it was already stifling hot, but here in Oregon, the weather still felt like spring, blue sky peeking between light gray clouds, the piney scent of evergreens. She sped down the sidewalk and headed straight for Stella's.

Unfortunately, the idyllic spring weather didn't change the fact that the bar didn't open until six. She slapped her hand against the rough wooden door and headed back to the Kaleidoscope Inn, where she turned off her phone and took off her pants before ordering a club sandwich from the inn's kitchen. Snuggled in the huge king-size bed, chintz be damned, she binged six episodes of a show on her laptop about a gay teenager in Georgia.

Eventually, though, when the sky started to go lavender, she got antsy. She was used to nights out on the city streets, waiting tables or keeping her hands busy by working on a piece, going to art events, or just hanging out in a bar until she found someone she liked. It didn't always end with a hookup—sometimes it was just nice to sit with someone and talk about nothing, anything.

She didn't like the quiet, the nights alone.

She flipped her laptop shut and slipped her pants and shoes back on. Five minutes later, she was heading down Main Street toward Stella's, the globed streetlights casting a golden glow over the cobblestone sidewalk. There were a few people out, couples and families, annual vacationers who'd come to stay in one of the few huge houses lining the river. Most of them were white, straight-looking, a weird number of them licking vanilla ice cream cones like they were posing for candids in *Good Housekeeping*.

Delilah sped up, ready for the noise and activity of Stella's. She was about halfway there when she spotted a messy bun through a store window, purple glasses catching the soft light. Books filled the window display, lots of colorful paperbacks promising summer sun and romance, a few thick cookbooks featuring lemony grilled chicken and watermelon salad with cayenne pepper on the covers.

River Wild Books, the sign said.

Of course, Delilah knew the store well. As a kid, it was one of the few places she could go in Bright Falls where she could breathe freely, disappearing in a way that felt like a choice rather than being ignored, happily spending hours reading fantasy novels and comic books in the back of the shop.

She paused, stepping closer to the window. Claire stood at the counter next to the register, flipping books into a stack, pausing to type something into the computer every so often. Inside, it was dim, a single Tiffany lamp on the counter and a strand of fairy lights around the store's perimeter the only light.

Before she could overthink it, Delilah pulled at the door, a relief she couldn't explain filling her chest when it swung open easily. A little bell chimed.

"Hey, sorry, we're closed. I meant to lock—"

Claire's words cut off as soon as she saw Delilah.

"Oh. Hi," she said, setting down the book in her hand.

Delilah glanced at her phone, the open door resting on her backside. "Closed at seven o'clock?"

Claire's mouth twitched. "Small town. But we get really wild and stay open until eight on Friday and Saturday."

"Whoa, edgy. Next thing you know, Stella's will be putting on a drag show."

Claire laughed. "If only."

Delilah laughed too, then they both fell silent. Claire hadn't told her to get the hell out, so Delilah took that as a good sign and came all the way inside the store, the door closing behind her. The smell hit her first—paper and glue, the faint whiff of something citrusy and fresh. It nearly knocked her back a few steps, the scent of her childhood. But unlike the perfumed aroma of Wisteria House, the store's clean air reminded her of safety, belonging.

The shop had changed a bit since she was last here. The dark shelves had been lightened to a blond wood and went all the way up to the ceiling now, with extra stock at the top and two matching blond wooden ladders, one on each side of the store, attached to an iron pole. The carpet used to be this thin industrial stuff, the kind you'd find in insurance offices and schools, but now smooth hardwood stretched the entire length of the small space. Fairy lights dangled here and there, and in the middle of the store, nestled between display tables and freestanding shelves, four dark brown leather chairs were arranged facing one another, a book-covered coffee table in the middle. A light fixture hung over the reading space, small round light bulbs hanging amidst glistening silver leaves on chains.

The effect was no small thing, brightening the shop in a way that made Delilah smile.

"This place is gorgeous," she said, running her hand along the counter where Claire stood. "It didn't look like this back when we were in high school."

"Yeah, I know," Claire said, fiddling with the books at her side. She stacked and then restacked them in a different arrangement, over and over. "When my mom remarried a few years ago, she and her husband wanted to travel, so I took over."

Delilah leaned her elbows on the counter. She remembered

Claire's mother—Katherine. She had soft brown eyes and round hips, and she had been one of the few adults in this town who had treated Delilah like a normal kid as opposed to a nuisance. There was no Mr. Sutherland. He had taken off when Claire was around nine, right before she and her mother moved to Bright Falls, if Delilah's memory served.

"You did all this?" she asked.

Claire met her eyes and stared for a few seconds. Delilah wasn't sure Claire was even aware she was doing it, and she watched Claire's throat bob in a hard swallow.

"Hello?" Delilah said, tapping the back of Claire's hand softly, just once before drawing back.

Claire jolted, then cleared her throat and looked down, fiddling with the book stack again. "Um, yeah, I did. I want to do more. Add a café, get some local art on the walls that people can buy, but that takes money."

"Most things do." Delilah took the top book off of Claire's stack and pretended to look at it. In truth, she was just thinking up ways to keep the conversation going, reasons she wouldn't have to leave. She felt weirdly at ease in here. Plus, she was enjoying the way Claire got all flustered around her a little too much. "Your mom still traveling?"

"Yeah. She's in"—Claire's eyes narrowed in thought for a second—"Colorado this month. But she'll be back for Astrid's wedding."

"Ah yes, the joyous occasion." Delilah turned and rested her hip on the counter.

"Have you met Spencer yet?" Claire asked.

"Haven't had the pleasure."

"Oh, it's a pleasure, all right." Sarcasm coated Claire's tone.

"That bad, huh?"

"I don't know." Claire waved a hand.

"If I recall correctly, you mentioned last night that you didn't like him," Delilah said.

Claire stiffened. "I'd rather not talk about last night, if you don't mind."

"'A total douche.' That's what you called him."

Claire sighed, pressed her eyes closed. "I shouldn't have said that. I thought—"

"That I was someone else."

"And you knew exactly who I was."

The words were sharp, ready, like Claire had been holding them in for a while. They looked at each other, the air between them so charged Delilah wondered if they might get a shock. She let the silence settle, let herself maintain eye contact. She had to play this delicately, or Claire would close up like a clam. There wasn't any denying what happened last night, no way Delilah could feign ignorance.

So she didn't.

Instead, she leaned into Claire's space—not too much to crowd her, but enough to notice a stray eyelash on her cheek.

"I did," Delilah said softly.

Claire's brows dipped. "So . . . so you just let me make a fool of myself?"

"Fool?" Delilah frowned and tilted her head. "You didn't make a fool of yourself. But would you have kept talking to me if you knew who I was?"

Claire pressed her mouth together.

"It's okay. You can say it," Delilah said.

"Say what?"

"That you would never have approached me if you'd known I was Delilah Green."

"I . . . That's not . . . You're twisting it around."

"Am I?"

Claire rubbed her forehead. "Okay, fine, no, I probably wouldn't have come up to you like that if I'd known."

"Well, there you go."

"There you go what?"

Delilah leaned just a little closer, whispering her next words. "The reason I didn't tell you who I was."

It wasn't a complete lie. True, Delilah had been a tad devious the night before at Stella's, letting Claire go on like they were total strangers, reveling in how she'd feel when she found out they weren't. But Delilah had also been turned on as hell, intrigued by adult, bi-sexual Claire Sutherland, a Claire who clearly thought adult Delilah was intriguing enough herself to approach in a bar.

The two women stared at each other for a moment before Claire pulled her gaze away and straightened her stack of books one more time.

"So that was quite an event today at Vivian's," Claire said.

"It was."

"Exciting."

"Ended with quite a bang."

Claire's mouth turned up at the corners—she was clearly trying to fight a laugh, which Delilah found completely delightful.

"So how mad was Astrid?" she asked.

"On a scale of one to ten?" Claire said. "Twenty-three."

Delilah nodded, couldn't help the smile that settled on her mouth. Claire watched her for a few seconds before clearing her throat.

"Thank you for your help today," she said. "With Ruby."

Delilah shrugged. "It was no big deal. She's a good kid."

"It was a big deal. We were ten seconds away from a meltdown over a bit of lace and satin in the middle of Vivian's."

"Would that have been so bad? Probably the most action that snore fest has seen since it opened."

Claire laughed. "Until you came along, that is."

Delilah flourished her hand in agreement.

"Still," Claire said, "Astrid bought that dress for Ruby. I just didn't want to add to her stress."

Delilah chewed on this, thinking back to when she and Ruby went into the bathroom with the dress. The girl had been sweet, yeah, but she'd also talked her ear off, and Delilah had let her. "Honestly, I think Ruby would've worn the dress as it was. She just wanted someone to listen to her."

"I listen to——" But Claire cut herself off, her mouth hanging open as she blinked over and over again. Then she let out a groan and dropped her head into her hands. "Oh my god."

Delilah laughed softly. "It's okay."

Claire looked up. "I'm turning into one of those moms."

"What kind of moms?"

She flapped her hands around. "The *ones*, the ones who never listen and think kids are idiots who can't think for themselves and just want things to be easy and quiet and oh my *god*."

"Do you think Ruby's an idiot who can't think for herself?"

"No!" Claire's eyes went soft, along with her voice. "No. She's so smart. You talked to her, right? She's a great kid."

Delilah nodded. "Seems to be."

"I just . . . I want her . . ." Claire sighed and looked down at her hands. "She hasn't had it easy. And I think some part of me thinks, the tighter I hold on to her, the more . . . I don't know, *organized* I make her life, the safer she'll feel. And I . . ."

Claire stopped, stood up straight, her posture suddenly rigid. "God, I'm sorry." She cleared her throat again. "You don't want to hear about this."

"Sure I do," Delilah said. She said it on instinct, the *right* thing to say to lure Claire into liking her, but as Claire sighed out a little laugh and straightened the books for the hundredth time, Delilah realized it was true. Back in New York, she didn't have any friends with kids. Everyone in her circle was an artist, aggressively single, and completely absorbed in their work. In fact, Delilah wasn't even sure she'd actually call any of them *friends*. They were colleagues, fellow artists, people she met up with at events, occasionally slept with. They were connections, hookups.

Friends?

Delilah didn't think she'd ever actually had one of those. Not a real one, someone she'd call if she was having a bad night or in trouble. She never went to college, never had a roommate to bond with. Jax had never been her friend—lover, chaos and passion personified, but not her friend.

Now, standing in River Wild with Claire Sutherland, of all people, she found herself leaning in, fascinated by this life Claire led, raising a tiny human, a person all her own. She wanted to ask Claire to go on, even if just to hear her voice, the way it was the littlest bit raspy, but before she could, footsteps clomped over the hardwoods from the back of the store.

"Mom, can we go home yet?" Ruby's voice called from somewhere among the shelves.

"Yeah, sweetie, I'm almost done," Claire said. She took the books and slid them to the back counter where there was some sort of gift-wrapping station, thick rolls of brown paper and simple striped ribbons. Then she came back to the register and started to shut the computer down. Delilah watched her, waiting for some eye contact, but Claire never gave it.

"Good, I'm starving," Ruby said, emerging from between the freestanding bookshelves, still in her lavender dress and boots. When she saw Delilah, her face broke out in a grin. "Hey! You're here!"

Delilah smiled at her, crossing her ankles as she leaned against the counter. "I am."

Ruby's eyes gleamed, her gaze roaming over Delilah's tattoos. Delilah could see the questions stacking up in the girl's mind.

"Which do you like the best?" she asked Ruby.

Pink spread over Ruby's cheeks, like she'd been caught. "Oh. Um . . ."

"It's okay," Delilah said. "I want to know."

"Well . . ." Ruby took a step closer. "I like this one." She pointed to the rain cloud thundering over the teacup.

"That's one of my favorites too."

"What does it mean?"

"It's a storm in a teacup," Delilah said.

Ruby furrowed her brow. "Huh?"

Delilah laughed. "It's an old phrase. It means . . . making a big deal out of something small. I got it to remind myself to have some perspective. That, most times, things aren't as devastating as they might feel at first."

The girl nodded, head tilted in thought.

"I like that one too," Claire said.

Delilah snapped her gaze to the other woman. She let a slow grin spread over her mouth.

Claire smiled and shook her head before kneeling down to grab her bag from under the counter, but Delilah swore she blushed a little.

"Ready?" Claire said to Ruby, coming around the counter.

"Finally!" the girl said, speeding toward the front door.

Delilah followed them both outside, hovering as Claire locked up the store. She looked down the sidewalk toward where Stella's waited a few blocks down, but the thought of going in there, alone, just to get half drunk at the bar, also alone, suddenly made her feel very tired.

"So . . . have a good night," Claire said as Ruby headed toward a little silver Prius parked at the end of the street. Delilah wondered where they lived, what their house looked like.

"Yeah, you too." She slipped her hands in her pockets and started walking backward, her eyes still on Claire.

The other woman opened her mouth once . . . twice . . . before finally asking, "I'll see you tomorrow, right?"

Delilah stopped. "Tomorrow?"

"Astrid's dinner? At your . . . at Isabel's house."

Delilah's tiredness morphed into exhaustion. "Yeah. You'll see me."

Claire nodded and fiddled with her keys. "Good. Okay, then."

"Okay, then."

"Bye."

"Bye."

Except neither woman moved. Delilah wasn't going to budge; she knew that. She was enjoying this fidgeting, addled Claire. Especially since Delilah was ninety percent positive she was the cause of the addling.

"Mom!" Ruby called from the car.

"Coming!"

Claire looked at Delilah one more time before finally turning her back and speed-walking toward her kid. Delilah stood in the middle of the sidewalk, ice cream lickers angling around her, watching with a smile on her face until Claire drove out of sight.

CHAPTER
EIGHT

DELILAH STOOD IN the driveway, Wisteria House rising up above her. It was dusk, the air a soft lavender, and it seemed like a few people were already here. She could not—*would not*—walk into that house with just Isabel and make small talk. Or, in Isabel's true medium, passive-aggressive talk. She wasn't even sure she could walk in there regardless, even with it full of other people.

Wisteria House had always been a confusing place for Delilah. On the one hand, she'd lived here with her father for two years, from ages eight to ten. She remembered that time, unlike the foggy, unformed pictures in her mind from her earlier childhood in Seattle. Her mother, dead by the time Delilah turned four, was just a shadow by now, a blur of curly hair and a soft hand on her cheek. But her father, Andrew, she remembered his face perfectly, his dark blue eyes, the way he laughed so loudly, from way deep down in his belly, always causing Delilah to laugh too, even if she didn't get the joke. Wisteria House was his, built and named for his new family, for his daughter he never got to see grow up.

But Wisteria House was also *theirs*. Isabel's. Astrid's. After Andrew died, Isabel's grief was heavy, a dark cloak over everything. She'd already lost her first husband to cancer—which was one reason she and Andrew had initially bonded: a shared grief over a horrible disease—and losing another so suddenly nearly killed her. Delilah remembered thinking, through her own sad haze, that Isabel might actually die of a broken heart and then she and Astrid would be left truly alone or maybe even sent away.

But Isabel survived, and as she slowly came back to life, Delilah kept waiting for the mother she needed. The parent. She waited for comfort and assurance. Hell, just a hand squeezing her shoulder in passing would've made her heart feel a little bit more at home in her own chest. Astrid sure as hell wasn't going to give it. But it never came from Isabel either. The woman fed her. Provided her with school supplies. Made sure she did her homework. Bought her Christmas presents. Clothed her with designer labels that Astrid loved and Delilah never cared for, but that was it. Basic needs, leaving love out of the equation altogether. Granted, she wasn't overly affectionate with Astrid either, but she was *involved*. Always asking about school projects, Astrid's friends, going to every single track meet during high school and cheering loudly, pushing Astrid to be better, faster. That was a kind of care, wasn't it? Astrid lapped up all that attention when they were younger, and then seemed to grow annoyed by it when they got to high school. Still, whenever Delilah sat next to Isabel on those metal bleachers, watching Astrid fly around a track with her blond ponytail flicking behind her, Delilah craved a question, any question, any push to greatness.

It never came. So when Delilah's fingers curled around her high school diploma to polite, dispassionate applause, she knew it was time to leave for good.

Now, just like each of the few times she'd been back in the last twelve years, she looked up at the lovely Georgian brick exterior of

Wisteria House and felt a low simmering panic just under each breath. She pressed her hands to her stomach and inhaled. She knew she had to go in, get through this just like she'd gotten through the brunch. She just needed a moment to prepare. But one moment turned into another, and she knew, any second, her phone would go off with Astrid screeching about professionalism and timeliness.

She took one step toward the front stoop, then another, and was nearly to the bottom of the stairs when a familiar car pulled into the driveway.

A silver Prius.

Delilah watched as Claire opened the driver's door and two other people got out of the car as well—Iris and some guy Delilah had never seen before. He was dressed in sleek gray dress pants and a black button-down, dark hair pulled into an impressive man bun. He wrapped an arm around Iris, and Delilah let out a breath of relief.

Which gave her enough space to actually focus on what she was seeing.

Claire, in red heels, red lipstick, and an incredibly tight vintage dress that seemed welded around every perfect curve. This was the kind of dress fantasies were made of, designed for bodies like Claire's, with its inch-wide straps hooking over her round shoulders and the sweetheart neckline showing off the perfect amount of cleavage. The black-and-white polka dots lent an air of innocence to the whole style, but shit, Delilah's thoughts right now were anything but innocent.

She felt her mouth drop open and couldn't do a single thing to stop it.

"That's exactly what I did when I saw her," Iris said to Delilah. "She looks just like Bettie Page, am I right?" She elbowed Claire.

"What?" Claire said. "No way. My boobs and ass are way bigger than Bettie Page's were."

"Yeah, and that's a good thing." Iris grinned at her, shaking her head.

Delilah dimly registered the conversation they were having—vintage model, boobs—because *dress*. All she could do was stare as Claire got closer.

"Hey there," Iris said when she stopped in front of Delilah. She tilted her head at her, like she was waiting for something.

"Can I help you?" Delilah asked after clearing her throat.

"You can. You're blocking the steps."

Delilah considered suggesting in a saccharine tone that Iris use *pretty please* in a sentence, but with the task of walking inside the house still hovering over her and Claire standing there looking like a pinup model, she didn't have it in her. She simply moved aside, flourishing her hand up the stairs.

"Hey, I'm Grant," the guy said as he passed by.

"Delilah," she said, and his eyes went wide. Her stomach clenched a little. "Yes, *that* Delilah."

"Oh, um, yeah, nice to meet you," he said, rubbing the back of his neck.

"Smooth," Iris said, taking his arm. She glanced at Claire, nodding her head toward the door. "We'll meet you inside?"

"Yeah," Claire said, then she just stood there as Iris and Grant disappeared, shifting from one foot to the other and pulling on the straps of her dress.

"It looks amazing," Delilah said.

Claire froze. "What?"

"The dress." She motioned to Claire's hand still on the left strap. "It looks good. Really good."

She watched as a little smile curled one corner of her mouth. "Yeah?"

"Oh yes."

Claire pursed her lips, clearly trying to fight a larger smile, but her cheeks went pink. She let her hand drop. "Are you going in?"

Delilah sighed and looked up at the house, at red-brown brick and shiny windows. "Eventually. You?"

"Well, I value my life quite a lot, so, yes."

"Astrid always gets what she wants, doesn't she?" The words came out quieter than she meant them to, sadder, and Claire's brows dipped as she searched Delilah's face. Delilah tried not to look away, but damn this woman, she had some very deep eyes, their brown like a bottomless pit, and Delilah didn't feel like falling tonight.

She pushed her gaze down, adjusted the camera bag on her shoulder. She needed to gain control of this situation, of what she was and was not doing with Claire Sutherland, one of Astrid's mean girls, for god's sake, but *control* was never something she felt when she was at Wisteria House.

"We could walk in together?" Claire said, more a question than a statement.

Delilah considered it. Claire's shoulder pressed to hers as she went through the front door, a buffer. But also . . . the look on Astrid's face when she saw them come in together.

Delilah smiled. "Yeah. We could definitely do that." Then she looped her arm through Claire's and pulled her body close, just for good measure.

⌒

DELILAH'S SHOULDERS CREPT up to her ears as they walked through the door and into the wide foyer. The smell hit her first.

Lavender and bleach, like chemicals attempting to tame something wild. Then the temperature curled around her, frigid cold, the air-conditioning blasting to the point of rustling hair and skirts. Finally, there was the view, the entryway still painted a light gray, the dark hardwood floors still gleaming and pristine, the walls still dotted with the most boring paintings imaginable, neutral-colored abstracts and boring riverscapes. In between these masterpieces, there were, of course, posed photographs of Astrid at all ages. Black and whites in driftwood frames of a blond princess in her ballet costume, her track uniform, her hunter-green graduation gown loaded down with gold and white honors stoles.

There was one picture featuring Delilah—an eight-by-ten family portrait of her and Astrid around age nine on the white sofa in the living room, Isabel and Delilah's father perched on either side of them, his blue eyes sparkling. A plain antiqued gold frame surrounded the happy scene, set on the console table near the staircase and half covered by a velvety succulent in a ceramic pot.

She felt dizzy for a moment, but that wasn't all that unusual. She just needed a minute to get her bearings, coat herself in her usual Isabel-and-Astrid armor—sarcasm and disdain. She rolled her shoulders back, her arm tightening on Claire's as she did so.

"You okay?" Claire asked, watching her.

"Peachy," she said, but she didn't let go of Claire.

And Claire didn't let go of her.

At least, not until Astrid appeared around the corner that led into the living room, her eyes immediately narrowing in on Delilah's and Claire's arms. Only then did Claire untangle herself, straightening her dress and clearing her throat.

"Hey," Claire said.

"Hey, yourself," Astrid said back as she came closer. She was wearing a strapless ivory jumpsuit with wide legs, sleek and expensive. Ironically, it paired perfectly with Delilah's own strapless black jumpsuit.

The angel and the devil.

If Astrid noticed, she didn't say anything. Instead, she air-kissed Claire's cheeks while she side-eyed her stepsister.

"You made it," she said to Delilah.

"Miraculously," Delilah said.

"Well, I wasn't sure if you remembered where it was."

Delilah just tilted her head at her stepsister. "Point me toward the champagne tower?"

"There isn't one," Astrid said, her tone laced with venom.

"Pity."

"Okay, so," Claire said brightly, "everything's set up outside?"

Astrid seemed to unclench and nodded, so Delilah let herself shift into professional mode and mentally ran through the lens she'd need for that kind of light. The champagne tower incident was therapeutic, but she wouldn't put it past Isabel to fire her ass, and at the end of the day, she had to get paid. A fact Astrid knew full well.

Wisteria House had a huge backyard, flat and green with a pool area just below the porch and a vast space of green lawn that rolled down into the banks of Bright River. There was a dock with a couple of Adirondack chairs set up, a little skiff that Isabel strictly forbade anyone from using when they were kids, and a tire swing that hung from the huge oak whose thick branches arched over the silver-blue water.

"Any particular shots you want me to get?" Delilah asked, but before Astrid could answer, a man appeared around the corner in dark gray pants and a blue button-down, both of which had that *very expensive* sheen to them. He was tall and lean, his golden blond hair cut short on the side and a little longer on top. He sauntered toward them, hands in his pockets until he reached Astrid, then he hooked an arm around her waist and tugged her closer.

"There you are, babe," he said, while Delilah watched his fingers dig into Astrid's hips. She fought an eye roll—cishet white men and their proprietary pet names.

Astrid, though, immediately curled into his side, putting a hand on his chest. "Spencer, this is Delilah."

His eyebrows rose. "Delilah, huh?"

"In the flesh," Delilah said. She didn't lift her hand to shake his. For his part, though, neither did he.

"I never thought I'd have the pleasure," he said, but he didn't give Delilah time to respond to that little tidbit. Instead, he turned to Astrid, hoisting her closer, and said, "I need more champagne, babe. Help a guy out?"

"Sure, of course," Astrid said, then looked at Claire and Delilah. "Do you two want some as well?"

"God, yes," Delilah said, but it echoed. She looked at Claire as she realized they'd both said the exact same thing at the same time. Claire laughed.

"Okay, I'll take that as a yes, then," Astrid said, her brow furrowed. "Coming right up."

She click-clacked toward the kitchen while Spencer just stood there watching her go, his legs wide and his hands on his hips.

"She's a good girl," he said, and Delilah's jaw clenched even tighter.

"I think you mean woman," she said. Claire shifted, her shoulder just touching Delilah's.

Spencer turned back to them. "Excuse me?"

"Woman." Delilah waved to where Astrid had disappeared into the kitchen. "Astrid, your fiancée, is a woman. Nearly thirty years old, if I recall correctly."

Spencer's eyes narrowed, just slightly, but then he smiled. "Astrid said you were . . . fiery."

"And Astrid said next to nothing about you." The words just came out, rude tone and all. She heard Claire's quiet intake of breath and knew she should shut up—she was on thin ice with Isabel already—but something about this guy felt like sandpaper rubbed over a sunburn. No one could ever accuse Delilah of feeling affection for her stepsister, but she felt even less for assholes who so obviously wielded their dicks like swords.

His smile didn't budge, his stance still space-taking. Finally, he swung his gaze to Claire, eyes flicking to her chest for a split second and then back to her eyes. "Good to see you, Claire."

"You too, Spencer," Claire said, her voice like stone.

And then he sauntered down the hall until he reached the back door, disappearing onto the porch, where a dozen human-shaped shadows undulated in the dusky light.

Next to her, Claire exhaled so heavily, Delilah was sure she'd crumple to the ground. She shook out her hands and shivered. Delilah watched her, waiting to see what else she'd do.

Claire caught her looking and shook her head. "Sorry. I just . . . well, now you've met Spencer."

"Is he always such a dick?"

Claire stilled. "*Is* he a dick?"

"Um, hell yes," Delilah said.

"God." Claire clutched her stomach. "I'm so glad to hear someone other than Iris and me say that."

"It's not obvious to literally everyone?"

Claire deflated, her shoulders slumping south. "Well, Astrid's one of the smartest people I know, and she's marrying him."

Delilah wrinkled her nose.

"Plus," Claire went on, "Iris and I have really only hung out with the two of them a few times. If she's not with us, they do their own thing. I was hoping he'd grow on me as time went on."

"How'd she meet him?"

"She redesigned his office late last fall. He'd just moved here from Portland, took over Dr. Latimer's practice after he retired."

"Dr. Latimer only just retired last year?"

Claire laughed. "God, I know, he had to have been in his seventies when we were in high school."

"At least."

"Anyway, Spencer asked Astrid out after the job was done in January. Iris and I met him a couple weeks after their first date, and they were engaged two months later."

"Two months? Jesus. So they've only been engaged since March?" Delilah now remembered when Astrid called her about photographing the wedding—it had been cool in New York, winter just loosening its hold over the city.

"I know, right?" Claire said. "It took her a year to pick out a couch for her living room."

"What does Isabel say?" Delilah asked, even though she already knew. Rich, prestigious career, nice golden-boy hair. Isabel loved Spencer, and Claire confirmed as much.

"I can never put a finger on it," Claire continued, "but he just . . . He's . . ."

"Smarmy?"

"Yes!" Claire reached out and grabbed Delilah's arm in solidarity but quickly dropped it. "But like . . . in a sneaky way. Like, right now, what just happened with him all"—here she fluttered her hands around her boobs—"what would I say about that to Astrid? 'Hey, your future husband *looked* at me'?" She shook her head. "Even Iris, who will legit say anything to anyone, can't figure out how to word it."

Delilah ran her brain through what *she* would say—*Your fiancé's a douche, he looks like a Ken doll, he ogled your BFF's tits, you turn into a sycophant when you're around him*—but each and every observation that popped into her mind would only piss Astrid off, which, now that she thought about it, might be a delightful way to spend an evening.

And a sure way to get fired.

Still, the idea of Astrid's wedding falling apart and all of Isabel's money and plans and dreams of the society event of the season crumbling before her face-lifted eyes? Well, let's just say it made Delilah feel all warm and fuzzy inside.

"Spencer never does anything concrete," Claire said. "It's just a feeling, the way she acts around him." She rubbed her forehead. "God, she'd kill me if she knew I was saying any of this to you."

"Not exactly how a maid of honor wants to feel about the groom, I guess."

"No. No, it's not."

Delilah watched as genuine worry settled on Claire's features. Then, as Astrid's heels echoed down the hallway again, it bled away just as quickly. Lines smoothed out, and Claire smiled at her friend. But that was genuine too, the grin crinkling up her eyes and pressing a single tiny dimple Delilah had never noticed before right next to Claire's mouth. This woman loved Astrid with her whole heart.

God only knew why.

"Cheers," Astrid said as she handed flutes of golden bubbly to Delilah and Claire, keeping one back and looking around. "Where's Spencer?"

Delilah took a sip of her drink then said, totally deadpan, "Hopefully, taking a flying leap off the dock into the river."

Claire choked on her champagne.

Delilah felt a rush of pride, but then she saw the look on Astrid's face.

She expected angry or annoyed. She didn't expect . . . crestfallen. Her stepsister's mouth went slack, and her eyebrows dipped in confusion. Delilah's stomach already felt wobbly from walking into this house, but now, suddenly, it was a pit of writhing snakes, and she didn't like it one bit.

"What?" Astrid asked.

"Nothing," Delilah said, waving her free hand, preferring Astrid's professional indifference to this unfamiliar wounded version standing in front of her. "You want me to take some pictures before dinner, right?"

"Yeah," Astrid said, her eyes flicking to Claire.

"Let's go out back, then," Claire said, clearing her throat. Then she hooked her arm through Astrid's and took a step to pull her away.

Delilah readied herself to be left behind, to go farther into the house on her own. She'd done it before. She'd spent ten years in this house, eight without her dad or any other ally. She could certainly walk through a goddamn foyer as an event photographer.

But this house, Astrid, Isabel, all of those things stirred together in one pot was a potent brew; one sip was all it took to make her feel like an odd, lonely teenager again.

She closed her eyes for two seconds, breathed in some lavender-bleach air, and ordered her feet to move. Before she could, though, before she even opened her eyes again, she felt soft fingers curl around her arm.

Delilah blinked to find Claire, one hand still holding on to Astrid and the other . . . smoothing down Delilah's tricep to her elbow. Astrid frowned at her, though her expression was more curious than angry, and Delilah felt something uncoil in her middle.

"Come on," Claire said gently. "Ready?"

No, Delilah wanted to say. She never was.

But as Claire's fingers tightened on her skin, just a little, her feet unfroze and she took one step, then another, then another. Before she knew it, she was through the white-couched living room where she'd spent many a Christmas morning digging through her stocking in silence, and outside on the wide back porch, fairy lights casting a soft glow over the whole space.

There were at least fifteen people out here. Delilah recognized some of the women from the brunch, Spencer's family, and of course Isabel, who was holding court while perched on a patio chair, champagne sparkling in her hand. Astrid kissed Claire on the cheek before shooting Delilah her usual irritated look and breaking off to join Spencer on the far end of the deck, where he was laughing with a group of three other guys, all of them dude-bro-ing it up with their preternaturally white teeth and perfect hair.

Delilah waited for Claire to break off too, speeding toward Iris or some other friend Delilah may or may not know, maybe Josh, though she didn't see him anywhere.

But . . . Claire didn't move. She stayed right where she was, her fingers cool and soft around Delilah's arm, like she was waiting for Delilah to break away too.

CHAPTER NINE

CLAIRE WAS STILL holding Delilah's arm. She didn't know why. She told herself to let it go more than once, but she worried that if she did, Delilah might float away or crumple to the ground or just stand there looking as lost as she had in the foyer.

Or maybe she just liked the silky feel of Delilah's skin under hers.

The thought was a lightning bolt, forcing Claire to finally yank her fingers away, sloshing a bit of her champagne onto the slatted porch floor as she did.

Delilah didn't seem to notice. As she looked around and took a sip of her drink, she didn't float or crumple, but her expression was still a bit wide-eyed. It was fascinating to see this bold, brash woman look like a deer wandering in the woods. Claire wasn't sure what it was all about, but she really wanted to know, which was exactly why she swallowed her questions with a too-big gulp of alcohol.

"Hey!" Iris called from across the porch, pulling Grant by the arm toward Claire. "What took you so long?"

"It's been like ten minutes, Ris."

"Which is ten minutes too long to leave me alone with this

crowd." Iris waved her own champagne toward the posh group of people. "God, have you ever seen so much Louboutin in one place? Are we seriously the only normal people in Astrid's life?"

Claire laughed. "You know we are."

Isabel Parker-Green had money and a lot of it. Her first husband had family money, which passed to Isabel after he died, and her second husband, Delilah's father, had been a pretty successful architect in Seattle before he moved to Bright Falls. He opened up a small boutique office here, which Isabel promptly sold (and possibly cursed) after he died. She was all about charities and philanthropy, but Claire always got the impression it was for the clout, rather than the actual do-gooding.

Isabel liked control, liked beauty and power, and she made sure Astrid knew it.

Back when Claire first met Astrid, the other girl had constantly clung to her mother, desperate for affection and attention. Claire supposed she understood it. Astrid's stepfather had just died, and Isabel was locked in her own grief, and she could tell Astrid was terrified her mother would leave her too. But as the years went on and Isabel not only lavished Astrid with attention but nearly smothered her with it, Claire remembered countless nights in high school with Astrid crying into Iris's lap while Claire rubbed her back, words like *I hate her* and *Can't she just leave me alone?* stuttering through Astrid's sobs.

Since coming back from college and getting her own place, Astrid and Isabel's relationship had mellowed, but it wasn't what Claire would call close. It was civil. Polite. Still, Claire caught that look in Astrid's eye sometimes, the need to impress, to please.

"Just think," Iris said, waving her glass at the crowd. "By this time tomorrow, it'll just be the three of us with copious amounts of wine at a five-star-rated spa."

Next to Claire, Delilah cleared her throat. "I should get some shots before dinner," she said before trailing off to a darker corner, setting her drink on the nearby table, and kneeling down to get out her camera.

"Iris," Claire said, smacking her friend on the arm.

"Ow. What?"

"You said *the three of us.* Delilah's going too."

Iris's mouth parted, but then she shrugged. "I doubt she actually wants to. Astrid's paying her. It's a job."

"Easy, Iris," Grant said.

"Oh, come on," Iris said. "The woman would rather chew on broken glass than be here. It's obvious."

Claire shook her head, her stomach clenching as she glanced at Delilah again. All she saw was her back, bare shoulders, and tattoos, but the other woman's posture seemed tight.

"I knew it," Iris said.

Claire turned to find both Iris and Grant staring at her. "What?"

"You're into her," Iris said.

"I am not."

Iris waved her hand over Claire. "The dress, walking in with her. You like her."

Claire tugged on one of the dress's shoulder straps while Iris smiled triumphantly. She'd ordered the garment months ago from one of her favorite vintage clothing sites, drawn in by the way she knew it would make her hourglass figure look even curvier. The designer called it a wiggle dress, because you had to literally wiggle it on, and had named it "Vixen." Claire wasn't sure she'd ever have the occasion—or the courage—to wear it, but tonight seemed like a good chance. It was classy and sexy at the same time.

Not that she was going for sexy.

"I like this dress, Ris," she said. "I wore it for me."

Iris's smile fell. "Honey, of course you did. I'm just saying—"

"And just because I'm being nice to someone and not acting like a total bitch doesn't mean I'm *into* them."

This time, Iris's mouth dropped open. "I'm not—"

"Yeah, you sort of are," Grant said.

"Hey," Iris said, hitting him on the chest. He released an *oof* sound, capturing Iris's hand and slipping his fingers between hers.

Iris let him, her expression growing pensive as she looked at Claire. "Okay, fine, I'm not a huge fan. Neither were you the last time I checked. She barely even spoke to Astrid growing up, or did you forget?"

"I didn't forget," Claire said, but she turned away, watching as Delilah wove through the crowd snapping pictures, drawing everyone's gaze as she went.

———

DINNER WAS MOSTLY uneventful. Claire sat next to Iris near the end of the long table the caterers had set up in the backyard, tiki torches lighting the area, and ate her mushroom risotto and organic green bean salad while everyone in Isabel's posh circle asked Astrid and Spencer about their honeymoon, where they were going to live, how many kids they were going to have.

Astrid answered it all with a smile, Spencer's arm tight around her shoulder the entire time. He even ate his food like that, cutting into his lemon-pepper chicken with his fork one-handed. When Astrid deflected the kids question, however—"Oh, I don't know, we're not in any rush"—Spencer laughed long and loud, like Astrid was a stand-up comedian putting on a show, and said, "Three boys, as soon as we settle down in Seattle."

Everyone oohed and aahed at this, as though the idea of Astrid popping out three white boys into this white-boy world was *just the cutest.* But Claire's mind caught on the word *Seattle* way more than *three boys.*

She turned to Iris, her mouth open, but Iris looked just as confused, her eyes pinned on Astrid.

"What the fuck?" Iris whispered, but Astrid probably knew Iris well enough to know what she was mouthing in her direction. Their best friend's face went crimson, a truly miserable expression settling on her features. She mouthed back, *I'm sorry*, which only meant it was all true.

"He's taking her to Seattle?" Claire asked.

"I . . . I don't know," Iris said.

"Why wouldn't she tell us?"

"Probably because she knew we'd freak the fuck out."

"She hates Seattle," Claire said. "The crowds, the grit mixing with all that rain. It's her worst nightmare. She barely survived Berkeley during college."

A chilled white wine had replaced the champagne once the meal started, and Claire slugged back the rest of her second glass. God, she was going to need a stronger liver to get through this wedding.

Seattle. It wasn't that far away, about four hours by car, but still. Seattle wasn't Bright Falls, and Bright Falls was where Astrid's whole life was. Her business, her friends, her family.

"Completely odious," Iris whispered next to her, and Claire didn't have to ask what—or rather, who—she was talking about.

"Did we ever like him?" Claire asked. "Like, when Astrid first introduced us?"

"Hell no," Iris said. "I mean, okay, he looks like a god with that hair and those biceps, so maybe we were a bit distracted by that at first. You know, beautiful people getting away with murder and all that."

"God, I hope he's not a murderer."

Iris laughed. "I'm pretty sure all he's actually guilty of is sitting on his ass with a Scotch and a cigar while Astrid vacuums the living room. In Seattle."

Claire cracked a smile but continued to simmer. Ever since the engagement, she'd been wary about Spencer, but suddenly, it all seemed to be coming to a boil. Hearing Delilah, someone who didn't even *like* Astrid, confirm that Spencer was a total jerk just made it all the more real. And Seattle? Taking her away to a city she hated? God only knew how long she'd been hiding that tidbit from her friends.

"We can't let her marry him," Claire said.

Iris froze with her mouth on her wineglass. "We . . . Say what now?"

Claire lowered her voice even more. "You know we can't."

Iris shook her head. "Hang on. I thought we were just going to talk to Astrid about Spencer. Let her know our concerns. Where's this *blow up the wedding* plan coming from? You know Astrid is gonna Astrid."

"Yeah, and that woman right there"—she waved her hand toward where their best friend was legit spooning some of her own risotto onto Spencer's plate—"isn't Astrid."

Iris's eyes narrowed on the scene then locked back onto Claire's. A million versions of the same question passed between them silently—*how, how, how*—as the party broke up around them.

Iris stood and pulled Claire with her, sighing very dramatically as she pressed their temples together. They stood there for a second like that, watching all of Isabel's friends drift off toward the far end of the patio while the caterers started cleaning up. Claire's eyes found Delilah, camera pointed directly at Claire and Iris before the other woman lowered it and checked the screen. Delilah pressed some buttons on her camera before looking up at Claire, the smallest of smiles on her lips.

Claire felt a swoop in her belly, but she couldn't tell if it was embarrassment at being photographed or . . . something else.

"Ris, Claire," Astrid called near the stairs that led into the yard. "Come on, we're going down to the dock." Spencer and his buddies were already bounding in that direction in a sea of khaki and Top-Siders. "You too, Del."

"Oh goody," Claire heard Delilah say, and couldn't help the smile that settled on her face.

"Indeed," Iris answered back.

"I don't have to hang out with them, do I?" Grant asked from next to Iris, his eyes trained on Spencer and Co. as they stood on the dock in the distance, the amber sun slipping underneath Bright River and turning everyone into backlit shadows.

"No, sweets, you can stick with me," Iris said, patting his arm.

"Oh, thank god," he said.

Claire laughed as Iris topped off their glasses and they headed toward the water. She was aware of Delilah behind her but didn't turn around until they reached the dock. Delilah's camera swung from her neck, a very full glass of wine in her own hand. She didn't look at Claire though. Instead, she leaned against one of the tall pines that bordered the bank—god, this woman was always *leaning* on things—and watched Spencer laugh with his friends.

Astrid stood next to him, sipping her drink and smiling, but for the first time, Claire noticed something icy about her expression. Practiced. Or maybe it was just wishful thinking. Maybe it was too dark out here to see anything clearly. The sun had gone completely to sleep, turning the gently rushing water into ink, and the few electric tiki torches that lined the bank were the only light.

"Can we leave for the vineyard *now*?" Iris asked next to her.

"I wish," Claire said, but that just caused a whole other set of worries to bloom into her mind. It was only a two-day trip, but Ruby was staying with Josh overnight again, and Claire would be four hours away if anything went badly.

It wouldn't, she told herself. She had already roped Iris into asking Grant to casually check in on Josh around eight o'clock the next night, stopping by Josh's apartment for a random beer when really, she'd given him strict instructions to make sure the oven was turned off and there were no candles aflame.

"Shit, these goddamn horseflies," Spencer said, pulling Claire out of her thoughts. He swatted at his cheek, then his ear.

"Good horsefly," Iris muttered.

"Go get some bug spray, will you, babe?" Spencer said.

Then he tapped Astrid on the ass. Not a slap, necessarily, but hard enough to jolt her. One of his friends laughed but then covered it up quickly with a swig of wine.

"Sure," Astrid said evenly. "It is pretty buggy out here."

When she swept off the dock toward the house, Claire seized the moment, grabbing Astrid's hand as she passed and pulling her close.

"What's going on?" Claire asked softly.

"What do you mean?" Astrid asked.

"Seattle?" Iris said. "What the hell is that about?"

Astrid sighed. "We're not going right away. It's just something we're talking about."

"You love Bright Falls," Claire said. She couldn't help the hurt that rose up in her throat.

"Spencer doesn't," Astrid said. "He took over the practice here, but he wants to expand, and Bright Falls isn't built for that."

"So you're just going to follow him?" Iris asked, voice raising. "What about your job?"

Us? Claire thought, but couldn't get the small word off her tongue.

"I can do more in Seattle," Astrid said. "It's a bigger market, a bigger—"

"You hate bigger," Iris said.

Astrid rubbed her forehead. "Look, it's not definite, okay? We're just talking about it. And we wouldn't go for another year or so anyway."

"Yeah, but—"

"Babe! Where's that spray?" Spencer called out.

Astrid waved at him, then pressed a kiss to both Claire's and Iris's cheeks before hurrying off toward the house.

"Do you know a good lawyer?" Iris asked.

"What?" Claire said, watching Astrid's form disappear up the porch steps.

"A lawyer. Preferably criminal law," Iris said.

"Oh Jesus," said Grant, who'd hovered off to the side as they'd talked to Astrid but now slung his arm around Iris's shoulder.

Claire turned to her friend. "What the hell are you talking about?"

Iris gritted her teeth. "I'm talking about how I'm going to need a really damn good lawyer in about two point four seconds, because I'm going to murder that shit boot." She waved her glass toward Spencer, who was chatting with his friends, teeth shining in the dark.

"Shit boot?" Claire cracked a smile.

"An Iris original," Grant said.

The three of them laughed, but Claire still felt uneasy, helpless. It was true that Astrid hadn't brought Spencer around them all that much since they'd been together. A dinner here and there. Mostly, though, she was either only with Iris and Claire or only with Spencer.

Now, Claire was starting to see the reason for Astrid's little boxes, especially with Seattle in the mix. Astrid knew her friends would cause more than a fuss over some guy dragging her off like a caveman to a town she loathed.

"Take these."

Claire startled to see Delilah suddenly right in front of her, holding out her phone and camera. "What?"

"Just hang on to them, okay?"

But before Claire could answer, Delilah closed Claire's fingers around the phone and looped her camera around Claire's neck before sauntering farther down the dock, wineglass held lazily in one hand, hips swaying. More than one of Spencer's friends checked out her ass as she passed, which, for some reason, made Claire clench her teeth together.

"Well, if it isn't the wicked stepsister," Spencer said as she approached. He stood at the dock's edge, dark water lapping underneath.

"Only I get to call myself that," Delilah said, but Claire could tell she was smiling. "So tell me about yourself, *Spence*," she went on, voice like maple sugar as she reached out to squeeze his arm.

But then she seemed to . . . wobble. Her heel caught on one of the rough wooden planks, and she stumbled into Spencer.

"Shit," she said, latching on to his shoulders as he grabbed her arms to steady her.

"Whoa, easy," he said, but her body just kept moving forward like a ball down a hill. She twisted, wineglass clanking unbroken to the ground as she tried to get her balance.

"Oh my god," Iris said. "Are they going to—"

But she cut herself off, because yes, yes they were.

Spencer and Delilah tumbled into the river in a twist of limbs and profanity.

"Dude, you okay?" one of Spencer's friends said, and they all crowded to the end of the dock. Claire rushed over too, Iris and Grant close behind. She elbowed her way through the frat boys to see Delilah and Spencer spluttering in the inky water, both of them completely drenched and looking like drowned rats.

"What the fuck?" Spencer said as he swiped his wet hair back and found his footing. The water wasn't that deep, but even standing, it still came up to his chest.

"I'm so sorry," Delilah said, her voice measured and calm. "I don't know what happened."

She treaded water as Spencer's friends all leaned down to help him out of the river. His silky shirt was ruined, his leather shoes waterlogged, and his expression looked like a thundercloud.

"Oh my god, Spencer, what happened?" Astrid said, coming up behind them all with a green can of bug spray.

"Nothing," he growled, shaking off his friends and moving past her. "I need to go change." And then he stomped off down the dock and into the grass, heading up toward the house.

Everyone was silent for a few seconds, but then . . . a snort of laughter.

"Holy shit," one of Spencer's friends said—Peter or Patrick or something. "He loved that shirt."

"And those shoes," another one said.

"Need some help?" Peter/Patrick asked Delilah, who was still in the water.

"I'm fine, thank you so much," she said, voice still dripping in sugar.

He shrugged, and the guys all moved off toward the lawn, leaving Claire, Iris, Astrid, and Grant alone on the dock.

And Delilah in the water.

"What happened?" Astrid asked, glaring down at her stepsister.

"I tripped," Delilah said, making her eyes almost comically wide. "It was an accident."

If Claire didn't know better . . . Well, the fact was she actually *didn't* know better. She didn't know Delilah at all. But with the woman's phone and camera strategically in her possession and Delilah swimming slowly toward the ladder at the end of the dock, she was pretty sure this whole thing was orchestrated.

"Are you okay?" Claire asked as Delilah climbed the ladder.

"Never been better." Delilah wrung out her hair. "Water's damn refreshing. I might need a change of clothes though." She glanced at Astrid and grinned. "Got some sweats for your sis?"

Iris snort-laughed before leaning close to Claire and asking, "Is she for real?"

"I think she is."

Astrid just gaped at her, then grabbed Claire's relatively full glass of wine and knocked it back in three swallows. She shuddered, handed the empty glass back to Claire, then stomped off toward the house.

"I don't know why the hell I thought this was a good idea," she said as she went, Delilah following behind obediently after collecting her things from Claire. Delilah didn't make any eye contact, but once she was off the dock, she turned her head and looked back, just for a second. It was dark, and Claire couldn't be sure, but she thought the woman winked.

And not only winked, but winked at her.

Claire felt a laugh bubble up in her chest but managed to push it down.

"Damn," Iris said as they started toward the house too. "Not that I want our precious BFF to be all pissed off, but that was—"

"Brilliant?" Claire said.

"Yes. Yes, it fucking was."

CHAPTER

TEN

"I'M SORRY, WHAT?"

Late Tuesday morning, Delilah watched as Astrid's eyes bulged to insect-like size, her slender fingers gripping the sides of the front desk at Blue Lily Vineyard and Spa. The whole building was like an oasis, all smooth tawny wood inside with white upholstery and sea glass–blue accents, from the jar that held the pens on the concierge desk to the paintings on the walls, images of clear rivers and lilies swaying in the sun. Windows lined the entire main floor, and behind a very terrified receptionist named Hadley, Delilah could see the Willamette Valley stretching out in a swath of green in the distance, neat rows of plumping grapes directly below them.

"Three rooms?" Astrid said. "No, I distinctly remember booking four."

"Oh shit," Iris muttered under her breath.

Delilah, for her part, leaned against the counter and kept her face impassive. She was exhausted. Honestly, she could use a massage. The whole drive up here, that's what she'd focused on—massages, a really good pinot noir, her very own chintz-free room overlooking the vineyard where she could just *be*, free of Astrid and Bright Falls and all the emotional sludge her visit to Wisteria House last night had left gunking up her veins.

Granted, she was technically here to get some photos of the three BFFs, probably to hang in their cave as they performed their spells for everlasting beauty and power, but she'd take the free massage regardless.

She'd never been so tired as she had been these past two days, and that included her first few months in New York at eighteen, when she first discovered other queer people and bars and didn't sleep for a week. But so far, this trip to Bright Falls had left her feeling boneless and not in that blissed-out, postorgasmic way. More like she couldn't find her footing, wobbling all over the place.

The only relief she'd really felt was when she pulled that tosser into the river last night.

God, that was fun.

Astrid didn't think so, of course, which was an added bonus. As her stepsister had shoved a pair of spare sweats into Delilah's arms last night, Astrid's expression held none of the crestfallen hurt Delilah had glimpsed in Wisteria House's foyer. No, it was all irritation, familiar and life-giving. The gods had gifted Delilah with a brand-new way to get under her stepsister's skin, and she planned to milk it for all it was worth, which had to be done carefully, artfully, if she was going to keep her job. But thinking of creative ways to piss off Astrid's beloved just made it all the more fun. Plus, Spencer was a walking golden-haired advertisement for the patriarchy, so it wasn't like any cleverly disguised insults she could toss his way weren't justified.

Her determination grew even more as she stood there in the resort's lobby, fighting to keep her face neutral as it became more and more clear that Astrid hadn't actually booked four rooms. She'd booked three for herself, Iris, and Claire, and Delilah hadn't even been an afterthought. She tried not to notice how her heart tripped in her chest, her throat grew a little thicker, a horrible cocktail of anger, annoyance, and hurt.

Claire stepped a little closer to her, and Delilah tried not to notice that either. Her body, however, had other plans, and she felt herself straightening and then leaning toward the other woman, just enough that her shoulder barely brushed Claire's.

"Delilah Green," Astrid said to the unfortunate receptionist, enunciating every syllable. "Look again. I know it's there."

"I'm so sorry, Ms. Parker," Hadley said, "but the reservation here clearly says that you called on April 4 and booked three rooms for one night, one for yourself, another for a Ms. Iris Kelly, and a third for a Ms. Claire Sutherland. I don't see anything for a Ms. Del—"

"All right, I understand," Astrid said, sighing heavily. "But surely there must be another room available."

Hadley winced. Delilah almost felt bad for her. "I do apologize, Ms. Parker. Summer is our busiest season, and we're all booked up tonight. But if anything becomes available, you'll be the first to know."

Astrid stared at the poor woman for a good five seconds, like the mere force of her gaze would make a vacant room appear out of thin air. Hadley, for her part, held her smile, but when Astrid's shoulders slumped in defeat, the receptionist audibly released a breath.

"It's okay. I'll just sleep with the grapes," Delilah said.

Astrid slowly turned but didn't meet her stepsister's cool gaze. Instead, she looked at the floor and inhaled several times in a row, like she was trying not to completely lose her shit.

Delilah folded her arms. She'd rather like to see Astrid lose her shit, right here in front of Hadley and the calming spa-blue color palette.

"It's fine," Claire said, laying a hand on Astrid's arm. "It'll be fine. The beds are king-size, right? Delilah can stay with me."

Oh my god, this was too perfect. Astrid's head snapped up, her eyes going wide.

"No, no, it's my fault," she said. "She can stay with me."

"Astrid," Claire said. "You deserve a room to yourself."

"So do you," Astrid said.

"Well, *I* sure as shit deserve a room to myself," Iris said, and Delilah nearly laughed. Honestly, in another life, she probably would have liked Iris a whole hell of a lot.

"Astrid," Claire said, closing her hands around Astrid's upper arms. "I don't mind. And I insist. It'll be great."

"Yeah, Ass, it'll be great," Delilah said. She met her stepsister's gaze and lifted a single brow, something she knew Astrid couldn't do and wished she could. They stared at each other, Delilah's little bet about getting Claire into bed hovering between them. Granted, this wasn't exactly what Delilah meant, but it was a start. It was a damn great start.

Astrid closed her eyes briefly, and in that tiny space of time, Delilah knew she had won.

There was something else there too though. Something other than the satisfaction Delilah felt knowing Astrid was inwardly seething, and she was pretty sure it was excitement. Claire was fun, sweet, and sexy as hell. She was interesting. And Delilah couldn't stop thinking about last night in the foyer at Wisteria House, that split second where Claire could've walked away with Astrid, leaving Delilah to deal with her demons all by herself, just like Delilah was used to doing.

Only she hadn't.

Claire had turned back, brown eyes wide open and honest, and she'd waited for Delilah. She'd walked her through what could've been the worst moment of her trip back to Bright Falls, and turned it into a simple stride down a hall.

And for the first time since her father died, Delilah hadn't felt alone in Wisteria House.

CHAPTER ELEVEN

CLAIRE HAD NO clue what she'd been thinking.

Well, *Help Astrid.* That was the spirit behind her whole *share a bed with Delilah Green* idea—keep her best friend from completely melting down during the one pre-wedding activity Claire and Iris were actually looking forward to. She'd seen it brewing, the freak-out, Astrid breathing like a bull facing a matador, and she knew how terrible Astrid must be feeling for leaving Delilah out.

What's more, Claire saw Delilah's disappointment. Or, not disappointment so much as . . . she wasn't sure. But something had been behind Delilah's eyes when it was clear what had happened. Her face remained expressionless, bored even, but her eyes had flickered, like a strong wind nearly snuffing a candle out before the flame reared back to life.

So, of course, offering to bunk up with Delilah seemed like the best course of action. Iris surely wasn't going to do it, and if Delilah and Astrid shared a room, the trip would probably end in some sort of bloodshed.

Claire was the obvious choice.

But now, as the door shut behind the two of them in their room, a pang of nervousness shot through Claire's belly.

"This is nice," Delilah said, rolling her suitcase to the bed and flopping down on the crisp white linens, spreading out like a starfish.

"Um, yeah" was all Claire could seem to get out. In her flopping, Delilah's black tank top had ridden up, revealing a stripe of smooth, pale skin. A belly button. Hip bones.

Claire turned away. Breathed. She set her own suitcase on an armchair in the corner and unzipped it, rummaging pointlessly through her clothes in an effort to do something, anything, other than watch Delilah snow-angel on the bed.

The room *was* nice. Dark hardwood floors, light gray walls with bright-toned artwork to offset all the neutral colors, a huge bed with a white duvet cover and sheets, blue accent pillows arranged just so. A wide window covered most of the back wall, and the view was incredible, all shimmery distant valleys and rows of juice-filled grapes rolling like green-leafed waves. And as Claire brought her toiletry bag into the bathroom, she walked into what was pretty much a mini spa with its sea-glass tile floors and huge glass shower, a dual vanity with white porcelain bowls and bronzed nickel fixtures.

She turned on the water in the far sink, running her fingers under the cool stream while she got her head on straight. The suite was ridiculously huge for one person, the bed like the state of Oregon itself. She and Delilah would hardly even notice each other.

Probably.

Maybe.

"Hey."

Claire jumped as Delilah appeared behind her.

"Whoa, sorry," Delilah said, dropping her own toiletry bag onto the marble counter. "You okay?"

"Yeah, fine." Claire managed to smile at her, but then Delilah *leaned* on the counter and she had to look away.

"I guess we should get undressed, huh?"

Claire dropped the little pot of lip gloss she'd mindlessly opened, finger swirling through the shimmery pink just for something to do. It clattered into the sink with the water still flowing, soaking the gloss before Claire could snatch it back.

"What?" she asked, grabbing a fluffy hand towel and wiping the pot dry.

In the mirror, Delilah's eyes flicked to the lip gloss and back to Claire. "Massages? Thirty minutes?" She brandished a creamy rectangle of paper that detailed the services Astrid had already arranged for them. This schedule, thankfully, did include Delilah.

"Oh," Claire said. "Right."

Delilah looked down at the paper. "It says here we're supposed to undress and put on the robes provided before we head downstairs to our assigned massage room." She set the paper on the counter and grabbed the two fluffy white robes that hung on the wall next to the shower, holding one out to Claire.

Claire took it, curling it to her chest, and then she just stood there, staring at Delilah like she was waiting to see who would start undressing first.

Delilah cleared her throat and Claire jolted.

God, *was* Claire waiting to see who would start undressing first? She was officially a disaster. A horny, stressed-the-hell-out disaster.

And from the small smile that lifted the corners of her mouth, Delilah knew it.

"You want to change in here and I'll take the bedroom?" she asked.

Claire nodded way too vigorously. "Yes. Good. Perfect."

That little smile again. "Good. Perfect," Delilah said before leaving and closing the door behind her.

Claire slumped against the counter, rubbing her forehead with the robe. She had to get a grip. It was just a robe. It was just a spa. Delilah was just a person. A gorgeous person, true, but a person nonetheless, like Claire. A person she had absolutely no business thinking about naked or what the skin just under her ear might taste like.

"Do you think we're supposed to leave on our underwear?" Delilah called from the other room, her voice completely guileless.

Claire groaned into the robe. "I don't know!"

"Hmm. I'm taking mine off."

Oh, for god's sake.

Claire stripped down to her undies and bra—decidedly leaving both on—and splashed some cold water on her face. Then she wrapped the cloudlike robe around her, securing the tie around her waist, and sat on the edge of the huge soaker tub while she took a few deep breaths. What she really wanted to do was call Ruby, but her phone was out in the bedroom. While she sat there, trying not to think about tonight or nakedness or Delilah's underwear on the floor, a knock sounded on the outside door.

"Who is it?" she heard Delilah call.

"Me."

Claire recognized Iris's voice and stood up.

"Me who?" Delilah said.

"Iris."

"Prove it."

Claire cracked a smile and opened the door into the bedroom an inch, just to make sure Delilah was robed—she was, and sat on the end of the bed scrolling lazily through her phone—and then went to let Iris in. She was thankful for the distraction in the form of her best friend, her voice of reason when it came to Delilah Green.

"Hey," Iris said with her own fluffy robe in place, her red hair piled on top of her head just like Claire's. She glared at Delilah. "Are you always like this?"

Delilah looked up. "Define *this*."

"Annoying bitch?"

"Iris," Claire said.

Delilah's smile was beatific. "For you, I put my best foot forward."

Iris sighed and popped her hands onto her hips. "Fine. Whatever, I'm sorry. So what's the plan?"

"Plan?" Delilah asked.

"Yes, plan," Iris said.

"To . . . get massages and a mud mask?" Delilah said.

Iris shook her head. "To dethrone lover boy."

A pit opened up in Claire's stomach. Last night, she and Iris had definitely decided that they needed to get serious about Astrid and Spencer. But the decision had been alcohol-induced, fueled by witnessing his covert dickishness and empowered by seeing Delilah haul him into the river. Actually doing something about it in the sober light of day, essentially ruining their best friend's wedding, was a whole other matter.

Claire pressed her hands to her stomach. "Iris—"

"Oh no," Iris said, pointing at her. "Oh *hell* no. You are not backing out now. You're the one who said we couldn't let her marry him."

"I'm not backing out. I'm just . . . thinking."

"You're backing out. Even Delilah can see he's a ghastly excuse for a human being."

Delilah tapped her chin. "I'm going to choose to take that as a compliment."

"Choose away," Iris said, but then continued staring at Delilah. "Will you help us?"

"Help you get rid of Spencer?"

"Not *get rid*," Claire said. "Just . . . maybe—"

"Yes. *Get rid*," Iris said. "Our darling Claire here is too kind-hearted."

"*Get rid* sounds so violent," Claire said. "We just need to talk to Astrid."

"And three is better than two," Iris said. "After last night, I like your style."

Delilah flashed a grin at that but then grew serious. "What do you plan on doing? Tossing *Astrid* in a river?"

"Of course not," Iris said.

"Oh, I know," Delilah said, clasping her hands together under her chin and fluttering her lashes dramatically. "Sit her down for a nice heart-to-heart and convince her that her true love is still out there somewhere over the rainbow."

Claire and Iris looked at each other. This wasn't *exactly* what they planned on doing, but it was close.

"Do you have a better idea?" Iris asked.

Delilah looked at them both for a few seconds before answering. "Maybe I do."

Iris stared at her. "Care to share, oh wise one?"

Delilah sucked her teeth. "I haven't decided yet."

"Which means you've already thought about this," Iris said, lighting up like a firework. "You have, haven't you?"

Delilah waved a nonchalant hand. "Why would I care who Astrid marries?"

"Trust me, I know you don't care," Iris said spitefully, and Delilah lifted a brow.

"Okay, enough," Claire said, then looked at Delilah. She could've sworn the other woman's gaze softened. "Look, we do want to talk to Astrid about this. We just don't know how."

"Aren't you two supposed to know her better than anyone?" Delilah said.

"Yes. We do." Claire grappled for the right words. "But Astrid's . . . complex. She doesn't open up easily, even to us." She looked at Iris. "Remember when she had a crush on Toby McIntosh for all of tenth grade? She didn't even admit it until graduation."

"I remember," Iris said.

"You don't have to do anything," Claire said to Delilah. "But, if you think of any ideas . . ."

Delilah stared at her for a second, Claire's heart in her throat. Finally, the other woman released a huge sigh. "Fine. Jesus. But if you're going to do this, you have to be careful about it. Astrid would have to be completely convinced that he's wrong for her, not just mad at him over something you say he did. It has to come from her."

"You mean we'd have to be manipulative," Claire said, wincing.

"No, I mean what I said. Careful. Get her to talk about him, ask her questions about what she likes about him, things like that. Help her realize it all on her own."

Iris paced, her thumbnail in her mouth. "Yes. That's perfect. It needs to be her idea or she'll never see it. You know Delilah's right, Claire."

Claire rubbed her eyes under her glasses. Delilah *was* right. Astrid would never, ever walk away from something she'd committed to unless it was her idea. Isabel raised her to be ruthless like that, always in control, always the one with the upper hand. Honestly, this die-hard trait was why Claire believed Astrid chose Spencer in the first place. He called the shots. He wore the pants. Astrid had been the perfect student, tried hard to be the perfect daughter, and now she was the perfect business manager. So for this one area in her life, she didn't have to work so hard. She didn't have to constantly be thinking about how to make her relationship succeed.

She just had to say yes to everything her already-perfect fiancé said.

Claire felt an almost unbearable sadness settle over her at the thought. She had to believe there were plenty of men out there who would love partnering with Astrid, working together to be successful together—or hell, even failing together—instead of this imbalance of power she had with Spencer.

"All right," Claire said. "It's a start, I guess."

"Exactly," Iris said. "So we're all agreed"—here she waved her hand in a dramatic circle to include Delilah—"that our plan is getting her to talk and think about Spencer and his douchebag ways."

Claire nodded while Delilah simply stood up, tightened her robe belt, and headed for the door.

Iris cleared her throat.

"What?" Delilah asked, dropping her phone into her robe's pocket and slinging her camera bag over her shoulder. "You want to come up with a secret handshake or something?"

Iris just glared.

CHAPTER

TWELVE

DELILAH HAD NO clue what she'd been thinking.

She'd had her own plan—annoy Astrid to within an inch of her life about the human germ she'd chosen to marry, becoming the proverbial thorn in Astrid's side during what should've been the happiest time in her life. Was Delilah an asshole for hatching this little scheme? Possibly. Okay, probably. But it was harmless fun, just little dips into the river and some broken glass, a way to hold on to a little bit of control, which Astrid—and Isabel, for that matter—always had in spades. Astrid was going to do what she wanted, no matter what her stepsister did, and Delilah had no doubt these two weeks would end with the happy couple sailing off into the sunset and Delilah heading back to New York with fifteen grand in her pocket, no harm, no foul.

Besides, what did she care if Astrid married this guy? What did she care if Astrid yessed her way to popping out a hundred babies in Seattle? What did she care if Astrid tied on an apron every night to cook her man's dinner? Maybe Astrid *liked* doing all those things.

Feminism, after all, was about equal respect for equal work, not en-suring a woman never baked a cake or fetched a cold one.

But then Claire had turned her doe eyes on Delilah. She'd been so . . . dammit, so *sweet* in her care for Astrid, her genuine worry, and Delilah had cracked like an egg. She'd never given in to anyone so easily in her life, and she still wasn't exactly sure what the hell had happened back in their room, how she'd ended up helping the fuck-ing coven break up her stepsister's wedding. She'd get paid no matter what—compensation was guaranteed even in the event of a wedding cancellation, a little clause she'd added to her standard contract es-pecially for her beloved stepfamily—and so here she was, collaborat-ing with Astrid's BFFs, helping them take down the patriarchy one dickbag at a time.

When they reached Astrid's door, Delilah hung back, leaning against the wall with her arms crossed. She'd agreed to help, but distance was good here. A *there's you and then there's me* sort of mes-sage to Iris and Claire.

But then Claire sidled up next to her, shoulder brushing hers, smelling like clean laundry and that meadowy scent Delilah remem-bered from that night at Stella's.

"Do you think this will work?" Claire whispered as Iris knocked on Astrid's door.

Her breath smelled like mint, and Delilah found herself wishing she'd thought to brush her own damn teeth.

"I have no idea," Delilah said, and then thought of adding some-thing salty like, *Maybe Astrid and Spencer are actually MFEO*, but then she turned enough to meet Claire's eyes, saw hope and something else in all that deep brown, that same flicker of interest as when Delilah had helped Ruby with her dress, and nerves fluttered low in her belly.

Actual nerves. She hadn't felt nervous around a woman since . . .

You actually thought we were going to get married? Are you fucking insane?

Jax's voice echoed between her ears—mean, incredulous, shaming—while a naked woman Delilah had only ever seen in Jax's old photographs lounged in Delilah's own bed, staring wide-eyed like she was watching a soap opera.

Delilah turned away and cracked her knuckles. She didn't think about that horrible last day with Jax five years ago very often, but when she did, she knew how to deal with it.

"I need a drink," she said.

"You and me both," Iris said as Astrid flung open her door and swept into the hallway with her own robe tied snugly around her thin frame, her blond hair in a stylishly messy bun.

As the four of them headed toward the massage rooms, Delilah could still feel Claire's eyes on her, but she didn't look at her again.

DELILAH SPENT THE rest of the afternoon in silent, massaged-and-mudded bliss. By her observation, so did the rest of her party, which made getting Astrid to talk about Spencer's misogynistic ways difficult. They all did everything together, rotating through seaweed wraps and saunas as a pack, but it was hard to bring up a life-altering decision when a person named Stormy was busy spreading pore-cleansing charcoal all over your thighs. Delilah could barely take any photographs, doing her best to capture a few in between treatments, particularly when Astrid's face was covered in complexion-brightening mud.

Still, throughout the afternoon, Delilah kept catching Iris's and Claire's eyes. She didn't mean to look at them, she swore, but whenever they'd all move to a new room or Astrid made a comment about something even remotely wedding-esque, like fittings or the chance of rain that day or how she was worried the salmon puffs she ordered wouldn't be fresh, the three of them would find one another, widen their eyes as though daring the others to say something first. Delilah, for her part, knew it would be easier to bring up Spencer if Astrid brought him up first, but she never did. Not once in four hours of pampering did she mention her dashing fiancé.

But that certainly didn't stop all the looks from passing between Delilah, Iris, and Claire. And every time it happened, something bloomed in Delilah's chest. She couldn't put a finger on it—nerves, irritation, pure adrenaline. Whatever it was, she didn't think she'd ever felt it before and wasn't quite sure she liked it.

By the time the four of them had showered and gathered again for dinner on the veranda overlooking the vineyard, Delilah was exhausted. Being around other people all day long, even if they hadn't talked all that much, was completely draining. She felt constantly *on*, and right now, all she wanted was a glass of wine the size of her head and a quiet room of her own.

Plus, there was that feeling again, right under her rib cage every time Iris and Claire so much as glanced at her or tapped her foot under the table, like something about to spill over.

"This is nice," Astrid said, propping her elbows on the wooden table and resting her entwined hands under her chin. "Isn't this nice?"

She was looking at Delilah when she asked it, so Delilah complied. "Nice. Wonderful."

And it was. This was the first meal at a wedding event she'd actually get to eat. Her camera was under the table, but she was so tired, she wasn't about to get it out of her own volition. She just wanted to sit here, in all the *niceness*. The patio only had a few other diners, and it was dimly lit with gas-powered lamps, flames flickering shadows over faces and arms. The sun was just dipping into the valley, turning the evening lavender and silver, and the air smelled like earth and rain, even though there wasn't a cloud in the sky. Everything felt verdant, alive.

And then there was Claire sitting next to her, dressed in a kelly-green linen romper, shorts falling mid-thigh and blouse-like top unbuttoned just enough to show a little cleavage.

Jesus, did this woman look bad in anything?

Delilah rubbed her forehead and took a gulp of 2014 Blue Lily Signature Pinot Noir. Despite the way she'd played with Claire earlier in the day, shouting through the bathroom door about the status of her underwear, she wasn't in the mood for any games tonight. She felt raw, like she'd been in the sun all day and needed to be wrapped in aloe, and Claire's meadowy scent wasn't helping.

"It's lovely," Iris said, looking at Claire and then Delilah.

"Gorgeous," Claire said, looking at Iris and then Delilah.

"Oh, for fuck's sake," Delilah said.

The three women froze—Astrid with her brows dipped in confusion and these other two yahoos with their eyes popped wide. Delilah felt a laugh bubble into her chest.

"What is it now?" Astrid asked, immediately irritated.

Under the table, Claire hooked her ankle around Delilah's, bare leg against bare leg. Claire's skin was smooth, cool, and made Delilah's stomach flutter more than she'd like to admit. It did the trick though. She took a deep breath and smiled, lifting her glass to her mouth and looking around as if for the server.

"I'm starving, is all," she said. "Don't they bring bread or something?"

Astrid visibly relaxed. "Oh, yeah, I think so." She flagged down the server who'd been taking care of them and asked for a basket of carbs, which was promptly delivered, along with a homemade honey butter that Delilah wanted to lick right out of the little stainless steel container.

She was on her second piece of warm brown bread when she realized Claire's ankle was still lightly twined around hers.

The knowledge was like an electrical shock. Delilah's spine went straight, and she couldn't keep her own gaze from finding Claire, who seemed to realize at the same time that she was still wrapped around Delilah like a koala. Claire jerked her leg back so quickly, her knee bashed into the table, rattling the plates and glasses and pulling a swear out of her pretty mouth.

"Shit, you okay?" Iris asked, steadying the vase of lilies at the center of the table.

Claire grimaced and nodded, rubbing her leg. "Yeah, sorry. Klutz over here."

Delilah cracked a smile, which Claire returned, a lovely blush spreading over her cheeks. Watching this beautiful, completely adorable woman under the sinking sun, the whole day suddenly seemed hilarious—the one-room-at-the-inn faux pas, Claire locking herself in the bathroom like a self-conscious teenager, this ridiculous team effort to take Spencer down. As three-fourths of a glass of wine rivered through Delilah's veins, her smile grew into a laugh she couldn't hold back.

"What's so funny?" Astrid asked.

Delilah shook her head, more laughter slipping through her mouth. Next to her, Claire started laughing too, her hand over her face and her shoulders shaking. Iris and Astrid just stared at each other, though Iris wore a tiny knowing smile that made Delilah feel a little less insane. Still, she had to get it together or Astrid would end up pouty and pissed, the opposite of what the three other women were going for.

Well, at least the opposite of what Iris and Claire were going for.

And right now, with the light and the wine and the laughs, all coupled with her own exhaustion, Delilah would give Claire Sutherland just about anything.

"Okay, so," Delilah said, knocking back another swallow of wine and propping her elbows on the table. She leveled her gaze at Astrid and fluttered her lashes like a school girl at a sleepover. "Tell. Me. Everything."

Iris choked on her wine, and Claire covered her smile with her hand. Astrid, however, didn't seem to notice. Her eyes went wide, and she released a nervous laugh.

"What?"

"Spencer," Delilah said, tearing a piece of bread in half and stuffing it in her mouth.

"Oh," Astrid said. She picked up her glass and tucked a piece of hair behind her ear. It did not escape Delilah's notice that Astrid's smile dimmed. Just a little. Just enough.

Apparently, it didn't escape Claire's notice either, as her leg nudged Delilah's once before retreating again. Delilah played along, pressing her thigh back against Claire's and then decidedly leaving it there. She heard Claire inhale slowly, but the other woman didn't move.

"We don't have to talk about him," Astrid said, waving a hand. "I babble on about him enough."

"Do you though?" Iris asked.

Delilah rolled her eyes. Iris was about as subtle as a kid on Christmas morning. But then, as Iris seemed to realize her less-than-suave prod and shoved some bread in her big mouth, something occurred to Delilah. A way in. A little gold nugget from her and Astrid's childhood, one of the few memories she had that wasn't laced with resentment.

"He's your Gilbert Blythe, right?" she said, daintily sipping her wine. "Must be a lot to say about him."

Astrid's mouth fell open. "Gilbert . . . Gilbert Blythe?"

"Yeah, from . . ." Delilah pretended to be stumped, waving her hand in the air. "What was it?"

"*Anne of Green Gables,*" Claire said. Her leg twitched against Delilah's but didn't move away. Something fluttered in Delilah's stomach, and she had to force herself to focus on the task at hand.

Delilah snapped her fingers. "*Anne of Green Gables.*"

"You remember Gilbert Blythe from *Anne of Green Gables?*" Astrid said.

"I remember how much you swooned over him," Delilah said. And that Anne and Diana were obviously super gay and hot for each other, which was precisely what she'd told Astrid back when she'd first read the books. They were thirteen and Astrid had finished *Anne of Green Gables* first before leaving it on Delilah's bed, something she sometimes did without any word of explanation. After reading the first four books in the series, Delilah had presented her Anne-and-Diana-are-queer theory over pizza one night while Isabel was at a charity event. Astrid hadn't even argued with her, just laughed and said she was probably right and then proceeded to ramble on and on about how much she wanted her own Gilbert Blythe one day.

"Who didn't swoon over Gilbert Blythe?" Astrid asked, and Claire and Iris both laughed.

Delilah raised her hand. "Gay as hell, remember?"

Astrid gave her a look and leaned forward. "You're telling me your heart didn't skip just a little when Gilbert rescued Anne on the river in her sinking skiff when she was pretending to be the Lily Maid or when he turned down the Avonlea teaching position so Anne could have it and stay with Marilla?"

Delilah tapped her chin. "Okay, maybe a little." Then she held out both of her hands in front of her chest suggestively. "But only if I imagined Gilbert with a nice pair of—"

"Okay, I get the picture," Astrid said, rolling her eyes.

"My heart *did* skip a few beats when Anne broke that slate over his head for calling her 'Carrots,'" Delilah went on. "I thought, that's my kind of woman."

Iris snorted a laugh.

"Okay, but his proposal was amazing," Claire said.

"Yes!" Astrid said, swallowing more wine. "Twice he proposed! She shot him down, and then he asked her again years later, telling her she was his dream." She tipped her glass at Delilah. "Come on, even you have to admit that's romantic."

Another leg nudge. "Yep. I sure do have to admit that."

Claire lowered her head, and Delilah only knew she was silently laughing because her body shook a little.

"So how did Spencer do it, then?" Delilah asked. "Was it as romantic as all that?"

Astrid's smile dipped again, but she covered it with a sip of wine.

"Oh, come on, I haven't heard this story," Delilah said, and immediately knew her voice was way too chipper. She sounded like someone out of a Jane Austen novel. Astrid full-on frowned, and Iris just looked at her like she was on drugs. Only Claire seemed to be enjoying the spectacle, her thigh warm and *right there* and her mouth pressed flat to keep from laughing. Delilah felt her own laughter trying to bubble up from her chest into her mouth, and she took a large swallow of wine to keep it inside. She felt oddly relaxed though, less edges and more rounded corners, that raw feeling from earlier fading at every stolen glance with Claire.

Or maybe it was just the seventy-dollar bottle of wine.

"We haven't either," Iris said after throwing both Delilah and Claire a *get your shit together* look.

"Yes, you have," Astrid said.

"No," Iris said. "At the end of March, you texted us to meet you at Stella's, and when we got there, you showed us the ring and said he proposed and immediately started babbling about wedding plans. You'd even already set a date by the time we found out."

Astrid's expression went from questioning to hurt in two seconds flat. Delilah could feel Claire's worry radiating next to her, the warmth of it like a homemade quilt.

"We were so excited for you, I guess we forgot to ask for proposal details," Claire said, trying to save the moment. She reached across the table and squeezed Astrid's hand. "Tell us now."

Astrid relaxed, but only a little. She sighed and took two gulps of wine before waving her hand through the air. "He asked and I said yes. That's about it."

"That's about it," Iris said, her voice flat. "And you let him get away with that? You, who once dumped a guy, *at* prom, mind you, because he forgot to get you a corsage?"

Jesus, Iris did not understand the concept of a gentle hand.

"Oh my god, I remember that," Claire said, laughing in what Delilah assumed was an attempt to lighten the increasingly darkening situation. "Poor Henry Garrison didn't know what hit him."

"A boutonniere in the face, that's what hit him," Iris said, and she and Claire cracked up.

Astrid didn't laugh, but her cheeks reddened, and Delilah didn't know if she was getting flustered or pissed or if the wine was kicking in. And then, like a storm rolling across a plain, Delilah could see it happening—the famous Astrid shutdown.

"You know, I'm actually a little tired," she said, scooting her chair back. "I think I'll head to my room."

"What?" Iris said. "Our food isn't even here yet."

"Yeah, I'm not all that hungry anymore." Astrid stood, glass in hand, and managed a smile. "Too much bread."

"Astrid," Claire said, taking her hand. "Come on, sweetie, sit down. What's wrong?"

But Astrid shook her head. "I'm just exhausted, that's all. I'm fine. Just . . . wedding stuff, you know? I'm going to call Spencer and try and get some sleep. See you in the morning for yoga?"

Claire nodded as Astrid kissed her on the cheek, then came around the table to do the same to Iris. Delilah, she completely ignored, and then took the half-full wine bottle with her as she left.

The three of them sat there for a few minutes in silence, letting what happened settle around them as the evening grew darker.

"Well, that was a disaster," Claire said. Her voice was small, thick-sounding.

"Train wreck," Iris said, collapsing back in her chair with a sigh.

"Are you both kidding me?" Delilah asked. "That's exactly what you wanted."

Claire stiffened, her thigh moving away from Delilah's. "No, it's not. We wanted . . . we—"

"Wanted her to question what the hell she's doing with Spencer when he's the complete opposite of everything she's ever dreamed of?" Delilah said.

Claire's whole body slumped, which sent her leg into Delilah's once again. "Yeah, but not like this. Not like . . . like she's hurt."

"Honey," Iris said softly, leaning forward. "If Astrid realizes she's made a mistake with Spencer, it's going to hurt."

Claire's face crumpled, but only for a second before her expression cleared and she nodded. "I know. I just . . ." She groaned and rubbed her eyes under her glasses. "Goddammit, why do men have to suck so much?"

"Not all of them do," Iris said.

"Most of them do," Delilah said.

Iris tapped her chin in thought for a second, then blew out a breath. "Okay, yeah, you're right. Most of them do. Thank fuck I'm bi."

Claire laughed, leg pressing more firmly against Delilah's. Delilah had to fight to keep her hand in place, the desire to reach out and squeeze the other woman's thigh almost irresistible. Claire was ridiculously adorable. And sweet. Jesus, how did she get so sweet? Being a teenage mom, raising a preteen daughter mostly on her own, running a business, dealing with her half-assed ex—Delilah would be a complete disaster if she was in her shoes. And yet, here Claire was, agonizing over her best friend's heart.

Iris lifted her glass. "To shitty men and the women who put them in their goddamn place."

"I'll drink to that," Delilah said, raising her own glass.

Claire followed suit, and the three women clinked over the lilies and drank, then dug into their food, which arrived a few minutes later. They proceeded to talk about easier things—movies, books, how they could cut through the filet mignon like it was butter. They laughed about how every time Iris drank even just one glass of red wine, her face blazed bright red and with the heat of a million suns, always leaving her with a wicked headache, but she loved the stuff anyway. They talked about Ruby and how she still slept with the stuffed purple unicorn Iris had given her when she was born and Claire was dreading the day she stopped.

Delilah had completely cleared her plate and drained her third glass of wine before she realized it.

She'd been laughing.

A lot.

With Claire and Iris.

Like they were actually friends and not a tangle of complicated histories simply tolerating each other for the night.

CHAPTER
THIRTEEN

CLAIRE FLOPPED ONTO the bed, her head pleasantly fuzzy, a smile still on her lips from the fun night.

Well, mostly fun. Thinking about Astrid made her stomach hurt, but the wine was helping keep the ache at a distance.

So was the fact that Delilah was in the bathroom right now, changing into . . . whatever she slept in. Pajamas? A nightie? Nothing at all?

Claire squeezed her eyes shut. She'd already completed her nightly routine—teeth, face, lotion—and was now keenly aware that she was wearing a pair of sleep shorts and a tank top with no bra. She hadn't even thought about it when she was changing in the bathroom a few minutes ago. The wine, the constant laughing at dinner, it had all distracted her from this very moment when she and Delilah would both slide in between the sheets, their skin inches away from each other, and—

Ruby.

She needed to call Ruby.

It was only ten thirty, and she was almost positive her daughter would still be up, probably stuffing her face with raw cookie dough and watching an R-rated movie. For once, she was glad for Josh's lax rules. She sat up, ignoring the sound of running water in the bathroom, and tapped Josh's name on her phone's favorites list. Ruby didn't have her own phone yet, and Claire refused to cave to her whining about it. She shuddered to think of her daughter on social media, but knew it was coming, looming like a storm just offshore.

"Hey," Josh said.

"Hey."

"How's the spa? Please tell me you got a massage. Or five."

"Ha ha. And yes, I did."

"Five?"

She felt a smile tug at her lips. "One, but it was a very good massage. Can I talk to her?"

"Oh, um . . . well. No, not exactly."

Claire sat up straight. "Excuse me?"

"She's indisposed."

"Indisposed? What does that mean?"

"It means she can't come to the phone."

There was the hint of a laugh in his voice, and it made her wish she could transcend space and time and strangle him right here and now. Her pulse started racing, her mind swirling with all the scenarios of why her daughter was *indisposed* at ten thirty at night.

They're at some wild party with Josh's baseball bros from high school.

They decided to take a road trip and Josh left Ruby at a gas station.

Josh completely forgot that she was spending the night and dropped her off at Claire's house and someone kidnapped her off the front porch and now Ruby was in the clutches of—

The bathroom door opened, and Delilah stepped out dressed in nothing but an oversize white cotton tee that fell at mid-thigh, her hair up in a clip. The sight jolted Claire back into the room and cleared her head. Delilah gave her a weird look—Claire was definitely huffing like a hyperventilating rhino—and froze on the spot.

Claire waved a hand as if to say *I'm fine.*

"Josh, put my daughter on the phone right now."

"Claire."

"I don't care where you are or what the hell you're doing."

"Claire."

"I swear to god, I will take a dull knife to your manhood if you so much as—"

"Jesus, Claire, she's asleep."

Claire stilled. "Asleep."

"Yes."

"In a bed?"

"Seriously? Yes."

"In her bed at *your* apartment?"

He sighed. "Yes."

She closed her eyes, warm relief spreading through her body.

Quickly followed by a chilly irritation.

"Then why the hell didn't you just say so?" she said. "Goddammit, Josh."

"I'm sorry. I was just playing around. I didn't think you'd freak out that much."

She let a beat of silence pass, because this guy. She chanced a look at Delilah, who was still standing by the bathroom door watching her with a concerned expression on her face.

"Okay, fine," Josh said. "Now that I think about it, I probably should've realized you would freak out. I'm sorry, really."

She inhaled deeply for what felt like the hundredth time in the past ten minutes, her shoulders dropping. Delilah must've taken that as a sign that things were okay, because she stepped close to the bed and rested one knee on the mattress. Her shirt inched up a bit, which Claire definitely did not notice.

"It's all right," Claire said, suddenly exhausted. She dropped her head into her hand and pressed her fingers to her temple.

"Want me to wake her up?"

"No, no, I'll talk to her in the morning."

"Okay. Hey, the oven's off."

She dropped her hand into her lap. "What?"

"The oven? I . . . I turned it off as soon as I was done cooking dinner. Even before you had Grant stop by and check on me."

"I didn't—"

"And Ruby's been in bed since ten o'clock. I know it's later than nine thirty, but I figured, summer and all. Ten is good, right?"

She wasn't sure what she was supposed to say to all this. Did he want a medal for performing basic parenting duties and pressing a button on the stove? After years of disappearing, staying gone for months, and barely even calling once a week, all in the name of *I'm not good for anyone right now*?

"Okay, Josh," she said. "I'll talk to you tomorrow."

And then she hung up before he could say anything else, setting the phone on the nightstand while she got herself back together.

"Everything all right?" Delilah asked.

Claire closed her eyes just for a second, then looked up and smiled. "Yeah. Fine."

Delilah narrowed her eyes at her, clearly not buying it. "So he's a dick, is that it? We need to take him out too?"

"No." The answer came so quickly. A reflex. Because Josh wasn't a dick. Not by a long shot. This would all be so much easier if he was. "He's just . . ." She shook her head. "He's a guy who had to grow up too soon."

Delilah pulled a face. "No sooner than you had to."

"I know. But I'm . . ." She closed her mouth, unsure why she was making excuses for him. She didn't mean to, but she knew that her relationship with Josh, Ruby, this little oddball family she had, wasn't as simple as Josh being a jerk and ghosting. It was a hurt-layered, terror-filled, love-for-your-kid-addled mess.

"You're what?" Delilah asked. "The mom? The woman? So that means you have to give up your whole life and he doesn't?"

Claire looked at her, a spark in the other woman's eyes that felt suddenly addictive, like sitting by a warm fire after a year in a frozen wasteland.

"Maybe," Claire said softly, her cheeks burning with the admission. "I know it's not the right way to think about it, but I . . . well, all he did was have sex with a faulty condom. I'm the one who grew Ruby in my own body."

Delilah pursed her lips and tilted her head at Claire. "All the more reason you deserve good things."

Her voice was so soft, so intense, it was like the world stopped spinning for a second. Claire could only stare at Delilah, her simple words swelling Claire's throat. She'd never been great at putting herself first, at going after the things she wanted. After all, she adored her daughter, couldn't imagine life without her. What else was there to go after?

But as Claire stared at Delilah, *want* curled in her belly, so strong her mouth watered and her chest ached with some emotion she couldn't even put a name to.

"Do you want to talk about this?" Delilah asked, breaking the spell.

Claire huffed a laugh. "Not really, no."

"Then we won't."

She didn't say it like it was a relief, or like she didn't want to talk about it in the first place. She said it gently, like she understood hard things and how, even though talking about them could be therapeutic, the words themselves were a labor and, sometimes, one just didn't have the bandwidth for them.

Claire nodded and met Delilah's eyes as the other woman took a large banana clip out of her hair, wild tresses haloing around her head. Claire meant to offer a smile of thanks, but a laugh burst out of her instead.

Delilah flinched.

Claire clapped a hand over her mouth, then spoke through her fingers. "Oh my god, I'm so sorry. It's just . . . you . . . your . . ." She waved her free hand around her head, indicating Delilah's hair, which was *huge*. No, what was bigger than huge? Gigantic. Ginormous. Her curls had frizzed in the evening air, but she must have clipped it up to wash her face, and now that it was set free again, it seemed to have a mind of its own. She looked like she'd been electrocuted.

Delilah's eyes lit with realization, but still she smirked and folded her arms across her chest, which drew attention to the fact that she was, most definitely, not wearing a bra.

A fact Claire did her best to ignore, locking her eyes on her Bride of Frankenstein hair.

"What's wrong, Claire?" she said, her voice a teasing lilt.

Another laugh escaped.

"Do I have something on my face?" Delilah patted her cheek, before smiling and pulling at her locks, stretching them out even bigger. "Oh, that. Yeah, do you have a hair tie I can borrow? I left all of mine in the Kaleidoscope Inn's floral hell, and all I have is this clip." She held up the black clip, then tossed it into her suitcase.

Claire nodded. "It looks amazing, just for the record."

"Sure it does."

"It does. It's unique. Not like my boring straight hair. I always liked your hair when we were teenagers."

Something flickered in Delilah's expression, but it was gone just as fast as it arrived. She cleared her throat. "So, a hair tie?"

"Oh yeah." Claire motioned to her own suitcase on a chair in the corner. "I know I have some in my toiletry bag, but I think there's one or two floating around in there too. I never leave home without them."

"A lesson I should learn," Delilah said, heading toward the turquoise-and-navy-striped suitcase, and Claire felt a spike of anxiety. Everything in her bag was organized, folded neatly. Claire was pretty sure her underwear was tucked away in a zippered pocket, and she hadn't brought her vibrator—

Her spine snapped straight.

Because she hadn't planned on packing her vibrator. It hadn't been on her list, but then she'd thought about how she'd be at a five-star spa and vineyard, enjoying a room of her own and probably trying very hard not to think about a certain big-haired, blue-eyed woman she couldn't for the life of her figure out.

She'd tossed the thing in last minute.

"Delilah, wait, I'll get it—"

"Oh. Wow."

Crap.

Delilah turned around, a black satin hair tie in one hand and Claire's bright pink California Dreaming Malibu Minx vibrator in the other.

Claire's face ignited. She knew a lot of people used vibrators. Hell, Iris had gifted her the very one that Delilah now held, raving about its abilities. Iris even forced the thing upon Astrid and asked often if it was collecting dust in Astrid's nightstand drawer. But Jesus Christ.

Of all the people to find her sex toy, clearly well used if Claire packed it for an overnight trip, it just had to be Delilah Green.

"Um . . . that's . . ." Claire trailed off, unsure of how to play this. She knew her cheeks were bright red, and she could feel the sweat beading on her upper lip.

But then Delilah smiled and nodded. "Oh, I know. I've got the same one. Amazing, isn't it?"

Then she tossed California Dreaming back into Claire's suitcase and piled her hair on top of her head, wrapping the tie around her messy locks with a *snap*.

CHAPTER

FOURTEEN

GOD, THIS WOMAN was adorable.

Delilah finished wrapping her hair, all the while keeping her eyes on Claire as her light pink blush burgeoned into a deeper red. The other woman didn't say anything else about the admittedly very large battery-operated dildo in her suitcase, so Delilah didn't either. Which was fine, because watching Claire fight a laugh when Delilah threw the toy back into the suitcase, then proceed to be simultaneously embarrassed, was . . .

Well, it was just about the cutest fucking thing Delilah had ever seen.

Her stomach suddenly felt a little unsettled, fluttery, like it did before the Fitz show or every time she approached an agent at an event or hit send on an email. She hadn't felt this belly-churning sensation over a woman since Jax, and she wasn't a fan. But, she supposed, Claire wasn't just some woman Delilah had met at an event or in a bar. She was Astrid's BFF, had known Delilah as an awkward teenager. It was a different context, that was all.

At least, that's what Delilah told herself as she tried to calm what felt like a million bees flying around in her stomach and grabbed her digital camera out of its bag. Her hands needed something to do as she approached the bed, something to focus on when she pulled the covers back.

A king mattress was like an ocean, but still. Claire was *right there*, and Delilah suddenly forgot how to make her limbs get into a bed like a normal person. She slid her knee in first, but then realized she'd be sitting on her legs, so she kicked her foot out from underneath her, which made her very nearly topple over on one elbow since her camera was still in her other hand.

Graciously, Claire ignored the awkwardness and picked up her phone, staring at the screen, but Delilah swore one corner of her mouth lifted a little. Delilah finally got settled in the cool sheets and flicked her camera to life. She began scrolling through the images she'd taken so far from the other wedding events, cringing at some bad lighting and then grinning at how, sometimes, that bad lighting made Isabel look like a crypt keeper.

"Have you gotten some good photos?" Claire asked, dropping her phone into her lap.

Delilah kept her eyes on her camera. "Yeah, I think so."

"Can I look at some? I don't think I've ever seen a photograph of yours."

Delilah glanced her way. Glasses, makeup-free face, hair in a pile on top of her head with her bangs brushing her eyelashes. One strap of her tank top had slid a little down her shoulder, and Delilah fought the urge to put it back in place.

Or slide it down even farther.

She cleared her throat and focused back on her screen.

"Sure," she said, but then those damn bees were back, their wings filling her stomach to the edges. She flipped backward to the brunch images, looking for something special, something beautiful. She wasn't sure why she cared what Claire thought about her photography skills, only knew that she did.

Finally, she landed on the perfect one.

She handed over the camera, which Claire took carefully, like she was handling a precious jewel—which she sort of was for what Delilah had paid for the thing—and then watched Claire's face as she reacted to the image.

First her mouth parted, eyes widening, but then everything softened.

"Delilah," she said. That was all. One word, but it was part voice, part sigh, and it was enough to make Delilah's arms break out in goose bumps, which she tried to hide by curling them around her knees.

"I thought you'd like that one," she said.

Claire nodded, eyes still glued to the black-and-white image of her and Ruby, sitting side by side at their table in Vivian's. Ruby was looking down, her long lashes on her cheek and the smallest smile lifting the corners of her mouth, while Claire had her arm wrapped around her daughter's shoulder, her nose pressed against Ruby's hair. Claire, too, wore a little smile. Delilah had managed to zoom in on their faces while preserving the light, cutting out most of the plates and glasses in front of them on the table.

The photo was just them.

Mother and daughter.

"I love it," Claire said, eyes still roaming over the screen. Finally, she lifted her gaze to Delilah. "You're good."

Delilah laughed and took back the camera. "You sound surprised."

Claire shook her head. "Not surprised. Just . . . impressed."

"The Ghoul of Wisteria House has talent, as it turns out."

It was the wrong thing to say. Claire immediately stiffened, the air between them growing tense, but Delilah wouldn't take it back even if she could. The bees had stilled their wings, and she needed to get her control back. She hadn't lost her shit over a woman in five years, and she didn't plan on starting now.

But then Claire said, "Delilah," and goddamn if that one word, her name on this woman's tongue, didn't stir up the whole hive again.

Delilah waved a hand and set her camera on the nightstand. "We should probably get some rest."

She flicked off the lamp and burrowed down into the sheets, her back to Claire. Next to her, she could tell the other woman hadn't moved.

"How . . . how did you get into it?" Claire asked. "Photography?"

Delilah didn't answer at first. But as her eyes adjusted to the dark, moonlight drifting in through the sheer curtains and silvering up the room, she found herself turning over, tucking her hands under her cheek, and arching her neck upward to see Claire's face.

Claire looked down at her, a safe distance away, but then she shifted. She slid down, fluffing her pillow once and then settling on her side too, her hands underneath her own cheek, a mirror image of Delilah. Her movements had pushed her a little closer to Delilah, only about a foot of space between them. The air changed again, thickened with something close and new.

"You really want to know?" Delilah asked, keeping her voice low and quiet. Too loud and this whole spell might break, and she hadn't decided yet if she wanted it to or not.

"I wouldn't have asked if I didn't."

"Oh, I don't know. You're a nice person. Nice people ask questions sometimes just because they think they *should*, not because they really give a shit."

Claire's brows pulled together. "I give a shit, okay?"

Delilah knew she should shut this down. She wanted to sleep

with this woman, not bond over origin stories and childhood griev-ances, and this whole day had sent her off-balance. Between Astrid just plain forgetting to book her a room, Claire offering her own, and the sudden camaraderie she felt tonight with Claire and Iris—a feel-ing she wasn't sure she'd ever experienced with women she wasn't screwing—her heart felt larger in her chest, more tender, like a sun-burn that screamed at the slightest touch. The words were all right there, the how and why of her life since Bright Falls, and she wanted to release them. Let them go. Let someone else carry them for a while. Or at least know. It had been so long since she told anyone her secrets. Just thinking about it now, all this solitary *knowing*, sud-denly made her so tired.

All the more reason to turn back over, just say good night. But as she locked eyes with Claire, who was staring at her like she really did give a shit, Delilah simply didn't want to.

"It started in high school," she said. At those few words, Claire seemed to relax, sink into the bed a little, like she'd been holding her breath. And so Delilah kept talking, telling her about her fascination with still images, freezing moments in time. She'd saved up money from doing odd jobs for Ms. Goldstein—her art teacher and the only adult in her life who ever seemed to give her a second look—and bought a Polaroid, just to see what it did. She walked around her cavernous house, echoes of Astrid's and Iris's and Claire's laughter pinging off the walls, and snapped pictures of anything she thought was interesting. A kitchen cabinet knob. A sliver of stained glass in the library. The molding on the fireplace. Expressions when no one knew she was watching. She'd caught Astrid's coven in so many un-flattering poses—mouths hanging wide open, eyes squeezed shut, tongues lolling out to lick the edge of a dripping Dr Pepper can.

Not that she mentioned those specific details to Claire right now. "I took a few pictures of Astrid too, just here and there" is what came out of her mouth, and she left it at that. But she remembered how she hoarded all of her photographs of the girls away, studying them for clues of what made them so acceptable and her such an odd duck. Other than a little bit of makeup and clothes from Nordstrom, she could never figure it out.

"I taught myself the photography basics in high school," she said. "Ms. Goldstein helped. Then, once I left Bright Falls, I knew I wanted to make it my life."

Claire nodded, eyes wide and dark as Delilah went on to tell her how she worked nine-hour shifts six days a week at a diner down on Grand Street just to afford her shitty apartment, but on her day off, she would wander the city, memorializing its sensuality, its passion, its queerness. All the things she'd been missing in her life. All the things she'd never had, never even dreamed were possible. It all came tumbling out in a rush of vulnerability and truth.

"And you started doing weddings?" Claire asked, still miraculously interested.

Delilah nodded. "Weddings, Bar and Bat Mitzvahs, anniversary parties, birthday parties. Anything I could get, really. I still waited tables—I still do, actually—but events pay pretty well, especially after I got some references. I've only been really trying to do the artist thing for the past few years."

"What do you mean the artist thing?"

"Photographic art, pieces I can sell, series, getting an agent to help navigate the art world. It's hard to break into though. Really hard."

Then her show at the Whitney fluttered into her mind, the relief and excitement associated with it. She told Claire about it, how it could be her big break.

"That's great," Claire said. "I wish . . ." But the other woman trailed off, brows lowering as she swallowed. Delilah didn't press her, and soon Claire was moving on.

"How did you know you wanted to make art?" she asked.

Delilah hesitated. The truth was . . . sensitive. And she wasn't sure she wanted to go there with Claire tonight or ever. There was no reason for her to know. None at all, other than the simple fact that Delilah wanted her to. Still, she wasn't sure how Claire would react.

But as she hesitated, Claire scooted a little closer and said, "Come on, I want to know."

So she told her.

"I got my heart broken," she said.

Claire's brows popped into her bangs. "You did?"

Delilah nodded, her throat thickening, but the words just kept coming. "I've only had one girlfriend. Her name was Jacqueline—Jax—and we met at a wedding I was working. She . . . she was the maid of honor."

Claire's mouth parted, and the irony here wasn't lost on Delilah, the fact that she was spilling her guts to another maid of honor she couldn't seem to shut up around.

"We moved in together, dated exclusively for two years."

"What happened?" Claire asked.

Delilah took a breath, wrapped her mind around the words she'd never said to anyone. After she and Jax broke up, there was no one else in her life to tell. Plus it was just embarrassing as hell, the fact that she hadn't been enough.

The words rushed out anyway.

"I caught her cheating on me."

"Oh god."

"With her ex. Whom, apparently, she'd never gotten over."

Claire covered her mouth with her hand. "Oh *god*."

Delilah nodded. "I was out of town for another wedding I was shooting. But the wedding got canceled—groom's cold feet—so I came home early and found her . . . well, she was in our bed and she wasn't alone."

The memory was still fresh and bright, like a high-res photograph. Jax—the only woman she'd ever loved and actually thought about marrying someday, creating the kind of family Delilah always dreamed about but never had—in the apartment they shared with her head between Mallory Prescott's legs. Delilah still remembered the vision of Mallory's blond head tossed back, her mouth open, and her aqua-painted nails curling around Delilah's own fucking pillow as she came.

"Apparently, it wasn't the first time," Delilah said. "She'd been cheating for months, trying to figure out how to dump me, and I just couldn't see it."

"Jesus," Claire said.

"Anyway," Delilah said, desperately wanting to get the conversation back on track. "I needed to get out of the city for a while, so I came back to Bright Falls. I thought . . . I don't know." She hadn't felt like being alone. That's what it had been, and she stupidly imagined the familiarity of Bright Falls, the family she had there, however odd and distant, might soothe some need in her she couldn't articulate. It hadn't. Astrid had been busy with her own life, and Isabel . . . well, Isabel was obviously very put out about finding Delilah on her doorstep, blaming some Junior League event she was hosting for why Delilah just couldn't possibly stay at her own house. It was the first time Delilah had had to check into a hotel in her hometown.

Turns out, it wasn't the last.

"I just needed a change of scenery," she said. "Brought my camera, walked around town hoping for some . . . I don't know. Inspiration, I guess."

"Did you find it?"

Delilah smiled and paused, because honestly, this was the part she was worried about. Not her heartbreak, though that was humiliating enough. But this, her art's origin story. Delilah hadn't done anything wrong, but still . . . it could come off as weird, and Delilah was already weird enough in Claire's eyes. But again, some gut instinct, some need, pushed her forward.

"I did," she said. "I found you."

Claire visibly flinched, head jerking back a little. "Me?"

Delilah nodded and told her how she'd been in town for about a week and she was walking along the riverbank, trying to work up the courage to go back to New York. And then suddenly, there was Claire, wading into Bright River up to her knees, fully clothed in a dove-gray dress with a lace overlay, shivering in the cold March wind. She'd started screaming. At the sky, the water, the evergreens on the other bank. Delilah lifted her camera and began snapping. She got at least a hundred shots, and Claire never saw her, never noticed her shifting behind her, lying on the sandy bank to get different angles.

Back in New York, she worked for hours editing the photos. Days. And it was from these images, Claire, beautiful and in pain in the river, that Delilah got the idea for a series that would define her style, her whole career.

Queer women, turmoil, and water.

She watched Claire take all of this in, looking for subtle shifts in her expression—shock, disgust, horror—but in the silver light, all she saw was . . . awe. A little sadness. Claire's brown eyes like bottomless depths as they stayed locked on Delilah in silence. She stayed silent for so long, in fact, Delilah began to panic—her heart, which had already crept into her throat, now felt like a tiny, trapped hummingbird, wings whirring.

"Are you . . . Is that . . . I mean, does that freak you out?" Delilah asked. "I never used the photos. I wouldn't do that." And she hadn't. She'd wanted to. Claire was gorgeous in them—sad and despairing and just fucking angry, something Delilah could relate to. But no way was Delilah going to have her sign a waiver, no way she was ever going to admit to Claire five years ago that she'd fascinated Delilah that much, that Delilah had captured what might have been one of the most painful moments in her life, immortalizing it forever.

And now, she'd admitted it all to her secret subject. The woman who, for all intents and purposes, had been Delilah's muse.

Claire just kept watching her, brows dipping a little in thought, for what felt like forever.

"Claire, I'm—"

"I remember that day," she said. Then she took a deep breath, let it out slowly. "Josh had just left again. I'd just *slept* with him again. And my six-year-old daughter was at home with my mother, crying her eyes out for her dad. Again. The one thing I've never been able to fix for her, just like my mom could never fix it for me."

Delilah sucked in a breath. She knew whatever had driven Claire down to the banks that day wouldn't be a happy story. Of course not. But this, the pain in Claire's voice even now as she talked about it, the image of a littler, even more vulnerable Ruby confused and hurt, it clawed at Delilah's own heart. And then there was the *slept with him again* comment that stirred up something totally different— something hot and angry, something that felt a lot like jealousy. Delilah shoved it aside and focused on Claire, searching for the right thing to say.

"Ruby's lucky to have you" was the only thing she could think of. And it was true. A mom like Claire, always thinking of her daughter, always trying to protect her, always, always, always. She was every kid's dream, wasn't she? At least, that was what kids like Delilah dreamed about, the kids who knew the alternative, the void where a loving parent should be.

"I can't believe you were there that day," Claire said.

Delilah swallowed thickly. "I'm sorry. I know it was a private moment, and I—"

But her words were cut off when Claire pressed a finger to her lips. Soft, feathery light.

Delilah heard herself inhale sharply, her mouth parting as Claire's hand slid down, pulling on her bottom lip just a little, her forefinger settling on Delilah's chin.

She left it there, and Delilah couldn't breathe. Couldn't think. Her heartbeat was everywhere—in her throat, her chest, her fingertips, between her thighs. Their breaths filled the room, soft and shallow and shaky. Claire's gaze searched her own, then flicked down to her mouth before returning to her eyes, over and over, a dance that made Delilah want to laugh or cry or . . .

Claire shifted. Closer. The finger on Delilah's chin slid to her jaw, then Claire's whole hand skated across her face, to her neck, and around to her nape. Delilah's eyes fluttered closed, every inch of her skin covered in goose bumps. This was what she wanted—Claire, wanting her—but she thought she would feel triumphant, laying out a plan and succeeding. Instead, her entire body felt like it was coming apart and knitting itself back together.

When she opened her eyes again, Claire was inches away, gaze searching her own, fingertips soft on Delilah's neck.

Delilah realized she was waiting for permission, waiting for Delilah to say she wanted this too. She forced her head to move, offering a single nod before she bridged the space between them and touched Claire's mouth with her own. She kissed her, soft and slow, her mouth closing around Claire's bottom lip. The other woman inhaled sharply, then seemed to let go, gently pressing back.

It was nothing like Delilah's normal first kisses. Usually, by this point, things were frenzied, desperate, wild and alcohol-infused, nothing but sensation and skin, and Delilah loved every minute of it.

But this. The way Claire exhaled into her mouth, fingers sinking into Delilah's hair, sliding her body closer so that every part of them aligned, everything slow and electric . . . this wasn't like any first kiss Delilah had ever had. Not even with Jax.

She cupped Claire's cheek and deepened the kiss, sucking on her bottom lip for a moment before turning her head for a new angle. Claire tasted like mint, a trace of wine, and something else totally different, totally Claire. The other woman released a tiny moan, and the sound shot straight to Delilah's center, made her feel wild even as the two women continued to move like they were underwater. She slid her hand to Claire's neck, then to her shoulder, gliding down her bare arm to rest at the swell of her hip. Claire shifted even closer, both hands now buried in Delilah's hair and opening her mouth more and letting her tongue tangle with Delilah's.

That was all it took to send Delilah over the edge. Soft was nice—beautiful even—but god, this woman. Delilah needed more, closer, harder. Fuck soft. Fuck everything but Claire and the way her breath hitched when Delilah slid a leg between her thighs. Now that—that raspy, desperate sound—was goddamn beautiful. Claire's own hands roamed down Delilah's shoulders to her hips, then dipped under her T-shirt before skating over the bare skin of her lower back.

"Is . . . is that okay?" Claire asked against Delilah's mouth.

"Hell yes," Delilah said, the breathy nature of her own voice surprising her. "Is this?" She lifted Claire's tank, fingertips ghosting over the supple skin of her stomach. Claire nodded, keeping her eyes open as Delilah's hands went higher . . . then higher still. Delilah could feel the imperfections in Claire's skin, soft ridges that felt like stretch marks, and they all seemed like heaven to her, sexy and curvy and perfect.

She wanted to move her hand higher, feel all of her, but she wanted this to last. Hell, she could've kissed Claire all night, nothing else, and been totally happy. The thought was so strange, so unlike her, she pulled her mouth back from Claire's, staring down at her for a few seconds. Claire stared back, her body shaky and needy. Her leg curled around Delilah's calf and her brows dipped.

"Are you okay?" she asked.

Delilah swallowed. She wasn't sure. She was . . . god, she was nervous and turned on as hell and wanted nothing more than to eat Claire for dessert right now, but under that simmering layer of lust was something else, something she couldn't put a finger on. She shook her head, trying to push it out of her mind. She'd done this dozens of times before. She knew how to fuck a woman. Knew how to make her cry out, knew how to make sure she herself had a good time, knew how to think of nothing but skin and mouths and coming.

Delilah crushed her mouth to Claire's. Tongues, hands, thighs.

Claire met her, touch for touch, shuddering when Delilah's fingers reached the lower curve of her breast. Delilah paused, but Claire pressed their mouths into another kiss, pushed her hips against Delilah's in clear acquiescence, so Delilah kept going and let her thumb sweep over Claire's hardened nipple.

Claire ripped her mouth from Delilah's, her chest rising and falling so rapidly Delilah was almost worried she was going to hyperventilate.

"You okay?" she asked.

Claire nodded.

Delilah grinned, then tugged Claire's bottom lip between her teeth, which pulled a groan from deep in Claire's throat so fucking sexy, Delilah had to release her own.

This. This was what she understood. Pure animal need. She knew her underwear was soaked and was pretty positive Claire's was too, but god, she wanted to know for sure. She squeezed Claire's nipple gently before soothing it with one more sweep of her thumb, then let her hand drift southward. Claire's hips undulated against hers and her own hand drifted down to the top of Delilah's ass, covered only by her royal-blue cheekies.

Delilah's fingertips had just dipped under the band of Claire's sleep shorts, her mouth on Claire's neck and the most perfect whispered sounds falling from Claire's lips, when someone knocked on the door.

Both women froze, humid exhales swirling between them.

That better have been my fucking imagination, Delilah thought. But then another knock echoed through the quiet room, followed by the worst possible sound in the entire world—her stepsister's voice.

"Claire? Delilah? Are you awake?"

"Oh my god," Claire whispered, scrambling out from under Delilah like she was on fire. She was out of the bed, straightening her tank top and fixing her hair on top of her head before Delilah had even sat up. "Shit."

"It's okay," Delilah said. "Take a minute."

"Claire?" Astrid called again, knocking even harder.

"Yeah!" Claire yelled, clicking on the lamp. "Just a sec!"

She stood there with her hands on her hips while Delilah watched. When Claire's gaze fell on her, her eyes widened.

"Your hair."

Delilah lifted a hand to her locks, feeling the curls Claire's fingers had pulled loose from the hair tie. "It's a mess, huh?"

"It's sex hair," Claire said, panic lacing her voice. "Can you fix it?"

Delilah never broke eye contact as she fully released her hair and then pulled it back up into a neat, sexless pile.

"Claire—"

"We can't tell her," Claire said, twining her fingers together. "Okay?"

Delilah just stared at her. That *something else* feeling from before started closing in on her thoughts. This had happened before. A potential partner shutting things down for some reason or another. Delilah always handled it fine. Shit happened. People were complicated. She was disappointed, but she got it, and she'd simply go home and rub one out, and that would be that.

But this . . . didn't feel like that. This felt different, a hollow feeling expanding in Delilah's chest, and she wanted to scream. Claire was just another lay. A vengeance lay at that.

But something in Delilah's face must've given her away, because Claire's shoulders slumped and she took a step closer to where Delilah still sat in the bed. "It's not . . . It's just . . . with Spencer and the wedding, we can't . . . She'd freak out and I—"

"I get it," Delilah said calmly, but that hole in her chest just kept growing, eating up all her normal. She looked away, inhaling quietly and slowly while she fixed the tangled bedsheets and draped them serenely over her lap. When they were smooth and crisp, when her heart had retreated back to its rightful spot behind her ribs, she looked up at Claire and smiled. "Okay, you can let her in."

Claire opened her mouth to say something, but before she could, Astrid pounded on the door again. Claire straightened her tank top one more time before hurrying toward the door. Astrid swept inside, eyes scanning the room like a mother looking for a teenage boy in the middle of the night.

"Are you okay?" she asked, looking at Claire.

"What?" Claire asked. "Me? Yeah, I'm fine." She waved a hand through the air, made a *psh* noise with her mouth, then rested that same hand on her shoulder.

Delilah would've bust out laughing if her throat wasn't doing this weird thick, achey thing.

"What are you two doing?" Astrid asked, turning her gaze on her stepsister.

Delilah tilted her head, the truth right on the edge of her tongue. This was what she'd wanted, wasn't it? To prove Astrid wrong about herself and Claire. To win. True, she and Claire hadn't had sex, but in some ways, what she and Claire had done was even more profound. More intimate, the slow slide of mouths, fingertips shyly ghosting over skin. This was Delilah's moment, her chance. Sure, Claire had asked her to keep it between them, but what did that have to do with Delilah, really? What did she care what Claire Sutherland wanted of her?

She didn't.

She *couldn't*.

But as her eyes found Claire's, her lashes thick and wide and pleading around all that deep brown, Delilah couldn't get the words around that cavern in her chest.

"Nothing," Delilah said. "Just talking. About to go to sleep, I think."

"Yep," Claire said, her eyes still locked on Delilah. "I'm pretty beat."

Astrid looked between the two of them, frowning. "Well, good thing I caught you, then."

"Caught us?" Claire said, her cheeks flushed.

"Before you went to sleep," Astrid said, and Delilah noticed Claire's shoulders loosen. "There's a room available. For Delilah."

Claire squinted at the clock on the bedside table. "At eleven thirty?"

"I told Hadley or whatever her name was to let us know anytime. Apparently, someone just called in and canceled their night's reservation. Delayed flight or something."

"Oh," Claire said.

Delilah couldn't tell whether Claire was relieved or disappointed, but she wasn't going to stick around to find out. She needed to get out of here. Now.

"Great," she said, tossing the covers back and grabbing her camera off the bedside table. She packed it into its bag, then headed into the bathroom to get her toiletries.

"Wait," Claire said. "I can go. You stay."

"Oh no," Delilah said, shaking her head as she came back into the bedroom and tossed her bag into her suitcase. "This is your room. I'll go." She zipped up her suitcase and headed for the door. "Room number?"

"Two twelve," Astrid said, handing her a key card. "I'll go with you, it's right next door to mine."

"Fabulous," Delilah said, opening the door and hurrying down the hall, suitcase rolling behind her. She heard Astrid tell Claire good night, heard the door close and Astrid's telltale purposeful footsteps over the hardwood, but she didn't look back or slow down until she was outside her door.

"Delilah, hang on," Astrid said.

Delilah pressed her eyes closed as she fumbled the key card into the slot. "What is it?" she said without looking at her stepsister.

Astrid slid up next to her, leaning against the wall while Delilah fought to get the damn red light to go green. "Look, I'm sorry."

Delilah paused in her battle. "For what?"

"For the room situation."

Delilah finally looked at her. Her stepsister had her arms crossed over her chest, as usual, and looked extremely uncomfortable with this apology. "Are you?"

Astrid seemed to deflate, shoulders drooping. "Yes. I didn't leave you out on purpose. When I made the reservation, I wasn't sure you'd actually show, okay? I was going to call back, and then things just got busy and I'm not used to . . ." She trailed off, but Delilah knew what she was going to say. She wasn't used to considering Delilah at all. That old, lonely feeling from childhood crept back up on her, piling on top of everything that had just happened with Claire.

"I get it," Delilah said. "It's fine."

"I just—"

"It's fine," Delilah said again. Her tone was so sharp, Astrid flinched, but she didn't want to talk about this right now. Not with her breath stuck in her chest like this, her legs still wobbly from having Claire's mouth on her neck.

The damn light finally blinked green. Delilah opened her door and disappeared inside before either of them could say another word.

CHAPTER FIFTEEN

FUCK.

Fuck, fuck, fuck.

As soon as she was alone, Claire tore off her clothes and all but threw herself in the shower to try to calm herself down. She turned the water all the way to cold, maybe to freeze off the memory of Delilah's mouth on hers, her hands, the way she'd tasted, how her neck had smelled like spring, like rain and fresh grass.

How Delilah's face had gone still as a stone, her fiery gemstone eyes dimming to a dull blue, the moment Claire asked her to keep what had just happened a secret.

Why the hell had she done that?

Because Astrid would have completely lost her shit, that's why.

One didn't simply make out with one's best friend's estranged sister and then announce happily that it was the single hottest fifteen minutes she'd ever experienced, and that included the time she and Josh frustration-fucked on her backyard patio table three years ago while her mother had taken Ruby to a movie. Tonight, she hadn't even come, Delilah hadn't even ventured below her hip bone, and

Claire still felt like she was about to explode just standing here under the water.

But that didn't matter.

It didn't matter that the whole thing had felt like so much more than just kissing and touching, or that even an hour later as she lay in bed wide awake, she was still wetter than she'd ever been in her entire life, her body humming and twitching like a live wire.

None of that mattered at all because what happened tonight absolutely would not happen again. It couldn't. Delilah lived in New York City. She was leaving in less than two weeks, for a huge show at a major museum no less. She didn't do relationships. Claire knew this from Astrid, just like she knew Delilah didn't care about anyone but herself and never had.

Claire grabbed the pillow Delilah had been using and threw it across the room. Then she got out of bed and turned the air-conditioning all the way down, hoping the cold would distract her from remembering the look in Delilah's eyes as she'd told her about Jax, about photographing Claire on the shores of the river. A look that seemed like the exact opposite of not caring.

CHAPTER SIXTEEN

THANK THE GODDESS for AirPods.

Delilah spent the entire drive back to Bright Falls with a sapphic fantasy audiobook blasting in her ears. After an afternoon of touring the vineyard and snapping photos of Astrid, Iris, and Claire tasting all sorts of fancy wines and then hocking them back into what can only be described as a spittoon, and trying her best to ignore Claire while making it seem like she totally wasn't ignoring Claire, all she wanted right now was her chintz-covered couch at the Kaleidoscope Inn, some liquor she could actually swallow, and a nice long session with her California Dreaming Minx.

Iris sat next to her in the back seat, which Delilah would also thank the goddess for except Iris legit kept writing messages to her on her phone's Notes app, then thrusting the thing under Delilah's nose.

What now?
We have ten days.

> Come on, I'm sure you can think of something really
> devious.
>
> Hello?
>
> If you don't answer me, I'll just get more annoying.

When Delilah did nothing but glare, Iris did indeed get more annoying. She snatched Delilah's phone right out of her hands and started tapping at the screen with a smirk on her face. Delilah fumed silently, not wanting to draw attention to whatever the hell Iris was doing. She finished with a final jab of her forefinger, and Iris's phone immediately buzzed with a text.

And so did Claire's.

Delilah snatched her phone back, her book still playing, and looked at her screen. Her messages were open, and there was a new group text that included her, Iris, and Claire, because of course Iris had just gone ahead and put everyone's numbers into Delilah's phone. Iris had named the chat OSB, whatever the hell that meant, and apparently, *Delilah's* first text to the other two women had been You're both queens and I live to serve you.

Claire shifted in the front seat, turning slightly to look over her shoulder at her.

Delilah quickly tapped out a text.

> **DELILAH:** I hate you both.
>
> **IRIS:** That's not what I heard.

In the front seat, Claire choked and went into a coughing fit. Delilah felt her cheeks go red. Had Claire fucking told Iris what happened between them last night? No. She wouldn't. Not if she was so set on Astrid not finding out. Iris was clearly not a great secret-keeper, as evidenced by her texting the two of them right now while Astrid sat in the driver's seat and babbled on and on about some design job she was doing for a law firm.

> **IRIS:** You just said we were queens.

Delilah relaxed a little while Claire chugged her water and made *uh-huh* sounds at Astrid.

> **CLAIRE:** Ris, what are you doing?
>
> **IRIS:** Um, texting?
>
> **DELILAH:** What the hell is OSB?
>
> **IRIS:** Operation Shit Boot
>
> **DELILAH:** Shit boot?
>
> **IRIS:** SHIT. BOOT.

Delilah looked at Iris, half irritated and half amused. Iris just smiled, then went back to texting.

> **IRIS:** What's our next move?
>
> **CLAIRE:** I think we can wait to talk about this until Astrid isn't two feet away from me.
>
> **IRIS:** We could, except we only have ten days and last night did not go as planned.
>
> **DELILAH:** Last night went exactly as planned.

Claire cleared her throat, and Delilah wanted to roll her eyes. She opened up a thread with just Claire.

Not what I meant.

I know, Claire texted back.

IRIS: Are you two texting on your own?

CLAIRE: No.

DELILAH: Maybe.

Claire huffed out a breath, and Delilah couldn't help but smile.

IRIS: Okay, no secret conspiring. I don't care if you two do want to bang each other's brains out.

Delilah choked on her own spit, which caused a coughing fit. She pounded on her chest while Claire's thumbs flew over her screen.

CLAIRE: Ris! For god's sake.

IRIS: I said what I said.

"Who are you texting?" Astrid asked, glancing at Claire's phone white-knuckled between her hands.

"No one," Claire said. "Josh. He's . . . bringing Ruby over to the house."

Astrid nodded and Claire retreated toward the window, her phone abandoned in the cup holder.

Delilah fired off one final text.

I still hate you both.

AFTER ASTRID HAD dropped off Iris and Claire, Delilah remained in the back seat.

"I'm not your chauffeur," she said as she pulled away from Claire's house on Linden Avenue. Delilah just stared at the window, taking in the Craftsman that looked exactly like something Claire would love. Small and cozy, with a large front porch and bright white trim, natural stone base and dusky-blue shingled siding. Claire walked up the front walk without looking back, her hips swaying under her tight jeans in a way that made last night rise up in Delilah's mind like a flash flood.

Christ.

All morning and afternoon, she had tried not to think about it. She'd kissed Claire, felt her up good and proper, and now she could move on. It didn't matter that Astrid didn't know and wouldn't know until after the wedding—or the non-wedding or breakup or whatever the fuck Iris was trying to accomplish—Delilah knew. And Delilah had gotten through life by putting herself first, only concerning herself with what she knew was true, because she'd learned a long time ago that she couldn't control anyone but herself. She couldn't change anyone's mind, couldn't make someone love her who had no interest in doing so, and couldn't keep someone from leaving her if that's what they wanted to do. She couldn't make agents see her. Couldn't make art lovers buy her pieces.

She couldn't make Claire feel unashamed over what had happened. And she couldn't change the fact that she was stuck with the woman and her lovely hips for another ten days. All she could do was mind her business and take the damn photos.

Except as Astrid pulled away, Claire paused on her porch and turned. She met Delilah's eye through the window, and Delilah felt it—that *look*—shoot down her legs. It was that same look Claire shot over her shoulder at the brunch. Interest. Intrigue. Fuck, it was *want*.

"Hello?" Astrid said.

Delilah swallowed and looked away, sighing heavily. "The inn is what? A mile from here? Just drive and I'll be out of your hair."

Astrid released her own sigh. "I asked you if I could see some of the photos you've taken so far."

"Oh." Delilah rubbed her forehead. She had to get her shit together. It was a kiss. A really good one. A *great* one, but still, it was just lips and tongues. Delilah had kissed a hundred people, heard a hundred people gasp into her mouth like she was the air and they'd been drowning.

Or . . . well, fine, she hadn't heard a *hundred* people make that sound when she was kissing them, but surely, she'd experienced it before.

"What the hell, Delilah!"

She jolted in her seat. "God, sorry."

"Where are you, back in New York?"

Delilah rubbed her hands down her face. "If only."

Astrid pressed her mouth flat and turned onto Main Street, which was bustling with the predinner crowd. The sky was a marbled gray and white, the promise of rain and an earthy scent in the air.

"That's Claire's shop," Astrid said as they passed by River Wild Books. A few customers milled around inside, a woman with blue hair manning the counter.

"Mmm."

"You went there a lot as a kid, didn't you?" Astrid asked.

Delilah leaned her head against the back of the seat. "Mmm."

"It's different now. Claire's turned it all modern and beautiful."

"Mmm."

Astrid huffed an irritated breath that made Delilah smile. She pulled up outside the Kaleidoscope, and Delilah leaped out like the car was on fire.

A bath. That's what she needed. A bath, some room service, a huge glass of wine. But when she turned to wave goodbye to Astrid, spit out something polite like *thanks for the free spa treatments even though you'd rather I hadn't been there at all as evidenced by your three-person reservation*, her stepsister had rounded the car, purse on her shoulder, eyes wide with expectancy.

"Um . . . are you staying here too?" Delilah asked, jutting a thumb toward the inn. "Spencer snores, huh? Or wait, he makes you sleep on the couch when you've eaten garlic and you just can't handle that lumpy sofa anymore."

Astrid, unfortunately, did not take the bait. "I'd like to see the pictures I'm paying a fortune for, if you don't mind."

"You mean Mommy Dearest is paying a fortune for."

Astrid just pursed her lips and continued to stare at Delilah. The woman would win a national blinking contest, hands down.

"What, you don't trust me?" Delilah said, pressing her hand to her chest. "I am an artiste. A visionary. An intrepid explorer through the wastelands of time. A veritable—"

"I'll just get the key from Nell," Astrid said, brushing past Delilah and heading into the three-story brick building.

"Oh, well played," Delilah said, following after her.

Once in her room, she tossed her suitcase onto the bed and removed her camera from its bag. Hooking it up to her laptop on the desk, she clicked around on the camera until all the photos she'd taken so far started uploading into Lightroom, which she'd always preferred over Photoshop. Less flashy, but simple was good in Delilah's opinion. Cropping, exposure and white balance, contrast and color, vibrancy and saturation. That's all she needed to play with. The real art was in the eye, the angle, the moment she hit the shutter.

"Keep in mind, these aren't edited," she said as Astrid sat at the desk and watched as images flipped onto the screen, piling into Lightroom like a deck of cards.

Delilah felt a flare of nerves. She'd never shown Astrid her work. Not once. Not the unflattering photos Delilah had taken of her and her coven back when they were teenagers, not a single wedding shot or portrait or a black and white of a piece of gum on the sidewalk. But now, she was going to see a lot. Wedding stuff, sure, but also just random shit Delilah snapped when she was walking through town after talking with Claire in River Wild, images she took just because they caught her eye, like a lollipop stick in the grass and a crack in a wineglass and—

Delilah's posture snapped straight.

And Claire when she didn't know Delilah was watching. Lots and lots of images of Claire when she didn't know Delilah was watching.

Well, shit.

"Um, what do I do?" Astrid asked when a notification popped up announcing the upload was complete.

Delilah didn't move, wondering if she could make some excuse as to why Astrid couldn't see the photos yet, but there was nothing. They were right there already, in front of Astrid's eager face, and the woman was like a dog with a very expensive bone when she wanted something. No way she was letting go.

It was fine. Delilah had taken candids of Astrid and Iris too . . . hadn't she?

She leaned around her stepsister and tapped on the first image,

then showed Astrid where to click to move to the next. Astrid leaned
in as the photos of everything Delilah had taken over the past three
days bloomed onto the screen.

Delilah perched on the side of the bed, her stomach suddenly in
knots, not just over the photos of Claire—which she could totally
play off as an attempt at intentionally driving Astrid bonkers, which
Astrid would have no trouble believing—but over her perfect stepsister digging through her work, her brain, her heart.

Jesus, Delilah, your heart? Get a damn grip.

So she did. She gripped her thighs and stared down at her jeans
while Astrid silently clicked . . . and clicked . . .

. . . and clicked.

God, she was taking forever.

"I need a drink," Delilah said, shooting up from the bed and removing the complimentary bottle of sauvignon blanc she'd found in
their room at Blue Lily last night from her bag. She nearly cried in
relief when she saw it was a twist cap. Filling one of the paper cups
stacked up by the mini Keurig to the brim, she gulped the first three
swallows, shuddering as it hit her bloodstream.

Then she paced and drank some more until she saw Astrid land
on a photo of herself and Spencer at the Wisteria House dinner.

It was a good photo. Black and white, Spencer's arm around her
shoulder while they sat side by side at the table. The light was soft
and lovely, the glow of candles and fairy lights curling around the
couple like a blanket. The saturation needed some adjusting, the contrast, but other than that, it was the perfect candid.

Except for one thing.

The bride.

Delilah stepped up behind Astrid, peering closer at the screen.
Spencer was laughing, his smile broad and bright, eyes twinkling on
someone in front of him. His fingers curled around Astrid's

shoulders—some might say protectively, but Delilah wouldn't. *Possessively* was the right word here, and it seemed like Astrid felt it. Her body in the photograph was rigid. Not so much as to draw attention during the actual event, but looking at the image now, frozen in time, she did anything but radiate warmth and happiness. Her smile was there, but it was plastic, didn't reach her eyes at all. Delilah had even managed to capture the subtle way her fingertips bled white, ever so slightly, on her wineglass.

God, she was good.

Still, Delilah felt anything but pride as Astrid continued to stare at the image. She felt a sinking in her stomach. A sick, heavy thud. She tried to shake it off—after all, Astrid's misery had always been her delight. And this clear horror Astrid was experiencing over seeing herself as a Stepford Wife in black and white would probably make Iris and Claire happy.

But even as Delilah thought it, wondered why the hell she even cared if Claire was happy or not, she also knew it wasn't true. Claire wouldn't be happy. She'd be heartbroken for her friend. Iris might gloat a little, revel in being right—god, Iris and Delilah really could've been friends in a different world—but she would've eventually settled down and supported Astrid no matter what, come up with a plan of action.

But Delilah wasn't Iris, and she sure as hell wasn't Claire.

"Astrid," she said, just to shake the woman out of her stupor.

Her stepsister startled, clearing her throat before skipping to the next photo. "These are beautiful."

Delilah blinked at the compliment. "Okay . . ." she said slowly.

"I really love the details. Like this one." She pointed to the photo on the screen, a sharpened image of Isabel that brought out every wrinkle the Botox just couldn't seem to reach.

Delilah snorted a laugh, and Astrid looked over her shoulder, a grin on her own face. They watched each other for a split second, something passing between them that made Delilah's breath catch. Something that felt young and almost hopeful.

Astrid turned back around and clicked to the next photo.

One of Claire.

Just Claire, the night of the Wisteria dinner. Evergreens crowded behind her, and the sun obscured part of her body, her face shadowed, but there was no doubt it was a lovely photograph.

There was also no doubt that she was looking right at the viewer. Delilah remembered taking the picture, Claire turning her head a split second before Delilah hit the shutter, a smile on her face at catching the wedding photographer in the act.

A smile that most definitely reached her eyes.

"This one is . . ." Astrid started, but then cleared her throat again. Then she scooted her chair back so fast, she nearly ran over Delilah's toes. She stood up and dug her phone out of her bag and checked the screen. "I should go."

"Oh, did Spencer summon you?"

As soon as she said it, she wished she hadn't. Instead of rolling her eyes or volleying a sharp comment back at Delilah in their perpetual barb match like Delilah expected, Astrid looked down, like she was embarrassed, and said nothing. Her throat worked around a hard swallow as she motioned toward the photo of Claire still on the screen.

"You should put that one on your Instagram," she said. "People would really love it."

"My . . . wait, you know about my Instagram?"

Astrid's mouth twitched, and when she spoke, her voice was soft, tentative. "How do you think I knew I would love your wedding photos?"

Surprise shot through Delilah's veins. Of course Isabel and Astrid knew Delilah worked as a wedding photographer. They knew she did portraits and waited tables in one of the most expensive cities in the world. But they didn't know about her art, her ambitions, her desire to be a name among American photographers. That's what her Instagram was for. A showcase of what she could actually do when she wasn't doing someone else's bidding and snapping pictures of couples mooning—or in Astrid's case, not mooning—over each other. Delilah had never told them about any of that. Not that a simple Google search wouldn't pull up her social media, but to even do that, Astrid would have to give half a shit to type in her name.

"Hang on," Delilah said. "You—"

"See you later," Astrid said, then swept out the door, leaving Delilah with a tight feeling in her chest that wouldn't go away no matter how many paper cups of wine she tossed down her throat.

CHAPTER SEVENTEEN

THE NEXT EVENING was Thursday and kicked off a whole six days without some godforsaken wedding event. Claire and Ruby came home from the bookstore to find Iris and Delilah sitting in their kitchen sipping on lemon LaCroix.

Claire froze, her heart suddenly in her throat.

"Hey!" Ruby said, barreling farther inside to meet them.

"Hey, Rubes," Iris said, pressing a kiss to the top of her head. Delilah smiled at the girl, but her eyes flicked to Claire, who felt her stomach lurch up to join her heart.

"Help yourself to that key under the planter anytime you want, Ris," Claire said.

"I shall," Iris said. "Got your mail too. Looks like your mom sent you another package."

Claire set her bag on the center island. "Oh Jesus, what is it this time?" In her vagabond retirement, her mother had gotten progressively into crystals and tarot. She burned sage to *cleanse her space* and talked about blocked chakras whenever she and Claire spoke on the phone. Not that Claire begrudged her the interest—she was glad her mother had a passion after handing her beloved River Wild Books over to her daughter's control. Claire just didn't have the time or brain space to really understand it all. Lately, her mother had taken to sending her things in the mail, everything from rose quartz neck-laces to books on meditation, convinced Claire simply needed a little spirituality in her life to set everything straight.

"I want to see what Grandma sent," Ruby said, picking up the padded envelope. She ripped it open and pulled out a box about the size of a small book. Her eyes scanned the front, reading the text. "The Literary Witches Oracle."

"Oracle?" Iris said, standing and taking the box from Ruby. "Like future telling?"

"I have no idea," Claire said, taking her turn with the box. "'Dis-cover divination using the magic of literary genius,'" she read from the back, where it showed the image of a card featuring Zora Neale Hurston, next to another card with an apple on it. Just that. An apple.

"How very magically bookish of Katherine," Iris said.

Claire laughed, peering at Zora. Underneath her image was the word *story*. "This actually might be something we could stock in the bookstore." She set the box on the island to deal with later before opening the refrigerator and taking out a beer.

"Oh, thank god," Iris said, holding out her hand for one as well. "I was trying to be good, but this sparkling water isn't cutting it."

Claire put a cold can in her hand and then looked at Delilah. "You want one?"

"I'm okay," Delilah said. "But thanks."

"I'll have one," Ruby said, folding her arms over her chest and glaring at Claire. This had been happening all day long. The glaring. The huffing. The arm folding. All thanks to Josh, once again, who told Ruby he wanted to take her on a camping trip this weekend before he talked to Claire about it, which now meant that any objection Claire had would automatically turn her into the fun-sucking, hundred-year-old worrywart mother she always felt like she was around Josh.

And that was exactly what happened when Ruby informed her about the trip this morning and Claire responded with a very calm "Honey, I don't know." She hadn't even said no yet, but Claire had still spent her day angry texting with Josh and dodging her daughter's dagger stares while working on invoices and redoing endcaps.

"Oh, ha ha," Claire said, reaching out to smooth Ruby's hair. The girl ducked out of her reach though, sliding gracefully to the other side of the counter next to Delilah. Iris shot her a look, but Claire waved her off. She was used to this by now. What was one more explosive fight with her eleven-year-old?

Delilah nudged Ruby. "Hey, want to show me your room?"

Ruby's eyes lit up. "Yeah!"

Then she bolted off toward the back of the house while Delilah got up and adjusted her very tight gray jeans. As she passed Claire, she didn't look at her, not even a smile, but her shoulder brushed against hers, sending Claire's stomach plunging to her feet. She chugged three swallows of beer.

"Jesus, what is up?" Iris said.

"Nothing."

"You're a horrible liar."

"What gave me away?" Claire deadpanned, knowing she looked like shit and was making very little effort to hide the fact that she felt like shit too. She'd barely slept last night, again, thinking about Josh and then Delilah before switching to Astrid and Spencer, then back to Delilah again. This morning, she hadn't even done anything with her hair after showering, just piled it all on top of her head.

"Josh?" Iris asked.

Claire nodded. "Camping trip. This weekend. As in the woods, with bears and ravines and rushing river rapids."

Iris made a *yikes* face. "You can't just say no?"

"I can if I want my daughter to despise me."

Iris sighed. "Oh, honey. What if you went along?"

Claire had considered this, but if she went along, there was a ninety percent chance she and Josh would end up doing something she regretted after Ruby went to sleep.

Delilah flashed in her mind, soft fingers on her skin, the way she'd pulled Claire's bottom lip between her teeth and—

She shook her head. "I don't know."

Iris reached out and squeezed her hand. "How about I order us all some dinner, huh? You don't look like you could heat up a Lean Cuisine right now, much less cook for your kid."

Claire squeezed back. "Yeah, that'd be good. Thanks."

Iris clicked around on her phone and was done ordering pizza before it even dawned on Claire to ask her what she and Delilah Green were doing at her house.

"I've been texting you all day," Iris said, sipping her beer.

"Oh damn, that's right. I forgot to look at them." Claire got out her phone and opened up the OSB thread. There were several unread texts between Iris and Delilah about a *plan*—mostly Iris demanding one and Delilah responding with nonsensical emojis like a robot and a nineties-era pager. "Sorry. I was caught up texting with Josh all day."

Iris nodded. "I figured you were busy. Hence our visit."

"I'm amazed Delilah agreed to come."

"Oh, she consented rather quickly when I suggested it."

Claire forced herself to ignore Iris's tone, and absolutely, one hundred percent, *not* to look at her friend right now, even while what felt like a huge grin fought to take over her face.

"Ten days left," Iris said, sipping her beer. "And the next wedding event isn't until the bachelorette party two days before the rehearsal, which means we probably won't see or hear from Astrid until next Wednesday while she spins around like a robot in heels."

Claire groaned. "I don't know what to do, Iris. She's barely spoken to either of us since the dinner at the vineyard."

"Unless it was about wedding shit. She barely shut up the whole ride home."

"You know what I mean. Like, actually talk to us. I texted her this morning—just a *hey, how are you*—and she didn't respond until three in the afternoon, and even then, it was a thumbs-up emoji."

Iris's eyes went wide.

"Yeah," Claire said. "An *emoji*, from the woman who has to spell out *laugh out loud* in her texts instead of *LOL*."

"I texted her and got nothing back."

"This isn't great."

"This is what I'm saying."

"We can't very well get her talking if she won't talk to us."

They both took a slug of beer, then fell into a stressful silence. Claire's thoughts swirled, too many things at once. A smart person would get very drunk right now, but that would only make her a sloppy, gooey mess around Delilah, which would immediately give her away as a sloppy, gooey mess around Delilah.

"So, camping, huh?" Delilah said as she came back into the room, then stopped when she saw Claire and Iris staring despondently at their beer cans. "Shit, what happened?"

"Astrid, the unfeeling ice queen, happened," Iris said.

Delilah pulled a face and settled onto a barstool next to Claire, one leg pulled to her chest. "And this is a new revelation?"

Iris glared. "For those of us with hearts, yes."

"Ris," Claire said, then glanced at Delilah. "Ruby told you about the camping trip?"

Delilah nodded. "Bagby Hot Springs. Sounds fun."

Claire nearly choked on her beer. "Hot springs?"

"I take it Josh didn't mention that part?" Iris said.

"No, nor did my adoring daughter," Claire said. "I guess I was too busy imagining a bear gnawing my kid's face off in the middle of the night because Josh left the hot dogs out. I didn't even *think* about boiling-hot water."

Delilah winced. "So, not so fun, then."

"I'm sure it's a blast for anyone other than a man-child in charge of our daughter." Claire went back to rubbing her temples. She couldn't deal with this right now. Not with Delilah Green and her tattoos and her fingers and her mouth just sitting here in her kitchen, as though they didn't make out like teenagers two nights ago.

"I've got it," Iris said, her spine going ramrod straight and her eyes popping so wide, Claire worried they were about to roll onto the counter.

"Herpes?" Delilah said.

Iris flicked her off without skipping a beat. "The solution. We all go camping."

Claire blinked at her. "All . . . all of us?"

"All of us," Iris said. "You, me, Goth Queen over here, Ruby, Josh . . . and Astrid."

Delilah spluttered her sparkling water all over the counter. "Shit, sorry."

She started to get up for a paper towel, but Claire put a hand on her knee, freezing her in place. Claire kept her eyes on Iris, but she could feel Delilah's warm skin through her jeans. Delilah sat back down, and Claire told herself to move her hand, but she couldn't seem to connect her fingers to her brain. Only when Iris flicked her gaze down to Delilah's leg was Claire able to slide her hand back into her own lap.

Next to her, she heard Delilah release a breath. Or maybe she just imagined it. Maybe she was already drunk off half a beer.

Finally, Delilah cleared her throat. "Astrid Parker. In the woods. Sleeping in a tent."

"This is what I'm saying," Iris said.

"Are you high?" Delilah asked. "She'd never go for that. She needs her cold creams and feather duvets."

"No one calls them cold creams anymore," Iris said. "What are you, eighty years old?"

"Both of you, stop," Claire said.

"She'll come," Iris said, looking at Claire. "If you tell her you need her, she'll be there."

Claire's shoulders slumped. "Ris. That's manipulative."

"Not if it's true. You want Ruby to be able to go camping with Josh without sending you reaching for a Xanax every five minutes while they're gone, right? So the only solution is to go too, but you don't want to be with Josh by yourself because, let's face it, the man is fine and you never make great decisions when he's around—"

"Wait, what?"

"—and so we all go, for moral and sexual support, and get Astrid talking more about Spencer in the meantime."

Iris mimed dropping a mic, then grinned at the both of them.

"Sexual support?" Claire asked, a sinking feeling in her stomach.

Iris reached out and pinched her cheek. "Like I said, you're a horrible liar."

Next to her, Claire felt Delilah go very still. Her knee, which had been brushing Claire's hip, just barely, moved away, and Delilah finally got up to get those paper towels and clean up her spill.

Claire's cheeks warmed, blood rushing to the surface of her skin. Iris knew about all the times she'd slept with Josh after they broke up. And if Iris knew, then Astrid knew. And now Delilah knew, and

Claire wanted to climb under a table with the emergency bottle of bourbon she hid in the cabinet above the refrigerator.

Iris reached out and squeezed her arm. "It's okay, honey. I'd probably bone him too if I had the chance."

"Ris," Claire groaned, dropping her face into her hand. She didn't dare look at Delilah. Not that it should matter. Not that she and Delilah were anything. Not that the other woman would care at all about who Claire slept with.

Claire sat up straight and shook her bangs out of her eyes. She needed to focus. Because as much as she hated to admit it, Iris's solution was the only way to avoid a war with Ruby. On top of that, everything Iris said was true—Claire did need her friends there if she was going to go on this trip, and it wouldn't be lying or manipulative to tell Astrid exactly that. If they all ended up talking about how Spencer was an asshole in a tailored suit, then so be it.

"Okay, let's call her," she said.

Iris grinned and pressed her phone to her ear. "Already had her number pulled up."

CHAPTER

EIGHTEEN

MIRACULOUSLY, ASTRID AGREED to the camping trip. Delilah watched it all unfold while leaning against the kitchen sink. It took three calls and a few text messages before her stepsister answered the phone, but Iris could be damned determined when she wanted to be, and when Claire got on the call, explaining how she needed her friends there to support her, especially since she couldn't be trusted around Josh, Astrid apparently caved like a hollowed-out cream puff.

I can't be trusted around Josh, Astrid. You know I can't.

That's what Claire had said. Quietly, as though she was loath to admit it, but Delilah still heard it, loud and clear, like a church bell ringing through the town square.

She hadn't even wanted to come to Claire's in the first place. At least that's what she told herself the entire Lyft ride over here. She'd been perfectly content to reply to all of Iris's annoying-as-hell text messages with random emojis, but the woman had to go and suggest they meet at Claire's to regroup, and suddenly, a DNA strand emoji just didn't feel like the right response. Then she'd been the one to cave, agreeing and bolting out of her too-quiet room at the inn before she could even think through what she was doing.

Going to see Claire again, that's what she was doing.

She didn't give two shits about Iris's plan or Astrid and Spencer. But now, standing in Claire's cozy kitchen with its butcher-block counters and farmhouse sink, watching her pace around her living room, which was covered with books and soft throws and photographs of Ruby all over the mantel, she could admit it.

She'd wanted to see Claire.

Ever since Astrid left her room yesterday, Delilah had felt unsettled. She craved something, something sweet, something she didn't have to constantly try and maneuver around, figure out, strategize about. And after that kiss with Claire at the vineyard . . . well, Delilah didn't feel very calculating at all.

She just felt fucking lonely.

And now Claire was telling Astrid how she needed her so she wouldn't screw her ex on a camping trip.

Okay, maybe Claire wasn't using those exact words, but the effect was the same, and Delilah couldn't seem to get rid of this burning sensation in her chest, no matter how many deep breaths she took. It was the same kind of oily dread she'd felt five years ago when she'd unlocked the apartment she'd shared with Jax, moans she didn't recognize already filtering under the door.

Which was ridiculous. She'd been with Jax for two years. She'd kissed Claire once, hadn't even slept with her. It wasn't nearly the same thing.

Still, she went to Claire's refrigerator and took out a beer. She'd been determined not to drink, to keep a clear head around Claire so she didn't do anything too terribly stupid, but now, as memories of Jax and Mallory melded with brand-new visions of Claire and Josh humping like rabbits in a tent under the stars, she needed something to calm her nerves.

"Okay," Claire said, ending the call with Astrid. "It's done."

"You should probably tell Josh," Iris said. "Make sure he reserves enough camping spots."

"Oh yeah, I probably should." She handed Iris back her phone, then grabbed her own from the center island. She looked at Delilah, opened her mouth, but nothing came out. Delilah held her gaze this time. She wanted Claire to . . .

To what?

Tell her Josh meant nothing to her?

Invite her to share a sleeping bag?

Kick Iris out and kiss her senseless?

Fuck.

Yes. Yes, Delilah wanted Claire to do all of those things.

She looked away first, taking a long pull of her beer. God, she needed something stronger. She needed . . . to not feel like this. She didn't do relationships. She did flirting. She did sex. And she did it damn well. So maybe she needed to do what she did so well with Claire, and this hard knot in her stomach would untangle. Perhaps it was just a lust knot. True, she'd never heard of or experienced a lust knot before, but hell, there was a first time for everything.

Claire took her phone and drifted off down the hall while Delilah drank some more. Iris eyed her from where she'd landed on the couch.

And kept eyeing her.

"Can I help you?" Delilah asked.

Iris lifted a brow, but before she could say anything, the doorbell rang.

"That would be our pizza," Iris said.

"Awesome." Delilah didn't budge, even though she was closer to the door. Finally, Iris huffed an annoyed breath, making Delilah smile and feel a bit more like herself, and got up to get the food.

———

DELILAH KNEW SHE should probably just go back to the inn, but after the pizza arrived and Ruby came into the kitchen with Claire, positively beaming from the news that they were all going camping together, the girl hooked her arm through Delilah's and asked her to sit next to her while they ate. There was no way Delilah could tell her no, not with those hazel puppy dog eyes and the "tattoo" she'd apparently inked on the inside of her arm after Delilah had left her room earlier.

"That's cool," Delilah said, motioning to a black-penned rose near Ruby's wrist. It was actually a pretty amazing drawing, the petals detailed, the thorns dripping with dew.

"Oh, um, thanks," Ruby said as they sat down at one end of Claire's farmhouse kitchen table. A blush spread into her cheeks.

Claire, who was sitting across from Delilah next to Iris, smiled, but said nothing of her daughter coloring all over her skin. Delilah was glad, and she could tell, by the way Ruby's shoulders relaxed a little, that Ruby was too.

Delilah took a bite of mushroom spinach pizza. "Do you like to draw?"

Ruby nodded and shrugged at the same time, her chin ducking to her chest. God, Delilah felt the girl's awkwardness in her bones, a familiar ache of not knowing where or how to fit.

"I should get you to design a tattoo for me," she said.

Ruby's head snapped up. "Really?"

"Yeah. You're good. Do you have any other drawings I could see?"

Ruby blinked at her then leaped up from the table and sprinted toward her room.

"You just made her year," Claire said, leaning across the table a little.

Delilah swallowed a bit of pizza and shrugged. "I'm not placating her. She's good."

"I know. And so does she. That's why you made her year."

Claire smiled at her, eyes soft behind her glasses, cheeks a little flushed. Something low in Delilah's belly fluttered, a moth around a light.

"No one would ever suspect you of placating anyone, D," Iris said, stuffing a whole crust into her mouth.

Delilah flipped her off right before Ruby sailed back into the room, hugging a notebook to her chest. As she sat back down, she kept the book under the table and slowly opened it, shoulders hunched. Delilah didn't try to take it out of her hands. It was hers, and Delilah knew better than anyone how much the art you did as a kid—whether it be drawings or photographs or songs—felt like spilling the contents of your heart out into the world. Hell, it still felt like that as a grown-up.

She leaned closer to the girl, tilting her head to see the drawings as Ruby flipped the pages in her lap. Black-and-white sketches filled each page. Plants, flowers, tea mugs and stacks of books, candles and cats and planets. Then the faces started—Claire, Josh, Iris, Astrid, younger girls who must've been her friends from school, her own face in various expressions, everything from smiling to despairing to distorted, a whole range of emotions and feelings and thoughts.

"These are great," Delilah said, her voice low and just for Ruby. She nudged her shoulder with her own, coaxing a proud smile out of the girl.

"Thank you," Ruby said softly, then looked up at Delilah. "Can you teach me about photography?"

"Sure. What do you want to know?"

"Everything. Like, lighting and framing and . . . everything. I love your photos."

Delilah tilted her head. "You've seen my photos?"

The girl's blush deepened. Delilah shot a glance at Claire, but the other woman just shrugged.

"I . . . um . . ." Ruby said. She looked suddenly scared, more than just nervous.

"Hey, it's okay," Delilah said. "Photos are meant to be seen."

Ruby blew out a breath, nodded. "Well . . . after Aunt Astrid's brunch, I looked you up on my laptop and I found your Instagram."

"Ah."

"Your account is amazing."

"You have an Instagram?" Iris asked.

Delilah tilted her head at her. "I'm a photographer. Of course I have one."

A purely evil grin spread over Iris's mouth, and she picked up her phone.

Oh god. Delilah wasn't ashamed of her Instagram account. It was pretty much a must for any visual artist these days. She just wasn't prepared for the whole of Bright Falls to be scrolling through her photos. Some of them were pretty raw, and the last people she'd considered when she posted them were Astrid and her coven. Just the thought of sitting here while Iris Kelly—and inevitably, Claire Sutherland—dug into her art made her want to puke.

"Hey, you know what?" she said to Ruby. "The light outside is perfect right now. Want me to show you a few tips for taking photos with a phone?"

Ruby's shoulders slumped. "I don't have a phone yet."

"But you will," Claire said, holding her water glass between two hands.

"When?" Ruby said, her posture going straight.

Claire laughed. "Someday."

"Ugh, you're the worst."

"I love you too," Claire said, eyes shining at her daughter.

"Oh my god," Iris said, eyes bugging out on her phone. "You have two hundred thousand followers?"

"And that's our cue," Delilah said, then waved her own phone at Ruby. "What do you say?"

"Okay, yeah," Ruby said, grabbing her notebook and leading the way through the living room toward the back porch.

"Holy shit," Delilah heard Iris say behind her. "Claire, look at this."

Anxiety spiked in her chest, and she hurried out the door. She wasn't sure if that was a good *holy shit* or a bad one, but either way, she didn't want to hear what Claire had to say about her photos at all.

Outside, the air was cool and damp, the sun just starting to sink, creating a twilight-lavender glow that was perfect for a certain type of photo. Delilah and Ruby went into the backyard, the grass a little long and the flower beds a little weedy, but there was a hammock strung between two maple trees, a strand of colored lights hung along the porch railing that could've been left over from Christmas or could've been a regular fixture. Either way, the yard was charming. Imperfect. It was lived-in and homey, the kind of backyard Delilah remembered from her and her father's house in Seattle, but which she'd never had at Wisteria House.

"Okay," she said to Ruby, once she'd taken a deep breath to calm her stomach. "Look around. See if anything catches your eye."

Ruby frowned at her. "Like what?"

"Anything. Photography isn't so different from drawing. When you go to do a sketch, you either see something interesting you want to draw, or you think of something interesting in your mind, right?"

Ruby nodded.

"Same thing with photographs. You see something and you want to capture it in a new way, a way only you can see it, and then show that to the world."

Ruby's frown deepened, but it was more a look of curiosity and thought than confusion. She glanced around her yard, then started walking through the grass slowly, her notebook still tucked against her chest. Delilah let her roam, watching the girl search through her tiny world.

"This," Ruby said, stopping at a stone birdbath in the corner of the yard. It was dingy, full of stagnated water and dead leaves, but right in the center a single white flower floated. Delilah couldn't tell what flower it was, some sort of weed probably, but the effect of a little life hovering above death . . . well, it was striking.

"Perfect," Delilah said, smiling at Ruby, then handed the girl her phone, already open to the camera app. "Let's see what you got."

Ruby took it and set her notebook in the grass, her expression uncertain, but after a few minutes of staring and head tilting, she got to work. It took a while. The girl was meticulous, careful, experimenting and then shaking her head softly when what she saw in the photo didn't match what she wanted in her head. Finally, she looked up and handed the phone back to Delilah.

Scrolling through her images, Delilah smiled. "These are good. I like your point of view here." She held out the phone so Ruby could see the birdbath's edge, the viewer nearly eye level with the dirty water, the flower the only thing in focus.

"Can you show me how to edit them?" Ruby asked.

Delilah glanced up at the house and saw Claire standing on the back porch, forearms resting on the deck railing like maybe she'd been there for a while.

Iris was nowhere to be seen.

"I should probably go," Delilah said, her stomach-moths taking flight again.

"What about on the camping trip?" Ruby asked.

Delilah frowned. She hadn't even thought about going on the trip. When Iris had said *we'll all go*, Delilah didn't take her literally. Plus, there wasn't another wedding event until next Wednesday, which meant Delilah had a blissful five days ahead of her without a single Parker or Parker-Green lavishing her with their disappointment. She was of half a mind to fly back to New York for the duration, except there was no way she could afford the round-trip ticket.

"Oh, sweetie, I don't think I'm going on that."

Ruby's face fell. "What? You have to!"

"I just think—"

"No, you have to go. You're fun and I like talking to you."

Delilah smiled, her chest warming. "Your mom is fun, right? Iris and Astrid?"

Ruby rolled her eyes. "Yeah, they're about as fun as a bag of rocks."

Delilah laughed at that, but Ruby was smiling. On the porch, Claire leaned her elbows on the porch railing, the colored lights illuminating her face with blue and green.

"What's so funny?" she called.

"See?" Ruby said, jutting her thumb toward her mother and lowering her voice. "Rocks."

Delilah narrowed her eyes at the girl, a smile still on her lips. "We'll see, okay? About the camping trip. But either way, we'll work on your photo soon, okay? I promise."

Ruby's shoulders sagged, but she nodded.

Then she stepped forward and wrapped her arms around Delilah's middle. For a second, Delilah didn't move. She couldn't remember the last time someone had hugged her. Years. Jax was probably the last person, and toward the end of their relationship, it was more mindless screwing than anything else. Stress relief for both of them. Lord knows, that's all Delilah had done since—thoughtless touches, desperation for skin without any real heart behind it.

This, though. This . . . embrace. From an almost-teenager, no less, and everyone knew almost-teenagers hated everyone. It took the breath out of her. Literally, for a few seconds as Ruby rested her head against Delilah's chest, arms tight around her waist, she couldn't find enough air, her eyes stinging with a swell of sudden tears.

But then she moved her arms around Ruby, pressed her cheek to the top of her hair. She exhaled what felt like a decade's worth of anxiety, and accepted the girl's love.

CHAPTER
NINETEEN

CLAIRE WATCHED IN awe as Ruby threw her arms around Delilah. She'd come out here about ten minutes ago to tell her daughter that Tess's mom had called and asked about a sleepover, but then she saw Ruby and Delilah talking, how the younger girl pressed her face into the air between them, eager and searching and fascinated. Ruby had taken Delilah's phone and started circling around their old birdbath, the one Claire had been meaning to clean out for ages but, in the grand scheme of things, was relatively low on her priority list.

Now she was glad she hadn't.

There was something beautiful in that leaf-filled bath, and Delilah was helping Ruby see it. Or maybe Ruby had already seen it and Delilah was just a guide. Either way, Claire felt breathless as the process unfolded, how Ruby bent and twisted with the phone, how Delilah quietly watched her with this look that Claire could only describe as pride.

And then . . . Ruby had hugged her. For the past couple of years, Ruby didn't give away her affection easily. She loved lying in bed at night with Claire right next to her, snuggling and talking when her body was less alert and ready for rest. During the day, though, her kid was on the go, always moving, talking, observing, wondering, and whenever Claire reached out for a hug, Ruby would pat her mother on the back and then dart off like the Flash to the next thing. She barely even let Iris or Astrid hug her anymore.

And yet.

Claire felt an ache in her throat, watching her daughter reach out into the world and have the world . . . reach back. She took a shuddering breath as Ruby and Delilah broke apart, shook her head to clear it, wiped the sudden wetness from under her eyes.

"Hey, Rabbit?" she called.

Ruby turned and looked at her mother. "Yeah?"

"Tess called. Want to spend the night?"

"Yeah!"

Her daughter raced toward her, Delilah forgotten, but as she pounded up the porch steps, she stopped and turned back to the other woman.

"Thanks," she said.

Delilah smiled. "You're welcome."

Then Ruby dashed inside, flip-flops loud against the hardwood. Claire watched her disappear around the corner to her room and then turned back. Delilah was ambling across the grass, her lithe limbs graceful, like she was moving over water instead of earth.

"Where's Iris?" she asked as she approached the porch.

"Gone. She and Grant had a movie night planned."

Claire might have imagined it, but she swore Delilah's steps halted for a split second at the news. But then she kept going until she was right next to her on the deck. Claire's stomach was in knots, and she couldn't figure out why. Could be any number of things. Josh. This camping trip. Astrid.

Or Delilah.

It could be Delilah, standing *right there* and watching Claire with a soft look in her eyes, and how Claire knew if she pressed her face to Delilah's neck, she'd smell like rain and grass.

It could be Delilah and the soon-to-be-empty house behind them. Claire realized with a cold wash of nerves that she owed Tess's mother a drink. She wanted Delilah to stay. She wanted to be alone with her. She knew it was stupid, knew it could never go anywhere, but ever since their kiss at the spa—no, before that, way before that—she couldn't stop thinking about Delilah. And it wasn't just physical either. There was something about Delilah that made Claire's throat ache, made her want to spill her secrets, made her want to reach out and swipe her thumb over the other woman's cheek like a lover would. Around Delilah—even just *thinking* about Delilah—Claire felt young and wild, unbound in a way she hadn't experienced since before Ruby was born.

Delilah bit her bottom lip as she gazed at Claire.

Okay, maybe in a way she'd *never* experienced. Not even Josh made her feel this crazed, this desperate just to brush her fingers over the pulse under another person's ear.

Which was a problem, because Delilah didn't do anything but physical. Claire knew this—whatever *this* was—could only ever end, but she couldn't help it. She still wanted this. She wanted Delilah. Maybe Claire could do casual. Maybe she didn't need dates and squealing with her friends. Maybe she really did just need a good lay.

Even as she thought the words, though, something flickered in her chest. She ignored it. She could do this. It would be good for her. She could reclaim what was supposed to have been her wild twenties while she was busy changing diapers and pushing swings at the park.

"Want to stay for a glass of wine?" she said, but at the exact same moment, Delilah had also spoken, "So I guess I should go" falling out of her mouth like a bomb.

"Oh," Claire said, again, at the same time as Delilah's own "Oh."

The two women looked at each other, then started laughing. Claire's cheeks heated, and she was thankful for the dim lighting that covered her blush. At the same time, she wanted to know if Delilah was blushing too.

Probably not. She couldn't imagine Delilah Green blushing over anyone.

"Sorry," Claire said. "Do you need to go?"

"Not right away, I guess," Delilah said. "I'll take that glass of wine."

"Oh. Great."

"Great."

"White or red?"

"Whatever."

Claire nodded, then continued to stand there like a doofus as Delilah tilted her head at her. "Right. Yeah, let me see what I've got."

Delilah laughed. "Lead the way."

They walked inside just as Ruby tore down the hall with her backpack, heading for the front door. "Mom, I'm going!"

"Hey, hang on, Rabbit," Claire said, walking over to her.

Ruby halted and endured a hug from her mother. Claire smiled into her hair, pressed a kiss to her head.

"Mom."

"Okay, okay. Have fun. I'll see you in the morning."

Ruby waved at Delilah and then bolted through the door. Claire stepped outside on the front stoop, watching her daughter walk down the sidewalk to the navy blue bungalow three houses down. When Ruby was safely inside, she stepped back into her own house and closed the door.

The quiet hit her first.

Then the pop of a cork, the glug of liquid into a glass.

She turned to find Delilah in her kitchen, lifting a glass of white wine to her lips.

"I found this already open in the fridge," Delilah said, angling the pale yellow contents from a bottle of pinot grigio into a second glass. "Hope that's okay."

"Totally fine," Claire said, watching her for a beat. Delilah's face was her usual calm, but also . . . there was something else there, something in the way she inhaled a slow breath before she took a sip of her drink, the way her cheeks puffed out, just a little, as she exhaled even more slowly.

Was Delilah . . . nervous?

The thought felt like a warm spring rain on a cool afternoon. It opened up a space inside Claire's chest, made her walk over to the kitchen island and pick up her glass, take a long gulp.

"Does it feel like all we ever do is drink around each other?" Delilah asked.

Claire laughed. "Yeah, a little bit. But, you know, wedding."

Delilah nodded. "Wedding."

"And diabolical plans."

"Those too."

"So . . . maybe we should do something else, then," Claire said.

Delilah's eyebrows lifted, a little smile tilting the corners of her mouth. Claire felt blood rush into her cheeks. God, she was the opposite of smooth. She hadn't even meant *that*. Not that she wasn't thinking about *that*, constantly and fervently ever since their kiss, but in this moment, all she wanted was to not think at all. Not worry. Not wonder.

Not need.

Before she could think through it, she grabbed the oracle cards her mother had just sent and held them up. "Want to try these out with me?"

Delilah took the box and looked at the front, which featured a woman with dark hair parted down the middle. "Is that . . . Emily Brontë?"

"Very nice, you know your female Victorian authors."

"More like I was forced to suffer through them during senior English."

Claire placed a hand on her chest, gasping dramatically. "Suffer?"

"*Suffer.*"

"Okay, I'll give you that *Wuthering Heights* is the least romantic book in the history of Victorian romances, but *Jane Eyre*?"

"Is that the one where the douchebag hid his wife away in the attic and then lied about it to the girl he wanted to bang who was, like, half his age?"

Claire winced. "Well, when you put it like that."

"I didn't put it like that. Brontë put it like that."

"Okay, fine, yes, Victorian literature was a little messed up."

"Poor Jane," Delilah said, sipping her wine. "She deserved better."

"Let's see how she's been immortalized, shall we?" Claire wiggled the box.

"She better damn well have some wisdom beyond *stand by your man* is all I'm saying," Delilah said as she grabbed the wine bottle and followed Claire to the couch. Claire settled into one corner, and she definitely did not notice how Delilah sat close enough to her that their knees touched, even though it was a full-size sofa and there was plenty of room to spread out.

Nope, she didn't notice that at all.

"Okay, how does this work?" Claire said, removing the plastic wrap around the box. Inside was a small coral-colored guide book and a hefty stack of smooth, thick cards. There were thirty cards featuring female writers and forty cards that depicted what the creators called "witch's materials."

"Have you ever had a reading done?" Delilah asked. "Tarot or anything?"

Claire tapped her chin thoughtfully. "Does my amateur mother count?"

"Depends. How'd the reading go?"

"I think true love and great wealth were mentioned more than once."

"Well, damn, let's put these babies to work," Delilah said, grabbing a card from the top of the pile. She frowned at it. "It's . . . a praying mantis." She turned the card so Claire could see it—indeed, against a cream background, was a solitary praying mantis.

Claire laughed. "Oh my god, are you going to bite my head off later?"

Delilah's brows went up again, though it took Claire a second to realize what she'd said.

Praying mantises only bit off their lovers' heads.

"I hadn't planned on it," Delilah said, her voice low and a little growly.

Heat pooled into Claire's cheeks—as well as a few other places—and she flipped through the guidebook until she found the praying mantis.

"Actually," she said very formally, "the praying mantis symbolizes wit, manipulation, and fun."

Delilah blinked.

"So . . ." Claire went on, "you're going to use your unsurpassed wit to manipulate someone for the hell of it."

"Shit, I sound like a real piece of work."

The two women stared at each other for a second, all seriousness, until Claire finally broke and both of them dissolved into laughter.

Delilah's shoulder brushed hers, the scent of summer and blueberries swirling between them like a drug.

"I don't think we're doing this right," Claire said when they recovered. She flipped to the directions, reading all about shuffling and intentions and splitting the deck into three intuitive stacks. They went through the ritual, then Claire chose a card off the top.

It was a praying mantis.

Both women immediately started cackling. Claire laughed so hard, tears bloomed into her eyes. She couldn't remember the last time she'd had this much fun, felt this . . . carefree. Praying mantis notwithstanding.

"Okay, okay, there has to be more than lover-eating, manipulative insects in here," Delilah said. "Let's do it again."

Delilah went through the motions before pulling wildflowers, which symbolized renewal, romance, and awakening; a peacock for splendor, the divine, and craving; and Gertrude Stein, who apparently represented perspective.

"So I'm a butch lesbian goddess looking for love," Delilah said, shrugging as though to say *obviously*.

"Oh yeah, that's the clear message here," Claire said, and Delilah winked at her.

God, that wink.

Once Claire recovered and had taken another sip of wine, she shuffled the cards and pulled her own: an apple, Sappho, and a volcano. Her stomach flipped at Sappho—she knew the ancient poet represented something homoerotic. Before she could look up what the apple and volcano symbolized, though, Delilah slipped the guidebook from her hands.

"Hey!" she said, making to grab it back.

"Oh no. You read mine, I read yours."

Claire pursed her lips, but they still managed to twist into a smile. Flirting. This was flirting, wasn't it?

"Okay, let's see here," Delilah said, flipping through the book. "Sappho . . . well, we all know and love her, don't we?"

Claire laughed, fighting a blush. "We do."

"She represents the beloved, desire—of course—and taking flight."

"So it sounds like I'm running away from what I want?" The interpretation flowed out of her mouth before she could stop it, the first thing that popped into her head.

"I don't know, are you?" Delilah asked, the teasing lilt to her voice completely gone.

Claire cleared her throat and picked up both the apple and volcano cards, peering at them carefully. "But I'm also very hungry and . . . am . . . simmering with anger?"

Delilah flipped through the book. Her eyebrows popped up, a little grin settling on her face. She flipped from one page to the other, back and forth, over and over.

"Oh my god, what?" Claire asked, reaching for the book again, this time succeeded in taking it back. She found the apple.

The senses, hunger, and . . . sex.

Her belly tightened, but she didn't look at Delilah, turning to the page with the volcano card.

Patience, repression, and—oh, for fuck's sake.

Lust.

She blinked at the pages. Next to her, Delilah was silently cracking up, one hand over her pretty mouth. Claire waited to feel embarrassed, even mortified, but she didn't. Instead, she felt like smiling, like flirting and playing. Hell, like telling the truth and being unashamed.

"Okay, so, I'm extremely horny," she finally said, shrugging and tossing the book into Delilah's lap. "So what?"

"But you're really patient about it," Delilah said, tapping the volcano card.

"Or incredibly repressed," Claire said, and they both laughed, poured more wine, and that was that.

For the next hour, the women lost themselves in the cards. They pulled chickens and Sylvia Plath, teacups and gloves and Octavia Butler. They made wild and unlikely interpretations—as well as a few that felt soft and gentle, like a whisper. They'd barely touched their most recent glasses of wine, but Claire's head was still perfectly fuzzy. She wasn't drunk, but she was definitely something. It took her a few minutes to come up with the right word.

Happy.

She was happy.

"So," Delilah said, tapping a card featuring a ghost against her knee. "You're heading out tomorrow?"

Claire sighed, leaning her head against the back of the couch. "Looks like it. I'm not sure what Iris thinks is going to happen on this camping trip. Astrid hates camping."

"You don't say."

Claire grinned at her. "Hey, she could do outdoorsy stuff."

"As long as there was air-conditioning and a soaker tub waiting for her after the hike."

"Okay, true. But she'll sleep in a tent for me."

Delilah tilted her head. "That I believe."

Claire watched her for a second. "You're coming, right?"

"Camping?"

She nodded.

"I don't think that's a good idea."

"Why not? Ruby wants you there."

"Astrid probably doesn't. It's not a wedding event, and the whole point is to get Astrid nice and vulnerable so she realizes that she's not in love with Ken."

Claire frowned. "Ken? His name is—"

"I know, Claire. Ken as in a Ken doll."

"Oh." Claire laughed and rubbed her forehead. "God, sorry. I'm usually better with jokes than this."

"Well, you've got a lot going on. With Josh and everything."

Delilah's tone was suddenly razor-sharp, cutting through all that previous *happy* and making Claire freeze. She looked at the other woman, at the cool expression on her face.

Too cool.

Delilah's mouth was tight and her fingertips were white on her full wineglass. She seemed to realize quickly that she was all locked up, because she suddenly stood, tossing the ghost card onto the sofa before grabbing the wine bottle and heading into the kitchen.

"Your stress is understandable, is all I'm saying," she said as she went.

Claire got up too, stacked the oracle cards on the coffee table, and followed her. "Delilah."

Delilah set the bottle and glass on the counter, then waved a hand like she hadn't just spit Josh's name out like she was talking about the bubonic plague.

She was . . . jealous.

Holy shit, Delilah Green was jealous of Josh.

Claire's pulse picked up, her breath short and fast in her lungs. She needed to figure out what to do here, and quickly. On the one hand, she was positive Delilah wanted her to act like it had never happened, but on the other, Delilah's jealousy made Claire want her even more, made everything in her hum and pop.

She set her own wine aside and then rounded the island so she was perpendicular with Delilah. Not quite next to her, but closer. Baby steps.

"Are . . . are we going to talk about the other night?" she asked. The perfect segue, and dear god, she actually really needed to talk about the other night.

Or replicate it immediately. Either one.

Delilah sighed, tucked her hair behind her ears. Her locks were so thick, the strands popped right back out. Claire had a desperate urge to reach over and push her hair out of her face herself.

"We probably shouldn't," Delilah said.

"Why not?"

"Because I drew the praying mantis card and that could mean terrible things for you."

"Well, I drew every single sex card in the deck, apparently," Claire said, laughing to try to bring back the lightness between them.

Delilah didn't laugh though. "We shouldn't talk about it because . . ." But then she didn't finish her sentence. She just looked at Claire, gaze searching, flicking down to her mouth, lingering there before moving back to Claire's eyes.

"Because?" Claire said.

"Because Josh," Delilah said.

"He's my co-parent," Claire said. "He's not . . . We're not like that."

"But you have been? I mean, since you've broken up?"

Claire blinked but wanted to be honest. "Yeah. But not for a while. Over two years ago."

"But it's still complicated."

"Why do you care?"

The question slipped out, spoken sharply and softly at the same time. Delilah watched her for a second and then slid around the island's corner, closer and closer. Claire's body shifted with her until they were standing right in front of each other, her lower back pressed against the quartz.

Delilah stepped into her space, arms on either side of Claire's hips, braced against the counter and hemming her in. Instinctively, Claire's hands went to Delilah's waist, fingers curling through the cotton of her shirt. She tugged a little, pulling Delilah that much closer. Their hips aligned, breasts, not an inch of space between their bodies.

Delilah leaned in, her bottom lip barely whispering against Claire's.

"I don't care," she said.

And that was all it took for Claire to slide a hand into Delilah's hair and close the last bit of distance between them.

THIS KISS WASN'T like the one at the vineyard. That kiss had started slow and tentative, a crawl toward a walking pace.

This kiss was a starter pistol, a leap off the block into a sprint. Tongues and teeth, gasps into open mouths. Claire had never felt so desperate to get close to someone. She wanted to climb this woman, rip her clothes off, and lick a stripe from her navel to that pretty dip in her collarbone. She buried both hands in Delilah's curls, tilting her head to get a new angle, tongue sweeping and tasting, wine and spring rain, a whisper of mint. Delilah's hands roamed, sliding up Claire's arms to her face, then back down again to her hips. Her fingers curled under Claire's shirt, skin against skin. Goose bumps erupted, and a moan slipped out of Claire's mouth into Delilah's.

"Get up here," Delilah said, pulling Claire up toward the countertop. Claire jumped while Delilah lifted, and immediately parted her knees as soon as her ass hit quartz. Delilah slid her hands up

Claire's jean-clad thighs, thumbs dipping into the creases where her hip joined her legs as their mouths met again. Delilah's hands moved up to Claire's waist and under her shirt, skating across her ribs and then over her bra.

Claire leaned back just enough to start unbuttoning her blouse, but Delilah stopped her.

"Let me," she said.

Claire smiled and rested her palms against the cool counter. Delilah kept her eyes on Claire's as her fingers popped one button and then the next, revealing the black lace bra underneath. Claire felt a rush of gratitude that most of her bras were pretty, bordering on sexy. Her underwear was a different story, but she'd worry about that later. Because right now, Delilah was spreading her shirt wide open and, as Claire sat a little bit above her now, the other woman was in the perfect position to press her mouth to Claire's sternum, which she did, flicking out her tongue for a little taste. At the same time, her hands came up, cupping Claire's breasts and sweeping her thumbs over her already hardened nipples.

Claire moaned and tipped her head back. She clamped her mouth shut, trying to rein it in, but she'd always been noisy in bed, and she had a feeling Delilah was going to pull out every scream that had been locked in her chest since her last non-self-induced orgasm.

"God, your tits are perfect," Delilah said, pulling down a bra cup and sucking a nipple into her hot mouth.

"Oh god," Claire said, tightening her legs around Delilah's hips. She tried to focus. "Really?"

"Mm-hmm."

"You . . . you don't think they're too . . . ?"

Delilah paused, releasing Claire's nipple, much to her chagrin, and looking up at her. "Too what?"

Claire swallowed, her lungs pumping like a marathon runner.

"Just . . . you know, they've always been big, and I've had a kid, so they're not what they used to be and—"

Delilah rolled her nipple between her thumb and forefinger, causing Claire to suck in a ragged breath. Then Delilah slid the straps down her arms, unhooked the back, and threw the bra deftly over her shoulder.

"Perfect," she said again, massaging Claire's tits as she kissed her, sucking her bottom lip between her teeth. Delilah's fingers stayed busy on her nipples, squeezing and sweeping until Claire was literally panting into her mouth, her underwear so wet she could feel the dampness on her thighs. She pulled away, plucking at Delilah's black T-shirt. She needed skin on skin, sweat and fingertips and tongues.

"Off," she said. "Now."

Delilah grinned up at her, then leaned back far enough for Claire to pull her shirt over her head.

Claire groaned out loud at the sheer yellow bralette covering Delilah's smaller, but just as perfect, breasts. Her nipples showed through, dark pink peaks already hard and waiting for Claire's mouth and hands. Her tattoos were gorgeous, art unfurling over her skin, including a delicate but heavily thorned rose on her sternum.

Claire reached out, touching the thorns, the petals, causing Delilah to shiver.

Suddenly, being shirtless wasn't enough. As much fun as sex on the kitchen counter sounded, she wanted space to move, to feel Delilah's thighs around hers, the curve of her ass, and how wet she was between her legs.

Oh god, they were actually doing this.

"You want to move to the bedroom?" Claire asked.

"Hell yes."

Delilah backed up so Claire could hop down, but then yanked her flush against her hips, kissing her hard as she started moving them toward the hallway. Claire walked backward, her bare breasts rubbing against Delilah's bra and creating a delicious friction.

"I don't know where I'm going," Delilah said against her mouth as she entered the hallway.

Claire laughed and turned them around so she could lead, but didn't let go of Delilah. She couldn't. If she did, she might wake up, or Delilah might change her mind, or hell, *she* might change her mind, and all she wanted right now was to not think about anything except getting this woman on her back.

Claire directed them into her room, then kept moving until Delilah's legs hit the bed, causing her to fall back onto the mattress, laughing.

Which was exactly how Claire wanted her.

She climbed on top of her, unbuttoning her jeans and pulling them down her thighs. Delilah had on a pair of hot pink lace cheekies, because of course she did. Claire's mouth literally watered as she ripped Delilah's pants off her feet and then glided her hands over Delilah's firm stomach, thumbs brushing over the top of her underwear. She started to pull those down too when Delilah sat up and flipped Claire onto her back.

"Oh no. Your turn to lose these pants," Delilah said, unzipping and sliding just as Claire had done, revealing her plain white cotton undies, her dimpled thighs, and her stretch marks.

A wave of self-consciousness flooded over her. She'd always been full-figured, and she'd been happy to be so, confident even, but the first time in bed with someone new always sent a brief wave of shyness through her. She went to cover her stomach with her hands, but Delilah caught her arms, moving them until they were settled above Claire's head. Then she sat back, knees on either side of Claire's legs, and looked her up and down. Claire felt her face burn, but her pulse throbbed between her thighs at the look in Delilah's eyes, like Claire was dessert and Delilah was still very hungry.

Delilah shifted, sliding up her body to kiss her. "Do you know how sexy you are?" she asked into Claire's mouth.

Claire let out a little laugh. "Um . . . well . . ."

Delilah's tongue blazed a hot path to her neck. "Very. Very fucking sexy."

Claire feathered her hands down Delilah's back, then pulled her bralette over her head. Both women released a soft moan as their breasts touched.

"Just so you know," Claire said. "I . . . I haven't done this in a while."

Delilah lifted her face from where she'd been nipping at Claire's collarbone with her teeth. "This?"

"Sex."

Delilah just smiled, then slid one leg between Claire's, pressing her thigh into Claire's center.

"Oh . . . my god," Claire said, gripping a fistful of her duvet cover as a bolt of pleasure shot up her spine. She could feel Delilah's arousal on her own leg, wet and warm even through her underwear.

"I think we'll be just fine," Delilah said, undulating her hips again, causing friction right where they both needed it. "Fuck," she said into Claire's neck. "I need to taste you. Tell me I can."

The rumble of Delilah's voice went straight between Claire's legs, and the idea of that hot mouth closing around her clit—

"God, yes," Claire said, body rolling upward, seeking more pressure.

Delilah pressed a kiss to her throat, then started a slow, tortuous journey down her body. Tongue, lips, teeth, pausing to explore one nipple, then the other, before continuing a wet glide down her stomach. Claire watched those dark curls descend, feeling every scrape of Delilah's nails as her fingers hooked through the top of her underwear and tugged the cotton down her thighs and off her feet. Claire's legs fell open, her hips rising to meet Delilah as the other woman settled between them.

"Goddamn," Delilah whispered, pressing a kiss to the inside of Claire's thigh. "You're gorgeous." The other thigh, another kiss. "And very wet."

Claire released a shaky laugh. Fuck yes, she was wet. Her clit throbbed, desperate for contact, but Delilah seemed to be in no hurry, brushing her mouth gently against Claire's center, tongue darting out for a taste everywhere except where Claire needed it. When Delilah licked a slow path from her entrance to her clit, then blew a puff of warm air over her and—holy hell—*hummed* against her skin, Claire nearly lost it.

"God, Delilah. Please."

Delilah grinned up at her. "Please what?"

Claire groaned in frustration, hips reaching for the ceiling.

"Tell me what you want," Delilah said, her mouth so close, that warm breath sliding over Claire's skin again.

"Fuck me," Claire said, fingers tightening through Delilah's hair. "Please, fuck me with your mouth."

It turned out, Delilah was excellent at taking directions. She hooked her arms around Claire's thighs, pulling her closer. Then her mouth got to work, doing exactly what Claire had begged her for. She kissed and licked, her tongue slipping into Claire like silk. A low keening sound ripped from Claire's throat, a sound she didn't think she'd ever made before, but fuck, she didn't care, because Delilah's fingers replaced her tongue, curling inside Claire and pressing against her wall. Delilah's mouth closed around her clit and sucked, then licked, then sucked again. Claire's thighs trembled, her hands pulled at Delilah's hair in a way she hoped wasn't too hard, but she couldn't think, couldn't worry, couldn't do anything but gasp and moan as Delilah's teeth and tongue and mouth lapped at her, fucked her just like she'd asked until she finally broke. Her legs tightened around Delilah's head, nails digging into the other woman's scalp as she yelled obscenities at the ceiling.

Delilah stayed with her until her body stilled, gentling her back down to earth, soft presses of her mouth to Claire's sensitive skin. Finally, when Claire could see straight, she pulled Delilah up her body and kissed her, the taste of herself on the other woman's tongue like striking a match low in her belly.

"Good?" Delilah asked.

Claire just laughed into her mouth.

"You were loud as hell, so I'll take that as a yes," Delilah said, and Claire froze.

"Oh. Shit, I'm sorry, I—"

But Delilah cut her off with a tug of her teeth on Claire's earlobe. "Are you kidding me? That was the single fucking hottest thing I've ever heard in my life."

"Really?" Claire could hardly believe it. Delilah had surely heard a lot of women coming underneath her in her time.

But Delilah just nodded, tongue flicking out to taste the sweat on Claire's neck. Her hips pulsed, seeking and needy. Claire tugged at her curls again, pulling a low, rumbling moan from Delilah's chest, which, okay, was maybe the single hottest fucking thing *Claire* had ever heard in her life. It made her feel feral, desperate, and she wanted to make Delilah come as hard as she had. She pawed at the other woman's underwear, which was, ridiculously, still on her body. Delilah quickly caught on, angling away from Claire and yanking the lacy cotton off with very little grace before throwing it into a dark corner of the room.

"Good call," Claire said, running her eyes over Delilah. The other woman was shaved, nothing but a perfect dark landing strip to guide the way. Claire gripped Delilah's hips and nudged her legs apart, pulling her until she was sitting up and straddling Claire's thighs, palms braced on Claire's ribs. When the hot slide of her center met Claire's mound, both women groaned.

"Best fucking decision I ever made," Delilah said, her breath ragged.

Claire rolled her own hips, then circled them so her pelvic bone hit Delilah right where she needed it. Delilah gasped and threw her head back, all of her undulating for friction. Claire felt her own desire building up again, a coil tightening in her lower belly more and more each time Delilah released those lovely, breathy gasps. Claire couldn't take her eyes off Delilah sliding over her body. She reached a hand between them, fingers playing in Delilah's soaked heat.

"Oh god," Delilah said to the ceiling. "Yeah."

She lifted her hips just enough for Claire to slide first one, then two fingers inside her. She was so tight, so perfect, and the back of Claire's hand pressed into her own clit.

Delilah leaned back and pumped her hips. "Fuck. Yes," she said, before her body clenched tight. She tangled one hand in her own hair, pulling the curls down over her face as she cried out, causing her body to press into Claire's hand so hard and perfect, Claire came too, their moans mingling with the smell of sweat and sex, their bodies arching and slowing, their breathing rough and ragged.

Delilah's hand closed around Claire's wrist between them, removing her hand and holding it to her chest before—dear god—she opened her mouth and licked Claire's fingers clean. The feel of Delilah's tongue, the way her eyes closed as if in bliss, almost had Claire ready to go again, but she was exhausted enough to simply enjoy the view, marveling at this woman in her bed. She pulled her hand free, wet fingertips lingering on Delilah's lips before settling on the woman's upper thigh. Delilah collapsed onto the mattress next to her, and they lay like that for a few minutes, legs still entangled, their lungs' pulls for more oxygen the only sound in the quiet room.

· Delilah lifted her head and met Claire's eyes. "Holy shit."

"Holy shit is right," Claire said. She curled her arms around Delilah's waist, not wanting the moment to end, but then saw Delilah's hair.

It. Was. Huge. Haloing around the other woman's face, the curls were tangled and frizzy and wild, the very definition of sex hair.

And it was just about the cutest fucking thing Claire had ever seen.

She let out a long laugh, relieved and sated and just plain happy, cupped Delilah's face—after she found it beneath all that hair—and kissed her hard.

CHAPTER

TWENTY

A BUZZING ON the nightstand woke Delilah. She lifted her head, the room unrecognizable for a split second before the entire night flooded back to her.

Claire.

She was at Claire's.

In her bed.

With Claire wrapped around her like a pretzel, her face pressed to Delilah's neck and breathing soft, sleepy breaths. She was totally zonked out, which wasn't any wonder. By the time the two women had fallen asleep after midnight, exhausted and boneless, they'd both come two more times and Delilah had discovered that Claire had an extremely talented mouth.

Now, Delilah had no idea what time it was, but it was still dark outside, and Claire's phone was making a hell of a racket on the nightstand.

"Claire." She shook her gently.

"Hmm." Claire just burrowed in deeper, her arm flopping over Delilah's waist.

"Claire, your phone. Hey." She moved the other woman's hair out of her face, moonlight filtering in through the gauzy curtains and silvering her skin.

Fuck, this woman was gorgeous.

Bzzz.

Delilah reached over and grabbed the phone, an unfamiliar name flashing across the screen.

"Claire, it's Maria." Whoever the hell that was.

"What?" That got her attention. Claire sat up, blinking, the sheet falling down to her waist. "Where?"

"On the phone?" Delilah handed it over, and Claire scrambled out of the bed, naked and perfect, before she grabbed her robe from a chair by the window. She slipped on her glasses and then pressed the phone to her ear. "Maria? Is Ruby okay? Oh no. Yes, put her on, absolutely." She turned to face Delilah, worrying her thumbnail in her mouth. "Ruby? What's wrong, honey? Okay . . . sweetie, calm down. Take a deep breath for me . . . You sure you can't just go to sleep and . . . Okay . . . Yes, of course you can come home. Tell Tess's mom I'll meet you on the sidewalk . . . Okay, honey. It'll be all right."

Then she hung up, sloughing off her robe and pulling on a pair of yoga pants and a tank top.

"Everything okay?" Delilah asked.

"Yeah, yeah, that was Tess's mom. Tess and Ruby had a fight, and she wants to come home. Says she can't sleep."

"Oh."

"They've been arguing a lot lately." Claire shook her head and rubbed her eyes, her hair a total mess and falling around her shoulders. "I'll be right back."

"Sure."

Claire paused at the door. "Um . . . stay in here, okay? I'll get Ruby to bed fast. She's probably exhausted. Just . . ." She trailed off, her eyes uncertain as she bit her lip.

Delilah understood what she was saying. *Please don't let my eleven-year-old know we're sharing a bed.* Delilah got it, but still, her chest sort of tightened up, and she suddenly very much wished she was wearing clothes.

"I should probably just go," she said. She rarely stayed overnight after sex anyway. Why should this time be any different? Still, she couldn't seem to move her ass off the mattress.

"No, don't," Claire said. "Just give me ten minutes, okay?"

Delilah nodded and then Claire was gone. Delilah heard the front door open and close, and she exhaled into the empty room. She really should go. She'd had sex with Claire, scratched the itch, and now she was done. Satisfied. And she'd definitely proven Astrid completely fucking wrong with her whole *Claire would never go for you* proclamation.

Yeah, this was over. Claire didn't want her here with Ruby in the house anyway. Delilah shoved the covers back, located her bra and underwear, her jeans, but her shirt was nowhere to be found, because it was still in the middle of the kitchen floor.

"Shit."

She went to the door, but before she could open it to try and sneak out, reclaim her clothing, and possibly bolt out the back door like a teenage boy running from a dad with a shotgun, she heard the front door open and shut again, Claire's and Ruby's voices mingling as they neared the hall.

"I . . . just . . . she's . . . so . . . mean . . ."

Ruby was crying, words falling out in stuttering breaths.

"Honey, shh. Let's just go to sleep, okay?" Claire said. "We can talk tomorrow and figure it all out. I promise."

"Can . . . can I sleep with you?" Ruby asked.

Delilah stiffened. She looked around the room, wondering if she needed to dive into the closet or jump out the window.

This was ridiculous.

She was two seconds from crawling under the bed when Claire spoke.

"Oh, honey, I think you'll sleep better in your own bed. But remember, we're going camping tomorrow, and you can share your tent with whoever you want, okay?"

Ruby said something in response, but Delilah couldn't hear the words as their voices faded down the hall. She slumped back onto the mattress, her head in her hands. Had she seriously been about to hide under the bed?

Yes. Yes, she absolutely had been.

The door opened and Claire slipped inside. "Hey."

Delilah sighed. "Hey."

"Sorry. She's in bed now. Do you—"

"I should go."

Claire froze, her mouth open. She stepped closer to Delilah, twisting her fingers together. "Yeah, I guess you probably should."

Except neither of them moved, and Delilah didn't know what to say. Sex had never made things so . . . awkward before. And she sure as hell had never been a secret. Attached women occasionally came on to her in bars, one too many glasses of Chablis running through their veins, but Delilah had a strict policy that she never slept with anyone else's monogamous partner. She knew what it was like to be on the other end of that raw deal, and no orgasm was worth inflicting that kind of pain.

That overwhelming feeling of not being enough.

She rubbed her forehead, that same feeling—from all her years in Wisteria House and again from Jax—creeping up on her now. How the fuck had this happened?

"You can stay for a few more hours if you want," Claire said. "Get some sleep."

"But be gone by first light, right?" Delilah looked up at her, a bitter smile on her mouth.

"Delilah. That's not fair."

"No, I guess it's not."

"I'm careful about who I bring around Ruby, that's all. The last person I dated, she never even met Ruby. Not once. And I dated her for over a month."

"But I'm already around her."

"Not like this." Claire motioned to Delilah's topless state, the bed in disarray. "Not like someone who means—" She cut herself off and closed her eyes. When she opened them again, her voice was quiet, low. "Again, why do you care? This is just sex, isn't it?"

Delilah frowned at her. She'd never told Claire it was just sex. She'd never hinted that she was only looking for a hookup, even though she absolutely was. It couldn't be more than that. They lived three thousand miles away from each other, she had the Whitney and her art, and hell if Delilah was ever going to put herself in the position again to be heartbroken by a woman who wasn't over her ex. She didn't know what Josh meant to Claire, but he had to mean something. He was the father of her kid. He was hot. And he'd always be in her life.

"Yeah," Delilah said, standing and starting for the door. "It is."

Claire blocked her path. "Okay, then what's wrong?"

"Nothing's wrong."

"Something is. I can tell."

"You can't tell shit, Claire. You don't know anything about me. You want to stuff me in a closet—"

"A closet? What?"

"—and oh, I assume I've got to keep all this *sex* a secret from Astrid, right? Wouldn't want to upset Princess Perfect. Now, if you'd kindly move, I need to get my shirt and go back to my floral hell of a hotel room."

Claire didn't budge. In fact, she seemed to dig in, brow furrowing as she reached out and grabbed Delilah's arms.

"Hey. Stop for a second, okay? Just slow down."

Delilah chewed on her bottom lip, but she stopped. Her chest was tight, and pressure built behind her eyes, like they needed to release something. God, she hadn't felt like this in so long, like she was shrinking, like everyone around her was more important than she was. She was just tired. Exhausted and tired and, okay, maybe a little overwhelmed by the fact that she may have just had the greatest sex of her life. One didn't just walk away from the greatest sex of one's life.

"I don't want you to go," Claire said. "Okay?"

"Why not?"

Claire's eyes searched hers. She searched back.

"Because I need this," Claire finally said, sliding her hands down Delilah's arms to tangle with her fingers. "And it was . . . *fun.*"

Delilah smirked.

"And I get that you're into casual," Claire went on. "That's fine with me. Totally fine. After Astrid's wedding, you'll go back to New York and I'll stay here and that'll be that. But we're here now. And I . . . well . . . I want to see you again."

"You want to fuck me again, you mean," Delilah said, but she was smiling. This she knew. This she understood. She'd had lovers she'd seen for multiple days, even weeks, before one of them broke it off for some amiable and practical reason.

Pink spilled into Claire's cheeks. "Okay, fine. Yes. Don't you?"

"Want to fuck me?"

"Delilah."

She laughed, then moved their entwined hands around Claire's waist, pulling the other woman closer. When their mouths touched, she whispered, "Yes. I want to fuck you again."

Claire smiled against the kiss. "Good. We're agreed, then."

"Should we sign something?"

"Like a fuck-buddy pact?"

"Sure." She slid her mouth down Claire's neck, nipped at her earlobe. "You don't want me spilling your dirty little secret, do you?"

Claire stiffened and leaned back so they were eye to eye. "Delilah. It's not about you being a secret. It's just—"

"You don't want people to know about us."

"Yeah."

"Which is a secret."

Claire wiggled out of her embrace. "Are you telling me you actually *want* Astrid to know?"

Delilah thought about it, the look of shock that would fill Astrid's eyes, the pure, unadulterated thrill of victory. But then she thought about how Claire was probably right—Astrid would be upset, and with more than just Delilah. She'd be upset with Claire, and then this whole sex thing Delilah and Claire were doing would come to an abrupt end.

And Delilah didn't want it to end. For the ten more days she had to spend in this soul-sucking town, she actually had a distraction now. A beautiful, sweet, amazing-in-bed distraction.

Who was she to look a gift horse in the mouth?

"No," she said. "No, I guess I don't."

Claire relaxed, but then narrowed her eyes at Delilah, concern creasing her brow. "It's not because I'm ashamed of you."

Delilah laughed. "Okay. Sure. The Ghoul of Wisteria House is in your bed. No big deal."

Claire's eyes flashed with something that looked like hurt . . . even regret. "Delilah."

She waved a hand. "Forget I said anything."

"I don't want to forget it."

"Sure you do."

"Hey." Claire took her hand, squeezed it. "I'm not ashamed of you. But I'm allowed to have something that's just mine, aren't I? I don't have to tell my best friends everything."

"But you usually do, right?"

Claire sighed. "You and Astrid . . . It's complicated."

Delilah just stared at her.

"Isn't it?" Claire asked.

In answer, Delilah simply unbuttoned her jeans, peeled them off her legs, and got back into bed. If she was going to talk about this, she definitely needed to be lying down. Claire watched her settle on her back, then followed her, pulling the sheet over both of them and propping her head on her elbow, eyes on Delilah's face.

"It didn't feel complicated," Delilah said. "Growing up with her. It felt extremely simple."

"What do you mean?"

Delilah stared at the ceiling, like she'd done so many nights before, listening to Claire and Iris and Astrid laughing in Astrid's room, like she'd done while Isabel hosted dinner parties Delilah knew her stepmother didn't really want her to attend.

"It was simple," she said again. "My mother was gone. My father died. Isabel resented that she had to raise me alone. Astrid thought I was too strange to include, too sad, too much on the outside of her perfect world to be part of anything in her life. You were there for most of it. You saw it."

There. It truly was so simple. Embarrassingly so. She actually couldn't believe she'd just said all that out loud, admitted her . . . unlovability.

Claire was silent for a beat, and Delilah didn't dare look at her. An ache started in her throat.

"I did see it," Claire said. "Astrid . . . she's a hard person to know. She holds things really close. I think Isabel just drilled into her this idea of never letting them see you sweat, you know? Or cry or show any kind of weakness. Vulnerability is hard for her, but when she does let you in, she's loyal and strong and would do anything for you. That's who I saw, and I guess I just . . . never understood why you didn't."

Delilah's chest tightened. "Because she didn't let me in, Claire. You just said it yourself, she's a hard person to know and she didn't give two shits about me knowing her."

Claire frowned but had nothing to say to that.

"And by default," Delilah said, "neither did you or Iris."

"Delilah," Claire said softly, leaning close to her so that her chin rested on Delilah's shoulder. Which just made the ache worse. It made this whole thing the opposite of *just sex*. "I'm sorry."

Delilah shook her head. "Don't say that just because we're screwing. It's cheap."

Claire pressed even closer. "I'm not saying it because we're screwing. I'm saying it because I feel it. I'm sorry I didn't try harder. I could've . . . I don't know, pushed Astrid to include you more."

"No one pushes Astrid to do anything."

"Then *I* could've included you more."

Delilah scoffed. "No, you couldn't have. Because you didn't want to."

Silence filtered in between them, Claire left with no response in the face of the truth. Delilah waited for the awkwardness of it all to push them finally apart, for Claire to sigh and admit that maybe this was all a big mistake. She even waited to feel some of that old anger flare up, the resentment that had fueled her relationship with anyone in Bright Falls for over two decades.

Instead, she just felt sad, desperate to not feel that way anymore.

Claire reached out and slid a finger down Delilah's cheek to her mouth before sliding her palm around the back of her neck. Instead of pushing her away, she pulled Delilah closer and pressed her forehead against hers.

"I want to now," Claire said, then pressed her mouth to hers, gentle and slow.

Too gentle and slow.

Delilah hadn't meant for the conversation to turn this direction. It's not like it mattered. She didn't want or need Claire's apology. She didn't want to hear excuses for whatever Isabel did to Astrid to fuck her up proper. Delilah was fucked up enough herself. She rolled over on top of Claire, settling between her thighs, and turned all that gentle and slow into hard and fast. She didn't let either of them come up for air for the next hour.

Later, as they both lingered in that place between awake and asleep, the first touches of lavender light trickling through the window, Claire entwined her fingers with Delilah's.

"Come camping with us," she said softly. "Ruby wants you there."

Claire's eyes were free of her glasses and hazy with sex and sleep. Delilah brushed her bangs off her forehead with her other hand.

"Ruby wants me there, huh?" she said.

Claire smiled. "Yep. Just Ruby."

CHAPTER
TWENTY-ONE

IT WASN'T ONLY Ruby who wanted Delilah on the camping trip, and they both knew it. Still, even in that intimate space between them in bed, Claire didn't want to admit it out loud. And when Josh's truck pulled into her driveway the next morning and Ruby sprinted outside to greet him, she told herself she was only looking out the window and down the street for Iris and Astrid, who were both coming separately and were due any minute.

Delilah had agreed to the trip. As she stood in Claire's room at five o'clock that morning, pulling on her clothes, she'd grunted a *fine, what else have I got to do* when Claire asked about it again, but Claire barely knew the woman, and Delilah didn't have the best reliability track record. At least twice, she remembered Astrid getting in a huff because Delilah hadn't shown up for a holiday, complaining about wasted food she'd ordered or tickets she'd procured to the symphony in Portland. Claire kept telling herself it wasn't a big deal if she didn't come—it was one day and this thing between them was just sex and it wasn't like they were going to have a chance to engage in a bunch of *just sex* while surrounded by Claire's best friends, daughter, and her co-parent ex-boyfriend.

Jesus.

She rubbed her sleep-deprived eyes as Iris's Subaru wagon pulled up. What had Claire been thinking? No, it was definitely better if Delilah didn't come. Maybe she should even call Delilah and tell her—

Claire gripped the curtain tighter as Iris's passenger door opened and Delilah stepped out, clad in another pair of gray jeans and a burgundy tank top that made it very clear she wasn't wearing a bra.

Okay, so they were doing this.

Claire pressed a hand to her stomach, memories of last night washing over her like warm rain. The way Delilah had looked when she was talking about her childhood being simple. How lonely she had sounded. How her eyes—

No.

No, she was not going to think about Delilah's *eyes*, for Christ's sake. This thing between them was casual. Transient. Completely carnal, no hearts involved whatsoever. Claire took one . . . two . . . three cleansing breaths, then grabbed her backpack stuffed with her bathing suit and a change of clothes, her water bottle dangling from the side by a carabiner, and walked outside.

"Morning, sunshine," Iris called, but as she came closer, her smile dipped. "God, you look like shit."

"Thank you, darling," Claire said.

"Surely, you've looked in a mirror," Iris said, cupping Claire's chin and peering into her face.

"I just didn't sleep much last night," Claire said. She met Delilah's eyes over Iris's shoulder, and her stomach fluttered.

"Why not?" Iris asked.

"Just . . . stuff with Ruby. She spent the night at Tess's but then came home in the middle of the night. They had a fight."

There. That wasn't a lie. She wasn't lying to her friends about having the best sex of her life—several times—all night long. She was simply . . . keeping it for herself.

Which, Claire realized, she would do even if Delilah wasn't who she was. This thing with Delilah was new, temporary, but intense. And Claire was a grown woman. She was allowed to hold things close, keep them to herself until she figured out how to handle them.

"Oh, honey, I'm sorry," Iris said. "She okay?"

Claire sighed. She'd tried to talk to Ruby this morning about Tess, but her daughter had refused to go into it. Looking at her now, up in Josh's truck bed and helping him arrange the camping gear, she looked happier than Claire had seen her in a while.

"I think so, yeah," she said.

"Okay, good, because we need to focus," Iris said, waving Delilah over. "I picked up Cranky Pants this morning—"

"Cranky Pants?" Delilah said when she reached them. "What am I, five?"

"—and it's imperative that we share a tent with Astrid."

"That you two share a tent with Astrid," Delilah said, circling her finger at them. "I'm sleeping in that hammock I just saw old what's his name throw in his truck."

Claire lifted her brow. *Old what's his name?*

Delilah lifted a brow right back, and Claire had to fight a smile.

"Look," Iris said. "It's go time, all right? We're a week from doomsday, and we have to—"

Iris cut herself off when a car that most certainly wasn't Astrid's pulled up along Claire's curb. It was silver and sleek, its Mercedes emblem shining under the morning sun. Astrid stepped out of the passenger side, a Louis Vuitton weekender bag on her elbow, and walked around to the driver's door.

"Please tell me that is the fanciest fucking Lyft in the history of all Lyfts," Iris said.

The driver's door opened, and Spencer stepped out, aviator sunglasses like mirrors over his eyes.

"Maybe he's just dropping her off," Claire said, but her palms had started to sweat.

Astrid hooked her arm through his, smiling as they walked up the drive, an expensive-looking leather duffel bag dangling from Spencer's hand.

"Or maybe," Delilah said, slinging an arm around Iris's shoulder, "Astrid just really, really doesn't want to share a tent with you two."

BAGBY HOT SPRINGS was located deep within Mount Hood National Forest. Claire surveyed the spot Josh had reserved for camping, which was pretty perfect, she had to admit. The forest floor was wide and flat for the tents, evergreens and pines rising high above them and hemming them in, creating a shaded area that was cool and quiet. The springs and the bathhouse, which boasted newly renovated wooden tubs for soaking, were just a short hike away, about a quarter of a mile, and there were plenty of trails to explore during the day.

It was the perfect getaway.

Or at least it would be if Astrid wasn't glued to Spencer's side right now as he set up their tent. She'd barely spoken to Claire or Iris since they had arrived, taking only a moment to ask what the hell Delilah was doing on the trip, to which Claire had fumbled a very unsmooth response about how Ruby had taken a liking to her and, goodness, who could resist Ruby's adorable hazel eyes when she really wanted something? Astrid had grunted a response, then promptly flocked to Spencer, who was calling out orders for tent stakes and some of the sparkling rosé that Iris had immediately popped open as soon as they arrived.

There were two more tents—one for Josh and Ruby and one, ostensibly, for Iris, Claire, and Delilah.

Claire decided not to think about that right now, how in approximately twelve or so hours, she was going to be stuffed in between her best friend and the woman she was secretly sleeping with.

Both of whom were now arguing over how to stick a stake in the ground.

"At an angle, you imbecile," Iris said, yanking a thin metal stick out of the dirt and repositioning it through one of their tent's nylon loops. "Haven't you ever been camping before?"

Delilah sat back on her butt, wrapping her arms around her knees. "Oh yeah, Isabel was a real wilderness kind of mom, let me tell you. She was also a Girl Scout troop leader and caught fish with her bare hands."

Iris glared at her for a beat before she cracked up. "God, I would've loved to see Isabel Parker-Green eating jerky and drinking out of a tin cup."

"The eighth wonder of the world."

Iris laughed and Delilah laughed too, and for some reason, the whole scene made Claire's chest feel warm and heavy, like honey flowed through her veins. She watched them for a second before heading over to Josh and Ruby, who were putting up their tent next to a pile of gear Josh brought along to feed them all—camping cookware, two coolers full of food, and a huge backpack Claire knew he used to carry all his spices and nonperishables.

"How's it going over here?" she asked, ruffling her daughter's hair.

"Great!" the girl said as she slid a thin black pole through a little tube in the nylon tent, erecting it into a dome-like shape. "Dad's teaching me all about camping stuff."

"Yeah, like what?"

"Like how to put up a tent," Josh said, then winked at Ruby. When his eyes shifted to Claire, she could've sworn his smile dipped a little.

"You always did love the woods," she said.

He nodded tightly. "I still do. I'd love to live out in a cabin someday, a little creek in the backyard."

"You?" Claire said, surprised. Loving the woods was one thing; settling down miles from anyone and anything was quite another. She couldn't imagine Josh, the man who always fled his own small town to find something better, something greater, living like a hermit in the Cascades.

"Yeah, me," he said, zipping the tent's door shut with a bit more fervor than Claire thought was necessary. "A little place over in Sotheby or Winter Lake. I've been doing a lot of work with Holden over there and those areas are pretty great."

"Really." Sotheby and Winter Lake were about thirty minutes outside of Bright Falls, north and northwest respectively. They were roughly the size of pinheads and known for fishing, quaint downtowns, and houses spread out so far apart in the surrounding woods it felt as though one lived on their own planet.

"Yes. Really." Josh's voice grew even tighter, and he shook his head while flipping the rain hood over the top of the tent.

"Josh, what—"

"Rubes, can you go grab those towels out of my truck?" he said. "I'm ready to hit the hot springs. How about you?"

"Yeah!" she said and dashed off toward the truck.

Once she was out of earshot, Claire turned back to him. "What is going on?"

"Nothing." He secured the rain hood and then threw the now-empty tent bag inside. "I'm taking my daughter to the springs. Is that okay with you?"

She just blinked at him, her pulse spiking. She knew the hot springs were completely safe for swimming. There was a bathhouse for soaking, but there was also a natural pool about half a mile off the trail where you could spread out a little more. Still, drowning could happen to anyone, anytime, anywhere.

"No, I can see it's not actually okay with you," he said, shaking his head.

She sighed. "Josh, I just—"

"I'm going to do it anyway. You've got your friends, some dude over there I don't even know in fucking leather . . . What the hell are those? Sneakers?"

Claire glanced back at Spencer, who was indeed wearing what could only be described as the fanciest sneakers Claire had ever seen. They had laces and white rubber bottoms, but the tops were a smooth brown leather, so soft and buttery-looking, she knew they had to be expensive.

"I thought you were fine with them coming along," Claire said, turning back to Josh.

"Oh yeah, this is a dream come true."

"What does that mean?"

He grabbed his own backpack from the picnic table and threw it over his shoulder, then he waved at the other four people in the campsite. "It means, what the hell is this, Claire? This was supposed to be a trip with *my* daughter. Her and me. One night. Simple. Next thing I know you're calling me up and telling me you're coming along too? Oh, and Astrid and Iris. And now Delilah and Douche Canoe over there."

Claire opened her mouth with the sudden urge to verify that he could tell Spencer was indeed a douche canoe from first glance, but she knew that would be the wrong thing to say at this moment. She tried to focus on what he was actually upset about, which seemed to be that she and her friends crashed his camping trip with Ruby.

"I'm not going to apologize for wanting to make sure my daughter is safe," she said. Hurt flashed across his face, but she refused to feel guilty. He was the one who'd put her in this position in the first place, after years and years of flaky parenting.

"Is that really what this is about? Safety?"

"What does that mean?"

He sighed, grabbing the straps of his pack and staring at the ground. When he glanced up, he looked wrecked, exhausted.

"I'm never going to be good enough, am I?" he asked softly.

Her mouth dropped open, but no words came out. Nothing. He nodded, then walked off toward Ruby and wrapped his arm around her shoulder as they headed for a clearly marked trail.

Claire watched them go, waiting for her daughter to turn back and at least smile or wave goodbye, but she didn't. Panic flared in her chest, but she forced it down. Josh was good at this kind of stuff, after all. Growing up, his parents had taken him and his brother camping all the time, and Claire vaguely remembered a trip he took to Mount Rainier with his best guy friends right after high school graduation. No one died or got lost. No one even got so drunk they fell into a river and nearly drowned.

So yes, Ruby would be fine. Maybe she would've been fine all along and Claire didn't even need to be here.

Maybe that's what she was actually afraid of.

CHAPTER
TWENTY-TWO

DELILAH WATCHED CLAIRE stare after Josh and Ruby for what felt like a long time. She wanted to drop the sleeping bag she was holding, some mothball-smelling thing that Iris said belonged to Grant, and go over to the other woman and kiss her within an inch of her life, make her forget whatever Josh said or what he might mean to her.

She didn't.

She pushed her feet into the pine straw–covered ground, forced herself to ignore the panic that laced through her chest like a fire.

Claire wasn't Jax.

And Claire and Delilah sure as hell weren't Jax and Delilah. They weren't together. Weren't emotional about this. They were fucking; that was it. Secretly, she might do well to remember. The fact that Delilah felt like hitting something right now—hitting, or pulling Claire off into the woods and showing her exactly why Josh wasn't worth wasting any time on—was purely biological. Something territorial in Delilah was rearing its primitive head. That was all.

That was one hundred percent all this slightly nauseous feeling in her stomach was about.

"She's been through it with him."

Delilah blinked, turning to pull a face at Iris, who had come up next to her and was gazing at Claire as well. "What?"

"Josh and Claire. Ruby. They've been through a lot."

"Yeah, so I've heard."

Iris lifted a brow. "From?"

Delilah shook her head, but then realized she could tell the truth. "Astrid."

Iris's eyes narrowed, but she nodded, then gestured toward Claire. "She deserves something good. Someone good. Someone who really sees her, you know?"

This conversation was not helping her nausea or the tight feeling in her chest.

"So does Astrid," Iris went on.

"And so do we all. Yes, it's all so precious and touching," Delilah said, rolling her eyes.

"Maybe not all of us," Iris said, but she was smiling and then slapped Delilah on the butt with her water bottle. Delilah couldn't help but laugh in relief, this slightly bitchy rapport she had with Iris comforting and familiar by now.

"Hey!" Astrid called, glancing at them with an annoyed look on her face. "Are we hiking to the springs or what? Spencer and I want some exercise."

"Yeah, ladies," Spencer said, rubbing his palms together. "We didn't come out here to talk about lip gloss and hair dye."

"Oh damn," Iris said, snapping her fingers. "I thought we were giving you a makeover, Spence?"

He laughed. "Not on your life. And it's Spencer."

"Sure thing, Spence."

He opened his mouth to say something else, but Astrid took his hand and led him into their tent to change, shooting Iris a look over her shoulder as they disappeared inside.

"God, I hate that guy," Iris said.

"Why? He's such a peach," Delilah said as Claire came up next to her. Their arms brushed, and Delilah felt the immediate rush of goose bumps over her skin, Claire's meadowy scent filling her senses.

She stepped a little closer to Iris. Jesus, she needed to get a grip.

"I guess we should get ready to hike, huh?" Claire asked, folding her arms.

"Maybe there's a ravine Delilah can push him down," Iris said.

"Oh sure," Delilah said, "make me the murderer."

"You could make it look like an accident." Iris nudged her arm. "Like the river? Pure brilliance."

"Um, in case you don't recall, *I* also went into the river. I'm not taking a tumble down a ravine to break up a wedding. I'm here to ruin some happiness, not, you know, die."

"Ruin some happiness?" Claire asked, brow furrowed.

Delilah sucked her teeth. She'd nearly forgotten who she was with. For a second there, it felt like she was simply talking with . . . friends. Bantering. Laughing. Joking. All things she'd never really had before, but Iris and Claire weren't really her friends. They were Astrid's.

"Spencer's," Delilah said, forcing a smile.

Problem was, Delilah wasn't even sure what she was doing anymore. Astrid and Isabel had dragged her back to Bright Falls, dangling money and her father's memory just to exert some sort of sick control over her, and when Claire and Iris wanted to get rid of Spencer, the thought of witnessing the Parker-Greens facing a canceled society wedding was just too delicious to pass up. Now, though, seeing Claire looking at her so sweetly, remembering Astrid's devastated expression as she'd stared at the unhappy photo of herself by Spencer's side, verbally sparring with Iris in a way that usually ended in laughter—it all felt like something so much more than a two-week trip to the place she hated most in the world.

It felt like the start of something.

Which couldn't be right. Her *something* was in New York City. Her *something* was huge crowds and dive bars and women whose names she only occasionally remembered. The Whitney. Fellow artists. Potential agents and sales and making a name for herself.

"I'm all about some Spencer-ruining," Iris said as she unzipped their tent's door and took the sleeping bag out from under Delilah's arm, tossing it through the entrance. "I'm going to get changed."

Then she disappeared, leaving Claire and Delilah alone for the first time since Delilah sneaked out of Claire's house this morning while the first streaks of light silvered across the sky.

As soon as the door zipped closed, Claire closed her hand around Delilah's wrist and tugged her across the campsite, behind Josh and Ruby's tent and out of view. Before Delilah could ask what was going on, Claire's mouth was on hers, soft and warm. Her arms settled on Delilah's shoulders, fingers slipping into her hair. Delilah's hands found Claire's hips, pulling her closer. She opened to her, tongue sliding over Claire's like silk, pulling the gentlest moan from Claire's throat.

God, this woman made her crazy. She felt wild, unhinged, like a horny teenager chasing her next make-out session.

"I've been wanting to do that all day," Claire said when they broke apart.

"Yeah?"

"Yes."

Another kiss. Another soft moan.

"Better be careful," Delilah whispered against her mouth, sliding her hands down to Claire's ample ass. "I'm about to take you right here, right now."

Claire stiffened and pulled back.

"Calm down. I won't," Delilah said.

"That's not what I . . ." Claire closed her mouth, her eyes searching Delilah's. "I want to be alone with you."

Delilah grinned, pressed her mouth to Claire's neck, growling a little into her skin. "Me too."

Claire laughed. "Not for that."

Delilah's tongue traced a path up to her ear, and Claire sucked in a sharp breath.

"Okay, not only for that," Claire said. "But I want . . . I want to talk too."

Delilah pulled back, alarm tightening her stomach. "What about? I won't tell anyone what we're doing. I already told you that."

"No, that's not it."

"Then what?"

Claire sighed and pressed her forehead against Delilah's shoulder.

"Hey," Delilah said, pressing a kiss to her temple. "What is it?"

Claire lifted her head and smiled, but it didn't reach her eyes. "Nothing. It's nothing."

"It's not nothing. I can tell."

Claire shook her head. "No really . . . I . . ." Then her brows lifted, just a little. "I want to see that picture. The one you took of me by the river five years ago."

Delilah's eyes widened. She had a feeling that's not at all what Claire actually wanted to talk about, but she let it go. "Really?"

Claire nodded and her arms tightened, hands sliding down Delilah's back. "Of course I do. You know Iris and I plundered your Instagram, right?"

Heat spilled in Delilah's cheeks. She still hadn't gotten used to the idea of anyone other than total strangers roaming through her art.

"I had a feeling," she said.

Claire frowned. "Is that okay?"

"Yeah. Yeah, it's just weird."

"Well, it shouldn't be. You're really talented, Delilah. Even Iris likes your work. The way you use light and your angles. I don't know anything about photography, but your stuff . . . I don't know. It's emotional. Angry and sad and empowered. It made me feel something."

Like any artist, Delilah viewed her own work with a dizzying mix of self-loathing and self-aggrandizement, so Claire's words nestled like an ember deep in her chest and stayed there, glowing warm and bright.

"Really?" she asked.

"Really," Claire whispered. "Your pieces at the Whitney are going to be breathtaking." Then she kissed her softly, slowly. That ember in Delilah's chest flared, igniting into a full flame. In that moment, Delilah didn't care about secrets or Josh or Astrid or the way Jax had pulverized her heart or how the idea of showing at the Whitney and *still* not advancing in her career made her want to curl into a fetal position and suck her thumb. She only cared about this, Claire in her arms, whispering things that made Delilah feel seen for the first time in . . .

Shit.

Maybe this was the first time she'd ever felt this seen. Or, no, not this exact moment, but every tiny moment with Claire since she'd been back in Bright Falls—talking with Claire at the bookstore, lying with her in bed at Blue Lily, listening to her talk about her worries over Josh, telling her about Jax, watching how Claire's eyes literally sparkled when she talked about Ruby. Hell, even letting the woman unknowingly hit on her at Stella's.

Then last night, her skin, her body, her touch. *Just sex* that suddenly felt like anything but.

Delilah leaned into the kiss, trying to shut down her thoughts with her mouth, her tongue, her hands sliding into the back pocket of Claire's shorts.

It didn't work. Claire, sighing into her mouth, like she was *happy*. It all swirled in Delilah's mind like a hurricane gathering strength. She pulled back, needing air, needing space. Needing to get her head back in this casual sex game.

Claire frowned at her. "You okay?"

Delilah didn't say anything. She didn't have to. Zips echoed through the campsite, followed by Spencer's booming voice directing Astrid to fill up his water bottle.

"Better get this happiness-ruining going," Delilah said as she turned away, swallowing around the infuriating thickness in her throat.

CHAPTER

TWENTY-THREE

SHE'D COME ON too strong. That must be what it was. Delilah could tell that what Claire had really wanted to talk about was *them*, what this thing between them was, even when they'd already established it was sex, sex, and more sex. Why else would Delilah have pulled away from her like that, gasping for air like Claire was smothering her? She knew this was a mistake. Claire couldn't do casual, and now Delilah was freaking out and realizing that Claire was starved for love and wanted nothing more than to climb inside Delilah and set up shop.

Except Claire didn't want that.

She couldn't.

This was *Delilah Green*, her best friend's stepsister who took off on her family twelve years ago and barely looked back, and Claire knew too well what it was like to love someone who couldn't stay. Who wouldn't stay.

Only . . . after listening to Delilah talk about Astrid last night, how she and Astrid weren't complicated at all, how Astrid and Isabel simply hadn't wanted her . . . something about it rang true. Not that she blamed Astrid for it. She'd already lost her own father, then a stepfather, and Isabel wasn't the kind of mother who doled out love easily. Delilah *was* strange as a girl, cold and distant, but she'd lost both parents by the time she was ten years old.

Wouldn't that make anyone strange and cold and distant?

And now, as an adult, Delilah was anything but. A little rough around the edges, sure. Prickly. But something about her made Claire's blood hum, apart from the amazing sex, even if they were just talking. Delilah was brilliant and funny and strong, and Claire wanted to wrap herself around her, soak her up, help fill that haunted look in the other woman's eyes with something soft and gentle.

Claire rubbed her eyes under her glasses, trying to press back all of these damn *feelings*. She had always wanted to be one of those people who could sleep with someone and let it be just that—sex, feeling, skin. She knew it wasn't a bad thing that she'd never been like that—she'd had a kid young, and there had always been too much at stake or simply not enough time in the day, but it always sounded so fun, hearing about Iris's exploits in her early twenties. Even Astrid had had a few one-night stands, and those were only the ones she'd told Iris and Claire about.

You're just not wired for casual, and that's okay.

Iris's words from that night at Stella's rang through her skull, but she ignored them. She could be wired any way she pleased, and right now, what pleased her was Delilah in her bed. She straightened her clothes and rolled her shoulders back, determined to play it cool with Delilah from now on.

Sex, she told herself. *Just think about sex.*

"What are you doing?" Iris asked, frowning at her as she stepped out from behind Josh and Ruby's tent.

"Oh. Um, just looking for a water bottle I can use," she said, making a show of glancing around. "Josh usually brings a million."

"Yes, except *your* water bottle is with your backpack," Iris said, pointing to Claire's pack leaning against their tent, a purple Nalgene hooked onto one of the straps.

"Right," Claire said and left it at that. She grabbed the bottle and took a long pull of the now lukewarm water.

"All right, let's hit it," Spencer called, clapping his hands like they were cattle. Then he smacked Astrid on the butt when she started toward the trailhead. He grinned at her, then pulled her into his arms and kissed her.

Claire watched, teeth gritted, as Astrid kissed him back. But her best friend wasn't smiling. And her arms seemed stiff around Spencer's shoulders while his hands roamed down her backside. She wasn't enjoying this, not in the least, but then again Astrid had never been one for PDA. Where most mothers teach basic manners, Isabel had hammered propriety into her daughter like a nail through wood.

"Is it too much to ask for a large rock to just, I don't know, fall on his head?" Iris asked as she tied up her hiking boots.

"If only we were the praying kind," Claire said.

"I'd be willing to convert if it got that shit hat out of our lives."

"Now he's a shit hat?"

"He's a shit-all-types-of-clothing. Shirt. Belt. Jacket."

"Shit shirt has a nice ring to it."

"It really does."

Claire laughed, but her eyes trailed over to Delilah without her permission. The other woman was sitting on the picnic table, scrolling through her phone. Claire forced her gaze away.

"Ready?" Astrid called, pulling back from Spencer.

"Yep," Iris said, linking her arm with Claire's and squeezing her tightly. Together they walked over to the trailhead, but when they arrived, Delilah still hadn't moved from the picnic table.

"Are you coming, Del?" Astrid asked.

Delilah glanced up, a bored expression in her eyes. "Nah. Looks like it might rain."

"It's the Pacific Northwest," Spencer said. "It always looks like it might rain."

"Oh my god, you're so right." Delilah looked around at the trees, wide-eyed, her voice saccharine. "I almost forgot what part of the country I was in. Thank you so much."

Iris snort-laughed, but then Spencer muttered something that sounded suspiciously like *bitch* under his breath, and Iris's smile turned into a murderous glare. Claire heard Astrid take a deep breath, then turn away and gulp from her water bottle.

"I'm good here," Delilah said, going back to her phone.

"Are you sure?" Claire asked. She took a step back toward the campsite, willing Delilah to look up at her.

She didn't. Instead, she just nodded, and Claire felt her stomach plunge to her feet. Iris pulled Claire's arm toward the trail, and she went, but she couldn't get rid of the panic bubbling into her chest. First Josh, now Delilah. She felt marooned, out of control, and very much like she was about to burst into some extremely embarrassing tears.

Five minutes into the hike, she pulled her arm free from Iris's. "You know what? I'm going to go check on Ruby at the springs."

"What?" Iris asked, her face going pale.

"Yeah, I just . . . I'm nervous, you know? About her and Josh and I just . . ." She didn't know how to say it, that she simply needed to *go*, that she needed to cry, to wrap her arms around her daughter, the one thing in her life that she was sure of.

"Sweetie, is everything okay?" Astrid asked, stepping closer to her. "Do you want us to come with you?"

Claire shook her head. "You go hike. Have fun."

"You heard her," Spencer said, taking Astrid's arm. He started walking her up the trail, leather sneakers and all. "She's fine. Let's go."

"Claire," Iris said, widening her eyes with meaning. "Are you serious right now?"

"I'll see you back at the campsite, okay?" she said before Iris could say anything else. Guilt swirled in her gut, but still, she turned away from her friend and ran back along the trail.

SHE BURST THROUGH the trees and into the campsite's clearing, breathing heavy, eyes searching. Delilah was still perched on top of the picnic table, phone in her hand. Her head snapped up when she saw Claire, brow furrowing in what Claire could only hope was concern and not annoyance.

"I thought you were going to hike?" Delilah asked.

Claire tried to calm herself down as surreptitiously as possible as all the wrong answers flitted through her head.

I wanted to see you.

I was worried about you.

I was worried about us.

But she knew she couldn't say any of those things. Those weren't *casual* answers to Delilah's question.

"I decided not to," Claire said. "I'm going to go to the springs and check on Ruby."

There. A perfectly breezy response. Her voice didn't even shake.

Delilah nodded, and Claire moved off toward their tent to change into her bathing suit. She ducked under the door flap, zipped it closed, then pressed her fingers to her eyes under her glasses. The tears welled, and she tried to push them back. This was ridiculous. She fought with Josh all the time. And Delilah had every right to stay back from a hike, to stay back from *her.*

But Claire had never been great with conflict. When she was young, her parents fought nonstop, her mother completely miserable for most of their life in San Francisco. After her father took off and she and her mom moved to Bright Falls, Claire spent years making sure her mother was okay, making their life as smooth as possible, always following the rules as much as she could.

Then she got pregnant.

Even then, her mother supported her—they'd been all each other had for so long—and everything ended up okay. Wonderful even. But then she and Josh started arguing, two stupid kids with huge adult problems, and she always ended up crying when they fought, always ended up feeling pathetic. And now Iris was most certainly pissed off at her for abandoning her with Shit Trousers, so essentially, Claire had just made everything worse. Still, she couldn't have gone on that hike without doing what she was doing right now—letting a few tears fall to get some release and heaving some shuddering breaths. She just needed a few minutes, then she'd be fine. She'd be ready to find her daughter, ignore whatever Delilah was doing, and figure out a way to make it up to Iris. She'd be—

The tent door unzipped, and before Claire had a chance to wipe her face dry or at least pull her shirt over her head to hide what were probably very blotchy cheeks and red eyes, Delilah was ducking into the tent.

"Oh, hey," Claire said. Calm. Breezy. Except her voice sounded thick and watery. She turned her back to the other woman, squatting down to unzip her pack and find her swimsuit.

"What's wrong?" Delilah asked, her voice so gentle it made Claire want to cry even more. Which she absolutely was not going to do.

"Nothing." She found her red-and-white polka-dot one-piece and clutched it to her chest as she stood up. "Just . . . I think I'm allergic to something out here."

God, she was getting good at lying.

"Claire, that's bullshit."

Okay, apparently not good enough.

She sighed and turned to face Delilah. "I just . . . I had a fight with Josh. It's not a big deal, but it threw me off."

Delilah's eyes went soft. The inside of the tent was hot, humid, despite the coolness in the June air outside. There wasn't a whole lot of space in here to begin with, and as Delilah took a step closer, Claire swore she felt their breaths mingling.

"What did you fight about?" Delilah asked.

Claire shrugged, her chest tight again. "Ruby. Us. The same thing over and over."

A little dip appeared between Delilah's brows, but she just nodded. "What can I do to help?"

Claire didn't expect that question. Not from Delilah. A nod of sympathy, sure. A joke about the universal awfulness of straight cis white men, perhaps. But not this caring offer, spoken while her arms slid around Claire's waist and pulled her closer. It made her want to bury her face in the other woman's neck, breathe in that smell that was all Delilah, sun and rain all at once.

"I . . . I don't know," Claire said. "Come down to the springs with me?"

The plea fell from her mouth before she could rethink it. It was a perfectly reasonable answer, but the way she said it, desperately and with a slight pant, made her want to curl up in a little ball again.

Except Delilah didn't seem to mind. She smiled, pulling Claire's hips flush against hers. Want fluttered low in Claire's belly.

"Is that all?" Delilah asked, then her tongue dipped into Claire's collarbone.

"Um . . . well . . ." Claire said, but when Delilah's teeth grazed her skin, a moan slipped out instead of any coherent words. She dropped her swimsuit and buried her hands in Delilah's curls.

"That helps, huh?" the other woman asked.

"A . . . a little."

"What about this?" Delilah's fingers went to the button on Claire's cutoffs. She flicked the clasp free, then worked the zipper down so slowly, Claire felt the vibration between her legs.

"That . . . yeah, that might help," she said. She pressed the back of one hand to her mouth to try and stay quiet as Delilah slipped a hand inside her shorts and palmed her over her underwear, fingers pressing and exploring.

"Already wet," Delilah said, lips on her neck.

God, she was. Claire felt like she'd spent this entire week soaking wet, anytime she was around Delilah Green, even before they started . . . whatever this was.

Delilah's fingers worked over the cotton in delicious circles. Claire gripped her shoulders, her legs wobbly, her hips pushing against Delilah's hand.

"Okay?" Delilah asked, fingers moving north to slowly glide along the waistband of Claire's underwear.

Claire could only nod in response, desperate for Delilah's skin on hers. The other woman didn't make her wait long, releasing her own quiet moan as she dipped into Claire's wet heat. Delilah circled this way and that, exploring slowly, tortuously, before she slid one finger inside and pressed her palm against Claire's clit.

Claire gasped, tipped her head back. Delilah's tongue flicked out to taste the skin just under her ear as she inserted another curling finger, pumping them so her hand rubbed right where Claire needed it.

"Faster," Claire whispered, nails biting into Delilah's bare shoulders. Other words flowed from her mouth, things Claire had never said during sex, complete and utter dirty talk, but she didn't care because this—this was what she needed. Fucking, hard and fast, nothing emotional about it.

She bucked her hips against Delilah's talented fingers, grinding against her hand until she broke. Her orgasm blazed through her, and she sagged against Delilah, her cries muffled by the other woman's neck. Delilah kept her hand in place until Claire stopped shuddering, and even when she was done, Delilah took her sweet time, fingers teasing and caressing as they slowly emerged from Claire's pants.

"Better?" Delilah asked, a smirk on her mouth.

Claire tried to smirk back, but she just ended up laughing, a space opening up in her chest she couldn't explain. "Much better." Her hand went to Delilah's jeans, more than ready to return the favor, but Delilah stopped her.

"Later," she said.

Claire frowned. "What? But I want to—"

"I know." Delilah took Claire's hand and wrapped it around her own waist, pulling them together even closer, mouths bumping as she spoke. "And you will. But right now, let's go swimming. You wanted to see Ruby, right?"

Claire exhaled against her. "Yeah."

Delilah nodded. "So let's do it."

She went to pull back, probably to get her own swimsuit, but Claire yanked her closer. She kept her eyes open as they kissed, soft and slow. Once they parted and turned away from each other so they could change into their swimsuits while keeping their hands to themselves, Claire could've sworn she saw a spark of something that looked a lot like happiness in Delilah's expression.

"IRIS IS GOING to kill me."

Claire glanced at Delilah as they walked along the trail toward the springs. She wore a black bikini top that put all of her tattoos on display, along with a pair of high-waisted denim shorts and her boots. She looked soft and badass all at once, and Claire couldn't stop staring at her.

It was a problem.

"Why?" Delilah asked, her own eyes on the pine straw.

"I left her alone with Spencer and Astrid," Claire said.

Delilah winced. "Yeah, she's not going to thank you for that. Not unless you somehow managed to further Operation Shit Boot from afar."

Claire groaned but then stopped abruptly, her hand flying out to land on Delilah's arm.

"That's it," she said.

"What's it?"

"Operation Shit Boot." She turned to Delilah, and what felt like a Cheshire cat grin curled her mouth.

"What about it?"

Claire flapped her hands around. "We need to . . . I don't know. Further it."

Delilah lifted a brow. "Are you talking about shenanigans?"

"Yes!" Claire clapped her hands once and then pointed at Delilah. "Exactly. Camp shenanigans."

"Like pouring honey all over his sleeping bag or something? Because I'm here for that."

Claire frowned. "Well, not exactly like that. I mean . . . he's sharing a tent with Astrid. I want to drive him nuts, not her."

"We could feed them both a sleeping pill and then pull his air mattress out onto the springs like in that movie *The Parent Trap*."

"Oh my god, I love that movie." Claire tapped her chin. "I don't think he has an air mattress though."

"And the water's not exactly dragging distance," Delilah said.

"Give him some sugar water for the bugs?"

"You know how he hates bugs."

They laughed, but nothing they'd mentioned felt feasible or, well, mature. But Claire didn't care about maturity right now. She cared about *this*. Delilah and her under the trees, plotting like teenagers to help their friend. It felt like something more than just planning a prank—it felt like getting something back, something fun and light and meaningful that they never got to have as girls.

Something Claire never even thought to try for.

But she could one hundred percent try for it now.

"Maybe we should consult the oracle," Claire said, taking Delilah's hand and lacing their fingers together as they started walking again.

"Ah, the all-knowing," Delilah said, smiling. "Now if Astrid could draw the praying mantis card, that would be ideal. Just bite his head the hell off and be done with it."

Claire laughed. "I seriously doubt she'd draw the apple."

"Well, she's not a horndog like you."

"Hey now." Claire bumped their shoulders together, and Delilah bumped right back. They walked like that for a while, nearly reaching the springs before Claire's posture snapped straight.

"I've got it," she said, turning them around and pulling Delilah back toward camp by the hand.

"I thought we were going swimming," Delilah asked.

"We are," Claire said, knocking a pine needle–covered limb out of her way. "But first we need to make a little stop by Josh's cooking supplies."

CHAPTER

TWENTY-FOUR

HALF AN HOUR later, Delilah couldn't stop smiling as they hurried along the trail toward the springs. Her fingers tangled with Claire's under the trees, and Claire kept releasing these little giggles that made Delilah feel like she was back in high school, but not any kind of high school she'd ever experienced. This high school felt like *belonging* and *friendship* and *laughter*. Delilah didn't even have those things now, much less back when she was a kid.

There were a million feelings curling in her gut, confusing and addictive. She wasn't sure what to do with them all other than ignore them, push them down, and focus on the way Claire's palm felt pressed against hers.

The way Claire seemed . . . happy.

It was a heady sensation, making a beautiful woman smile and laugh like that. So heady, in fact, that when the trees cleared and the small natural pool sparkled in front of them, Ruby squealing as Josh tossed her into the air, Delilah and Claire didn't let go of each other. Not at first. For a second it felt so . . . normal, to be holding hands in front of other people.

But when Ruby resurfaced, Claire pulled her fingers free. Delilah determined not to let it bother her, the secrecy. Claire was an adult who had a kid, and Delilah knew she was no one's idea of a dream partner.

She got it.

But as Claire walked away from her and toward the water, kicking off her shoes and sliding her shorts down her lovely thighs, Delilah was starting to think she didn't like it.

She didn't like it one bit.

DELILAH SPENT THE rest of the afternoon with Ruby. They swam in the steamy water while Claire spoke in low tones with Josh, Delilah pretending she couldn't hear the stress in Claire's voice the whole time. Later, when they got back to camp and changed into dry clothes, she sat with Ruby on a log and showed her how to edit the birdbath photo the girl had taken the night before.

"Whoa," Ruby said as Delilah adjusted the exposure. "That's amazing, how much of a difference it makes."

"Well, the trick is," Delilah said, fiddling with the saturation, "make it look like you didn't edit it at all. Figure out what to do so that the natural light, color, tone is all enhanced, not completely altered. Like, look at this part right here." Delilah pointed to the flower floating in the middle of the dingy water on the screen. "What would you do to make it look better?"

Ruby screwed up her face in thought. "I'd . . . I'd sharpen it."

Delilah smiled and nudged her shoulder. "Me too." She tapped the *Detail* tab and handed the phone over to Ruby. "Go for it."

The girl played around with the sharpening tool, watching how it changed the photo, before deciding on a setting that outlined the flower a little more clearly against the water.

"What else?" Delilah asked.

Ruby stared down at the phone. "The color. I want it to look kind of . . . faded?"

"Why?"

"Because . . . because it's sort of a sad picture? An old birdbath, a single flower, dirty water. It's not . . . it's not something birds actually use. It's forgotten."

Delilah's mouth parted as she watched the girl frown at her photo, her chest tightening. But not in a bad way. In a way that brought back that feeling she had with Claire earlier, like years reforming themselves. Ruby saw the world in a way that felt familiar to Delilah, an artist's point of view, and it could be a lonely way to move through life. Ruby wasn't alone, of course. She had myriad people who cared about her, so she and Delilah were different in that way. But in other ways, with this little birdbath and what it might symbolize, they were alike.

And it was . . . comforting.

Delilah felt a wild urge to reach out and tuck the girl's damp hair behind her ear. She didn't. Instead, she just nodded. "Yeah. Fading the color would be really powerful."

Ruby looked up at her. "Really?"

"Absolutely." She tapped on the *Color* tab. "You can adjust the temperature here—like cooler and warmer tones—and the vibrancy, which will leach out that color without making it full-on black-and-white."

Ruby nodded and started fiddling with the app. Delilah sat back, and when she looked up, she saw Claire watching them from the picnic table. She'd tried to appease Josh by offering to help with the chili he planned to cook, so now she was popping open cans of beans and dumping them into a pot while he seared some meat over the firepit. Claire had a little smile on her face, her eyes soft as she watched Ruby create.

Delilah got up, leaving Ruby to do her thing, and sat across from Claire at the table.

"Thank you for that," Claire said, prying open another can of black beans.

"Nothing to thank me for," Delilah said. "It was fun. She's an amazing kid, Claire."

Claire beamed. "She is."

"She's talented."

"You think so?"

"Hell yes. She draws really well, and she's got a good eye, good instincts."

Claire took a deep breath, but then her smile faded as she looked off toward the trail. "Should we be worried that they're still not back?"

Delilah frowned, picking up Claire's phone to look at the time. The hikers had been gone awhile. "Did you text Iris?"

Claire nodded. "And Astrid. Three times. But the signal's not great out here."

"Maybe they—"

But she was cut off by the sound of voices coming from the trail. The three hikers appeared, all of them scowling, and they looked . . . well, they looked horrible. Spencer was fully clothed and soaking wet, including his leather sneakers, which made a distinct squelching sound as he stomped into view. Iris had twigs sticking out of her hair, and Astrid's expression was a thunderstorm.

No, a hurricane.

"Uh-oh," Claire said, wincing. She stood up and started toward her friends, but stopped when Spencer flung his pack down with a loudly yelled "thank fuck that's over" and then disappeared into his tent.

"What happened?" Claire asked as Astrid took a deep breath and rubbed her eyes.

"Nothing," she said. "We just got a little lost."

"Shit," Josh said, standing up from where he was squatting by the fire. "Are you okay?"

"Obviously," Astrid said, her voice dripping with disdain.

Josh lifted his hands as though surrendering and went back to cooking, muttering something under his breath Delilah couldn't decipher.

"*We* didn't get lost," Iris said. "Spencer, oh great wonder of the outback, got us lost."

"Iris," Astrid said, sighing. "Just drop it."

"It's not my fault your fiancé can't stick to a trail," Iris said. "The path is clearly marked, but oh no, he just had to be Daniel Boone out there."

"He wanted to explore."

"That's how people die in the woods, Astrid, which I clearly told him."

"Well, we didn't die."

"No, we just got a million bug bites, saw a fucking black bear, and ran out of water an hour ago. Real good time exploring."

"Whoa, whoa, you saw a *bear*?" Claire asked.

"It was far away," Astrid said, rolling her eyes. "And it didn't even hear us."

Delilah grabbed her water bottle and walked it over to Iris, who snatched it out of her hands and gulped it noisily. Claire offered hers to Astrid, who took it with her eyes focused on the ground.

"The only good part was when Spencer Dearest took a little tumble after he decided he could never be a real man unless he forded the great rivers of the earth."

"Oh, for Christ's sake, Iris," Astrid said. "He was trying to fill up his water bottle."

"Good way to get cholera, that," Iris said.

Astrid shoved the bottle back into Claire's hands and stomped off toward her tent without another word.

"Jesus," Delilah said, fighting a smile. Nothing was more entertaining than an Astrid Parker off her poised game. But when she turned back around to see Iris glaring at Claire and Claire wringing her hands, her joy evaporated.

"You," Iris said, teeth gritted. "Left. Me."

"I'm sorry," Claire said. "I thought—"

"You left me alone with them, and you know I can't keep my mouth shut around that shit loafer."

"What did you say to him?" Claire asked.

"Which time? When he wouldn't shut up about his precious Italian leather shoes that he wore into the fucking woods or when he kept telling Astrid that there was no shame in using a walking stick since she was pretty out of shape? Or, no, wait, how about the time he started grilling me about why Grant and I aren't married and don't have any kids, even though Astrid asked him to drop it, and then he started waxing poetic about how my eggs were drying up?"

"Holy shit, he said that?" Claire asked.

"He said that. I'm just glad Grant had to work today and wasn't around to hear it." Iris's shoulders slumped, all her breath leaving her lungs as she rubbed her forehead.

Delilah felt as though she was missing something here, something important and best-friend-shaped, but she didn't know how to ask.

"Honey, I'm so sorry," Claire said, stepping close to Iris and rubbing her arms. "Josh and I fought and I just—"

"I get it," Iris said, her voice soft now. "But our plan, I fear, has gone to shit."

"I don't know," Delilah said. "Astrid didn't look happy."

"Yeah," Iris said. "With me."

Delilah tilted her head. "Maybe a little. But it sounds like Spencer was a real jackass. Maybe she's partly frustrated with him too."

Iris looped her arm through Claire's and rested her head on her friend's shoulder, her anger clearly forgotten. "Maybe. I did find out that she didn't ask him to come on the trip."

"She didn't?" Claire asked.

"Nope. When we got lost, they started arguing because Astrid wanted to turn back and he thought we should keep going. He snapped at her that the trip was her idea, and she snapped back that she hadn't asked him to come in the first place. That he just *had* to tag along because he didn't think she could brave the woods by herself."

"Oh my god," Claire said. "He actually said that to her?"

"Well, Astrid isn't exactly a wilderness girl," Delilah said.

Iris glare at her. "Not the point. The point is he thinks she's totally incompetent, and she knows it."

"Poor Astrid," Claire said. "What do we do?"

"We just need to talk to her, Claire," Iris said. "Enough is enough. You and me. Tonight."

Claire nodded, grabbing onto Iris's hand. Neither woman looked at Delilah or tried to include her in their BFF plan. And that was just fine with Delilah. Totally and absolutely fine.

She turned away and left them alone to plan out what they'd say to Astrid, and she sat back down next to Ruby to see what beauty the girl had created.

EVERYONE HAD CALMED down by the time they all sat around the fire to eat. Delilah sat with Ruby, who had taken a few more pictures with Delilah's phone and wanted to show her what she did with them. Delilah was more than happy to disappear into the world of color and angles and tone for a little while. These last few days had been a lot with Claire, and honestly, she could use a break from all the thinking and feeling. Josh sat on Ruby's other side, listening to his daughter tell Delilah all about her vision for an image of the evergreens against the sky. Delilah kept shooting glances at him, watching him for signs of boredom or disdain—or for signs that he couldn't keep his eyes off his ex—but he didn't rise to the occasion. Instead he oohed and aahed over his daughter's photographs, asking her questions here and there. Mostly, though, he shut up and let Ruby talk, let her have her moment. Delilah would say she was impressed, but she didn't feel like being so charitable toward him quite yet.

Claire was busy with Iris. They sat close together on a log, talking and laughing, but constantly looking over at Astrid, who was pressed against Spencer's side at the picnic table while he rambled on and on about all the bug bites he'd incurred on the hike.

Astrid barely responded, her eyes glazed over while she ate.

They'd all been eating for about ten minutes when Delilah noticed a sudden quiet. Spencer had finally shut his mouth, and a frown puckered his golden brows. She watched him shift on the bench as though trying to get comfortable . . . then shift again.

She cleared her throat, trying to get Claire's attention, but her face was turned away as she and Iris talked in low voices.

She cleared her throat again, then coughed.

"Do you need some water, Delilah?" Astrid asked, her tone already annoyed.

"Yes, thank you so much," Delilah said, then sipped from her water bottle. Astrid rolled her eyes and went back to staring at her food, while Spencer was most decidedly starting to sweat next to her. He couldn't sit still, and Delilah watched as he tried to adjust his crotch as surreptitiously as possible.

She coughed again. "Phew, this chili is *spicy*," she said loudly.

This, finally, got Claire's attention. She glanced at Delilah, who widened her eyes meaningfully and ticked her head toward Spencer.

"Really?" Josh said, frowning at his bowl. "I barely added any cayenne to it. Turns out, I didn't bring as much as I thought I did."

Delilah choked on a laugh, something giddy and girlish and just plain *fun* rising up in her chest. Claire covered her mouth with her hand, and Iris watched Spencer with a maniacal sort of glee sparkling in her eyes. Claire had clearly told Iris how she and Delilah had *borrowed* Josh's cayenne pepper and sprinkled a generous amount in all four pairs of Spencer's black Ralph Lauren boxer briefs, and now the three women watched as Spencer squirmed and sweated, wiping his brow with the back of his hand.

"Are you all right?" Astrid asked, finally noticing her fiancé's discomfort.

He nodded, but his face was quickly turning red, perspiration dripping down his temples.

"You're not," Astrid said, alarmed. "What is going on?"

"Just . . . ah, fuck!" This time he didn't even bother trying to hide the fact that he was pawing at his crotch. He scrambled off the bench, his body jolting this way and that to try and get some relief.

"What the hell?" Josh said.

"Is he okay?" Ruby asked.

"Oh, he's totally fine," Delilah said, waving her hand, but then Spencer yanked off his khaki shorts, revealing his boxer briefs and grabbing at himself in desperation.

"Whoa, dude, whoa!" Josh yelled, clapping his hands over Ruby's eyes.

"Spencer!" Astrid leaped up from the picnic table and pushed at her fiancé's chest, shoving him toward their tent before he could expose himself further.

"Water! I need water!" he screeched. Astrid grabbed her water bottle from the table and then continued to haul him toward their tent. Once they were safely tucked inside, his moans and groans and *what the fucks* echoing against the trees, the rest of the party sat in stunned silence for about ten seconds before Iris broke into a fit of laughter so vehement, she fell off the back of the log she was sitting on.

"Oh. My. God," she said, still cackling while lying on the ground, her arms splayed and her chili bowl safely tucked between her feet.

"What just happened?" Josh said.

Delilah locked eyes with Claire, her own laugh bubbling onto her tongue.

"Well, Josh," she said, "let's just say we owe you some cayenne pepper."

DELILAH COULDN'T SLEEP.

It was too damn quiet, too hot in this tent, and her mind was too damn busy. Claire was next to her, completely conked out and snoring softly, Iris on her other side. Earlier, after it became clear that Astrid and Spencer were not going to emerge from their tent for the rest of the night—and Iris stopped laughing like a villain in a Disney movie—they'd all settled down around the fire as the sun slipped behind the evergreens. They spent the next couple of hours drinking the beer Josh had brought in one of the huge coolers and listening as Josh spun campy ghost stories for Ruby, who didn't seem the least bit freaked out about a girl who found a spider bite on her cheek after a camping trip and then watched in her mirror at home as the boil burst and a million baby spiders spilled out.

"Josh," Claire had said at the story's conclusion, rubbing her cheek absently.

"What?" He smiled, then nudged Ruby, who couldn't stop laughing and babbling about what an amazing photograph that would've made.

"Wouldn't it, Delilah?" she asked.

"It totally would," she said, winking at the girl.

Claire shook her head, but her gaze kept drifting toward Astrid's tent, concern creasing her brow. Iris told her over and over not to worry, that they'd talk to Astrid tomorrow when they all got back to Bright Falls. She nodded, but Delilah could almost feel her stress on her own shoulders, which was a preposterous idea.

Delilah didn't care if Astrid was pissed about the pepper. And she certainly didn't care if Spencer was sporting a rather large rash on his crotch. She didn't care that Iris had sat next to her near the fire and leaned her cheek on Delilah's shoulder, still hiccupping from laughing so hard, and just . . . stayed like that. Delilah kept expecting her to say something about the pepper, but she didn't. Iris Kelly simply sat there for a good ten minutes, *snuggling* with the Ghoul of Wisteria House while she sipped her beer.

Delilah proceeded to chug her own drink, hoping the alcohol would calm her down and give her the courage to shrug Iris's face away, but it didn't. If anything, it made her more maudlin, and the word *friends* kept lighting up in her brain like June fireflies.

Once they all settled into their tents at the ungodly hour of nine thirty and Iris went to pee in the woods, Claire had curled toward her in her sleeping bag, stolen a kiss, and whispered in her ear about sneaking off to the soaking tubs once Iris was asleep.

"She's impossible to wake up once she's out," Claire had said.

Delilah had agreed, eager for . . . something. She felt unsettled and anxious, so maybe an hour with Claire's skin under her hands and mouth would do the trick. But Claire, exhausted after getting next to no sleep the night before, was completely unconscious within thirty minutes of announcing her midnight hookup plan.

So now here Delilah was, wide awake despite her own lack of sleep, staring at the tent's roof and nearly suffocating with the heat of three bodies under a June sky. Claire mumbled something and then flopped an arm over Delilah's stomach, pushing closer to her until her mouth was pressed right up against Delilah's neck. She was still asleep, her limbs heavy, but Delilah couldn't stop the slow spread of comfort that wound its way through her veins as she drifted her fingers over Claire's soft arm.

Finally, she sat up, her heart pumping too fast to sleep now. She wiggled out from under Claire, shucking her sleeping bag off her bare legs, and unzipped the tent. Cool night air flowed in, and she sat there on her knees in the entrance for a second, waiting for her heart to go back to normal.

About twenty feet away, remnants from the fire still glowed. Delilah crawled from the tent, heading toward Josh's coolers for another beer, but found them locked tight with a complicated mechanism she couldn't half see in the darkness.

"What the fuck?" she said quietly, squatting down to squint at the lock.

"It's so the bears don't get into it."

"Jesus Christ!" Delilah tumbled backward onto her ass, heart rate definitely pumping at full speed now.

"Nope, just me," Astrid said languidly, tipping her own beer can at Delilah from where she sat on a log by the fire. "Though that was worth it to see you fall on your butt and screech like a little kid."

"I did not screech like a little kid," Delilah said, standing up and brushing the dirt off her sleep shorts.

"You did. It's okay." Astrid blinked at her, a blanket around her shoulders, hair slightly less coiffed than it usually was, and a definite intoxicated gleam to her eyes. Of course it could just be the firelight, but her voice was also a bit fuzzy. Delilah had never seen Astrid Parker drunk. Not once, even during their teenage years when she would watch from her window at one in the morning as her stepsister, Iris, and Claire sneaked out on sleepover nights, meeting boys at Bryony Park a half mile down the road from Wisteria House. Astrid always came back stone-cold sober. So did Claire for that matter. Iris, not so much.

"Just lift the bottom latch and then twist it to the left," Astrid said, motioning toward the cooler.

Delilah watched her for a second before squatting back down and following her stepsister's directions. Sure enough, the cooler popped open, revealing a few beer cans floating in a sea of watery ice. She grabbed one and locked the cooler again before walking toward the fire. She settled on a log across from Astrid, far enough away to indicate she was not here to talk. There was just nowhere else to go, not in the dark of night with black bears and god knew what else roaming the forest.

"Spencer okay?" she asked, cracking open the beer. The question popped out, untried and impulsive. She wasn't sure what Astrid suspected about Spencer's little, er, problem from earlier. The pepper was odorless and was hard to see against the black cotton of his boxers, especially in the fading sunlight. It would probably look like a little bit of dirt if one peered closely. Either way, Delilah expected at least some backlash, narrowed eyes and some snarky retort, because that's how the two of them had always interacted, even if Delilah had simply asked about the weather. But Astrid didn't do any of that. She just sighed, took another swallow of beer, and shrugged.

Delilah watched her, brain automatically calculating what to say next to get under Astrid's skin, to piss her off, annoy her, passive-aggressively guilt her over one thing or another, all her usual mechanisms for interacting with her stepsister.

She came up with nothing. Astrid looked small, lost even, shoulders rounded and purple half-moons snuggled under her eyes. Nothing a little concealer wouldn't fix, but still. Delilah couldn't remember a time she'd seen Astrid look so disheveled.

Her fingers itched for her camera or her phone, the vision of Astrid looking like a character from a horror movie—at least by Astrid's own standards—almost too heady to resist. She didn't move though. After all these damned emotions from the last few days, she found she didn't have the clarity of mind for wicked-stepsister games tonight.

So she didn't play them. She drank her beer and let the cool summer breeze slide over her skin. She stared into the fire and tried to pretend Astrid wasn't even there. This proved impossible, however, as in the absence of any bitchy banter, Delilah's mind filled with all the things that led back to Astrid in one way or another—Claire, Iris, Ruby, the wedding and the money she'd be paid for it, even the show at the Whitney, which just reminded her how desperate she was to be something, someone in this world. Someone who mattered and who people remembered, who people wondered about and sought out, even if they were just strangers chasing the emotions her photographs evoked.

Usually, this line of thinking led to a steely resolve—produce mind-blowing pieces for the Whitney, work harder, think more creatively, forge more contacts with artists and gallery owners, be more, do more, don't stop until that piece sells or her vision for another series comes to fruition. Now, though, Ruby's wide-eyed wonder filled her thoughts. The girl's awe, excitement over creating. Claire slid right in there too, the way she felt in Delilah's arms, the sounds she made when Delilah touched her, the way she drifted toward Delilah even in her sleep.

Which had to have been accidental. Claire was a snuggler—Delilah knew that from their first night together—and Claire had simply been facing Delilah's direction. She would've burrowed against Iris had she been turned the other way.

Wouldn't she?

Fuck. Delilah rubbed her forehead and gulped her beer. Fresh air, it seemed, was doing very little to get rid of these goddamn *feelings*.

"What's wrong?" Astrid asked.

Delilah's head snapped up. "What? Nothing."

Now came the quintessential narrowing of eyes. "Bullshit."

"You're a real connoisseur of swear words lately."

"Hard to hold them in around you."

Delilah smiled at her across the fire. "Me? Are you sure about that?"

"Why wouldn't I be?"

"Well, you're out here in the cold drinking a beer, for god's sake. What did you call it once? A loaf of bread in a can?"

"That's just a fact. Have you seen the carb count on these things?"

"Meanwhile," Delilah went on, "your Prince Charming is sleeping under the stars cuddled up in his feather duvet."

"He didn't bring a feather duvet."

"Okay, fine, a silk duvet. Point is, maybe something else is pulling out all your *shits* and *fucks*."

She waited for Astrid's retort, something supremely bitchy and most likely demeaning, but she met Delilah's proclamation with nothing but silence. Her stepsister swirled her beer in the can, eyes downcast. It was the perfect situation, really, to keep annoying her, poking at her like a sleeping bear. Maybe it was the liquid bread, but instead, Delilah found herself suddenly wondering what Claire would say or do in this situation. It was a strange thought. Even stranger, she actually knew what Claire would say and do. She'd be sweet. She'd be comforting. She'd put Astrid's happiness before her own. She'd *care*.

And that had never been how Delilah and Astrid operated.

"Do you remember when my mother had the sex talk with us?" Astrid asked.

"Oh god." That was definitely not what she was expecting. "Why would you bring up such a horrible memory?"

A tiny smile ghosted across Astrid's mouth. "We were, what? Twelve?"

"And already knew about sex from Bright Falls's inept sex education curriculum. Thank god for the cheap romance novels our baby-sitter always seemed to leave stuck in the couch cushions, is all I'm saying."

Astrid laughed. "Oh my god. I just remember that one where the courtesan or whoever liked to tie her lover to the queen's throne."

"And then make him call her *Your Majesty*? If that didn't teach us all we needed to know, I don't know what would."

"Mom's version was a little different."

Delilah sat up straight, holding her beer can like a teacup and sticking out her pinkie. "Now, dears," she said with an affected British accent that sounded nothing like Isabel Parker-Green, "be sure you always use the little girl's room after being *intimate*, and for goodness' sake, *don't* let him talk you into getting on top."

Astrid laughed loudly, then clapped a hand over her mouth. "She did not say that last part."

"She was thinking it. Trust me."

Astrid's smile faded. "Yeah, she probably was." Then her voice took on a ghostly quality, eyes glazing over. "'It's not always pleasant, but it makes your husband happy, so I count it time well spent.'"

"What?"

"That's what she said." Her gaze met Delilah's. "You don't re-member that part?"

"Not verbatim," Delilah said. "Plus, by twelve years old, I already had a good feeling that the word *husband* would never apply to me, so I probably just zoned out whenever she went down that road."

Astrid nodded. "She said it. And I've never forgotten it."

"Wait, wait, wait," Delilah said, standing up and moving to a log next to her stepsister. "She really said that? In those words?"

Another nod.

"You know how disturbing this is considering she was married to my father, right?"

Astrid winced but smiled at Delilah, something like camaraderie blooming between them. Delilah felt suddenly young and hopeful, which was just silly. She wasn't that young anymore, and she'd never associated Astrid with hope by any stretch of the imagination.

"Sorry," Astrid said. "Yeah, that's weird, but . . . I can't stop think-ing about it for some reason."

"So Spencer's terrible in bed. Is that what this is about?"

Astrid groaned. "No, he's—"

"Because you know that's bullshit right? That a woman has to have sex with her man—or any partner—to keep them happy?"

"I know. It's not about the actual sex; it's the spirit behind what she said. Like I have to . . ." She trailed off, staring out into the space in front of her. Firelight danced in her wide eyes, and Delilah swore she saw a tiny swell of tears, but Astrid blinked it away before she could be sure.

"Like you have to what?" Delilah asked softly.

Astrid looked down, trailed her finger along the beer can's rim. "Say yes. All the time, no matter what. Be calm and poised and con-trolled and just say yes."

They sat in silence for a few seconds, Astrid's confession hovering between them. Delilah thought back to their childhood, their teen years, all the attention Isabel lavished upon Astrid with her grades and track, her monthly trips to the salon, balanced diets and French lessons, debate team in high school and early admission and a bachelor's degree in business. All the things Isabel had never bothered to push for Delilah. Well, that wasn't strictly true. Isabel had hounded her about her homework, made sure she ate a decent dinner every night, but regarding everything else, right down to Delilah's wild hair and disdain for anything resembling a sport, Isabel let her be. She accepted Delilah's refusals so easily, like they were a relief and she could focus her attention where it really mattered, on her perfect Astrid, who never put up a fuss about slipping into a satin gown and parading around a fundraiser like a princess.

Astrid was right. She never said no. But Delilah had always assumed she'd never wanted to.

"Astrid—" Delilah started, but her stepsister cut her off when she stood up abruptly.

"You don't care about any of this," Astrid said, waving her hand and offering Delilah a plasticky smile. She wrapped the blanket more tightly around her shoulders and swept off toward her tent before Delilah could say anything else.

CHAPTER
TWENTY-FIVE

CLAIRE DIDN'T TALK to Astrid or Delilah for the next two days.

Saturday morning at the campsite had been quiet, all of them except Josh and Ruby either hungover or sleep-deprived or, in Delilah's case, still zonked out in the tent by the time they were all ready to pack up. Astrid and Spencer left before Josh had even finished making breakfast over the fire, giving Claire and Iris zero chances to talk to her, and then Delilah slept the entire drive back to town.

Now it was Monday evening and Claire felt like she was coming out of her skin. She and Iris had texted a lot over the weekend, but it was mostly about how neither of them could get in touch with Astrid. Claire would've driven over to Astrid's house and confronted her there, but both she and Iris had been swamped with work at their respective shops, making up for the time off they'd taken for the spa and the impromptu camping trip. Plus, she didn't want to ambush her best friend. It was time to be honest about their worries, yes, but she and Iris agreed that they still had to approach the whole situation gingerly, particularly now that Astrid was clearly avoiding them and wouldn't make it easy.

All of that stress might have been manageable—after all, she'd been worried about Astrid ever since her best friend got engaged—but now there was Delilah, who had definitely not texted or called or come by the store since they got back from Bagby Springs. Granted, Claire hadn't called or texted her either. Calling or texting had a decidedly *dating* tone to it, and they definitely weren't dating. And since they weren't dating, reaching out in any form seemed more like a booty call, which didn't feel right at all.

Nothing felt right.

She knew this was what casual looked like, and she told herself over and over again that she was fine with it. She told herself she was fine with it when Ruby asked if Delilah could come over for pizza on Saturday night and she had to say no. She told herself she was fine with it when she rolled over in her bed on Sunday and could still smell Delilah on her pillow. She told herself she was fine with it as she scrolled through Delilah's Instagram on Monday evening while she lay on her couch and the rain came down in sheets outside, ignoring how the ache in her chest bloomed bigger and brighter with each beautiful image.

She was feeling particularly broody as she looked at a photograph of a gorgeous Black woman in a formal tulle-skirted dress standing barefoot in the watery rush of a New York City fire hydrant, a graffitied stone wall behind her. The hydrant's red popped against the woman's neutral clothes, the gray and muted blues and greens of the wall, the water droplets that looked like bits of crystal suspended in midair.

It was a lovely photograph. Wall worthy. Gallery worthy, even.

She'd just tapped on a new breathtaking image, really settling into her self-pity, when the doorbell rang. She shoved off her cocoon of blankets, cursing Josh for being early for once in his life. He was taking Ruby and Tess to a movie tonight, followed by a sleepover at his apartment, and wasn't due to arrive for another fifteen minutes. She pulled up the strap on her tank top that kept slipping down her arm, but didn't even bother to fix her hair, which she'd put up into a messy bun on top of her head once she got home from the bookstore but had now slowly given way to gravity.

"Ruby, your dad's here!" she called down the hall as she reached the door.

"Oh my god, he's early!"

"You hear that?" she said as she wrenched the door open. "You've officially shocked your—"

She blinked into the rain at the person standing on her porch under a pink umbrella with ruffles around the edges. A person who was mostly definitely not Josh.

"I've shocked my what?" Delilah said.

"Um. No one. I thought you were Josh."

"Sorry to disappoint."

"No!" Claire yelled it loud enough that Delilah startled a little. She forced herself to calm down, play it cool. "Sorry. No, I'm not disappointed. Just surprised."

Delilah nodded, and then they stared at each other for a few seconds, during which Claire became acutely aware that she was in a pair of dirty sweatpants, a tank top with an old mustard stain in the area of her left boob, and her hair looked like a wasp's nest. She had on some makeup, but with an evening of self-indulgent brooding and drinking boxed wine ahead of her, she hadn't bothered to freshen up after getting home from the bookstore.

"So, can I come in?" Delilah asked. "I took some photos today that I'd love to show Ruby."

Claire's stomach fluttered, but she backed up. "Yeah, sorry, come in. Though Ruby's about to head out with—"

"Well, hello, ladies." Josh jogged up the front walk in tight jeans, a plain gray T-shirt dappled with rainwater clinging to his chest and arms. "Lovely evening, isn't it?"

"Hey," Claire said. "Ruby's almost ready."

"Cool. Hey, Delilah."

"Hey."

"Nice umbrella."

Delilah glanced up, as though she forgot what the thing looked like. "It's the only one the Kaleidoscope Inn had to loan me."

"How very Strawberry Shortcake of them," Josh said. "What are you two up to tonight?"

"Nothing," Claire said.

"Nothing at all," Delilah said.

Josh frowned, his eyes flitting between the two of them. Claire could almost hear his mind whirring, and she just wanted him out of here. Luckily, Ruby came bounding down the hall at the exact right moment, kissing Claire on the cheek and saying hello to Delilah before launching herself into Josh's arms. Then they were gone in a flurry of Ruby's green rain coat and duffel bag and Josh's promise to have her back tomorrow morning by ten.

Claire watched as her daughter got into the back seat of Josh's truck and buckled up. She left the door open even after they'd pulled away and driven out of sight.

"Sorry," she said. "Ruby's staying with her dad tonight."

"So I gathered," Delilah said.

"Do you . . . I mean . . . Would you . . ."

She couldn't get the words out though. She wanted Delilah to stay, but she didn't want the other woman to think Claire just wanted her to stay for sex. Then again, they'd already established that they were just screwing, so surely, Claire could just ask her to stay without fear. Delilah was the one who'd shown up on her doorstep, for god's sake.

Still, Claire couldn't help but want something more right now. Dinner. A movie. Maybe just splitting a bottle of wine out on her covered porch, listening to the rain and talking.

But that was ridiculous.

That was . . . impossible.

"Do I want to what?" Delilah asked, taking a step closer.

Claire shook her head. "Never mind. I just—"

But then Delilah closed her umbrella and set it outside on the stoop and stepped inside. She pushed Claire's front door closed before crowding into her space, hands on Claire's hips and her mouth bumping up against Claire's bottom lip as she spoke.

"I missed you," she said.

Claire couldn't breathe. Didn't dare. "You did?"

Delilah nodded and then she kissed her—once, twice, soft and sweet that in no way indicated she was expecting to fall into bed immediately. In fact, this kiss, well, it felt like Delilah expected . . . *something more.*

CHAPTER TWENTY-SIX

DELILAH KISSED CLAIRE, then buried her face in the other woman's neck while wrapping her arms around her waist. She inhaled her meadowy scent, the slightest tang of sweat just underneath, and felt her own heart slow down for the first time in two days.

She'd tried.

She'd tried really hard to stay away from Claire ever since Iris dropped her off at the Kaleidoscope Inn on Saturday afternoon. No texts. No calls. And definitely no goddamn impromptu stops by her house. She knew she needed a break from all the feelings this woman stirred up inside her. She'd spent the time taking photographs around town, going through her online portfolio for the Whitney show, hanging out at Stella's last night until close to midnight, but Bright Falls wasn't the easiest town for her to be alone in. It was quiet and still, and while there was a certain charm in the introspection it inspired, Delilah had never been very good at soul-searching.

In fact, she'd staunchly avoided it for the past twelve years.

So it was no surprise that by this morning, she was going out of her mind. She couldn't stop thinking about Astrid and their conversation by the fire. Her entire childhood kept rolling out from where she'd kept it hidden for so long, the ways she'd neatly wrapped up Astrid's coldness and disinterest unraveling.

But maybe even worse than all this incessant *thinking* was this *want*. This pull toward Claire was getting absurd. And it wasn't only about sleeping with her again. Delilah simply wanted to see her, talk to her. Kiss her gorgeous mouth, sure, but even just standing right here in her foyer felt like diving into a cool lake after a walk through the desert.

"Are you okay?" Claire asked, settling her arms around Delilah's shoulders, hands drifting into her hair.

Delilah nodded, face still pressed to her neck. But the truth was, she wasn't sure. She didn't feel okay. She felt small and desperate, a little kid in need of a hug.

"Tell me what's wrong," Claire said.

Delilah finally lifted her head. "I said I was fine."

Claire tilted her head. "And I call bullshit."

"You do?"

"Yeah, I do."

Delilah felt a small smile work its way onto her mouth. That Claire Sutherland could tell when she was bullshitting her—and what's more, seemed to actually care—suddenly felt like a small miracle.

"Let's go do something," Delilah said, pulling Claire closer, hands sliding down her backside. She kissed her, just once.

"Like . . . go out?"

"Yeah." Kiss. "Like go out." Kiss.

Claire laughed. "Where?"

Delilah grinned, an idea springing into her head. She knew Claire wanted to keep their relationship under wraps for now. If she let herself, Delilah could get very moody about the whole thing again, but she just wanted to have fun tonight.

She wanted to take the woman she liked out on a date, plain and simple.

"A place," she said, kissing Claire one more time, "where I can hold your hand."

⁓

"ROLLER SKATING?"

Claire laughed, her hands flying to her mouth as Delilah pulled Claire's Prius into the Sparkles parking lot. The roller rink was in Graydon, a town about twenty-five minutes east of Bright Falls, so there was very little chance of anyone they knew seeing them. Delilah remembered a couple of birthday parties here when she was in elementary school, before her father died and birthday parties were a thing she did like a normal kid.

"Roller skating," she said, getting out of the car and flipping up her ruffled umbrella, then jogging around to the passenger side to open Claire's door for her.

Claire raised her eyebrows at her as she stepped out, the rain and the neon lights from the rink's signage reflected in her glasses. After Delilah had suggested going out, she'd changed into a pair of jeans and a slouchy off-the-shoulder T-shirt, and brushed out her messy hair, which now flowed around her shoulders in soft waves.

"Thank you," she said.

"Let the record state that I'm gallant as shit," Delilah said.

Claire laughed. "I feel very wooed."

Then Delilah slipped her fingers between Claire's and they ran inside while the rain continued to pour down, like two teenagers on a first date. That's a little how Delilah felt as well—giddy and just . . . happy. It was a strange thing, to feel something you hadn't felt in a long time. It made her realize how much she'd missed it, how important the sensation was. For years, she'd been getting by, mistaking physical closeness with someone for a night as actual happiness. But holding Claire's hand right now, sneaking glances at her and watching Claire light up in response, this was something altogether different.

Delilah paid and they got their skates, storing their shoes in little cubbies along the carpeted floor. The shiny wooden rink glimmered under a disco ball, colored lights flashed, and eighties music moved all the skaters along as though on a river.

"I haven't done this in forever," Claire said, laughing as she stepped onto the rink.

"Me either," Delilah said, still holding on to Claire's hand, which turned out to be a mistake. Because when Claire wobbled, so did Delilah. And when the wobbling turned into full-on flailing, both women went down in a flourish of swear words and a tangle of limbs.

"Ow," Claire said, rubbing her ass as tweens and teenagers flew past them and laughed.

"God, it's high school all over again," Delilah said, but she was smiling. She managed to get to her knees, then her feet, pulling Claire up with her. "Okay, let's take this slowly."

"Good idea."

And so they did. Delilah held Claire's hand, and they pushed themselves along the floor, picking up speed after one time around the rink. It was a bit like riding a bike, muscle memory kicking in, and soon they were flying over the lacquered wood, air-conditioned wind in their hair while Whitney Houston sang about feeling the heat with somebody. Skating was so simple, even silly, but as Claire squeezed Delilah's fingers, laughed when Delilah tried to skate backward and landed on her butt again, kissed her quickly after helping her up, Delilah couldn't think of a time she'd ever felt like this.

Not with Jax. Not with anyone.

In the back of her mind, Delilah knew this wasn't a good thing.

She knew this whole deal with Claire was based on the fact that it would end. She knew, and yet, she couldn't stop herself from pressing her mouth to Claire's temple as they stood in line for soda and pizza. She couldn't stop her smile from crinkling up her eyes when Claire tucked an errant curl behind Delilah's ear. She couldn't stop herself from imagining a whole life, so different from the one she'd already made for herself hundreds of miles away.

THEY DIDN'T TALK the entire drive back to Bright Falls. They didn't talk when they pulled into Claire's driveway, or when Delilah flipped up her ridiculous umbrella and put her arm around Claire's shoulders, shielding her from the rain as they ran up the front walk.

They didn't talk as Claire unlocked her door and let them into the dark house, both of their shirts spotted with water. Claire didn't turn on any lights or offer Delilah a drink. She simply took Delilah's hand and led her to the bedroom. There, Claire undressed her, slowly and with this serious look on her face that made Delilah's throat go thick. Claire's fingers shook, and Delilah grabbed her hand, pressed her mouth to Claire's palm. Claire inhaled a ragged breath, but still, neither woman spoke. The room was dark, the only sound their breathing, cotton sliding over skin and puddling on the ground.

Claire pushed on Delilah's sternum, directing her to lie back on the bed. As Delilah obeyed, she kept trying to think of something to say, to laugh about, but none of this felt funny. It didn't feel desperate or like a distraction or something they both needed to relieve some stress. It didn't feel like a spillover of pent-up lust.

It felt like it was on purpose.

Claire pressed her mouth to Delilah's, their tongues touching in a slow, silky dance. They'd stayed like that for a while, just making out soft and easy. When Claire began to glide south, pressing kisses to Delilah's neck, between her breasts, just below her navel, Delilah watched her, hands trailing over any part of Claire's skin she could reach. Need thrummed through her body, not just between her thighs, but everywhere. Her gut, the middle of her chest. It knocked the wind out of her, and Delilah never wanted this to end.

"Wait," she said when Claire parted her legs and started to settle between them. She pulled on Claire's arms, guiding Claire's body north again until they were face-to-face. "I want to see you."

Claire pressed her forehead to Delilah's, kissed her slowly, then adjusted her body so their legs were entwined like pretzels, thighs pressing against each other's centers.

Delilah gasped at the contact. The wet slide of the other woman's skin against hers was almost too much to bear. It was hot and intimate, wild and safe all at once. Delilah rolled her hips, and Claire rolled back, a dance that pulled a moan from Delilah's throat. Claire released a sort of animal sound as Delilah gripped her ass, guiding her up and down and in circles, the press of their centers intense and perfect. Delilah's belly tightened, her clit aching as it slid against Claire's thigh. She sort of wanted to slow down, taste Claire, feel the heat between her legs with her fingers, but she reminded herself that they had time.

They had all night.

Claire arched her back, lifting her torso up a little so that her thigh pressed even harder right where Delilah needed it. She felt her orgasm building as Claire increased her movements, ran her thumb over Delilah's tight nipple. Still, neither woman hurried. Even as Delilah's physical need for release reached a desperate pitch, her veins felt honeyed. Delilah was wrong. She wasn't fucking Claire. They weren't fucking at all. This was something else altogether, though she wasn't sure what. All she knew was that as Claire's body responded to her touch, the other woman's breath quickening, her center pushing against Delilah's for relief, their gazes never left each other.

And when they both came, Claire biting her swollen lower lip, a low groan rumbling in her chest, she kept her eyes open and on Delilah the entire time.

It was the most gorgeous thing Delilah had ever seen.

She didn't untangle herself from Claire. Instead, she unfolded the quilt at the end of the bed and pulled it over their heads, cocooning them inside. She wasn't ready for the outside world yet. She wanted this to last. They had all night, sure, but one night didn't feel like enough. She didn't want the sun to rise, more wedding drama, the end of her two weeks in Bright Falls looming up ahead like a mountain she wasn't sure how to climb. She just wanted this. Claire curled her arms round Delilah's waist and pulled her close, no space at all between their heated skin. Their legs tangled, Delilah's head tucked under Claire's chin, her fingers trailing across Claire's back.

"Do you do this a lot?" Claire asked after a while, twirling one of Delilah's now-frizzy curls between her fingers.

Delilah lifted her head to look at her. "Do what?"

Claire smiled. "Wine and dine your dates."

"You call this wining and dining?"

Claire laughed. "I mean . . . the roller skating and then . . . I don't know . . . this." Claire waved a hand, indicating their curled-together status, which, if it were anyone other than her, Delilah would definitely categorize as cuddling.

The truth was, no, she didn't do this a lot. She didn't *date*. She hooked up. She didn't lie peacefully after sex and cuddle. She rolled over and fell asleep until two a.m., when she usually jolted awake trying to remember where she was before she collected her clothes and went home. She sure as hell had never taken a woman roller skating before. She'd never even taken a partner to dinner. Not since Jax.

Delilah watched Claire watching her. She couldn't be sure what Claire was thinking here, but this thing between them wasn't just casual anymore. Delilah was sure of it. And what was more, Delilah didn't want this to be only that, just kisses and coming. She wanted . . . this. Roller skating and amazing sex and this peaceful sort of talking and *not* talking, cuddling and questions and a place to belong.

A person to belong to.

She had no idea what to say or how this would work. If it *could* work, if Claire even wanted it to work. But for now, she framed Claire's face in her hands and pressed a soft kiss to her mouth.

"No," she whispered. "I've never done this before in my whole life."

Claire seemed to deflate, relaxing against her as she kissed her back, and they didn't talk again for the rest of the night.

CHAPTER TWENTY-SEVEN

TWO DAYS LATER, Claire still felt like she was drifting through a dream. It wasn't always a pleasant dream. Sometimes, it felt more akin to a nightmare, laced with panic and heavy breathing as she wondered how the hell she was going to get through this—whatever she and Delilah were doing—without a broken heart.

But there were decidedly dreamy moments too, remembering how Delilah had kissed her, touched her, how she'd held her hand while they flew over the glossy wood of the skating rink, laughing and eyes sparkling under the disco ball. Never in a million years would Claire think she'd go roller skating with Delilah Green, share a huge slice of greasy pizza and a Coke slushy, then make love in Claire's bed like the world was ending.

Because that's what it had felt like.

Making love.

Not sex and definitely not fucking.

Since Monday night, Delilah and Claire had spent every possible moment together. Delilah had left the next morning before Ruby came home, but then she came by the bookstore after lunch, armed with a camera roll of photos for her and Ruby to sift through and edit together, the two of them sitting on the beanbag chairs in the kids' section while Claire worked. Then Claire made beef stroganoff and the three of them ate dinner together at Claire's kitchen table, and it all felt so normal and right, Claire had to excuse herself to go the bathroom in the middle of the meal, splashing water on her face and forcing a sudden surge of tears back into her eyes.

Now it was Wednesday afternoon, and Claire hadn't seen Delilah since the night before. They'd watched a movie with Ruby after dinner, kissed a little after Ruby went to sleep, but that was it. Claire wasn't super comfortable with deliberate sleepovers with Ruby in the house, so Delilah had gone back to the inn, and Claire went to bed alone and she hated it. She proceeded to spend a restless night, her brain working through a million different ways to tell Delilah that she wanted her.

She never came up with anything very good.

"Ruby, we need to go!" Claire called down the hall. She was dropping her daughter at Tess's house for the night so she and Iris could take Astrid out in Portland for a small, staid bachelorette party. Delilah was coming too—at least Claire hoped she was—and Iris and Claire had already decided to talk to Astrid about Spencer tonight.

Which was a whole other set of problems.

"Mom, I can't get in touch with Dad," Ruby said as she came down the hall with her bag, her brand-new phone in her hand. Claire had finally caved about Ruby having a phone, and Josh had taken her out yesterday morning and gotten one set up for her. Claire had to admit that knowing she could contact Ruby any time she needed to, particularly when her daughter was out with Josh, decreased her stress level a little. All the parental controls smartphones came with these days decreased it a lot.

"What do you mean?" Claire asked, slinging her bag over her shoulder.

"I texted him like four times today, and he hasn't answered."

"Hmm." Claire took out her own phone and waved it in the air. "Send me a text and make sure it's going through."

Ruby tapped at her screen. A second later, Claire's phone pinged with the message.

"See?" Ruby said.

"Okay, well," Claire said, "I'm sure he's fine. Or his phone's dead. He's not the best at keeping it charged."

Ruby nodded, but her brow puckered with worry. Claire felt a pinch of panic. This was exactly how Josh skipped town the last time, two years ago. One day he was here, and the next he was gone. A few days after his disappearing act, he texted Claire his standard apology—*I'm sorry, I need some time, tell Ruby I love her, I'll be back*, blah blah blah.

Now, looking at Ruby, Claire knew her daughter was roaming through the same memories.

"It'll be fine," Claire said, swiping her thumb over Ruby's cheek. "I'm sure he's just busy. He has work, you know." The lie felt wrong on her tongue, but what could she say? She couldn't stand to crush her daughter's hopes just yet. She knew Josh would want the benefit of the doubt, knew he'd been trying, and honestly, he'd been doing pretty amazing this last week. If he really had disappeared again, Claire wasn't ready to face what that meant for their daughter either.

"OH SHIT," IRIS said as she pulled into the driveway of Astrid's small but immaculate Craftsman. Claire sat in the passenger seat and pressed her face against the window. They were supposed to pick up Astrid and then swing by the inn to get Delilah before heading down to Portland, but a bachelorette party seemed like the furthest thing from Astrid's mind right now.

She was standing on her front porch, Spencer next to her with his hands on his hips, and she was screaming.

And throwing clothes onto the lawn.

Men's clothes.

And several pairs of fancy Italian leather shoes.

"What is going on?" Claire asked.

"It doesn't look good, whatever it is," Iris said.

Claire gripped her friend's hand across the center console, her heart squeezing. She wanted to fling the door open and run to Astrid, help her somehow, but this seemed like a pretty personal moment between her and Spencer, and Claire wasn't sure what to do.

Iris pressed a button, and the driver's window rolled down about four inches. Astrid's voice filtered into the car.

". . . can't believe you thought that was okay. It's not. It never will be." Another shoe shot onto the lawn.

"Will you calm the fuck down?" Spencer said. "You're hysterical."

Astrid's expression went nuclear. "Hysterical? This"—she waved her hand around her face—"is a perfectly reasonable and logical reaction to what you did."

Claire sucked in a breath. "What did he do?"

"Who the hell knows with him?" Iris said.

"Should we leave?" Claire asked. "This feels intrusive. Like we're spying on her."

Iris shook her head and opened her mouth, but before she could answer, Spencer yelled again, all the while collecting his clothes.

"I did that for *you*. For us. You need to get out of this town and everyone in it."

"That's not—"

"Your mother? Total nightmare. You're like a rag doll around her. And your friends are fucking miscreants."

Iris's posture snapped straight. "Damn right we are, you shit sock."

"Don't you dare talk about my friends," Astrid said.

"I did you a favor, buying that house in Seattle," Spencer went on. "You're content to be nothing in Bright Falls, Astrid. I'm just trying to get you to see that."

"Holy shit," Iris said.

"He . . . bought a house in Seattle?" Claire asked. Her stomach splashed to her feet, Spencer's proclamations rolling through her like a bulldozer. "I thought they weren't leaving for another year."

"By the looks of it, I think Astrid thought the same thing," Iris said.

Astrid didn't say anything. She just picked up a pin-striped suit jacket and launched it onto the grass.

"That's Armani!" Spencer shrieked, jogging down the steps and collecting the garment.

"That doesn't belong in my house anymore," Astrid said, pointing at him. "And neither do you. Enjoy your new house in Seattle."

"What are you going to do, cancel our whole wedding? Our whole life?" Spencer said, spreading his arms. "We're getting married in three days. You wouldn't dare."

Astrid's face sobered, and her chin started to wobble. Claire opened the car door, ready to intervene, but Astrid didn't give her a chance. She simply turned on her heel and went inside, slamming her front door behind her.

Spencer stared after her for a second, then snatched up the last of his clothes and thundered toward his shiny Mercedes, which was parked on the curb. He glanced at Claire and Iris in the car, flicked them off over a pile of dress shirts like the classy guy he was, then got in his sedan and drove away.

The two women sat in silence for a second before Iris finally spoke.

"I think . . . I think they just broke up?" she said.

Claire blew out a breath. "I think they did."

"That's what we wanted."

Claire nodded, but she felt terrible. Not guilty—Spencer dug his own grave, no doubt about it—but it was hard seeing a friend hurting. Plus . . .

"Isabel's going to kill her," she said.

"Yeah," Iris said with a sigh. "I think she just might."

"No reason for her to die alone, then," Claire said.

Iris squeezed her hand and smiled at her. "One for all, bitches."

They got out of the car and started up the sidewalk, Claire's heart pounding the entire time. Iris rang the bell but then pushed the front door open and stepped inside. Astrid's house, as always, was a vision of modern design and style. Cool gray walls, ecru sofas filled with throw pillows in various shades of blue, distressed wooden console tables, white quartz countertops, and stainless steel appliances. The living area, kitchen, and dining room were one huge space, and windows lined the entire back wall, revealing a small patio and a view of the river in the distance.

"Astrid?" Claire called. "Honey?"

No answer. She glanced at Iris before they both headed for the hall that led to the bedrooms.

Inside her room, Astrid sat on her queen-size bed facing the window, her back to the door. Evening light streamed in through the glass, turning all the grays in the room to lavender.

"Sweetie?" Iris said, walking inside slowly. "We're here."

Astrid didn't move. Her shoulders were rounded, her posture very un-Astrid-like.

"Honey?" Claire said. She moved around Iris so she could sit next to Astrid. The bed dipped, and her friend's shoulder pressed into hers. She moved her arm and wrapped it around Astrid, holding her tight. Iris settled on her other side.

Astrid wasn't crying, but her eyes looked a little red rimmed as she stared vacantly out the window. Claire caught Iris's gaze over Astrid's blond head, a *what do we do?* look passing between them. They didn't know. Finally, Iris's arm came around Astrid's shoulder as well, so that the three of them were locked together, just like they'd always been.

Astrid took a deep breath. She opened her mouth a few times, but it took several tries before she actually spoke.

"I don't love him."

Iris and Claire widened their eyes at each other.

"And I should love the person I'm going to marry," Astrid went on without looking at either one of them. "Shouldn't I?"

"Yes," Claire said softly. Iris smoothed a hand down Astrid's hair.

"I should trust him, be excited about marrying him."

"Also yes," Iris said.

"And I don't. I'm not."

Claire leaned her head against Astrid's.

"He bought a house," Astrid said. "An entire house without telling me. Asking me. He just . . . did it, like I didn't even exist."

"Well, that's a shitty thing to do," Iris said.

"Do you . . . do you remember when my mother signed me up for tennis when I was thirteen?"

Claire caught Iris's eye again, both their mouths pressed flat. Of course they remembered. Astrid hated tennis. She always had, ever since her gym teacher had done a unit on it in fourth grade and a ball hit her square in the nose. But Isabel didn't think track—which had been Astrid's preferred sport since middle school—was a very lady-like activity. It wasn't . . . posh enough. So she'd signed her up for tennis at the Bright River Club, private lessons, crisp white pleated skirts, the whole nine yards.

And Astrid did it for a year before it was clear she was terrible. Only then, when Isabel's reputation for having a clumsy-on-the-court daughter was on the line, did she relent and let Astrid return to track and cross country.

"Yeah," Claire said. "We remember."

Astrid sighed. "She never asked me if I wanted to play. Never even thought about asking me, if I had to guess."

Claire rubbed circles on her back.

"She never asked me about French lessons or what color dress I wanted to wear to all of her events. Never asked me what kind of cake I wanted for my birthday. She just always bought angel food."

"God, I always hated your birthday cakes," Iris said.

"Iris," Claire hissed, but Astrid just laughed.

"No, she's right," Astrid said. "Angel food cake is the worst. But it was what my mother wanted, just like everything else, like taking over Lindy Westbrook's business, like—"

"Whoa, wait, what?" Iris asked. "I thought taking over for Lindy was what *you* wanted?"

Astrid sighed, waving a hand. "My point is, she doesn't ask. No one ever fucking *asks*, and Spencer never asked me either."

Claire's heart ached for her friend. She tucked a piece of blond hair behind Astrid's ear. "About the house?"

Astrid shrugged. "About the house. About moving to Seattle at all. He just assumed I'd say yes, because I always say yes. Don't I?"

They sat silently for a bit, Claire totally unsure how to answer that. Because Astrid wasn't wrong.

"I don't want to go to Seattle," Astrid finally said.

"Then don't," Iris said. "You don't have to."

"I . . . I don't know how . . ." Tears finally welled in Astrid's eyes, spilling down her cheeks so quickly, it was as though they'd been waiting for years to be set loose. "I don't know how to say no. I don't know how to do it."

"We'll help you," Claire said. "We'll do whatever you need us to do."

"I'm awesome at saying no," Iris said.

Astrid cracked a smile, but it faded quickly, and she wiped her eyes. "God, my mother. She—"

"Will get over it," Iris said. "This is *your* life, not hers."

"Jesus, what a mess," Astrid said, then her posture went ramrod straight. "There's so much to do. I need to call the caterers. And the florist. God, Delilah. I need to—"

"Stop," Claire said, pulling her friend closer. Her heart flipped at Delilah's name, but she ignored it. "We've got time. Right now, just . . . just sit here with us, okay?"

"Or," Iris said, "if you wanted to get some practice in saying no, you can tell us to go fuck ourselves right now and we'll get going on these phone calls stat."

Astrid laughed, then shook her head. "No. No, taking a minute is good, I think."

"See?" Iris said. "You just said no to me telling you that you could say no. An expert already."

Astrid laughed again, then flopped back onto the bed, her arms splayed above her head. A very un-Astrid-like motion, and it made Claire smile. She lay back too, followed by Iris, and the three friends hooked their arms together, relieved tears running down all of their cheeks and splashing into the thousand-thread count duvet.

CHAPTER

TWENTY-EIGHT

DELILAH WAS WAITING outside the Kaleidoscope Inn, something like worry coalescing in her chest at how late Claire was in picking her up and the three unanswered texts Delilah had sent her, when her phone rang. Already gripping the device in her sweaty palm, she slid her finger across the screen, relief filling her up at the sight of Claire's name.

"Hey," she said, pressing the phone to her ear. "Are you okay?"

"Hi," Claire said. "Yeah, I'm fine."

"Where are you?"

"We're . . . well, we're heading over to Wisteria House."

"What?" Delilah frowned, hitched her camera bag higher on her shoulder. "Why?"

"They broke up. Astrid and Spencer. About thirty minutes ago."

"Oh." Delilah sagged against the inn's exterior brick wall. "Holy shit."

"Yeah. Apparently, he bought a house in Seattle without telling her, showing her pictures, anything."

"And that was the straw, huh?"

"I guess so."

Delilah nodded, even though Claire couldn't see her. She waited to feel relieved, happy, even. This was what she'd wanted, what they'd all wanted, though Iris and Claire had different motivations from her. For Delilah, she could go back to New York now, get ready for her show at the Whitney. Fifteen grand richer, too. Per her contract, she still got paid in the event of a cancellation, and Isabel would fork over the money without a blink. Her stepmother would be too busy losing her shit on Astrid anyway, the called-off society wedding of her perfect daughter and a bona fide golden boy the stuff of Isabel Parker-Green's nightmares, no doubt.

Delilah was done.

Free.

She never had to set foot in this town again if she didn't want to.

So why was her back glued to this red brick wall like it was the only thing holding her up?

"What happens now?" Delilah said, her voice embarrassingly small. She cleared her throat, like a little bit of phlegm was the only reason for the near-whisper.

"Iris and I are going with Astrid to talk to Isabel," Claire said.

"Yeah. Sure. Astrid will definitely need help with that one."

"We thought so too."

A silence pressed between them, and Delilah hated it. If this was going to end, best end it quickly, like a beheading. Painless and fast.

"Okay," she said. "I guess I'll—"

"Come with us," Claire said.

Delilah blinked, then pushed off from the wall. "What?"

"Come with us," Claire said again.

"Astrid doesn't want me there."

"You know how Isabel is. Maybe you could help."

Delilah laughed, a bright, bitter sound. "Isabel definitely doesn't want me there."

"Well, I want you there."

Delilah closed her eyes. "Claire."

"Please. Just come, okay? I want to see you. And Astrid's your family. The only one you have, right?"

"You know it's more complicated than that."

"I know. And don't you wish it wasn't?"

Delilah frowned, at a loss for what to say to that. Sure, she wished her relationship with Astrid and Isabel was simpler. And once she went back to New York, it would be, nearly nonexistent, just like it always was between visits. But even as she thought this, something else nudged at the back of her mind. A different wish. One where *family* meant more than awkward encounters and avoided text messages. One where *friends* meant more than an acquaintance or a colleague or a one-night stand. One where *home* meant more than a fifth-floor walk-up and IKEA furniture.

But it was too late for that.

Wasn't it?

"Please," Claire said again, and goddammit, Delilah didn't want to say no to her. And if she was being honest, she didn't want to leave without seeing Claire one more time.

"Fine," Delilah said. "But meet me outside, okay? I don't—"

"Want to walk in alone. I know."

Delilah's eyes felt suddenly wet. She ended the call before Claire could hear the tears in her voice.

CLAIRE WASN'T THERE to meet her, though Iris's car was in the driveway. Still, Delilah stood frozen as her Lyft drove away. She should just turn around, go back to the inn, and book her flight home. She didn't belong here, and she never would.

And yet.

Delilah had taken her time getting to Wisteria House. She'd gotten a coffee at Wake Up, then walked slowly through downtown until she was sure Claire would already be at Wisteria.

She had stopped in front of River Wild Books, gazed through the window at all the colorful spines, the bare walls Claire couldn't decide how to fill. Brianne, Claire's manager, waved at Delilah from behind the counter, a bright smile on her face. Delilah waved back, found herself smiling too, which just made all the confusing feelings gathering in her chest like a storm swirl even thicker.

Now, standing in front of her home, she couldn't make herself turn away. For the first time since her father died, she *wanted* to go inside.

What the hell had Claire Sutherland done to her?

This wasn't okay. She needed to leave now. What did she care if Astrid was upset, if Isabel's perfect fairy-tale wedding was dissolving behind her parlor doors?

She didn't. Delilah Green didn't care. Because they'd never once cared about her.

She slumped against the door, pressed her forehead to the thick inlaid glass. Not caring was fucking exhausting.

Before she could stop herself, she twisted the thick brass door handle and stepped inside, lavender and bleach assaulting her senses like always. It was cool, nearly cold, and just as she suspected, the parlor doors to her left were closed, voices murmuring behind them. Once, the room was her father's office, filled with squashy leather couches and a huge oak desk Delilah used to curl up under with a book while her dad worked. Now, the room looked like something out of Versailles, settees and chaise lounges and fainting couches arranged just so. She walked up to the doors, placed a palm against the wood.

". . . any idea how embarrassing this will be?" Isabel was saying.

"Embarrassing for who, Mother?" Astrid said, her voice thick and watery-sounding. Delilah had never heard her voice sound like that. "For you or for me?"

"For the both of us," Isabel said, her voice completely calm. She didn't scream or yell. She never had in all the time Delilah had known her, but Christ, that woman could spit out an invective like no one else, her tone always measured and cold, which, honestly, made everything worse. More than once growing up, Delilah had tried to rile her stepmother into a frenzy, if only so Delilah wouldn't be the only one losing her shit.

"Well, I'm sorry," Astrid said. "But for once, just *once*, I need you to—"

Astrid's voice cut off, silence filing the space. Delilah pressed her ear against the door. She thought she heard "It's okay" in Claire's soothing tone, but it was so quiet she couldn't be sure. There was some sniffling, some shushing.

"Oh for god's sake, Astrid," Isabel said. "Stop crying. If this is upsetting you so much, call your fiancé and fix it."

"He's not upsetting me, Mom, you are," Astrid said.

"I beg your pardon?" Isabel said, her voice like a knife.

"Just once, please," Astrid said, "put me first."

"I have done nothing but put you first your entire life, young lady."

"No. You haven't. You've put your image first. Your money. Your social standing. And I'm tired, Mom. I'm tired. Delilah's tired."

Delilah jolted at the sound of her name. Her heart thrummed, adrenaline flooding her system hot and then cold.

"Don't you dare talk to me about that girl," Isabel said. "She made it very clear a long time ago how she feels about this family. You think I don't know she pushed poor Spencer into the river? And that debacle at Vivian's, my god. She's like a barn animal. I don't know where I went wrong with her."

"Mom, stop."

"If you ask me, this is her fault," Isabel said. "You were perfectly happy marrying Spencer before she came back to town. I warned you she'd just stir up trouble, but no, you just had to have your *sister* at your wedding, didn't you?"

Delilah frowned, blinking at the door and trying to process what she'd just heard. Even after all these years, Isabel's indifference toward her still stung. She wished it didn't, told herself it didn't matter, but she couldn't help it. Some childish, desperate need for love always rose up inside her when it came to Isabel. She said she didn't care, but the truth was, Isabel was the only mother she'd ever known, and the woman hated her. Or worse, felt nothing toward her.

Isabel didn't love Delilah Green, and she never would.

And she hadn't wanted Delilah at Astrid's wedding. She hadn't hired her as the photographer. She hadn't guilted Delilah into coming, indicating her father would've wanted her there. She hadn't offered her a ridiculous amount of money she knew Delilah needed.

Astrid had done all that.

Astrid had wanted her here.

Delilah shook her head and stumbled back from the door. She didn't want to hear any more. She *couldn't*. Her chest tightened and her eyes stung. She turned toward the front door, ready to flee, but she didn't want that either.

She wanted Claire.

She even wanted Iris.

Without thinking, she let muscle memory take over. Her feet moved her to the right and took her up the vast staircase, hand sliding along the oak bannister like it had done so many times before. Upstairs, she stopped in the doorway to her old room, but there was nothing for her to remember there. All of her things were gone, shipped to New York a month after she'd left Bright Falls at eighteen, when it was clear to Isabel she wasn't coming back. Her old space was a guest room now, white linens with gray-blue piping, bland paintings of rivers and waterfalls on the wall, sheer white curtains framing the window.

She moved on to the next room. The second she opened the door, she felt like she was walking into a museum of her past. Astrid's cavernous room looked exactly the same as it had when they were teens. All of Astrid's favorite books were still on the shelves, her duvet the same delicate lavender and yellow swirls, her white-wood vanity still sporting that Cinderella jewelry box she'd gotten when she was eight, the one Delilah secretly coveted but could never figure out how to ask for.

The only thing different was the few plastic tubs on the floor filled with various childhood items, notebooks and old school folders, award ribbons and medals from all of Astrid's accomplishments, movie ticket stubs and yellowing programs from the Portland ballet, stuff that had been sitting in Astrid's closet, forgotten, since she went to college.

Delilah stepped farther in the room and sat on the bed. Growing up, she hadn't spent a ton of hours in here. She and Astrid were never those kinds of sisters, of course. Still, there were times when she'd darkened the doorway and Astrid had waved her inside to borrow a book or watch a movie on the little TV that sat on Astrid's dresser, particularly when Isabel was hosting one of her parties and they were both dressed in ruffles and lace, tired of putting on a show and ready to simply be young girls again.

Long-suppressed memories curled through her, fuzzy as though she was waking up from a dream. She peered inside one of the tubs, which was filled with leather-bound books. Astrid's journals. Her stepsister was always scribbling in these books growing up. Delilah never asked what she wrote, but she was sure if she opened them up right now, she'd see an entry for every single day of Astrid's life. Delilah wondered if she still kept a journal, what she'd write for today, tomorrow.

She lifted the top book from the tub. It was dark brown leather, embossed with flowers and vines twining over the cover. Flipping it open, Astrid had written her name on the first page—*Astrid Isabella Parker*—along with the relevant dates, the first of which placed the start of this journal about three months after Delilah's father died when the girls were ten years old.

Delilah fanned the pages through her fingers, the paper crinkling from age and disuse. Astrid's neat scrawl, always in dark blue ink, blurred through her vision. She had no intention of reading the journal. This was Astrid's, filled with her private thoughts, and even Delilah Green wouldn't cross that line. But then, as the letters rolled by, her eyes snagged on a certain word.

Delilah

Her thumb caught in the middle, and she opened the book on her lap, flipping a few pages and scanning for her name again.

It was everywhere.

Not on every page, but on a lot of them. She blinked down at the writing, knowing she should close the book and walk out of the room right now, but something kept her there. Something childish and curious, a little girl looking for something to ease this knot in her chest.

Or, maybe, to pull the knot even tighter.

She swallowed, took a breath, and started reading on a page where her name appeared several times.

September 25th

I went to Delilah's room tonight, thinking maybe she'd want to do our homework together or watch TV, but when I knocked on her door, she didn't answer. And then, when I peeked inside, she was just lying on her bed, staring at the ceiling, which seems pretty boring to me, but then she's always staring at stuff. I guess I don't blame her. She's sad. I know she is, just like Mom is and I am too. I don't know how to help anyone though. When I asked her if she wanted to watch a movie, she just rolled over on her bed and faced the window. She doesn't want my help.

October 3rd

The leaves are starting to change and it's my favorite time of year. I wanted Delilah to come to Gentry's pumpkin farm with Claire and Iris and me today, but I never got the chance to ask her. When Claire and Iris got here, Delilah had been in the living room watching TV, but as soon as the doorbell rang, she disappeared. She wasn't in her room when I went looking for her. Iris says she's a little weird, which I guess is true. I don't know what to say about her to my friends, so I don't say much of anything. It's kind of embarrassing that my stepsister doesn't seem to really like me at all. She doesn't like Mom either, though I guess Mom's not the easiest person to like. Even when Andrew was alive, Delilah was pretty quiet, but she wasn't like this. I don't know what to do.

Delilah set the book in her lap, lungs pumping hard, her memory reaching back, back, back for this time, mere months after her father's death made her an orphan. She remembered Astrid asking her to watch TV or do homework together every now and then, but this . . . this . . . *longing* that seemed to fill Astrid's writing, the worry and wonder and even hurt . . .

That was new.

That was . . . impossible. Astrid never felt like this. She never actually wanted Delilah to be a part of her family. After Delilah's father died, Delilah was just a burden, an orphan, a strange girl messing up Astrid and Isabel's perfect life.

Wasn't she?

She flipped forward a few pages, landing on an entry dated that next spring when they were eleven.

March 19th

Claire and Iris spent the night last night. I'm so glad they're my friends. Iris is so funny, and Claire is probably the sweetest person I've ever met. I don't know what I'd do without them, especially with Delilah still ignoring me most of the time. Claire asked me about her last night while we were making cookies, about why Delilah never hangs out with us or talks to me. My face got kind of hot, and I didn't know what to say.

My sister hates me?

My sister wishes she had a different family?

It was way too embarrassing to admit, even if it was true. So I just shrugged and said Delilah was a weirdo and that she just liked being by herself.

Iris nodded and called Delilah a super weirdo. Claire just

*frowned and went back to mixing the dough, and we didn't say
anything else about Delilah, but I knew my face was still really
red, because it felt warm for the next hour. My chest hurt too,
like it always does when I do something I know isn't right, like I
can't breathe the right way or something.*

Delilah slammed the book shut and tossed it onto the bed next
her. Then she dived into the tub at her feet, searching for another
journal. Her hands were shaking because none of this was right. It
couldn't be right.

She grabbed a hunter-green journal a few books down in the
stack. Opening it, she found the date, placing it when she and Astrid
were in high school, ages fifteen to sixteen. A quick scan of the first
pages filled her with relief—her name didn't litter the writing—until
she got to the middle, where *Delilah* seemed to appear every other
word.

January 11th

*I swear to god, I hate my mother. Sometimes I feel like I can't
talk, can't think for myself at all. I'm just a doll, programmed
only to say "yes, Mom" and "okay, Mom" and "whatever you
want, Mom." I'm so sick of it. Sometimes, I think Delilah had
the right idea—just be a total bitch to everyone, and eventually,
they'll leave you alone. I mean, Mom asks her about her school-
work and makes sure she won't do anything to sully the great
Parker-Green household, dragging her to a few fundraisers
here and there, but for the most part, Mom leaves her alone.*

Why can't she leave me alone?

*I wonder all the time what Delilah thinks about the horror
show that is my mom and me. She's probably relieved she doesn't*

*have to deal with it. Not that she'd tell me if she was. If we're
not at school or forced to the dinner table by Mom, Delilah's in
her room, reading or doing I don't even know what. Anytime I
try to get her to come out, she barely acknowledges my questions
with a grunt. Like last week, I asked her if she wanted to come
with me to the bookstore. I figured this would get her attention.
She loves River Wild Books. It's the only place she goes to in
town. Claire always tells me when she sees Delilah there, which
is at least a few times a week after school. But when I asked her
to go? It was a flat-out "No thanks." Even when I asked her
why not, she just shrugged and mumbled something about how
she was just there yesterday, like that's ever stopped her before.
Logical conclusion—she just doesn't want to go with me.*

*Which, fine, whatever. I learned a long time ago that
nothing I ever did would be enough for Delilah. I don't need a
sister anyway.*

Delilah dropped the book into her lap, the blue letters blurring
and swirling in her vision. Her chest felt tighter than it ever had
before. She had to get out of here. She needed *out*, right now.

Standing, she let the journal fall from her lap and onto the floor.
She rushed to the door, but before she could make her way through
it, Claire appeared, her wide eyes softening when she spotted Delilah.

"There you are," she said. "I'm so sorry I wasn't there to meet
you. I was watching out the window, but then Isabel——" She froze,
her expression shifting back into worry, even alarm as she peered at
Delilah. "You okay?"

Delilah nodded, tried to smile, tried to do anything that felt like
herself before she walked into this house. No, before that. Before she
came back to Bright Falls.

"Bullshit." Claire said the word so softly, so sweetly, even though it was a swear, Delilah felt herself crumple. Her mouth twisted and her eyes burned and she didn't know what to say or how to think about anything anymore, not Astrid, not herself, not her entire childhood.

"Hey," Claire said, reaching out and taking Delilah's hand. "What's going on?"

Delilah shook her head, but her fingers gripped Claire's. She swallowed over and over. There was way too much spit in her mouth. Maybe she needed to throw up. She was suddenly dizzy, her core thrown off-balance.

Claire read her like a book, leading her to the bed and guiding her to sit down. She rubbed slow circles on Delilah's back, and Delilah inhaled, then let her air out slowly.

"What happened?" Claire asked, fingertips trailing down Delilah's neck.

Delilah eyed the journal on the floor, then bent to pick it up. "Do you . . . What was I like back when we were kids? Do you remember?"

Claire frowned. Clearly, this was not the question she was expecting. "Um, yeah, I remember."

"And?"

Claire slid her hand down Delilah's back. "You were quiet. Sad. You . . . didn't seem like you . . ." She rubbed her forehead with her free hand. "I don't know."

"Just say it."

Claire sighed. "You didn't seem like you cared much about anything. About anyone here. Making friends or getting to know people. But you were just different, and I don't think anyone knew how to—"

"And Astrid? How was I with her?"

Claire winced. "What is this about?"

Delilah ran her hand over the journals. "I just . . . Have you ever wondered if you got it all wrong?"

"Got what wrong?"

"I don't know. Something big. Like maybe you just missed all the signs, or you didn't know how to interpret them."

"What do you mean?"

Delilah shook her head. "I don't know. I don't know what I mean." She thought about those first months after her father died, how alone she'd felt, how abandoned. Isabel was nursing her own grief, Astrid too most likely, so there was no one to help ten-year-old Delilah through the night, no one to hold her hand or wrap her up in their arms or tell her it was going to be okay. She remembered feeling invisible, lost, like maybe her body wasn't even real. By the time Isabel got it together enough to be a presence in the house, Delilah was already gone. In her mind, anyway. She knew she wasn't wanted. She knew Isabel never planned on raising a kid who wasn't even her own blood. A strange kid, at that.

And Astrid . . . *Had* she tried with Delilah? Did she actually want a sister and Delilah simply didn't know how to be one? How to be anything to anyone as a little girl who'd just lost the only person who'd ever made her feel wanted?

"It's okay," Claire said, pressing her lips to Delilah's temple. "Whatever this is, it's okay. Just talk to me."

Delilah turned to face her, searching Claire's brown eyes. All of that loneliness from childhood, all of those feelings of being unwanted, a burden, something to be tolerated, she didn't feel any of that when she looked at Claire.

She felt the opposite.

She had from that very first night in Stella's, before Claire even knew who she was and Delilah turned the whole thing into a hilarious joke, a twisty little revenge scheme. Even then, something pulled her to this woman, and she didn't want to miss it.

She didn't want to misinterpret or ignore or shut down.

Before she could think through it further, she leaned forward and pressed her mouth to Claire's. The other woman gasped in surprise, but then relaxed, cupping Delilah's face in her hands, her lips parting to let Delilah in. The kiss was slow and desperate at the same time, exactly what Delilah needed. She let the journal fall to the floor again, wrapping her arms around Claire's waist. They fell back onto the pillows, tangled like a knot. Delilah didn't want to come up for air to talk, knowing Claire would listen and understand and accept her. Right now, she just wanted to feel Claire's body pushing against hers, her fingertips drifting down Delilah's cheek like she was something precious.

"Hey," Claire said against her mouth, framing Delilah's face and pulling them apart a little. "Delilah, I . . ." She paused, doubt flickering in her eyes.

"What?" Delilah asked, bottom lip bumping against hers. She didn't like that doubt. She wanted to excise it like a tumor. "You what? Tell me."

Claire ran her thumb over Delilah's brow. "I . . . I don't want you to leave."

Delilah pulled back a little farther. "What?"

"I don't want you to leave. I don't want this to be casual or just sex or whatever we agreed it would be. I hate casual. Casual sucks. I don't see how anyone does it."

"Claire, I—"

"I know you live in New York and you need to be there and I need to be here, but I don't care. We can figure something out, can't we? We can tell Astrid about us. Iris too. I just . . . I think, I don't want—"

Delilah pressed her finger to Claire's mouth, cutting her off. She stared at the other woman, trying to parse this feeling in her chest, but it only took a second for her to figure it out.

Relief.

A little spark of fear that felt pretty normal for something this big. Happiness.

Before right now, when was the last time she felt really and truly happy? She couldn't remember. Getting the email about the show at the Whitney, maybe, but that was different. That was . . . success. This was blood-warming, bone-settling, brain-fogging *happiness.*

But she couldn't put any of that into words, not yet, so she pulled Claire closer, slid her hand up her back and around her nape, thumb swirling over her soft skin as she kissed her, pouring everything she didn't know how to say into every touch, every press of her body against Claire's.

Yes. Kiss. *Yes.* Kiss. *Yes.* Kiss.

Claire laughed against her mouth and wrapped one leg around Delilah's hips. Delilah slipped her hands under Claire's shirt, feeling her soft skin, completely forgetting where they were, why they were there. This moment was all that mattered, all she cared about, and—

"What the hell is this?"

For a split second, the voice, the angry tone, the words felt like a dream. Like a movie left on a TV no one was watching. But then Claire sucked in a breath, scrambled away from Delilah, and Delilah found herself alone on the bed as a tear-streaked Astrid Parker stared into her childhood bedroom, her mouth hanging open in shock.

CHAPTER
TWENTY-NINE

CLAIRE'S HEARTBEAT WAS everywhere, fingertips fizzing with too much oxygen. For a second, nothing felt real—her plea for Delilah to stay, her decision to tell her best friend that she was maybe, possibly, most likely in love with her estranged stepsister, and now this.

Astrid, gaping at her, hurt and anger radiating through her body. Iris stood behind her, an *oh shit* sort of expression on her face.

"Astrid," Claire said. "I—"

"Don't," Astrid said, holding up a shaking hand.

Claire sighed and stood up. Her shirt was twisted, but she definitely didn't want to call attention to her rumpled clothing in the moment. "Honey, let me explain."

"Explain what?" Astrid said. She didn't shriek or scream. Claire almost wished she would. Instead, her tone was quiet, exhausted. Sad. "That you're, what? Screwing my sister and didn't even bother to tell me?"

"No, Astrid, I—"

"So you're not screwing her?"

Claire blinked at her best friend, shame warming her face.

Astrid nodded. "That's what I thought."

"Sweetie, maybe let her talk," Iris said, squeezing Astrid's shoulder.

Astrid whirled around. "You knew about this?"

"No, she didn't," Claire said, but Iris just shrugged and said, "I suspected."

"What the hell is happening?" Astrid said. "What else are you two keeping from me? Oh, wait, I already know you hate Spencer."

"We don't hate him," Iris said. "We just don't like him for you. You deserve better than him. We've been wanting to talk to you about it all, but we didn't know how. And through the week, Claire and Delilah and I thought if we could just get you to think about what—"

"Hold on," Astrid said, lifting a trembling finger into the air. "You and Claire and *Delilah*?"

Iris's mouth hung open, then she closed her eyes. This was a disaster. Nothing was going right. Claire didn't know how to explain anything, her words a tangle on her tongue.

"She was with us all the time," Claire finally managed to say. "And she . . . well . . . she was . . ."

"I was good at making a mess of things," Delilah said quietly.

Astrid looked like she was going to throw up. She stared at all three of them in turn, but her gaze finally settled on Delilah. "I can't believe this. Twenty-two years we've been sisters. Twenty-two years of your distance and your *I don't give a shit about anyone but myself* attitude."

"Astrid," Claire said, alarm spreading through her as Delilah's face paled. "Hang on a sec."

But Astrid ignored her. "Twenty-two years of wondering what the hell was wrong with me, what I did, why you wouldn't give me a chance, why—"

"Why *I* wouldn't give *you* a chance?" Delilah said, standing up. "From the second my father died, your mother made it very clear what I was in this family. A ward. A girl without a home. An orphan. Someone she would feed and clothe and that was it. Not a family member. Not a daughter."

"That's *Mother*," Astrid said, then slapped her own chest so hard Claire flinched. "What about me?"

Delilah lifted her chin, almost defiant, but Claire noticed a slight tremble of her lower lip, the way she clenched her jaw to steady it.

Astrid shook her head. "I should've never invited you here."

"Why did you?"

"Because you're my goddamn sister! And I wanted you at my wedding. I thought . . . I don't know what I thought, but I certainly didn't expect this. Mom was right; you don't care about us. You don't care about me, you don't—"

"You never gave me a chance to," Delilah said.

"I gave you a chance the second I hired you for this wedding! I gave you a chance every holiday you never came home and every time I stopped by your room growing up, every time we had dinner, every time—"

"So now I'm supposed to be a mind reader? You ignored me for the entirety of high school. Middle school. You ignored me every time Claire and Iris came over to the house, making sure I felt like an outsider every step of the way."

Astrid blinked at her, tears falling silently onto her cheeks. When she spoke, her voice was fragile, shattered. "You ignored me first."

Delilah pursed her lips, turned her head away, her eyes glistening just a little. Claire wanted to curl her into her arms. She wanted to take Astrid's hand, get them to calm down and talk, but she didn't move. She didn't dare. This barbed-wire connection between Astrid and Delilah was so much sharper than she'd ever imagined. There was so much hurt here, so much anger, and she didn't know how to help either one of them.

"I didn't know I was ignoring you," Delilah finally said, her voice so soft, Claire almost didn't hear it. "I thought . . . I thought that's what you wanted."

Astrid shook her head, lifting her hands and letting them flop back to her sides. "So you come back to town, conspire behind my back with the only people in my life I really love, steal my best friend, just to what? Get back at me?"

Delilah rubbed her forehead, but she stayed silent.

"Oh," Astrid said. "I forgot. That's exactly what you did. You even told me you were going to do it. Didn't you?"

Delilah's hand dropped. "What? Astrid, Claire and I—"

"Let me guess. It just *happened*."

"Yeah. It did."

"I'm sure. She came after *you*, right? She wanted *you*. You're irresistible. You had nothing to do with it."

"I didn't say that."

Astrid sniffed. "So you didn't bet me you could get into Claire's pants before the wedding?"

It took Claire a few seconds to realize what Astrid had said, the words settling around the room like a sudden snow shower in April—quiet and cold and shocking.

Claire turned to look at Delilah. "You . . . you did what?"

Delilah pressed her eyes closed. "That's not what happened."

"Hang on, hang on," Iris said. "Delilah *bet* you she could sleep with Claire?"

"The morning of the brunch," Astrid said, gesturing at Claire. "She said you were looking well, and I told her to stay the hell away from you and she just *grinned*. Like it was a joke. Then she bet me she could get you in her bed in two weeks' time."

"And you took it?" Iris said, her mouth gaping.

"No! I told her to go fuck herself."

"That's not what happened," Delilah said again, but her voice sounded frail, unsure.

"So you didn't try to sleep with Claire just to get under my skin?" Astrid asked.

"You're twisting it around," Delilah said.

"Am I?"

"Wait," Iris said, stepping farther into the room. "This can't be right. What are we missing?" She frowned at Delilah, hurt furrowing her brow.

And still, Delilah said nothing. Nothing in defense. No explanation. She just stood there, her arms crossed, her eyes on the floor, teeth worrying at her bottom lip like she was trying to think of what to say. But if she even *had* to think, *had* to worry, then . . .

Claire couldn't process this. She turned to look at the woman she'd just begged to be *more* with her. The woman she couldn't stop thinking about, couldn't imagine letting go back to New York without a plan to be in each other's lives. She knew Delilah was rough around the edges. She knew Delilah was brash and brazen, and she actually loved all that about her. Plus, underneath all that, Delilah was . . . She was soft. And gentle and considerate and brave. She was real. It had all felt so real.

It *was* real.

Wasn't it?

But now, the truth of how unfeasible their whole relationship was settled on Claire's shoulders.

Claire had asked Delilah to stay. To try. To figure it out together.

And Delilah . . . hadn't said yes. She'd kissed Claire, touched her so gently and tenderly it made Claire's throat tighten just remembering it, but she hadn't said yes. Because she couldn't. Moreover, she didn't want to. Delilah was always going to leave, just like Josh, just like Claire's father. Regardless of how this started, no matter what she felt for Delilah or what she had hoped might happen, she couldn't give her heart to someone else just to have them disappear on her again.

Whatever this was between them—sex, *more*, nothing—it was over.

Because Delilah Green would never stay in Bright Falls for Claire Sutherland.

"Claire," Delilah said. "Please, can we—"

But Claire held up her hand, cutting Delilah off. Delilah flinched like she'd been slapped, and that's what it felt like to Claire too—her palm smarting, fingers shaking, adrenaline rushing through her veins.

Finally, Delilah nodded once, her jaw tight, and walked toward the hallway.

"Go ahead and walk away," Astrid said quietly. "It's what you do best."

Delilah paused in the doorway, her shoulders up around her ears. Claire wanted to scream, *no, no, no*, this wasn't right, but it was. It was, because Delilah didn't turn around, she didn't stay, she didn't push.

She just left.

CHAPTER THIRTY

JOSH WAS GONE.

Claire had to admit it now.

It had been two days since she'd heard from him.

It had been two days since a lot of things.

Two days since Astrid called off her wedding, since she'd walked in on Delilah and Claire. Two days since Delilah left Bright Falls. Two days since Astrid had spoken to Claire at all.

Iris had been the reluctant go-between, texting Claire with things she could do to help Astrid cancel the wedding. Since Wednesday, Claire had holed up inside her house, telling her manager Brianne she was sick while, really, she lay on her couch drinking lemon LaCroix until she switched over to wine around five p.m. each day, making phone calls to wedding guests and vendors or whoever Iris commanded via text.

Claire hadn't talked to Iris either. At least not in person. After Delilah had walked out of Astrid's room, Claire had tried to talk to Astrid, tell her about her whole thought process since things started up with Delilah, but Astrid hadn't wanted to hear it. And she was right—this wasn't the time for Claire to make excuses, no matter how justified Claire felt in her decisions. Astrid had just called off her wedding. She was heartbroken . . . though Claire didn't think her heartbreak was over Spencer. Not after everything that had passed between Astrid and Delilah.

So Claire's phone became an endless stream of cold, imperative texts, all of them void of any personal questions.

> Call the florist.

> Emailed you a list of guests to call.

> Cancel the Graydon String Quartet. Here's their number.

She'd done it all with a thumbs-up emoji and timely execution, completing whatever task she could to help Astrid take care of this mess . . . a mess she'd wanted, a mess she'd planned for with Iris and Delilah. She didn't have a justification for that, for why she never felt comfortable being honest with Astrid about her feelings toward Spencer, why she always shrank away from confrontation.

Now, as she texted Josh for the millionth time with no response, left him yet another voice mail, she wanted a fight. She wanted to push his stupid broad shoulders and scream in his face. Words scrambled in her brain, everything she would say to him, everything that was clouding into her chest like a storm.

I knew you would do this, I was right, you always leave, everyone always leaves.

She called him again, but it went straight to his voice mail, just like it had every time she'd tried to contact him in the past two days. Ruby was beside herself. She'd been calling and texting her father nonstop too, and he wouldn't answer. Yesterday, Claire had used the key Josh had given her a few weeks ago to let herself into his apartment, just to check things out and make sure he wasn't lying on the floor with a fatal head wound or something. Inside, most everything looked like it was in its place, but his truck was gone, as were his toiletries and the big duffel bag he always took with him when he skipped town.

Now, as Claire finished a tense call to the Bradfords in Portland, fielding a million incredibly intrusive questions about Astrid's sanity, she sat up on her couch and rubbed her forehead. Down the hall, Ruby was shut inside her room, sad music filtering from under the door. Claire felt like a piece of cloth stretched thin, fraying at the edges. She couldn't watch her daughter go through this again.

She couldn't go through this again.

She picked up her phone and opened her text messages, her thumb hovering over her thread with Delilah for the hundredth time since the other woman left. She wanted to talk to her. She wanted to tell her about Josh, to beg her to come back, but she couldn't. She wouldn't. Delilah was already gone, back where she belonged, and Claire . . . well.

Maybe it wasn't only Josh she couldn't stand to see walk away again.

And that's all that would happen if she reached out to Delilah right now, if anything happened at all.

Delilah doesn't care.

Claire said it to herself, over and over and over, ignoring the spark of doubt in the back of her mind. It wasn't doubt anyway. It was hurt, lust, maybe even a little longing, but it wasn't doubt.

She switched to her messages with Iris and finally swallowed her pride.

Can we talk? Please?

She hit send and held her breath, but those three little bouncing ellipses appeared immediately, Iris's response buzzing through soon after.

I'm already on my way over.

TEN MINUTES LATER, Claire opened her door and sucked in a surprised breath. Iris was there in a green sundress, her red hair long and flowing around her bare shoulders, but she wasn't alone.

Astrid stood next to her on Claire's front stoop, her arms folded and her sunglasses hiding her eyes. Her mouth looked tight, but Claire didn't even care. She was *here*, and Claire had never felt so relieved in her life.

She must've sagged against the doorframe, or maybe the dark circles she knew snuggled under her eyes gave away her current mental state, but either way, Iris stepped forward and gulped her into her arms. Claire fell into her, tears suddenly clogging her throat.

"Josh is an honorary shit boot," Iris said, smoothing circles on Claire's back.

Claire pulled back. "How did you know?" She hadn't mentioned his vanishing act to either of them—it never felt like the right time to drop that bomb via text.

"You gave your daughter a phone and our phone numbers," Astrid said, removing her sunglasses. "She's eleven; texting is her life."

Claire exhaled. "Oh god. I'm so sorry. I gave her your numbers for emergencies, and I—"

"Honey," Iris said, taking Claire's arms. "It's okay. We're part of Ruby's family. Of course we want her to text us when she needs to."

Claire flicked her eyes to Astrid, who gave her a terse nod, which was enough for Claire.

They came inside, and Claire opened up a fresh bottle of rosé. The three women settled on Claire's couch, which, over the past two days, had become a nest of blankets, books, glasses of water, and bags of chips.

"You're really set up for the long haul here," Iris said as she tucked herself into a corner.

Claire laughed. "You know I burrow when I'm depressed."

"I do know," Iris said, winking at her over her glass.

Astrid was on the other end of the couch, Claire in the middle, and her friend had yet to smile or relax her shoulders. Claire searched for what to say, how to make this right, but she wasn't sure anything would help.

"Astrid, I'm sorry," she said, making sure to look her friend in the eyes, because if nothing else, Claire owed Astrid this much. Astrid met her gaze but said nothing. "I know things are complicated with you and Delilah. When things started up between us, I . . . well, it was casual. It was just . . ." She forced the words out, no matter how untrue they felt. It was how it all started, and that was at least true. "It was just sex, and I knew it was temporary. I didn't feel like I needed to tell either of you about a hookup that would just end. And I didn't want to stress you out or make things harder for you with the wedding coming up."

Astrid tilted her head. "Is that really why you didn't tell me?"

Claire frowned. Next to her, Iris cleared her throat. "I . . . well . . . What do you mean?"

Astrid sighed and looked down at her lap. Now that Claire peered closer at her friend, Astrid looked deeply exhausted. No makeup, which was unheard of for Astrid Parker, and her hair looked a bit dull, like it hadn't been washed in a few days. What's more, she was dressed in black yoga pants and an old gray T-shirt that said *Bright Falls High School Track.*

"What I mean is . . ." Astrid turned to face Claire, tucking her legs underneath her. "I've been thinking a lot the past few days. *Soul-searching*, I guess you could call it."

"Oh, you could definitely call it soul-searching," Iris said.

Astrid shot her a look, but a tiny smile lifted one corner of her mouth. "Okay, I've been doing some soul-searching, and I realize . . . I'm not always the easiest person to talk to."

Claire frowned. "Astrid, honey—"

"No, let me finish."

"Yes, let her finish," Iris said.

"Would you shut up?" Astrid said, but there was no venom in her voice.

Iris presented her palms in surrender.

"I'm not always the easiest person to talk to," Astrid went on. "I'm demanding and inflexible and I've never . . . I've never shared certain things with the two of you. A lot of certain things."

Claire reached out and took Astrid's hand, relieved when Astrid didn't pull back. "Like what?"

"Like . . ." Astrid sighed. "Like how I felt about Delilah. I mean, *really felt* when we were growing up. How I wanted her to be my sister, but when she didn't seem to want the same thing, I just shut her out and how . . . how hard it was. How hard it still is, because it makes me feel . . ."

She swallowed, pressed her eyes closed.

"It makes me feel unwanted and like I'm not enough, and talking about it just made me feel like that even more."

"That's a lot of feels," Iris said.

"And you know how I hate those," Astrid said, smiling without humor.

"Sweetie," Claire said softly, but Astrid shook her head and pressed onward.

"When I found out about you and her, I just . . . I freaked out because, honestly, I thought, *Why her? Why Claire and not me?*"

"I think it should be clarified here that Astrid is *not* talking about you shagging her sister," Iris said, tipping her wineglass at them.

"Jesus, Iris," Astrid said.

"What? It needed to be stated."

Astrid focused on Claire, squeezing her hand. "I just mean that you clearly had something with her. She meant something to you, and you meant something to her, I could tell. And I . . . I didn't understand why *I* could never mean something to her. Not romantically, of course, but just . . . as something. As anything. We'd been through a lot together, had lost parents together, and I wanted to share that with her. I'd always wanted to share that with her, because she was the only one I *could* share it with, and when she constantly shut me down, it just felt . . ."

"Horrible," Claire finished for her.

Astrid nodded. "But I don't think it's entirely Delilah's fault. There was a lot about her experience I didn't understand either. Things I didn't want to see or try to understand. And when she pushed me away, I responded in kind, and then we just sort of fed off each other like that."

Claire nodded, her throat suddenly tight. "I'm still sorry that I hurt you."

Astrid released a breath and smiled at her. "Thank you."

"What about Spencer?" Claire asked.

Astrid closed her eyes for a second. "Yeah. Spencer. I think he was just an easy way out for me."

"He was a shit boot," Iris said.

"Not helping," Claire said, but Astrid laughed.

"No, Iris is right. He was a total shit boot."

"And a shit belt, a shit sock, a shit shirt, a shit—"

"Yes, we get it, Ris," Claire said, then turned back to Astrid. "I wish you would've let us in about him."

"I know. I'm sorry. I've been thinking a lot about that too. He made my life look how I was taught it should look. It was easy to just give in to him, knowing it made everyone else around me happy."

"Not everyone," Iris said.

"I know," Astrid said. "But he was everything my mother always told me I wanted, so when he came along, I *made* myself want him, because what the hell did I really want if it wasn't him? In the back of my mind, I knew he wouldn't make me happy, and I knew you two knew that from the beginning, which was why I never talked about him, hardly ever brought him around. I didn't want to hear it, that he was wrong, that *I* was wrong."

"I'm sorry we held back too," Claire said. "We should've just talked to you honestly from the beginning."

"I didn't make it easy," Astrid said.

"No, you sure as hell didn't," Iris said.

Astrid rolled her eyes. "Ris, you and I already had this conversation, so can you shut your piehole?"

"Fine, fine," Iris said, "but really, I just spoke up to hear Astrid Parker say *piehole*."

The three women all laughed, and then Astrid pulled Claire into her arms. They sat like that for a long time, Claire reveling in the familiarity of her best friend's embrace, her chin resting on Astrid's bony shoulder.

"Whew, okay, now that that's over with," Iris said, clapping once when the other two women pulled away, "what are we going to do about your little problem?"

She was looking at Claire as she spoke, and Claire felt herself deflate.

"I don't know," she said. "Ruby is devastated, and Josh is—"

"Not that honorary shit boot," Iris said, holding up a hand. "Because honestly, Josh is gonna Josh, and we've got you and Ruby, and we always will."

Claire frowned. "Then what are you talking about?"

Iris glanced at the ceiling, her mouth moving as though whispering a prayer to the gods for help, before leveling Claire with wide eyes. "Delilah, my darling, lovesick best friend. Delilah Green."

Claire shook her head. "Nothing. There's nothing to do about her."

Iris and Astrid eyed each other over Claire's head.

"What?" she said. "There's not. And I'm not lovesick. I'm just . . ." She looked around at her melancholy nest, all the signs of a devastating breakup littering her living room. "It doesn't matter. Delilah's gone."

"Oh, honey," Iris said. "If you think that woman isn't completely in love with you, you're even more clueless than I thought."

"What?" Claire said. "No. She's not. It was just sex."

"Claire, you don't do *just sex*," Astrid said softly. "And you never have."

"But she does. She made a bet," Claire said, ignoring Astrid's observation. "She made a *bet* that she could sleep with me, you said so yourself, and—"

"No one who's only out to piss off their stepsister looks at someone they're already sleeping with the way Delilah looked at you," Iris said. "On the camping trip? At the vineyard? Hell, even at Vivian's, she couldn't take her eyes off you."

Claire shook her head. "No. No, she doesn't care about me. She *left*."

Astrid sighed. "She left because she doesn't think anyone here wanted her to stay."

"I told her," Claire said, tears finally welling up and spilling over. "I told her to stay."

Neither of her best friends said anything after that. What was there to say? Delilah was gone; it didn't matter what Claire felt for her, or what she might have felt for Claire. New York might as well have been a universe away.

Claire knocked back the rest of her wine, but before she could get up to offer everyone another round, her phone exploded in a flurry of text messages.

All of them from Josh.

> Hey I'm heading out of town for a few days. I'll be back on Friday, I promise.

> What the hell? What are all these texts from you? Didn't you get my text?

> Shit, you didn't. It has one of those little red exclamation points next to it. Shit!

> Ruby's texted me a million times. I didn't get them until now.

> Claire, I'm sorry.

> I'm on my way to your house right now.

> I'm thirty minutes out.

> I'm pulling onto your street.

> Ruby won't answer her phone. Is it dead?

> Shit, shit, shit.

> I'm here.

Claire leaped up, eyes wide on her phone. "Oh my god."

"What?" Iris said, standing too. "Is it Delilah?"

"It's Josh. He's here." She rushed toward the front door and flung it open just in time to see Josh bolting out of his truck, door hanging open as he jogged up the sidewalk.

"Claire," he said, eyes wide with panic. "I'm sorry, I—"

But before he could get anything else out, Iris flew past Claire, her red hair flowing behind her like flames, and punched Josh square in the face.

———

BLOOD SPURTED EVERYWHERE.

"Shit!" he yelled, his hands flying to his nose. "Iris, what the hell?"

"No country for old shit boots," Iris said, pointing a pale finger in his face.

He flinched back, hands still covering his wound. Blood seeped through his fingers and down his arms. It was like something out of a horror show, and it took Claire a second to register what the hell had actually happened and what to address first.

Finally, the blood that was starting to dapple her sidewalk took precedence, aided by Astrid handing her an old towel she kept under the kitchen sink for just these kinds of staining messes.

Claire pressed the towel to Josh's nose, which he used to mop up most of the mess, then kept against his face to prevent any more spillage.

"What is going on?" she asked when he was more or less stable.

"Irith punthed me in the fucking nothe, that'th what'th going on," he said, his *s*'s thickened by the injury.

"And I'd do it again," Iris said.

"About time somebody did it," Astrid said.

He glared at the both of them, but then his expression fell when he looked at Claire. He shook his head. "I didn't leave. Not this time—I told you I wouldn't."

"But you did," Claire said. "You've been gone for two days without any explanation, and once again, I've got a devastated daughter I can barely get to come out of her room."

His eyes—as that was all Claire could see—tightened as though in pain. Then he dropped the towel, and the three women sucked in a breath. His face was smeared with now-drying blood, his nose already swelling, the space under his eyes darkened and hinting at the bruises that would soon form.

"That bad, huh?" he said.

"It suits you," Iris said.

Claire shot her a look but couldn't help but smile. She knew her friends were just as sick of Josh's mind games, his unreliability, as she was. And she was done letting him get away with it.

"You can't keep doing this," she said. Iris and Astrid both came up next to her, each friend taking one of her hands. "In fact, this was your last chance. I'm finished. Ruby can't take this, Josh. I can't take this. It's not fair, and I don't understand why you—"

"I built a house in Winter Lake," he said.

She blinked at him. Winter Lake was about thirty minutes northwest of Bright Falls. It was tiny, heavily wooded, and had a downtown the size of a button.

"You did what?" she asked.

"That's where I went. I've been working on a few projects there these past months, and one of them . . . well, it's mine. I had to go finish all the paperwork on Wednesday, then spent Thursday getting some things set up inside. When I was getting ready to leave on Wednesday, my phone was dead. I charged it up in my truck and sent you a text as soon as I could, but Winter Lake has shit reception—I'm going to have to change carriers when I move out there permanently—and I didn't realize the text didn't go through until I was on my way back today and all these texts started rushing in as soon as I hit I-5. I would've called Ruby while I was gone, but like I said, no signal, and I don't have my Wi-Fi set up yet."

She stared at him, her friends' hands still in hers. They stood by quietly, letting her take the lead.

"Why didn't you just tell me what you were doing?" she asked. "Before you left? All you had to do was *talk* to me, tell me what was going on. Hell, leave me a sticky note on my door!"

He sighed. "Would you have believed me? If I told you two months ago that I was building a house in Winter Lake?"

She pressed her mouth flat, her answer clear.

"That's why I didn't tell you any of this," he said. "I wanted it done. I know my words are cheap, Claire. I wanted to show you that I was serious this time."

He stared at her with his blackening eyes, never looking away.

"You really built a house in Winter Lake?" she asked.

He grinned. "I really did. And, if it's okay, I'd like to take you and Ruby to see it."

"Dad!"

Ruby appeared in the front doorway, her eyes wide and her smile infectious as she ran toward him and threw her arms around Josh's neck. He lifted her up, held her close while her feet dangled off the ground, his sore nose pressed into her hair.

"What happened to your face?" Ruby asked when he put her back down.

He waved a hand. "Nothing I didn't deserve."

"Aunt Iris finally punched you, huh?" she said.

"I'm glad to see my work is noted and appreciated," Iris said.

Josh rolled his eyes, but he was smiling. They all were, and Claire couldn't seem to stop. She was so relieved, so pleasantly shocked, she didn't know what to do with herself while Josh explained to Ruby what had happened with his phone and all about Winter Lake.

After a few tight hugs and a teary goodbye on Claire's part—along with plans to spend all of tomorrow together getting drunk and eating chocolate on the day that would've been Astrid's wedding—Astrid and Iris left. For the rest of today, Claire knew she needed to take some time for her daughter and Josh.

After Josh cleaned the dried blood off his face in the bathroom, Claire and Ruby piled into his truck, and they drove out to Winter Lake. It was a pretty short trip—a quick stint on Interstate 5, followed by a lot of winding back roads flanked by leafy woods. They passed through Winter Lake's downtown, a two-block affair complete with zero streetlights, one coffee shop, two hardware stores, and an amazing old-fashioned movie theater called the Andromeda. Despite that gem, the area made Bright Falls look like a booming metropolis. Finally, about ten minutes outside of downtown, they wound down a narrow road with little houses spaced at least a half mile apart, until Josh pulled into the drive of a log cabin that belonged on a postcard. It was bigger than she expected, with an A-frame roof, a wide front porch, siding the color of good whiskey, and a stone chimney that rose into the sky. Evergreens and pines surrounded the property, and Claire could see a tiny slice of silver behind the house—Winter Lake.

"Josh," she said, her voice breathy. "This is . . . this is . . ."

"Amazing!" Ruby said. "It's amazing!" Then their daughter flung open her door and ran up the front walk to the porch, peering through the windows before throwing herself into one of the rockers.

"It really is," Claire said, smiling at Josh. "I can't believe you did this."

He winked at her. "Wait until you see the inside."

They climbed out of the truck, and Josh unlocked the front door. Inside was . . . well, it took Claire's breath away. The entire back wall was completely made of windows, letting in the sinking sun and filling the house with an amber-lavender glow. The kitchen, living room, and dining room were all one big space, with the same pine-knotted log walls as the exterior paired with modern appliances and design. The kitchen was bright and rustic at the same time, with cream-colored cabinets interspersed between the whiskey walls, an island that featured a farmhouse sink and lots of workspace, and butcher-block counters. Soft, dark brown leather couches filled the living room, along with a squashy hunter-green armchair that looked big enough to fit two adults. Throw pillows in navy and green filled the space, and the artwork on the walls showcased lakes and rivers and forests in the same colors. A black-and-white photograph of Ruby sat on the mantel, along with a photo of the three of them—Claire, Josh, and Ruby—back when Ruby was around nine.

"Can I see my room?" Ruby asked. "Please, can I?"

"You bet, kiddo," Josh said, grinning. "I left it pretty blank, because I want you to pick out all your own stuff, okay? Maybe we can do that tomorrow?"

He eyed Claire and she nodded. Then Ruby took off down the hall off the living room.

"Can I have the room with the huge bed and the big bathroom?" she called.

"Not a chance," Josh called back, laughing.

"Ugh, fine," Ruby said, but Claire could tell she was teasing.

Claire continued to tour the space slowly, taking in all the little details. It was beautiful. There was no other word for it. And when Josh asked shyly what she thought, she told him so.

He beamed. "Come here. I want to show you the view from the back deck." He took her hand and led her outside. The deck was simple, just two Adirondack chairs and a table between them, but the view . . .

"Wow," she said, resting her forearms on the railing and watching the sun as it spun gold over the surface of Winter Lake.

"Pretty great location, huh?" he said as he came up next to her.

"I'll say." She turned to him, nudged his shoulder with hers. "I can't believe you did this."

He shrugged, eyes softly narrowed on the view from his very own porch. Then he dug into his back pocket and took out his wallet, extracting a small white card. "I did this too."

Claire took the card, felt the thick paper between her fingers, the glossy, navy blue writing slightly raised.

JOSH FOSTER HOMES, LLC

Her head snapped up. "Wait . . . the projects you've been working on . . . They weren't with Holden's company?"

He shook his head, then paused. "Well, yeah, the first couple were. But the last two, the ones I've been doing up here? All mine."

"You did it."

"I did it."

She smiled at him, her chest suddenly feeling tight and warm at the same time. "Josh, I'm . . . I'm sorry I didn't—"

He shook his head, putting up a hand to cut her off. "No, don't do that. I deserved your doubt. I know I did."

She released a breath, and he turned to face her.

"But I'm here now," he said. "I'm here for good. I'm not the same stupid kid I was when we had Ruby. Hell, I'm not the same stupid kid I was two years ago. I hope I can earn back your trust."

Claire reached out and squeezed his hand. "I hope so too. This is a hell of a start."

He laughed and squeezed back. "I want us to be a family."

She nodded. "Me too."

Then his face fell and his mouth dropped open a little. "But, I mean, not a *family* family."

She tilted her head at him, frowning.

"I mean . . ." He pulled his fingers from hers and scrubbed a hand through his hair. It was hard to tell in the dim light, but Claire could've sworn he was blushing. "I know sometimes when I've come back to town we've . . . well, we've . . ." He waved his hand between them.

"Screwed?" she asked. His eyes went so wide she laughed. "Oh, come on, Josh. We're adults. We can call it what it was."

His shoulders relaxed, and he laughed too. "Okay, yeah. But I don't think we should anymore."

She just lifted her brows at him.

He shook his head. "It doesn't help either of us be a good parent to Ruby. And honestly, in the past, I wonder if us having sex was half the reason I bolted. Not that any of that was your fault. It was all me, but well, the sex confused me. Scared me. And I just want to be a good dad and a good co-parent for you."

Claire nodded, honestly shocked at the wisdom he was spouting. "Yeah. All that makes sense."

"And we don't love each other like that. Not anymore."

"No, we don't."

"And I want to have that with someone someday."

She smiled. "I want that for you too."

"And there's the fact that you're completely in love with someone else."

Her smile dropped. "I'm sorry, what?"

He laughed. "Admit it."

"I can't admit to something I don't understand."

"Oh, please. Claire. You and Delilah. It's obvious."

"It absolutely is not. You saw us together, what? Once?"

"Once was enough. I know she's got a complicated past in Bright Falls," Josh went on, "but I've never seen anyone look at you like she did. Not even me. And you looked at her the same way."

"And how was that?"

"Like you'd follow her to the moon."

She chewed at her bottom lip and turned back to face the lake. She didn't understand why everyone couldn't let it go. Why everyone seemed to think the way Delilah merely looked at Claire meant she was madly in love. You couldn't judge that from a look. You couldn't judge anything from a look.

So why did she suddenly feel the need to cry long, shuddering sobs that would hopefully dislodge this ache in her heart? She shook her head, muttered *fuck* under her breath, because if any situation called for a good f-bomb, it was this one.

Josh nudged her with his shoulder. "What are you so afraid of?"

She laughed through her falling tears, wiping under her eyes. "Where do I start?"

He looked at her expectantly, and she realized he really wanted to hear her answer.

She sagged against him. "I'm scared of getting hurt. I'm scared of Ruby getting hurt. I'm scared I'll give her—give anyone, I guess—everything I've got, and they'll just end up leaving. I'm a lot, Josh. I've got a kid who's about to be a teenager, for god's sake. I've got you. I've got a business. And I've got . . . well, I guess I've got some major trust issues."

He nodded. "And a lot of that is my fault."

She didn't say anything to that. They both knew it was true.

"And my dad's," she said. "And Nicole's and, hell, I don't know. Every broken heart I've ever heard a sad song about."

He wrapped his arm around her, and she rested her head against his shoulder.

"Do you love her?" he asked.

"It doesn't matter."

He squeezed her a little closer. "Do you love her?"

She let the question settle between them for a while. The sun sank lower, turning the golden air to lavender to a deep violet. She knew the answer to Josh's question, but it was a ridiculous answer. Impossible.

Josh sighed. "Your whole life, you've been putting people first, Claire. Your mom. Astrid and Iris. Me. Ruby. It's okay to take something for yourself."

His words sounded like wisdom, like truth. They sparked something inside her that felt a whole lot like hope, and in any other circumstance, Claire might've agreed. But she'd already tried. She'd tried to take something for herself when she'd asked the woman she maybe loved to stay, to figure things out together.

And Delilah Green had left anyway.

But even though it was impossible to have what she really wanted, she liked this—her and Josh standing out on the deck he built himself, her head on his shoulder while they talked about the possibility of love.

CHAPTER

THIRTY-ONE

DELILAH WAS SURE she was about to throw up.

The sun was setting, casting a golden glow over Gansevoort Street, and a breeze blew over her skin, finally giving the city some relief from this mind-numbing summer heat. She was dressed in her favorite black jumpsuit, her hair big and wild, curls defined to within an inch of their lives with all manner of gel and curl crème. Her makeup was spot-on, if she did say so herself. Smoky eyes and winged eyeliner, a dark red lip that made her feel powerful and sexy, like a creature of the night in some paranormal romance novel.

Except this wasn't a romance. Because as she stared up at the Whitney, a towering gray building, all modern lines and glass, that she'd been inside of a million times before and twice since returning to New York nearly two weeks ago, her stomach churned like it regretted her last meal.

She swallowed, inhaled, then swallowed again, but nothing was making her feel calmer. Tonight, *Queer Voices* launched at the Whitney. She was ready. She'd been working her ass off since she got back to New York. She'd even gotten Michaela to cover her shifts at the

River Café. After her fee for the Parker-Hale wedding dropped into her Apple Cash account two days after leaving Bright Falls—no email from Astrid about it, no text, just a chunk of change that was rightfully Delilah's anyway—she'd pushed all worries of money and rent out of her head and gotten to work.

Ten pieces.

That's how many photographs the Whitney wanted, and by the time she'd returned to New York, she'd had one week to prepare before the museum needed everything for framing. Those seven days had been a blur—barely eating, catching cat naps on her couch, constantly poring over her existing body of work for pieces that showed the world who Delilah Green was, niche and all. But she'd done it. She'd even worked on a new piece, a shot she'd taken in Bright Falls after the camping trip during those long couple of days before she'd taken Claire roller skating. She'd gone out to the falls, about ten miles outside of town, a woodsy area where Bright River pooled under a series of small white waterfalls that cascaded down from a rocky cliff. She'd brought her tripod and her camera, then proceeded to spend the entire day lost in hundreds of shots of the natural world, herself in a soaked white blouse the main subject.

"Wow," Alex Tokuda had said as they'd stared at the photograph five days ago when Delilah had dropped everything off. Delilah had named the piece *Found*. She wasn't sure why, but it's the only thing that popped into her mind when she'd finished editing the shot she'd chosen.

"This is . . . powerful," Alex said, tilting the large rectangle of photo paper this way and that. Their hair was short and dark, and they wore a maroon suit with a silk black blouse, chic as hell. "Painful, even."

"Yeah" was all Delilah could think to say, but inside, she felt as though she was made of glitter, a feeling that only increased as Alex had continued to sift through her ten pieces, commenting simply but authentically.

Later that day, when she'd returned alone to her fifth-floor walk-up in Brooklyn, the space a mess of clothes and food wrappers, half-drunk glasses of wine abandoned on side tables for more nourishing gulps of water, she'd grabbed her phone and opened up to her texts with Claire.

A thread that had been silent for a week.

Her thumbs hovered, desperate to reach out, but unsure what to say. What was there to say? The bet with Astrid, of course, was stupid. It was mean and selfish. Even though Astrid hadn't taken it, and as soon Delilah and Claire started up their affair, Delilah rarely thought of those spiteful words she'd spoken to Astrid in her Kaleidoscope Inn room again.

Still.

It looked bad, she knew. When she thought about the trip, played every moment out like a movie, studying herself like an aspiring actress studied Hepburn, she saw it.

Her constant snarky comments.

Her meanness.

Her lack of care.

The way she lashed out at Astrid any moment she could, and for what? For revenge? For fun? It was no wonder Claire had let her leave, let her walk right out of Wisteria House and Bright Falls without a single question. Delilah didn't blame her, she supposed. She'd made every effort to ensure everyone in Bright Falls knew she didn't give two shits about them.

And she didn't.

But now, as she looked up at the Whitney, her chest felt strangely hollow. There was excitement there, of course. Professional excitement. Artistic excitement. This-could-change-everything excitement, which was no small thing. But she couldn't stop or ignore this tugging around her heart. The wish for something more. Some*one*, perhaps.

She closed her eyes, just for a second, and imagined what it would be like.

Life with someone's fingers entwined with hers for nights like this.

Life with her person.

But as Delilah imagined someone walking beside her in this huge moment, that someone took on a face, a familiar feel, soft skin and brown eyes shining behind her glasses.

Claire hadn't been like Jax.

She hadn't been like anyone in Delilah's life.

She'd been . . . She was . . .

Delilah shook her head, rolled her shoulders back. She had a job to do tonight, and she couldn't afford distraction.

She couldn't afford whatever Claire Sutherland was.

⁓

THE SHOW BEGAN at eight o'clock. By nine, Delilah had already spoken to four agents who had handed her their card and told her to email them her portfolio, connected with two other artists whose work had similar themes about some collaborative projects, and sold three pieces for more money than she could currently comprehend.

She'd also come dangerously close to breaking down into tears five different times.

There was no reason for the crying.

The night was perfect, the show a success. The exhibition room was brightly lit and soft all at once, artists and patrons sipping champagne and spilling out on the museum's veranda, which over-looked the city. There were incredible queer photographs hanging in the space, images that showcased resilience, pain, sex, determination, hope, despair, celebration, and love. It was the pinnacle of not only Delilah's professional life so far, but her queer life as well. Here, in this room, was everything she'd ever wanted or run from or feared.

So why this constant welling sensation, like something inside her was about to overflow? She couldn't tell if she was overwhelmed or happy or scared or sad. She'd finally gotten a moment to breathe and grabbed a glass of bubbly alcohol, which she very much hoped would chill her the fuck out, when she heard her name.

She turned toward the sound to see a woman with a blond pixie cut in a fabulous white bandage dress sashaying toward her.

"Lorelei," Delilah said when the woman got closer.

"You remembered," Lorelei said, clinking her glass against Delilah's, a knowing smile on her lips.

Delilah winced. "I'm sorry I never texted."

Lorelei waved a hand. "Oh please. I know how to have a casual hookup."

Delilah nodded, but something about the words—the implication of *just sex*—twinged something in her gut.

"I can't thank you enough," she said, shaking off the feeling. "For showing my work to Alex."

"It was my pleasure. I've known Alex for years. We went to Vassar together. And although I'm just one of the Whitney's many bloodsucking lawyers"—here Delilah laughed—"I know a beautiful photograph when I see it."

"Well, it was appreciated, nonetheless."

Lorelei nodded, her eyes on Delilah over her champagne flute. "Maybe we could get a real drink afterward? Perhaps even learn each other's middle names?"

Delilah opened her mouth to say yes. She always said yes when a gorgeous woman asked her out after an event or before an event or, hell, for any time during an event. But her response got stuck in her throat, wouldn't even roll onto her tongue.

Lorelei's expression fell. "I get it."

"I'm sorry," Delilah said, rubbing her forehead. "I . . . I want to say yes."

Lorelei tilted her head. "But . . . ?"

Delilah shook her head. "I don't know. I just . . ."

"There's someone else?"

Again, Delilah's mouth dropped open, this time a definitive *no* ready and waiting.

But she couldn't seem to get that word out either. Delilah blinked, swallowed, and tried again. Still nothing.

Lorelei smiled, oblivious to Delilah's inner turmoil, sighing and waving a hand at the crowd of nameless beauty all around them. "You're lucky, then."

And with that, she kissed Delilah on the cheek and sauntered off. Delilah watched her, suddenly battling a feral urge to call the woman back and drag her to some unused coat closet, then fuck her silly just to feel normal again.

She turned away, back toward her pieces on the wall. There were still at least two hours left, and she needed to focus. She couldn't blow this chance. She couldn't—

Delilah froze as she saw a familiar figure standing in front of *Found*. The woman's head was tilted as she took in the image, her hip popped out in her black pencil skirt, holding a glass of champagne with two fingers like it was the cheapest bilge she'd ever tasted.

Blinking didn't clear the vision, which Delilah had half hoped, half dreaded was just some stress-induced hallucination.

But no. Astrid Parker was here. In New York City. At Delilah Green's show.

Delilah stared for a few seconds, wondering if she could get away with simply turning around and walking straight out of the Whitney, but she knew she couldn't. Strangely, she didn't even want to. Curiosity trumped her horror, and she made her way over to her stepsister, approaching her slowly like one might a wounded animal.

When she got close enough, she decided silence was probably best, sliding up next to Astrid and looking up at her own face in black and white. She still loved this photograph, probably more than any other self-portrait she'd ever taken. Self-portraits were tricky; they took forever, as you had to set up the shot without its subject, then do it again and again until you got it right. Double the complications if water was usually a centerpiece of one's work. This one was no different, and it had paid off.

Alex was right.

It was powerful.

In the image, Delilah was in the water up to her waist, dressed in a thin white blouse that was completely soaked, and no bra. Her hair was drenched, slicked straight back as she leaned one arm on a rocky crag. Her body was turned to the side, her head resting in the crook of her elbow, while the falls pounded down upon her back. Water droplets flew into the air. The sliver of sky above was clouded, the trees thick and wiry. The pool rippled out around her, around the press of water from the falls. The entire setting was chaos. Nature, loud and lovely and powerful.

But the woman herself.

Delilah.

Her face was . . . serene. A third of her expression was hidden in her arm, but both eyes were visible, just off center of the viewer. Water beaded on her slightly parted mouth, her cheeks, the end of her nose. Even with all of that, she looked at peace. There was no smile on her lips, no ecstatic glimmer in her eyes. There was just . . . a quiet there. She hadn't meant for it to happen. She'd simply been wasting time, trying not to think about how much she wanted to see Claire, experimenting with the water depths and if she could pull off a self-portrait using a timer and a tripod set up in the middle of a three-foot deep river pool in Bright Falls.

The result had been this. A shocking calm in the midst of natural cacophony.

"Interesting title," Astrid said, motioning her glass toward the white placard below the piece identifying the artist and other pertinent information.

Delilah sighed. She couldn't explain the title—*Found*. Or maybe she could, and that's why she'd convinced herself, over and over in the past week, that the title had been arbitrary, something to fill the mandatory space.

"What are you doing here?" she asked.

Astrid didn't answer right away, and when she did, her voice was soft. "I'm not sure."

She turned then, her eyes finding Delilah's, and the two women stared at each other. It occurred to Delilah that this was probably the longest she'd ever really *looked* at her stepsister. She'd spent years perfecting the art of avoidance, of protection, of never letting Astrid see how much Delilah was hurting. If eyes were the window into the soul, Delilah's had long been shuttered.

Now, though, she made herself look, all those entries about Delilah in Astrid's journal fluttering through her mind. She wanted to say something about them, to understand, but she'd never been forthcoming with Astrid Parker.

Not once.

The fact struck her suddenly, something regretful and sad pulling down her shoulders. It was a weight, this burden of hurt and resentment, of misunderstanding. She was tired and sore, and she wanted to be done with it. The realization was almost a relief, even if Astrid laughed in her face—she was ready for this part of her life to be over, or, at the very least, to change. Maybe that meant she and Astrid were done for good. Maybe they just needed to say goodbye, wish each other well, and walk away.

She turned and looked at her own face again, an expression she barely recognized but wanted to see in the mirror every morning. She wanted the Delilah hanging up there on the wall to be the real Delilah. Strong and resilient. Battered by the world and circumstances beyond her control, sure, but instead of resentful and angry, that woman was calm. Peaceful. Serene. Grateful. She belonged somewhere, despite years and years of emotional displacement. She'd found something. She'd been found by someone.

Or maybe, by many someones.

"Astrid—"

"You know what I realized?" Astrid asked.

Delilah looked at her, relieved to have to hold off the words she wanted to say, because she wasn't sure how to say any of them.

"What?" she said.

Astrid took a breath. "I realized, in twelve years of you living in New York, I've never once come to see you until now."

Delilah blinked at her.

"I'd bitch and moan about you coming back to Bright Falls."

"Astrid—"

"Then I'd bitch and moan even more when you didn't show up, but I never planned a trip out here. I never even tried to bridge that gap, did I?"

She looked at Delilah, her bangs just touching her lashes. She looked tired, her outfit pristine and her makeup natural and minimal, but nothing hid the shadow of purple under her eyes. As they looked at each other, really looked, Delilah felt something inside her release.

"It was a pretty big gap to bridge," she said.

Astrid nodded. "Yeah."

"And I . . ." Delilah sighed, forcing herself to keep eye contact. It was intense, that welling feeling was back, but this also felt right. Hard and horrible and right. "I did my level best to make it as wide as possible."

Something flickered in Astrid's expression. Something like . . . pain. Like sorrow.

"I'm sorry," Delilah said before she could talk herself out of it. Two words of apology didn't fix it all; she knew that. But maybe it was a start. Because, no matter how hard her childhood was, how lonely, Astrid Parker was her family. Her sister. Delilah finally got that, twenty years after her father died and left her alone. She didn't have to be alone. Not unless she just wanted to be, and goddammit, she didn't. She was tired of trying to forget she even had a sister, tired of pretending like she didn't want to understand Astrid because caring about her might lead to pain or rejection.

But it might also lead to so much more.

"I'm sorry too," Astrid said. "I didn't make it easy either. I know that. You'd lost a lot. So had I, and we were just kids. I guess . . . well, I guess neither of us knew how to handle the other. How to handle the hurt."

"No, I don't think we did."

Then they both seemed to . . . let go. Literally. They exhaled, releasing what sounded like four lungfuls of air, tiny laughs filtering out on the ends.

"Good god," Astrid said. "That only took us twelve years to say."

Delilah smiled and shook her head, her shoulders suddenly releasing their hold on her neck. "Longer than that probably."

Astrid nodded and held up her glass.

Delilah clinked it with her own, and they both sipped, the air between them a little clearer, a little more buoyant. They stood there like that for a while before Astrid moved on to Delilah's next piece . . . then the next and the next. Delilah followed her, watching Astrid take in her work. She found she actually cared what her sister thought. Maybe she always had, which was why she'd never shared any of this with her before today. Not on purpose anyway, as she knew Astrid had been checking out her Instagram for years now.

"These are really lovely, Delilah," she finally said. Astrid had never been effusive with praise, so Delilah didn't expect any now. But that simple phrase held weight, an authenticity that Delilah felt in her stomach.

"Thank you," she said, and meant it.

"I especially like this one."

Astrid had stopped in front of Delilah's personal favorite piece, her own self-portrait aside.

Lace and Fury, it was called. In it, a twenty-five-year-old Claire Sutherland waded into Bright River in a lace dress, everything about her soft and beautiful, and at the same time, despairing and rage filled. Delilah remembered taking the photo, looking at her camera's screen after each shot, something in her connecting with Claire's rage. When Alex had seen it a few days ago, they'd just stared at it for a while, then shook their head.

"Pretty sure every queer person in the world can relate to that," they'd said, setting the photo aside and moving on to the next piece.

And they'd been right. That's why Delilah had taken the photo in the first place. Claire represented a contradiction, the discomfiting marriage of beauty and pain. But now, as Delilah looked at Claire through the glass, she realized she wasn't a contradiction at all. She simply *was*. Complexity and clarity, fear and hope, love and hate and indifference. She was everything.

"I like it too," Delilah said now, staring at Claire's profile.

"Are you in love with my best friend?"

Delilah snapped her head toward Astrid. "What?"

Astrid just lifted her brows.

"I . . . um . . . I . . ." Delilah blew out a breath, the right word hovering just out of reach. A simple word. A terrifying word.

Astrid nodded, as though Delilah had spoken the word anyway, then lifted her glass toward the photo of Claire. "Well, I wouldn't sell that one. I have a feeling there's someone who might like to see it."

CHAPTER
THIRTY-TWO

RIVER WILD BOOKS didn't open until ten, but Claire always arrived around nine, ready for her workday to begin. Some days, she was already perched at her desk by eight, sifting through invoices or perusing online catalogs, making schedules and trying to figure out how to work some e-commerce into the store's services. Especially this week, with Ruby staying at Josh's new cabin in Winter Lake, she needed a distraction. Iris did her best to be available, but she had her own life, her own relationship to stress over, and god knew Astrid had enough on her plate lately.

Now, three days after what Claire knew was Delilah's show at the Whitney, she unlocked the store's door and stepped into the fairy light–illuminated space at eight forty-seven. She left the main lights off, like she always did until they opened, and flicked on the two computers behind the front counter, listening as they whirred to life and booted up the shop's systems.

Her thoughts strayed as she waited, wandering without permission to Delilah, to how her show went, if she'd gotten an agent. In the past few days, she'd reached for her phone more than once, itching to text Delilah and ask about it, ask about her, ask anything. But she always stopped herself. There was no point, and as Delilah hadn't reached out to her either in the more than fourteen days since she'd left Bright Falls, Claire had to assume the other woman agreed.

She rubbed her forehead, exhaustion making her eyes swim. She hadn't been sleeping great lately, which made absolutely no sense, but there it was, nonetheless. She'd even bought brand-new sheets and a new coverlet, new pillows and a new quilt to fold at the end of the bed. Nothing helped. It was like Delilah's scent, the feel of her, was impressed into the walls, the mattress itself, and Claire's bed was damned expensive. No way she was replacing that.

The point-of-sale program bloomed onto the computer screens, and Claire logged in to both registers. She had just come around the counter and was starting to weave through the shelves to her office when she saw them.

Claire had been trying to decide what to hang on the walls for a while now. She wanted some local art, a way to bring the community together, but thus far, no one had expressed real interest in selling their work in River Wild. Either that, or the artist's style didn't fit with the bookstore's aesthetic, which Claire wanted to keep clean and simple. Over a year ago, she'd taken down her mother's choices, plastic-framed images of book covers, most of which were written by dead white dudes, and the walls had been blank ever since.

Until today.

She stood near the counter, her eyes roaming over the black-and-white photographs that now hung on her store's walls, all of them in distressed wooden frames the colors of a desert sunset—terra-cotta and sage green, the palest dusky blue. The images were large, at least twenty by forty, and Claire saw familiar faces behind the glass of each one.

Her and Ruby at Vivian's, Claire's face pressed into her daughter's hair.

Claire, Iris, and Astrid at the vineyard, Astrid in between the other two women, wineglasses in their hands, their mouths open in laughter, rolling rows of grapes blurred behind them.

Firelight in the darkness, Iris and Claire huddled on a log bench, Iris's mouth near Claire's ear as though sharing a secret.

Ruby on Josh's shoulders in the hot springs, her arms spread and the most beautiful, euphoric smile on her face.

Image after image, Claire's life surrounded her. Her friends, her family, her town. There was even a photo of the outside of Stella's, all rough wood and brass. She felt her throat thicken, and she was just about to call Iris and Astrid and ask them what the hell was going on when she saw one more photo.

A black-and-white image of one woman.

Claire. All alone.

Wading into Bright River five years ago in a lace dress.

She gasped, and her hand flew to her mouth. She spun around, eyes searching through the dim lighting. Astrid could've had access to all the other photos. She knew Delilah had sent her a file with the images she'd taken during her time in Bright Falls. And this was the sort of thing Iris would do for her—organize some amazing display of the exact kind of art and photographs Claire would want to populate her store.

But this photo, only one person could've hung it here. Only one person had it in their possession, and there was no reason she'd ever give it to Astrid or Iris. No reason Claire could think of anyway. She walked swiftly through the store, hope and dread mingling in her gut. She angled around a freestanding shelf that held reference books, the reading area she'd set up with soft brown leather chairs coming into view.

And in one of the chairs, Delilah Green sat with her elbows resting on her knees.

Everything in Claire froze—her body, her breath, her heart. That's what it felt like, her pulse pausing to see what was going to happen next.

"Hi," Delilah said.

Claire didn't say hi back. She couldn't. She just blinked, her mouth hanging wide open.

"I'm really here. You're not hallucinating," Delilah said with a little smile. She had on a pair of gray skinny jeans and a fitted black V-neck tee, her lovely tattoos on display.

Claire snapped her mouth shut.

Delilah's smile fell, and when she spoke again, her voice was soft. "Say something. Please."

Claire finally got a good breath into her lungs. Her brain worked hard, trying to process all of this. She noticed one other pale green wooden frame resting on the coffee table in front of Delilah. It was far smaller than the ones on the walls, maybe a five by seven, and it was facedown so Claire couldn't see the image.

"How . . . how was your show at the Whitney?" she finally said.

Delilah looked surprised. "Is that really what you want to ask me right now?"

"I . . . I don't know. I just . . . I've wondered."

Delilah's eyes lit up. "It went well. *Really* well."

Claire smiled. She couldn't help it. She wanted good things for Delilah, even if those good things didn't include Claire. But then again, Delilah was here. She was in Bright Falls, in Claire's store. Curiosity and confusion warred in her mind.

"What are you doing here?" she asked.

Delilah laughed, the sound small and a little nervous. "I thought you'd never ask."

Claire took a step forward, then another and another until she found herself sinking into the chair across from Delilah, the coffee table in between them.

"So?" she asked when Delilah didn't continue.

Delilah swallowed and nodded, then scooted to the edge of her chair, lacing her hands together. "First, I wanted to bring you these photos."

"You could've mailed them." Her tone came out harsher than she intended. Or maybe not. She felt her defenses rising, and maybe they needed to. She didn't think she'd even admitted it to herself yet, but this woman broke her heart when she left two weeks ago. She wouldn't go through that again. She'd already been there so many times with her dad, with Josh. So whatever Delilah's game was here, Claire wasn't playing it.

Delilah took a deep breath. "I could have, but that brings me to my other reason for coming here."

"And what's that?"

"You."

Such a tiny word, but it landed like a bomb. "Me."

"You."

"What about me?"

Delilah looked down at her boots as though gathering her thoughts. She chewed on her lower lip like she did when she was nervous, and Claire had to force herself to stay put, to *not* go to Delilah and touch her face, tell her it was going to be okay. She needed to hear whatever Delilah was going to say, and she needed Delilah to tell her on her own. Claire couldn't help her with this one.

"What about me, Delilah?"

Delilah reached for the frame on the table, sliding it into her hands and staring down at whatever image there was behind the glass.

"After I left," she said, "I didn't have much time to think about anything. The show at the Whitney was coming up, and I knew I couldn't blow it. I worked night and day getting photos ready, and then, when it was time for the show, time for everything I ever wanted, it didn't feel like I thought it would."

Claire frowned. "What do you mean?"

Delilah glanced up at her, eyes clear and bright, almost feverish, like maybe she hadn't slept very well in a couple of weeks either. "The night of the show was everything I dreamed. But it also wasn't, because I was . . . I was doing it all alone."

Claire felt something in her chest start to crack, but she rolled her shoulders back, lifted her chin. "I'm sure you could've found a date."

"Oh, I'm sure I could've too."

Claire pressed her mouth flat.

"But I didn't want a date," Delilah said. "I wanted you."

Claire shook her head, but she could feel those all-important defenses crumbling one by one, her eyes already starting to sting. "You left," she said, because it was all she could think to say. "You left without a single word of explanation."

Delilah nodded. "I did. And it was a mistake and I'm sorry."

Again, so simple, those words, but the way her voice curled around them, Claire found herself believing them, which was dangerous.

"And the bet?" she asked. "Did you really try to get close to me to annoy Astrid?"

Delilah watched her, and Claire held her breath.

"Yes," Delilah said after a second. "It was a shitty thing to do, and I won't make excuses for it. But I swear to you, Claire, after we kissed that first time at Blue Lily, it was only about you. About us. Probably even before that. You were so beautiful and sweet, but I was never very good with beautiful and sweet. I didn't know how to . . . I don't know. Accept it. Treat it well."

Claire's eyes filled, and she shook her head. She appreciated the honesty, but it still stung that this whole thing had started out as a game to Delilah.

But it hadn't ended that way, had it? It hadn't even progressed that way. Claire knew that was also true, because she felt it, because Delilah was sitting in her bookstore. She'd come back. She'd come back for Claire.

Delilah got up, photo frame still in her hands, and rounded the coffee table until she was right in front of Claire. She sat on the table, their knees barely touching, and leaned into Claire's space, just a little. Just enough that Claire leaned too, her body instinctively wanting to be closer.

When she was settled, Delilah flipped the frame around so Claire could see the image. It was in full color, a selfie of two women lying on their backs in a bed, dark hair a mess against the white and lavender linens, smiles on their faces, cheeks pressed to cheeks.

Claire and Delilah.

Delilah and Claire.

Claire remembered this photo, that last time they spent in bed before everything went pear-shaped, after their roller skating date and Delilah had spent the night. The next morning, they'd made love and then slipped on tank tops and underwear and eaten bagels in bed. Afterward, Delilah had grabbed her phone and taken photo after photo of the two of them, tickling Claire to get her to laugh, kissing her senseless to get her to be serious.

It was the perfect morning. The perfect way to wake up. The perfect everything.

"This is what I want," Delilah said. "My whole life, this is what I've wanted. A best friend. Someone who gets me, who accepts me. Someone who fights like hell to get me to see that they love me. Someone who lets me love them back. Someone who's so goddamn beautiful, she makes my toes curl. Someone who calls me on my bullshit. Someone who makes me laugh. Someone who makes me look at her like this and looks at me the same way. Someone who . . . who's my home."

Tears spilled freely and silently down Claire's cheeks. "But . . . New York. Your art. You—"

"I can take photos anywhere. I can take trips when I need to. You can come with me. We'll figure it out."

"You hate Bright Falls."

Delilah's shoulders fell a bit, but she shook her head. "I hated who I was here. How I felt here. But you changed all that. Ruby changed all that. Iris. Hell, even Astrid changed all that."

Claire frowned. "Astrid? Have you . . . have you talked to her?"

Delilah's smile was small, a little sad. "She came to New York. To the Whitney."

"She did?"

Delilah nodded. "And we talked. A lot. She stayed a couple days— not with me, hell no—and we had dinner and worked through a lot. We've still got a long way to go, but it's a start. It's what I want. She helped me get these photos shipped out so they'd arrive yesterday, and we actually flew back together last night. She let me into the store at the crack of dawn this morning."

Claire knew that Astrid hadn't been around for the past few days, but she always responded to Claire's and Iris's texts that she was fine, giving nothing away as to where she was or what she was doing.

Claire took the photo from Delilah's hands. In the image, she was so happy. God, she was happy. She was . . . she was in love. She could admit it now. More than she'd ever been in love with anyone in her whole life. But . . .

"I'm a lot, Delilah," she said softly, looking down at the photo. "I've got a kid, an ex who will always, always be in my life. I can't just fly off to New York at a moment's notice, and you're used to this wild kind of life. I'm a small-town girl. I always will be. Josh built a house—"

"I know. Astrid told me."

"Then you know I'm here to stay. Ruby comes first. Always, and I can't—"

"I'm not asking you to put her second. I would never do that." Delilah took the frame from Claire's hands and set it on the table. Then she twined their fingers together and pressed her forehead to Claire's. "*I'm* putting you first, Claire. In case you couldn't tell, that's what's happening here."

Claire laughed, more tears spilling over. "Really?"

"Really. I want to try this. I adore Ruby, you know I do. And I'll follow your lead for how you want to handle us when it comes to her. I'll do whatever you want. Astrid's already looking into a place for me to rent in downtown and—"

"But your art." Claire leaned back so she could see Delilah clearly. "You need to be in New York. If you get an agent, you—"

"I've got an agent." Delilah smiled. "Her name is Julia Vasquez and she's a goddamn shark and I've already told her I'll be spending a lot of time in a little Oregon town for the foreseeable future."

Claire squeezed Delilah's hands. "That's so amazing. I knew you could do it. Congratulations."

"Thank you, yes, it's all amazing, but did you hear the part where I said I'd be spending a lot of time here? Apartment? You? Me? A life?"

Claire grinned. This was happening. Delilah had left, but she'd come back.

For her.

For good.

Claire had no idea how it would work, *if* it would work. All she knew was that she wanted this. She wanted Delilah Green. And for once, goddammit, she was going to let herself have exactly what she wanted.

"Claire?" Delilah tilted her head to meet Claire's eyes.

"Can we stop talking now?"

Delilah frowned. "Um, I guess, but are you—"

Claire didn't let her finish. She closed the space between them and pressed her mouth to Delilah's, framing the other woman's face like it was a precious work of art. God, she'd missed her. And from the way Delilah gasped a little, then slid her hands to Claire's hips and pulled her to the edge of her chair, both of their thighs parting to fit together like puzzle pieces, Delilah felt the same.

"Is that a yes?" Delilah asked between kisses.

Claire pulled back. "To which part?"

"All of it. You. Me. Us."

"It's a yes," Claire whispered against her mouth. "Yes to all of it."

CHAPTER
THIRTY-THREE

STELLA'S WAS PACKED tonight. Of course, as the only gig in town, it usually was. Also as usual, the smell of sawdust and beer and cheap perfume permeated the air, the patrons loud and laughing as they relaxed at the end of a workday.

Delilah Green walked through the door in her jeans, boots, tank top, and bomber jacket, just as she had on so many other occasions. But something was different tonight. Tonight, Delilah, for the first time in her life, didn't walk in alone.

Claire Sutherland's shoulder pressed against hers, their fingers tangled together as they looked for the rest of their party.

"Over here, bitches!" Iris called from a table in the center of the room, her red hair in two Princess Leia buns and a vodka soda already in her hand. Astrid was there too, offering a much more staid wave, but a wave nonetheless.

In the three weeks that had passed since Delilah had come back to Bright Falls, she'd moved into an apartment over her father's former architectural firm. Josh's old apartment, incidentally. It was surprisingly clean and exactly what Delilah needed. Ruby had been helping her decorate it, slowly, because despite her sales from the Whitney and several new commissions her agent had arranged for her, she still needed to budget carefully. Iris even came over one evening, a bottle of bourbon in one hand and a paint roller in the other, and helped her coat the walls in a steely blue. The night ended with the both of them drunk off their asses and laughing hysterically over nothing and everything in the middle of Delilah's living room floor. The next morning, a hangover the likes of which Delilah had never experienced assaulted her head and stomach, but she couldn't seem to keep a smile off her face. Everything felt so new, every day— living in Bright Falls, Claire, Iris who felt like an actual friend. She'd even gone out to lunch with Astrid. Twice. Isabel was another story. Delilah wasn't sure she was ready to climb that mountain, but she kept telling herself she had time. Right now, she was discovering Bright Falls all over again, living inside this cozy town the way she'd always wanted to, the way her father had always wanted her to.

Now, Claire pulled Delilah toward the table, kissing her once on the mouth before they both settled into the chairs.

"Do you two have to be so damn cute all the time?" Iris said, rolling her eyes.

"Cute?" Delilah said. "You mean like this?" She reached over and hooked her finger into the collar of Claire's polka-dotted button-up and pulled her closer for another kiss. Closed mouth, no tongue, nice and soft and the cutest fucking thing this town had ever seen, if Delilah had to guess.

"Exactly like that," Iris said, then made a gagging face.

Claire blushed and grinned, and Delilah winked at her. It would never get old, making that woman's cheeks pink up like that.

Astrid just smiled and poured Claire a glass of wine from the bottle of Riesling already at the table. Delilah ordered a bourbon neat, and soon all four women had a glass in their hands.

"What should we toast to?" Iris said. "Oh, I know, I know—to Astrid getting her ass good and laid."

Astrid spluttered on her wine. "What?"

"It's been almost six weeks since you kicked shit boot prime to the curb," Iris said. "It's time."

"It's time for you to pull your nose out of other people's sex lives," Astrid said.

"I'll second that," Claire said.

Iris's mouth dropped open. "Excuse me? My *nose* is what got you two sickening lovebirds together." She motioned between Claire and Delilah.

"Wait, what?" Delilah said.

Claire groaned. "Iris."

Iris just cackled.

"What's going on?" Astrid asked.

"Oh my god, I forgot we never told you this story," Iris said, slapping the table.

"Hello, in the dark over here too," Delilah said.

Claire dropped her face into her hands while Iris launched into a story about trying to get Claire laid nearly two months ago in this very bar, challenging her to get someone's number, which resulted in her unknowingly hitting on Delilah Green.

"Is *that* how all of this started?" Astrid said, eyes wide.

"Well, my ass does look fabulous in a good pair of jeans," Delilah said.

"Oh my god," Claire said, and Delilah laughed.

Astrid shook her head. "I can't believe you didn't know who she was."

"It was dark!" Claire said, and the other three women gave her a look. "Darkish. And okay, fine, but come on, look at her." She motioned to Delilah, a smile on her still-blushing face.

"Aw, sweetheart, you thought I was hot?" Delilah said in a teasing lilt, taking Claire's hand and kissing her palm.

Claire pursed her lips. "I guess I did."

"And just look at them now!" Iris said. "So, my meddling worked, thank you very much, and now it's your turn, my darling Astrid." Then she stood up and cupped her hands around her mouth. "Hey, Bright Falls! Who wants a chance with this fine-looking lady next to me!" Here she motioned to Astrid. "She's in desperate need of a good fu—"

"Oh my god, Iris, shut up," Astrid said, pulling her friend down. Claire was too busy cracking up to defend Astrid, and Delilah just enjoyed watching all of this unfold, the dynamic of friends, old and new, the give-and-take. It was wondrous. A miracle, if she was being honest and a bit dramatic. But dramatic felt right. It felt perfect for a night like this.

"I'm not looking to date, okay?" Astrid said.

"Who said anything about dating?" Iris said, waggling her eyebrows.

"Well, I'm done with that too," Astrid said. "No more men, ever."

"Women, then?" Iris asked, and Delilah couldn't help but smile at the hopeful tone to her voice. An all-queer coven was probably Iris's dream come true, but Astrid just blinked at her.

"Okay, okay," Claire said after she'd finished laughing. She sat up straight in her chair and held up her glass of wine, her other hand resting on Delilah's thigh beneath the table. "A toast for real."

"About something other than my love life, please," Astrid said.

Iris stuck out her tongue.

Delilah lifted her bourbon and took a deep breath. "To us," she said. "All of us."

The other women looked at one another, small smiles on their faces.

"Perfect," Claire said.

"Hear! Hear!" Iris said.

Astrid nodded and lifted her glass, a tiny smile on her face as she looked at Delilah. "To us."

"To us," Iris said.

"To us," Claire said.

They all clinked glasses, the music and laughter and life bustling all around them. A full, happy feeling filled Delilah's chest as she looked at her friends, her partner, her home. She lifted her glass once more into the air, tipping it to each of them in turn.

"To us."

ACKNOWLEDGMENTS

Writing a romance novel has long been a dream of mine. Romance has seen me through many stages of my life, from a twenty-something who barely knew herself to the thirty-six-year-old woman who truly understood herself for the first time, thanks to a bit of romance between the pages of a book. So first, I want to thank romance writers. Thank you for writing those happily ever afters, for persevering in the face of derision, for believing that love, in all its forms, really can conquer all. I would not have written this book—nor would I be anywhere near as happy or self-aware as I am—without all of your words.

Endless gratitude to my agent and friend, Rebecca Podos. We've been together since my beginning. We've navigated the stormy waters of publishing in YA and MG, edited an anthology together, become colleagues in agenting, and they've now seen me safely into this wonderful world of adult romance. There's a reason this is now the second book I've dedicated to them, and I would be lost without their wisdom, humor, and camaraderie.

So many thanks to Angela Kim, my brilliant, kind, insightful editor. I could not imagine this book landing with a better person. You understood Delilah and Claire from the beginning, and I'm so thankful to have worked on this book—and hopefully many more—with you.

Thank you to the whole team at Berkley, including Christine Legon, Megan Elmore, Jessica Brock, Fareeda Bullert, and Elisha Katz, who have expressed passion and enthusiasm for this story in a way that has truly exceeded my expectations. You have made this dream of mine a reality and it has been a pleasure working with you all.

Thank you to Marianne Aguiar for your amazing copyediting skills. I'm forever in awe of the details you all keep in your heads and help authors fine-tune!

Thanks to Katie Anderson for the beautiful design of this book, as well as Alison Cnockaert, whose design for the interior pages is an absolute dream. So many thanks to Leni Kauffman, whose gorgeous cover illustration captured Delilah and Claire so perfectly, I gasped when I first saw what she'd created. She's so unbelievably talented and I'm so honored that this book features one of her creations.

Endless thanks to Talia Hibbert, Meryl Wilsner, Kosoko Jackson, Rachel Lynn Solomon, Karelia Stetz-Waters, Rosie Danan, and Lana Harper for their generous words. I'm such a fan of each one of you and so humbled and honored that you would read (and like!) Delilah's story.

Thank you to Courtney Kae for your enthusiasm and all-around kindness. You're a true champion of your peers and I can only hope to help you feel as confident in your work as you've made me feel in mine.

To Craig, Benjamin, and William, thank you for creating space for me to think, to create, and to be myself. You are my home and my respite, and my books would not be half of what they are without your support.

Finally, to you, dear reader, for reading, for sharing, for showing up. We've been through a hell of a time—I wrote this book during the pandemic because it made me happy. It gave me a purpose each morning. Now we've made it through (dear god, let it be true) the hardest of times, and I hope this book has also given you some happiness, some comfort, some laughs, and of course, some swoons.

Turn the page for a look at the next
romantic comedy by Ashley Herring Blake

ASTRID PARKER DOESN'T FAIL

Coming to Piatkus Autumn 2022!

ASTRID PARKER LOOKED perfect.

Well, as perfect as she *could* look, which these days meant a lot of concealer smoothed over the purple half-moons that had taken up residence under her eyes. But other than that bit of smoke and mirrors, she was pristine.

She hurried down the sidewalk, the April morning light lengthening her shadow along the cobblestones of downtown Bright Falls, Oregon. She couldn't believe the sun was out, warm on her pale skin, that she'd actually been able to leave her umbrella and galoshes at home in her front closet. This was the first rainless day they'd had in two weeks.

Born and raised in the Pacific Northwest, Astrid was used to the rain, used to gray and drizzle, but that the clouds deigned to part today of all days . . . well, it was encouraging, to say the least. Had Astrid actually believed in signs, she might've gotten a bit maudlin about the timing. Instead, she stopped in front of Wake Up Coffee Company and gazed at her reflection in the large picture window.

This morning, she'd woken up an hour earlier than she needed to and washed and blown out her hair, making sure she styled her recently trimmed blond fringe exactly the way Kelsey, her stylist, had shown her. The result was . . . well, it was perfect. Her wavy locks fell just past her shoulders, her bangs were shaggy and chic and shiny. Her makeup was minimal—concealer notwithstanding—and her jewelry understated and tasteful, just a pair of gold hoops swinging from her lobes.

Her dress was the real star, her favorite outfit and the most expensive thing she owned—she still didn't dare tell her best friends, Iris and Claire, how much she paid for it last year after she and Spencer broke up. It was a necessary purchase. A power purchase, one to make her feel confident and beautiful. As she took in the ivory pencil dress now, sleeveless and midi length, her reflection confirmed it had been worth every penny. Paired with her favorite black strappy three-inch heels, even her mother couldn't complain about the vision Astrid saw in the window right now. She was elegant and poised. Prepared.

Perfect.

Everything she should be for today's meeting and first filming at the Everwood Inn. A wobbly smile settled onto her mouth as she thought about the historic inn, which was now hers to re-create. Well, not exactly *hers*. But when Pru Everwood, longtime owner of the nationally beloved Victorian, had called two weeks ago and said that she was ready to renovate—and that Natasha Rojas's super chic HGTV show, *Innside America*, wanted to do an episode on the whole transformation—Astrid had nearly bitten her own tongue to keep from screaming with glee.

Glee and a good bit of terror, but that was just nerves, or so Astrid had been telling herself for the last fourteen days. Of course, she was excited. Of course, this was the opportunity of a lifetime.

The old mansion-turned-inn was a designer's dream—three stories of intricate eaves and gables, a wide front porch, an exterior that was currently the color of cat vomit but would shine beautifully under some lovely pastel hue, lavender or maybe a cool mint. Inside, it was a maze of dark-paneled rooms and cobwebs, but Astrid could already envision how she would lighten and brighten, the shiplap and accent walls that would replace the cherry wood wainscoting, the transformation of the rotting back porch into a sun-drenched solarium.

There was no doubt: The Everwood Inn was a dream project.

And currently, it was her only project.

She sighed, pushing her recent financial woes to the back of her mind, including the fact that she recently had to let her assistant *and* her receptionist go because Astrid could no longer afford to pay them. Bright Designs was officially a one-woman show, so she didn't have time for doubts, for inconsistency.

Since taking over Lindy Westbrook's design business when the older woman had retired nine years ago, Astrid usually had the perfect amount of work to keep her busy and solvent. But lately, things had been slow . . . and boring. There were only so many design jobs to go around in a town as tiny as Bright Falls, Oregon, and if she worked on one more doctor-slash-lawyer-slash-real estate agent's office, filling them with uncomfortable seating and abstract paintings, she was going to tear her own eyelashes out.

Not to mention, if she let Lindy's business fail now, particularly after her disaster of a failed engagement last summer, Astrid's mother would not only tear her eyelashes out for her, she'd make absolutely sure the entire town knew the professional deficiency was one hundred percent Astrid's fault, bringing her personal shortcomings out from behind the family curtain.

Lately, this endearing quality of her mother's had kicked into overdrive, Isabel's lip literally curling whenever Astrid had a hair out of place or reached for a bagel. Astrid was exhausted, had slept like shit for months, and needed a very, very long vacation.

Or she just needed it to stop—all of it, every single sigh, lifted eyebrow, and pursed mouth her mother aimed in her direction. Surely, if anything would appease Isabel—maybe even draw out a proud hug or a glowing declaration like *I had every faith in you, darling*—it was appearing as the lead designer on a prestigious show and bringing the beloved Everwood into the modern age.

So Astrid very much needed the Everwood job. She needed the money and she needed the clout that being on *Innside America* would bring. The place was famous—there were countless books and shows and documentaries featuring the legend of the Blue Lady who purportedly haunted one of the upstairs bedrooms—and featuring on *Innside America*, the brainchild of the design world's sweetheart, Natasha Rojas, could change everything for Astrid.

This was her chance to go from small-town designer with a failed engagement to something more. Something *better*. Someone her mother actually liked. She would prove herself with this project, she could feel it.

She offered her reflection one more smile and was straightening the buttery material of her dress when a fist banged on the glass from inside. She startled, stumbling back so that her ankle very nearly buckled from the height of her heels.

"You look hot as fuck!"

A pretty redhead grinned at her through the window, then made a show of waggling her eyebrows at Astrid's form.

"Jesus, Iris," Astrid said, fingers pressed to her chest as she tried to calm her galloping heart. "Could you *not* for one day?"

"Not what?" Iris yelled through the glass, arms propped up on the back of a turquoise-painted wooden chair.

"Not . . ." Astrid waved her hand around, searching for the right word. When it came to her best friend Iris Kelly, the right word rarely stuck for very long. "Never mind."

"Get your cute ass in here already," Iris said. "Claire and Delilah are whispering sweet nothings in each other's ears—"

"We are not!" Astrid heard her other best friend, Claire, call from somewhere behind Iris before she appeared in the window too, her dark hair up in a messy bun and her purple-framed glasses catching the sunlight.

"—and I'm slowly losing my will to live," Iris went on, her shoulder knocking into Claire's.

"Don't even pretend you don't love it." This from Delilah, Astrid's stepsister and Claire's girlfriend for the last ten months, whose presence Astrid was still getting used to in her life. She and Delilah had had a fraught childhood together, filled with resentments and misunderstandings. The healing process was long and, honestly, exhausting. They'd come a long way since last June, when Delilah arrived in town from New York City to photograph Astrid's doomed wedding and fell in love with her best friend instead. Since then, Delilah had moved back to Bright Falls and proceeded to make Claire happier than Astrid had ever seen her.

As though to further prove the point, Delilah glided into view and draped a tattooed arm around Claire, who promptly beamed up at her as though Delilah not only hung the moon, but created it as well. Astrid felt a pang deep in her chest. Not jealousy necessarily, and she'd long realized the problems she and Delilah had growing up were just as much her fault as they were her stepsister's, so it wasn't discomfort or worry on her best friend's behalf either.

No, the feeling was more akin to . . . nausea. She'd never admit it to Claire—or Iris and her brand-new girlfriend, Jillian—that the sight of a happy couple gave her the urge to vomit, but it was true, and her roiling stomach was the proof. Ever since she and Spencer had broken up last year, she felt squicky just thinking about romance and dating.

Which was exactly why she *didn't* think about romance and dating—much less engage in them—and had no plans to do so in the future.

"Come on inside, honey," Claire said, tapping at the window gently. "It's a big day!"

Astrid smiled, her nausea dissipating, thank goodness. When she'd told Claire and Iris about Pru Everwood's call—about *Innside America*, how Pru's grandkids were coming into town to help the older woman manage the whole affair, Natasha-freaking-Rojas—her best friends had promptly squealed with glee and helped her prepare for today's meeting with the Everwood family. Granted, *prepare* entailed several nights at Astrid's house, open wine bottles littering her coffee table while she worked on her design software and Iris and Claire grew increasingly giddy and obnoxious, but still. It was the thought that counted.

Today, they'd insisted on her meeting them for breakfast at Wake Up to fuel her with, as Iris put it, "bagels and badassery." Astrid would be lying if she said she didn't need a little badassery right now. She nodded at Claire and moved toward the front entrance, hand reaching for the tarnished brass handle. Before she could give the first tug, however, the turquoise wooden door flew open and something slammed into Astrid, yanking all the breath from her lungs and sending her flying backward.

She landed hard on her butt, palms scraping on the cobblestones, and a burning sensation grew in the center of her chest before slithering down her belly.

"Oh my god, I'm so sorry."

A voice sounded from right in front of her, but she was frozen, her legs splayed in a most inelegant fashion, the right heel of her favorite shoes snapped in half and hanging on by a literal thread, and—

She squeezed her eyes closed. Counted to three before opening them again. Maybe it was a dream. A nightmare. Surely, she was not sitting on her ass on the sidewalk in the middle of downtown Bright Falls. Her pencil dress—her gorgeous, lucky, just-shy-of-a-grand pencil dress that made her ass look amazing—was not covered in very hot, very wet, very dark coffee right now. Three soggy paper cups were not spinning on the ground around her, a drink carrier was not upturned in her lap, pooling more liquid all over the dry-clean-only linen, and there was most definitely not a woman with a tangle of short golden brown hair, light denim overalls cuffed at the ankles, and rugged brown boots standing over her with a horrified expression on her face.

This was *not* happening.

"Are you okay?" the woman asked, holding a hand out to Astrid. "I was in a hurry and I didn't see you there and, wow, that dress really took a hit, huh?"

Astrid ignored her babbling, ignored the hand. She concentrated instead on breathing. In and out. Nice and slow. Because what she really wanted to do right now was scream. Loudly. In this woman's face, possibly accompanied by a nice, firm shoulder shove. She knew she shouldn't do any of those things, so she breathed . . . and breathed.

"Are . . . are you hyperventilating?" the woman asked. "Do I need to call someone?"

She kneeled down and peered into Astrid's face, her hazel eyes narrowed. Her face was almost elfin, all delicate features with a sharp nose and chin, and her short hair was shaved on one side and longer on the other, swooping over her forehead and filled with messy tangles like she'd just woken up. She had a nose ring, a tiny silver hoop through her septum.

"How many fingers am I holding up?" she asked, presenting two fingers.

Astrid felt like responding by holding up one important finger, but before she could, Iris and Claire and Delilah spilled out of the café, all of their eyes wide when they spotted her on the ground.

God, was she *still* on the ground?

"Honey, what happened?" Claire asked, hurrying over to help her up.

"I happened," the woman said. "I'm so sorry, I was coming out and not watching where I was going, which is just so typical of me and I feel so horrible and—"

"God, will you shut up?"

The words fell out of Astrid's mouth before she could think better of it. The woman's eyes went wide, perfect winged eyeliner arching upward, her raspberry red mouth falling open in a little *O*.

Claire cleared her throat and tugged on Astrid's arm, but Astrid waved her off. Goddammit, she was going to get up on her own, preserve what dignity she had left. Passersby on their way to work or out for coffee stared at her, all of them probably thanking the gods or whoever that their mornings weren't going as badly as that poor lady with the ruined dress and scraped-up palms.

She hobbled to her feet, the woman rising with her and twisting her hands together, wincing as Astrid whipped off her broken shoe and inspected the ruined heel.

"I'm really—"

"Sorry, yes, I got that," Astrid said. "But your sorry isn't going to fix my dress or my shoe right now, is it?"

The woman tucked her hair behind one ear, revealing several piercings lining the delicate shell. "Um. No, I guess not."

Something that felt like despair, as irrational as it might be, flushed Astrid's cheeks and clouded into her chest. This one thing. That's all she wanted, this *one* morning to go perfectly, but no, this disaster of a woman with her cute hair and her nose ring had to come barreling into her life at the worst possible moment, obliterating any chances at perfection. Her fingertips felt tingly, her stomach cramped with nerves, and her words flowed forth in a panoply of venom and annoyance.

"How could you possibly not have seen me?" Astrid said.

"I—"

"I was right there, in *ivory* no less." Astrid fluttered her hands down her now decidedly *not* ivory dress. "I'm practically glowing."

The woman frowned. "Look, I—"

"Oh, forget it," Astrid said. "You've already ruined everything." She dug her phone out of her bag, tapped into her contacts, and shoved it in the woman's face. "Just put your number in here so I can send you the bill."

"Oh shit," Iris muttered.

"The bill?" the woman asked.

"Run away," Iris whispered at her, but the woman just blinked at both of them.

"The dry cleaning bill," Astrid said, still holding out her phone.

"Sweetie," Claire said, "do we really need—"

"Yes, Claire, we do," Astrid said. She was still breathing hard, her eyes never leaving this walking hurricane who couldn't seem to pass through a door without causing mayhem.

The woman finally took the phone, looking down at it while she tapped in her number, her slender throat working around a swallow. When she was finished, she handed the phone back to Astrid and started picking up the now empty coffee cups and drink carrier, dumping them all into a large trash can near Wake Up's entrance.

Then she walked away without another word.

Astrid stared after her as she hurried about half a block down the sidewalk. She stopped at a mint green pickup truck that had most certainly seen better days, and all but threw herself inside, peeling out of the parking space with a squeal of rubber, engine rumbling as she drove north and out of sight.

"Well," Delilah said.

"Yeah," Iris said.

Claire just reached out and squeezed Astrid's hand, which jolted Astrid back into what was actually happening.

She looked down at her dress, the coffee drying to a dull brown, her shoe dangling from her fingers. Fresh horror filled her up, but now, it wasn't from her ruined outfit, her destroyed perfect morning on the most important day of her professional life. No, she was Astrid Goddamn Parker. She could fix all that.

What she couldn't fix was the fact that she'd just ripped a complete stranger a new one over some spilled coffee, a fact that settled over her now like tar, thick and sticky and foul.

"Let's get you cleaned up," Claire said, trying to pull Astrid toward Wake Up, but Astrid wouldn't budge.

"I sounded just like my mother," she said quietly. She swallowed hard, regret a knot in her throat, and looked at each of her friends in turn, then let her gaze stop on Delilah. "Didn't I?"

"No, of course not," Claire said.

"I mean, what is *just like*, when you think about it?" Iris said.

"Yeah, you really did," Delilah said.

"Babe," Claire said, swatting her girlfriend's arm.

"What? She asked," Delilah said.

Astrid rubbed her forehead. There was a time when sounding exactly like Isabel Parker-Green would've been a good thing, a goal, an empowered way to manage the world at large. Astrid's mother was poised, perfectly put together, elegant and educated and refined.

And the coldest, most unfeeling woman Astrid had ever known. Astrid often feared her mother's overinvolvement in her life would have severe repercussions, Isabel's essence seeping into her daughter's blood and bones, becoming part of her in a way that Astrid had no control over. And here was the proof—when shit went down, Astrid Parker was entitled, arrogant, and an all-around bitch.

"Shit," she said, squeezing her temples between her thumb and forefinger. "I threatened her with a dry cleaning bill, for god's sake. I need to apologize."

"I think that ship has sailed," Delilah said, waving toward where the burned-rubber smoke from the woman's tires still drifted through the air.

"You'll probably never see her again, if it makes you feel any better," Iris said. "I didn't recognize her. I would've remembered someone that hot."

"Iris, Jesus Christ," Claire said.

"Oh, come on, she was empirically gorgeous," Iris said. "Did you see the overalls? The hair? Total queer core."

Delilah laughed and even Claire cracked a smile at that. Astrid just felt a dull sense of loneliness she couldn't explain. She'd been experiencing it more and more lately when she was around her friends, like they all understood something fundamental about life and love she couldn't seem to grasp.

"We all have bad days," Claire went on. "I'm sure she gets that."

"You are too pure for this world, Claire Sutherland," Iris said.

Claire rolled her eyes while Delilah grinned and pressed a kiss to her girlfriend's head. The whole scene caused Astrid's stomach to roil even more—the PDA, Claire's constant positivity, Iris's snark. The only one who gave it to her straight anymore was Delilah, and Astrid couldn't bear to look her in the eye right now, not after going all Isabel Parker-Green.

"I need to get cleaned up at home," she said, slipping off her other shoe to avoid limping down the sidewalk in one three-inch heel.

"I'll come help," Claire said.

"No, that's okay," Astrid said, untangling her arm from Claire's grip and moving toward where she'd parked her car. She needed to be alone right now, get her head on right. Disaster of a morning notwithstanding, she was still the lead designer for the Everwood Inn, she was still going to be on *Innside America,* and she was still about to meet Natasha Rojas. No way in hell was one collision with a clumsy coffee drinker and a moment of extreme bitchiness going to ruin that for her now.

She'd kissed her friends goodbye and was halfway to her car when she thought to look at her phone for the woman's name. Maybe she could send her an apologetic text, tell her, at the very least, that of course she would not be sending her the dry cleaning bill. She unlocked her phone, her bare feet coming to a halt as she stared down at the woman's contact information.

There was no name.

There was only a number, saved under *Delightful Human Who Ruined Your Ugly Dress.*

Do you love contemporary romance?

Want the chance to hear news about your favourite authors (and the chance to win free books)?

Kristen Ashley
Ashley Herring Blake
Meg Cabot
Olivia Dade
Rosie Danan
J. Daniels
Farah Heron
Talia Hibbert
Sarah Hogle
Helena Hunting
Abby Jimenez
Elle Kennedy
Christina Lauren
Alisha Rai
Sally Thorne
Lacie Waldon
Denise Williams
Meryl Wilsner
Samantha Young

Then visit the Piatkus website
www.yourswithlove.co.uk

And follow us on Facebook and Instagram
www.facebook.com/yourswithlovex | @yourswithlovex

PIATKUS